BREWER'S REVENGE

A SEA NOVEL

BREWER'S REVENGE

BY

JAMES KEFFER

www.penmorepress.com

Brewer's Revenge by James Keffer

ISBN-13: 978-1-946409_28-7 (Paperback)
ISBN - 978-1-946409-29-4 (e-book)

BISAC Subject Headings:
FIC014000FICTION / Historical
FIC032000FICTION / War & Military
FIC047000FICTION / Sea Stories

Editing: Chris Wozney
Cover Illustration by Christine Horner

Address all correspondence to:
Michael James
Penmore Press LLC
920 N Javelina Pl
Tucson, AZ 85748

PROLOGUE

Katherine Wilkerson decided she absolutely detested fog. Unfortunately for her, at that moment she was on the merchant ship *Mary Elizabeth* in the midst of a fogbank so dense she could not make out the quarterdeck from her position at the railing opposite the mainmast. The *Mary Elizabeth* was carrying Katherine, her family, and fifteen other passengers to the Dutch island of St. Eustacius, where her father was to take up a position as the British trade representative to the governor.

Katherine was beginning to get nervous, although she was determined not to let it show. Like everyone else aboard, she had heard stories of the pirates who roamed the Caribbean, capturing and looting ships by suddenly appearing out of just such a fog as this. The *Mary Elizabeth* had entered the fogbank just after dawn this morning; she had heard the captain tell her father that it looked too large to go around. When her father had expressed concern for the safety of the ship, the captain had replied that according to all the charts of this area, it should be safe to sail straight through the Windward Passage and on to their destination. Personally, Katherine thought it would have been better had they waited for the fog to dissipate.

"Do you think there are pirates out there?" a voice said, breathless with excitement.

Katherine rolled her eyes back in her head before looking

at the newcomer, eleven-year-old Bridget Mulroney. Katherine (who was all of fourteen) had spent a great deal of energy trying her best to avoid Bridget after the second day of the cruise, when she decided the girl was just too juvenile for her. *Well*, she thought, *it isn't just pirates that can ambush a body out of the fog.*

"What?" she said.

"Pirates!" Bridget exclaimed. "Do you think there are pirates out there? You know, hiding in the fog?"

"Of course there are! But why—" Katherine was interrupted by the clanging of the ship's bell, which Katherine supposed was meant to give a warning to any ships that might approach too close in the fog. "And that silly noise will probably bring them right to us!"

Katherine smiled at how the younger girl's eyes grew wide in an instant. Bridget turned and ran away along the fog-bound deck, and Katherine had to laugh when she heard the girl collide with a sailor and hurriedly apologize before running on. She looked out into the fog again and tried to suppress a shudder. Truth be told, she *was* scared at the thought of pirates appearing out of the fog. She knew that the captain had posted extra lookouts, but somehow it was of little comfort. She gulped down her fear and resumed her own watch.

Katherine was by no means alone in her fear of the unknown in the fog. Captain Edward Johnson was also nervous. The *Mary Elizabeth* carried no cannon at all; in fact, the only arms on the ship at all were two muskets, three pistols, four swords, and two dirks. The muskets he gave to men whom he positioned at the mainmast and the mizzen, and he, the mate, and the master each had a pistol and a sword. The bosun had the fourth sword and a dirk, and the senior midshipman had the other dirk.

The Captain was regretting his decision. He had not wanted to enter the fogbank, but he was contractually obligated to deliver the new British trade representative to his destination by the twenty-seventh, which was only ten days away. This left him with no room for delay, given how much the fog would slow them down. So he'd put on a brave face for the passengers and ordered the ship forward into the swirling grey that turned the day to twilight.

Now, after several hours of sailing virtually blind through pirate-infested waters, his nerves were stretched to the breaking point. Three fellow captains had disappeared in the last two years in these waters, and the wreckage of one of the ships had pointed to its burning by pirates; others had submitted to being boarded and looted, which had saved the ship but proven disastrous for their careers, he recollected. He had no way of knowing how much longer they would be in the fog bank, but he prayed the bright Caribbean sun would burn it off quickly.

A quarter-hour later he sighed with relief: the fog was thinning. Visibility was improving considerably. The captain began to dare to hope that this voyage would not end in mystery, disappearance, and death.

A cry from one of the port lookouts dashed his hopes.

"Ship off the port quarter! It's showing a black flag, sir!" he cried, pointed into the fog where a dark shape loomed. "There, sir! About two hundred yards!"

Johnson opened his telescope and raised it to his eye. A frigate by the look of it, and a large black flag aft, barely discernible through the fog. He felt the blood drain from his face as he watched ominous figures running out their starboard battery as they slowly overtook his ship. In the next minute, a shot was fired from the ship's starboard bow chaser, and a column of water spouted up ten yards off his own port bow. The message was clear: *Heave to or be sunk.*

Johnson looked at his sails in desperation, but he already knew it was hopeless. That approaching ship looked a lot like the French frigates he'd fought against during the Napoleonic wars. If it was one of them, he knew flight was impossible. At the same time, he had heard about what happened to women and children when their ship was boarded by pirates. He had four women and seven children—all girls—on board. How could he allow them to be taken?

The Captain studied the approaching ship for a moment, then called for his mate.

"You sent for me, sir?" the mate asked when he arrived.

"Yes, Mr. Leslie. We are going to have to heave to. There's no way we can outrun that ship."

"Agreed, sir, but what about the women?" The mate looked nervously around the deck.

Johnson looked toward the intruder and fought down his fear. "We shall have to fight them when they board." He looked ruefully at the mate. "I don't see any other way, Jack. If we even try to run, they'll put a broadside into us from half pistol shot. How many of the women would survive that?"

Lindsey sighed in resignation. "Agreed, sir."

"Good. Heave to, and then gather those of the crew who are armed, along with anyone else who can fight. We'll hit them as hard as we can when they board. Tell the women and children to remain below."

"Aye, Captain." Lindsey knuckled his forehead and ran off, shouting orders for the crew to take in sail and heave to.

Johnson was joined by Nathan Wilkerson, the new British trade representative.

"What is the meaning of this, Captain?" he demanded.

"What does it look like, sir?" the Captain answered, somewhat testily. "Pirates, that's what it is! They will be boarding us soon. I suggest you prepare yourself to fight."

"What?" Wilkerson exclaimed. "You're not going to run?"

Johnson exploded. "Use your eyes, man! That ship out there is the size of a frigate! Thirty-six guns, maybe more! Look down our deck! Do you see any cannon? If we try to run, they'll put a broadside into us." He looked to the pirate, now barely a hundred yards away and closing swiftly. "At least if we go down fighting, maybe they'll have mercy on the women and children."

"I hardly think that likely! I hope you do not expect—"

The Captain left his passenger blustering at the rail and went to the mainmast, where the mate had gathered perhaps eleven or twelve men, crew and passengers, set to sacrifice themselves. Those who did not have a pistol or sword had armed themselves with clubs. One man had the cast iron skillet from the galley.

"The devils will be on us in moments," he said to them. "Protect the women and children at all costs." He looked the group over, meeting each man's eyes in turn. "Take as many of them with you as you can." Several of the men nodded in grim determination.

Johnson turned in time to see the pirate ship swing alongside the *Mary Elizabeth* and pirates launching grappling hooks to pull the ships together. One of his crew ran with an axe to try to cut one of the ropes, only to be shot in the chest. He dropped the axe, groaning, and clutched at his bleeding breast before falling to his knees, then slumping backwards as the ships knocked sides.

The first wave of pirates bounded over the railing, yelling like savages out for blood. They were frightening to look at, and there was no mercy in their eyes.

"Attack!" he yelled and charged the invaders. His little force was already outnumbered, and he didn't expect to be alive in five minutes. He dove at the pirates, swinging his sword wildly, trying to inflict as much damage as possible. He heard screams behind him as others of his party were cut down, but he couldn't spare the time to look back.

He dodged a thrust and hacked his attacker's neck. He kicked the dying pirate out of his way and stepped forward, only to see a pistol pointed right at his head. The man who held it was dark complexioned, with black eyes and hair down to his shoulders. He was not tall but had a powerful build, and when the wind blew his hair, Johnson noticed he was missing an ear. In his other hand, he held a bloody sword.

"Surrender," he said, just loud enough for Johnson to hear, "or I shall kill every soul on board this ship."

Johnson hesitated, and the man cocked the pistol. Johnson dropped his sword and raised his hands in surrender, shouting over his shoulder to the others still fighting to give up. The pirate smiled.

"Good decision," he said.

Johnson was herded aft to the quarterdeck along with the other survivors of the struggle. His mate was not among them. He stole a quick glance down the deck and saw Leslie lying in a pool of blood.

Several pirates were dispatched below decks and soon bought the remaining passengers to join Johnson and his survivors. Women screamed when they saw their loved ones on deck, bloodied, wounded or dead, and two fainted. Johnson saw to it that they were comforted, and then he turned his attention to the man who had held the pistol on him.

"What do you intend to do now?" he asked the man.

"We shall search your ship to see what valuables or cargo you are carrying," he said with a vicious smile. "You better hope we find something we want."

Johnson's eyes narrowed at the implied threat. The man waved his pistol, and several laughing and shrieking pirates ran below decks again. The passengers huddled together as they heard their cabins being ransacked, the sounds of breakage and seizure punctuated by whoops and cackles from the pirates below.

Suddenly, a commotion drew their attention to the companionway stairs, from which two laughing pirates drug Mr. Wilkerson up on deck.

"Captain!" cried one of the pirates. "Look what we found hiding down in the orlop!"

"Unhand me, you cretins!" Wilkerson cried. "I'll have you hung before King George himself for this!"

The pirates laughed all the louder and threw him on the ground before their leader, the man with the pistol.

"And who might you be," the pirate Captain inquired, "to bring down such a punishment on us?"

Wilkerson pushed himself off the deck to his hands and knees. "I am Nathan Wilkerson, appointed by the King himself Special Trade Representative for the Caribbean. I am to work with the Dutch government on St. Eustacius."

The pirate captain laughed. "I'm afraid King George has very little authority here, Mr. Special Trade Representative. Tell me, what were you doing hiding down in the orlop like a craven coward?"

Wilkerson bristled, indignation mixed with shame as he rose slowly to his feet.

"You leave my daddy alone!"

All eyes turned to Katherine, who was being restrained by those around her.

"Oho!" the pirate captain crowed. "It seems we have *someone* in your family with an ounce of bravery! Too bad it's your daughter and not you, you sniveling dog!"

Without a second thought, the pirate captain shot Wilkerson right between the eyes.

Katherine screamed and Wilkerson's wife fainted to the deck. The pirate captain dropped his empty pistol to the deck, and one of his comrades tossed him another.

Johnson was outraged by the sight of Wilkerson dead on the deck, but when he turned to the pirate captain, he found himself looking once again down the barrel of the pirate's pistol.

"No man should be in a hurry to die, Captain," the man said. Johnson stood his ground and said nothing.

The pirates sent below began to come back on deck, carrying sacks less than half-full.

"Well?" their leader bellowed.

"Slim pickings, Captain!"

"No supplies in the hold worth takin', neither!"

"This is all we could get from their cabins!"

The pirate captain looked at Johnson again.

"That is not good for you, my friend."

"I am not your friend," Johnson said. "What are you going to do?"

The man smiled and said loudly to his men, "Take the women!"

Johnson's eyes went wide as several pirates cheered and the women wailed.

"Over my dead body," Johnson said.

"As you wish." The pirate captain raised his pistol and shot the merchant captain dead.

"Take the women," he ordered. "Kill anyone who interferes. Leave the brats."

His orders were met with laughs and cheers from his crew. Two of the *Mary Elizabeth's* crew were cut down trying to defend the women. The children cried out in terror and huddled together, hiding their eyes from the horror.

"Mama!" Katherine cried out, as her mother was torn from her arms and dragged away.

"No, little miss!" One of the crew grabbed Katherine to stop her pursuit of her mother. He pulled her in and hugged her close, burying her face in his chest.

"Don't worry, little one," a pirate laughed, "we'll see she's not lonely! Ha ha ha ha!"

"Katherine!" her mother cried, as the pirates dragged her over the rail. All her daughter could do was sob in rage.

The pirate captain turned back before his went over the rail. "Tell King George that El Diabolito rules the Caribbean! His ships are not welcomed here—but he is welcome to send us women!"

And, with a fiendish laugh, he was gone.

Chapter 1

Commander William Brewer sat in the stern sheets of the gig that was carrying him to his new command, HMS *Revenge*. She was formerly the *El Dorado*, a sloop taken from the pirate Jean Lafitte and only recently converted for use in His Majesty's navy. The ship was 110 feet on the gun deck and thirty feet across the beam—almost as big as a small frigate—armed with four 18-pound carronades and sixteen 12-pounder guns. Brewer felt a shiver go down his spine; he was nervous at the prospect of this, his first truly independent command.

He turned as he caught sight of HMS *Defiant* and felt a pang of regret. After the death of James Norman, Brewer had assumed command of the big frigate and had nursed fond hopes of having his appointment made permanent by Admiral Lord Hornblower. Unfortunately, Hornblower was unable to justify handing so powerful a warship to so junior a lieutenant, and *Defiant* had gone to Captain Sir Thomas Fell, formerly of HMS *Clorinda*. Brewer watched as dockyard workers swarmed over the ship, putting final touches on repairs from the engagement with the pirates. With a heavy sigh, Brewer forced himself to put the past behind him, and he turned back to face *Revenge*.

The sloop seemed small after *Defiant*, but Brewer felt his chest swell as he ran his eye over her from stem to stern. No matter how big or small she was, she was his, and that was what mattered. The admiral had signed his commission as Master and Commander, but Brewer would be known as Captain to all on board. He was fully aware of how fortunate he was to have such a command at his age and rank in the peacetime Royal Navy, and he knew he had Hornblower to thank for it.

His mentor had been pleased to inform him that *Revenge* was crewed by volunteers from *Defiant*, of whom there had been so many he'd had to turn some away! Brewer had almost blushed when the admiral said, "It's a great compliment many captains have gone their entire careers without seeing."

Even now, as the gig approached HMS *Revenge*, Brewer could scarcely believe it. He had no idea that his efforts on behalf of his men would produce such an outpouring of respect and loyalty. As he glanced around, basking in his good fortune, his eyes landed on the midshipman seated slightly forward of him, and Captain Brewer's mood soured. Sitting there was Noah Simmons, son of the governor of Jamaica and the newest midshipman assigned to HMS *Revenge*.

Brewer had taken the twenty-three-year-old into his ship at the admiral's request. The governor of Jamaica had asked Hornblower to get his son off the island; it seems the young man had committed a 'youthful indiscretion' with the daughter of a powerful local merchant and then refused to marry the girl to make it right. The governor thought honorable service in His Majesty's navy might be just the thing to mature his son, and the admiral had felt he could not refuse the request.

Brewer frowned. Twenty-three was very old to begin service as a midshipman, and Simmons acted as though he was not used to taking orders, if his conduct in the admiral's office was anything to go by. Simmons was tall, nearly as tall as Brewer, but very slim, as though he hadn't had a decent meal in weeks. His face was long, and not what anyone would call handsome, but he carried himself with an air of one accustomed to getting his way. Brewer got the impression that Mr. Simmons did not like the idea of his being here anymore than his admiral did.

Brewer looked ahead, a small grin appearing at the corner of his mouth. Simmons would be an interesting problem for Mr. Greene and Mr. Tyler to solve.

He came back to himself as McCleary guided the gig to the access port. The bowman hooked the chains on his first attempt, and Brewer climbed to the deck. As his head and shoulders cleared, he took in the sight of seamen lined up with swords drawn in salute. Lieutenant Greene stepped forward and removed his hat.

"Welcome aboard HMS *Revenge*, Captain."

"Thank you, Mr. Greene. May I present Midshipman Noah Simmons? Mr. Simmons is joining the ship. Mr. Simmons, may I present Mr. Greene, the First Lieutenant."

Once the introductions were over, Greene stepped back and to the side. "If you'll follow me, Captain?"

"Lead on, Mr. Greene."

Brewer was pleased to see Mr. Tyler, acting-lieutenant until he could appear before a commissioning board and currently *Revenge's* second lieutenant, standing alongside Mr. Sweeney, the sailing master, and Dr. Spinelli, the surgeon. Brewer greeted each man in turn, and Greene led him down the line to some familiar but newly promoted faces.

"Sir," Greene said formally, "may I present *Revenge's* gunner, Mr. Hodges; her carpenter, Mr. Ringold; and Mr. Snead, the bosun."

Brewer acknowledged their salutes.

Greene turned his attention to the next in line, an unfamiliar face.

"Captain, this is Mr. Allen, the purser."

"Captain," Allen saluted.

"Mr. Allen," Brewer said. "Welcome aboard."

Brewer followed Greene to the two young gentlemen standing at the end of the line.

"Your midshipmen, sir. I believe you already know Mr. Short, and this is Mr. Reed, newly arrived from HMS *Clorinda*."

The young gentlemen saluted. Mr. Short was smiling.

"Mr. Short," Brewer said, "it's good to see you again. Mr. Reed, welcome to HMS *Revenge*."

"Thank you, sir," both midshipmen said.

Brewer turned and surveyed the vessel. Though he had been aboard several times already, this time it was different. He inhaled deeply.

"Mr. Greene, have the hands lay aft, if you please."

The order was passed, and the hands made their way aft and crowded beside the small quarterdeck. Brewer eyed them curiously. He recognized many of them from *Defiant*; these were men who had fought for him as acting-captain and then volunteered to be part of his new command. .

He took his commission from his pocket. He spread it out slowly and deliberately on the rail, and in a loud voice began to read. The document required William Brewer, Esquire, to go on board and take the charge and command as captain in His Britannic Majesty's Sloop of War *Revenge*. He had heard Captain Bush read similar commissions twice before, once when taking command of HMS *Agamemnon* prior to the journey to St. Helena, then on HMS *Lydia* before going to fight Barbary pirates in the Mediterranean. He could still hear Bush's rich baritone echoing out over the deck. In contrast, Brewer was ashamed when he heard his own voice crack twice. Not a good beginning.

Somehow, he made it through to the end. He solemnly folded the document and returned it to his pocket without dropping it. "Mr. Greene, dismiss the hands."

"Hands dismissed!" Greene bellowed.

Brewer watched the men make their way forward to complete their various tasks for getting ready to go to sea. A dozen or so settled down to making rope—a never-ending need aboard ship—at several points on deck. The sail maker and his mates were working just forward of the mainmast, probably to enjoy the sea breeze that that ruffled the surface of the harbor.

"Mr. Greene," he said, "detail someone to show Mr. Simmons to the midshipmen's berth, then join me in my cabin. I want to meet the new personnel."

"Aye aye, sir," Greene said. He saluted as his captain went below, then looked around. "Mr. Short! Mr. Simmons!"

The midshipmen came over. Short saluted and, a moment later, Simmons followed suit.

"Mr. Short, please take Mr. Simmons here to the midshipmen's berth and see him settled in."

Greene watched Simmons follow the boy below and wondered what kind of seaman he would make. He looked around the deck until his eyes fell on the petty officer of the watch—what was his name?—Anderson? No, wait a moment...

"Mr. Abbott," he said when the name came to him, "you have the deck. I shall be with the captain. If you need anything, call Mr. Tyler."

"Aye aye, sir."

Greene went below deck and made his way aft, congratulating himself on remembering to duck and avoid the low clearance. He stopped in mid-stride when a thought came to him, and his eyes went wide: *Oh, no—the Captain!*

Brewer had gone below deck and automatically turned aft, only to be reminded that the deck beams on a sloop-of-war were much lower than on a frigate when he rammed his head into one. He was stunned only for a moment, but he cursed under his breath and hoped nobody had seen him. He cautiously made his way to his cabin. It was strange to see no marine guard outside his door, as there had been on *Defiant*. A sloop-of-war had no marines.

He entered the cabin and closed the door gently behind him. The stern cabin was painted white, and the furnishings seemed better suited for a bordello than a ship of war. Brewer knew them to be left over from when the pirate Jean Lafitte was captain. He had to wonder about the man's taste in furnishings.

Brewer turned when he heard someone clearing his throat. He saw a tiny man standing there, hardly more than a dwarf in size. The man said nothing as Brewer set his hat on the desk.

"Are you the steward?" Brewer asked.

"Yes, sir," the man replied. He pulled a note from his coat pocket and handed it to Brewer without a word.

Brewer unfolded it and read.

Dear Captain Brewer,

As promised, I am sending you a replacement steward with the blessings of Admiral Hornblower. His name is Alfred Thomas. Please do not be put off by his size; he can do wondrous things in the galley! I believe he will serve you well, Captain, although I

6

would advise you to avoid remarking upon his stature.

Your Ob't Servant,
Jenkins

Brewer looked up from the note. The little man was still there.

"Jenkins speaks highly of you."

The little man nodded. "Thank you, sir."

Brewer sat down at the desk and stared at a cup of hot coffee sitting there. He looked at his steward, but the man's face betrayed nothing; obviously, he had moved swiftly and silently to put the cup there while Brewer was reading Jenkins' note. He blinked; this was going to take some getting used to. He sipped the hot beverage and was impressed by how good it was.

"Well, Mr. Thomas—would you prefer Mr. Thomas, or will Alfred do?

"Alfred will do fine, sir."

"Yes, well, Alfred, this coffee is extraordinary!"

"Thank you, Captain."

Just then, there was a knock at the door, and Mac came in. He stopped as he saw the steward standing there, then looked to the captain for an explanation.

"Mac," Brewer said, "this is my new steward, Alfred Thomas. Alfred, this is my coxswain, Mr. McCleary."

McCleary stuck out his big paw. "Call me Mac."

Thomas had to reach up to shake hands, and Brewer smiled at the look on his coxswain's face.

"If there's nothing else, sir?" Alfred said.

"Thank you, that will be all," Brewer replied. The steward bowed and withdrew, closing the door behind him.

McCleary's eyebrows raised in wonder, as though he were watching a circus sideshow.

"*He's* going to be your servant?" he asked, jerking his thumb toward the closed door.

"Yes," Brewer said, holding up the note. "Jenkins recommended him."

Mac looked back at the door. "Can he reach the stove?"

"Careful, Mac," Brewer warned, waiving the note in the air. "Jenkins advised we make no mention of his stature."

Mac shook his head in disbelief. "Might be hard not to, sir."

Brewer shrugged. "Keep an eye on him for a while, make sure the crew doesn't give him a hard time."

Mac smiled and left the cabin.

Brewer enjoyed his coffee and considered the contrast between his competent new steward and recalcitrant new midshipman. This was certainly going to be an interesting two weeks.

Lieutenant Greene arrived at his captain's door and knocked. He heard the captain say "Enter," and opened the door to find Brewer seated at his desk, rubbing his temple.

"Hit your head, sir?" he asked. "I must apologize; I ought to have reminded you."

"I'll live," Brewer said. "Have you met my new steward yet?"

"Yes, sir, when he came on board. An interesting character."

"Quite. Brewer smiled. "Shall we put him to the test? Will you dine with me, Mr. Greene, and sample his fare?"

"An honor, Captain."

"Good," Brewer said. "Now, how about the crew?"

The two men spent the next hour going over the muster book and the watch bill. There was also a brand new Punishment Book, and both men pledged that it would never be a bad mark on their ship.

When they were satisfied with the ship's books, Brewer sat back in his chair. "Well, let's have our new senior midshipman in."

Greene rose, opened the door and called, "Pass the word for Mr. Reed."

Within minutes there was a knock at the door, and Mr. Reed entered. Brewer noticed his head cleared the low deck beams by nearly an inch. He had dark hair and eyes, which made him hard for Brewer to read at a glance. Thick, dark eyebrows gave his face a look of intense concentration. Brewer wondered if it was indicative, or merely a look.

Reed stood at attention. "You sent for me, sir?"

"Yes, Mr. Reed," Brewer said. "Please sit down." He saw Greene retreat against the door and settle in to listen. "I wanted to meet with you and hopefully learn more about you. I also wanted to take your measure and let you get mine as well. How old are you, Mr. Reed?"

"Eighteen, sir."

"And *Clorinda* was your first ship?"

"Yes, sir."

"How long did you serve there?"

"Eight years, sir. Two as ship's boy, six as midshipman."

"I see. You are to be senior midshipman, Mr. Reed. I trust you are up to the task?"

"Yes, sir!"

"Mr. Short knows his duty—he was with me in *Defiant*—but Mr. Simmons is brand new to the navy, so you will have to instruct him in his duties."

"Aye aye, sir."

Brewer rose. "Very well, Mr. Reed. The first lieutenant will be speaking to you."

To his credit, Reed heard the dismissal in his captain's words. He rose and made his way from the cabin.

After he was gone, Brewer said, "Well, Mr. Greene, what do you make of him?"

Greene shrugged. "He seems capable enough. He came with good reports from *Clorinda*."

"Well then, let's have our standing officers in, but save the purser for later."

After Greene passed the word for the gunner, carpenter, and bosun, the three men arrived so promptly Brewer realized that Mr. Greene must have had them cleaned up and standing by outside his cabin. Hodges and Ringold removed their caps as they entered; Mr. Snead was bareheaded. Brewer glanced at the Muster Book and noted that Hodges was the only one of the three to have a warrant. Ringold and Snead held acting-warrants, but that did not bother their captain. He knew their work of old and was glad to have them aboard *Revenge*.

Mr. Hodges was a compact man, short but stocky, and well muscled. As gunner, he was responsible for the maintenance of all the arms on board as well as the magazines. The ever-present danger of explosion by the black powder aboard required Hodges to follow strict rules in its handling and storage, as well as seeing it was kept dry. Brewer made sure the gunner understood he was to make regular inspections on the tackle and breeches for the guns and make reports to the captain on his findings.

The carpenter, Mr. Ringold, was a tall man with shoulders like an ox. Brewer wondered idly, with powerful shoulders like those, why Ringold wasn't a professional wrestler instead of a ship's carpenter. He was responsible for the maintenance of the hull and masts of the ship; he took care of plugging shot holes taken during action, and regularly checked the level of water in the well.

Mr. Snead stood out in any crowd for two reasons—his loud voice and the shock of unruly, bright red hair on his head. Snead's was responsible for the rigging, cables, anchors, sails, and boats. He motivated the crew (with his starter when necessary) and made sure their work on deck was performed satisfactorily.

After a few words with each man in turn, Brewer addressed the group. "Gentlemen, I want you to go over the ship stem to stern before we sail. We shall use this first cruise to work out any kinks in our routines. By the time we reach Jamaica, *Revenge* should be the best sloop in the Caribbean. Dismissed."

The standing officers filed out of the cabin.

"Mr. Greene, have the purser come see me, will you please?" Brewer said.

"Aye, sir." Greene gathered his hat and prepared to leave, but stopped as he put his hand on the door and turned back slowly.

"Captain, have you spoken to Dr. Spinelli lately?"

"The Doctor? I saw him when I came on board, but I haven't spoken to him in some time. Why do you ask?"

Greene just smiled. It was a sad smile, Brewer thought, the kind that regrets how far a friend has fallen.

"I think he could use a friend," the first lieutenant said, and he left the cabin.

Brewer sat for a moment, lost in thought. He had not noticed anything untoward about the good doctor; but come to think of it, the doctor had not said a word when Brewer greeted him. He'd just stood there, next to Mr. Sweeney, and ....

Brewer rose and went to the door. He opened it and stuck his head out.

"Pass the word for Mr. Sweeney!" he called. He shut the door and sat back down to wait.

In a few minutes, Mr. Sweeney was standing in the cabin with his captain. Brewer was coming to regard the old sailing master as a rock on whom he could rest, and he valued his counsel.

"Sit, please, Mr. Sweeney," Brewer said. "Port?"

"Thank you, Captain," Sweeney said as he sat down. Alfred appeared, holding a small silver tray with two glasses of dark liquid. He set one in front of each man and silently withdrew. Brewer picked up his glass and lifted it in a toast to his friend. The sailing master raised his glass as well, sniffing appreciatively before draining it. Sweeney sat back in his seat and waited for Brewer to explain his summons.

"Sweeney," Brewer said, "have you spoken to Dr. Spinelli lately?"

Sweeney looked down at his empty glass as though he wished it were full again. "Yes, I have."

Brewer's left eyebrow rose a fraction of an inch. "And what was your impression of him?"

Sweeney sighed and raised his eyes to his captain's. "In my opinion, sir, something is amiss. He's been withdrawn since reporting on board."

Brewer looked out the stern windows with a frown as he considered Mr. Sweeney's confirmation of Mr. Greene's statement. Definitely something he needed to look into, preferably before they left port.

"Do you think," Brewer hesitated, hating himself for prying, "do you think he's drinking again?"

Sweeney shrugged, his eyes going down to the empty glass. Brewer felt his heart sink, and he lowered his eyes for a moment as well, remembering the surgeon aboard HMS *Lydia*, whose life was destroyed by the bottle. Brewer had watched that surgeon die in *Lydia's* sickbay, tied down so as not to injure himself or others, screaming about the insects and beasts he thought were crawling on him, biting him.

Brewer shook his head hard, hoping to drive the memories away. He looked to find the sailing master staring at him. He smiled to hide his embarrassment. Brewer rose, and Sweeney did the same.

"Thank you, Mr. Sweeney," Brewer said. "Let's keep this between us, if you please. Our orders are to sail on the tide."

"Aye aye, Captain." Sweeney picked up his hat and left the cabin.

Brewer sat down again and tried to get some work done, but thoughts of his friend kept intruding. Finally, he set his pen down and sat back in his chair, wondering how to approach the good doctor as a friend and not as his captain.

His head began to ache, and he rubbed the lump rising on his head. He opened his orders and read them thoroughly, but they contained nothing beyond what he had been told. *Revenge* was to go on a two-week cruise to make ready his crew. He didn't think it would be hard. Other than Simmons and a few others, the entire crew had come over from *Defiant*; they knew how to work together, and it would not take long for them to adjust to the new ship.

Brewer held his orders in his hand, and his face grew grim as he remembered the rest of his meeting with the Admiral.

"Our main problem is still the pirates who roam the Caribbean," Hornblower had told him. "We hurt them in the recent battle, but the frigate got away. Our other problem is the French. I have received reports stating that they are moving to expand their influence in the area. I want you to put in at Martinique and introduce yourself to the governor.

See what you can find out about French intentions. Informally, of course; we don't want an incident with our new allies. Personally, I wouldn't put it past them to dealing with pirates if it advances their agenda. In any case, gather what information you can."

Brewer looked at his orders again, then glared into empty space. Two weeks would be enough. His crew would be ready the next time they ran into the pirate who ambushed *Defiant*, and Brewer would get the one thing he really wanted in this world.

Revenge.

CHAPTER 2

Mr. Short led Simmons down to the midshipman's berth. Simmons stopped as he entered the space, his mouth hanging open in disbelief. The area, which amounted to a couple small spaces forward of the officers' quarters, was dimly lit and stank. The furniture was little better than empty casks, and the floors were dirty as well as wet and slippery. The air was heavy and still, yet Simmons shivered in spite of himself. Tall as he was, he had to stoop in the cramped, low-ceilinged space.

Short sat on a sea chest. "This here's mine," he said, "and that one belongs to Mr. Reed. He's the senior midshipman. He just came over from *Clorinda*."

Simmons stood in the midst of the berth, the look on his face going from disapproval to incredulity. He turned back to Short.

"Senior?" he demanded sharply.

"Yes," Short said. "He's in charge of the midshipmen. We follow his orders."

"Yes, well," Simmons said, half under his breath, "we'll see about that." He looked around disdainfully. "I still cannot believe one wench could reduce me to this."

Short looked confused. "What's that you say?"

Simmons smiled. "Never mind. How old are you, anyway?"

"Fourteen."

"What's your first name?"

"William. What's yours?"

"Noah."

Just then, Reed entered the berth.

"Hello, who's this?" he said, walking over and extending his hand. "Jonathan Reed. I'm the senior midshipman."

"Noah Simmons." Simmons took Reed's hand and squeezed it hard. Reed's eyes narrowed.

"Good grip you have there, Mr. Simmons."

"Sorry," Simmons smiled and released his grip, then stood there looking down at Reed. He was almost a full head taller than the senior midshipman, although Reed was more heavily muscled.

"His father's the governor!" Short said.

"Is that so?" Reed said, without taking his eyes from Simmons. "William, I think Dr. Spinelli was looking for you. You'd better go see what he wants."

"Right-oh." Short got off his sea chest and left.

"Now," Reed said quietly to Simmons, "am I going to have any trouble with you?"

Simmons' face broke into a small smile, and his voice was menacing. "I don't know, *Mr.* Reed, are you?"

Reed stared into the newcomer's eyes and knew this come to a head sooner or later. He had just decided sooner was better when a ship's boy, popularly known as a Bobbin by the crew, skipped into the berth.

"Mr. Reed!" he said. "The first lieutenant wants you on deck!"

"Right away!" Reed said. He backed away and left the berth, never taking his eyes from his adversary. Simmons, for his part, watched the shorter man go and wondered what he had got himself into.

Slouching at his desk, Captain Brewer was roused from his thoughts by the knock at his cabin door.

He sat up and called out, "Enter!"

Mr. Allen, the purser, came in. He was a short, round man, like so many of his profession. He removed his hat, revealing an unruly mass of red hair. His nose was pointed; his eyes, dark and piercing, were sunk into his head. The most distinguishing thing about Mr. Allen—or the most disconcerting– was his perpetual, toothy grin. Brewer wondered what secret the purser was smiling about.

"You wanted to see me, Captain?" the purser asked.

"Yes, Mr. Allen, please sit down," Brewer said. "I wanted to talk to you about your job."

"Oh, yes?" Allen's grin flickered for a moment, then reasserted itself.

"How long have you had your warrant, Mr. Allen?"

"Three years, Captain," the purser said, with an air of confidence. "My last ship was the brig *Triumph*. She was wrecked in a hurricane last year. Since then, I've been working in the victualing office in Port Royal until the post came available in *Revenge*."

Brewer steepled his fingers. "Mr. Allen, I am not going to tell you how to do your job, but I am going to expect you keep me informed on the status of our supplies. I will tell you that I will be inspecting your work from time to time, just as I will the gunner or the carpenter." For a moment, his smile mirrored the purser's. "If I ever find you are buying bad food or meat rancid in the casks, I will have you stripped of your rank and flogged. Do I make myself clear?" There was nothing of levity in his tone.

The purser nodded, nonplussed. "Perfectly, sir."

"My responsibility is to the British navy and to the men under my command," Brewer said softly. "They cannot do their work if they are being poisoned by the meals that should nourish them. It is little enough they get in wages; the least we can do is to see to it that their 'three square meals' sustain their labors. And think on this: if we do run into pirates or other hazards, you own safety will depend on the well being and strength of these men. Do not undermine it with poor fare." His gaze was steely as he held the widened eyes of the purser.

He had meant every word he said. Too many pursers skimmed the cream for themselves by buying spoiled goods at a discount, reporting the regular price as paid, and pocketing the difference. Two weeks might not make a noticeable difference, but over time, poor fare could cause discomfort and disease. A captain who made sure his men ate well did a great deal for the welfare of the crew. He leaned back in his chair and called, "Alfred!"

The diminutive servant appeared in the doorway.

"Madeira, please," the Captain said.

"Yes, sir," Alfred disappeared.

"Do your job well, Mr. Allen," Brewer continued, "and you've nothing to fear from me. You are a major factor when it comes to crew morale, especially in these tropic climates."

"I understand, sir."

Brewer paused as Alfred reentered the cabin. He set two glasses of the wine on the desk. Brewer struggled not to laugh at his purser's expression when he saw the desk-top level with the steward's chest. Brewer hurriedly cleared his throat and made the proper introductions.

"Mr. Allen, purser, this is Alfred, my steward."

"Oh, ah," the purser stammered, "how do you do?"

The servant just looked at Allen. He turned to the captain. "Will there be anything else, sir?"

"No, Alfred, that will be all."

The purser watched the steward go, and when the cabin door closed, he looked at the captain. "Quiet little man, isn't he?"

Brewer smiled. "Yes, well, I've been advised not to make much of that."

"Which one—quiet or little?"

"Which do you think?"

The purser looked at the door again and shook his head. He saluted his captain with his glass and drained it in a single draught.

Brewer rose. "As I said, Mr. Allen, please keep me informed."

The purser rose and picked up his hat. "I shall, Captain."

Brewer stood as well, to let his height underscore his message, and watched his purser go. An inspection or two after the next few calls at a port would show Mr. Allen he was serious.

He gazed out the stern windows at the harbor and the landscape beyond, and his thoughts returned to his doctor. There was another man upon whom the entire crew depended. He sighed and stood. There was no point in uninformed speculation; he would have to visit the doctor and see for himself. Brewer hesitated; he had never made such a visit from a position of authority before, and he wanted to go as the doctor's friend and not his captain. He hoped the doctor would see it that way.

Brewer made his way forward, keeping his head low this time. He arrived at the doorway for *Revenge's* small sick bay and peered inside. It was dark within, but he could just make out a desk against the far bulkhead, and a bookcase crammed with what looked like medical books. He stepped a bit further and was drawn to a sound and a movement in the far corner of the room. There was a lantern on the desk, with a candle, and a box of matches beside it. He struck a match to life, lit the candle and set it into the lantern, which he held high to get a better look around the sick bay. It was a small space with little furniture save the doctor's desk and medicine cabinet, along with a long table that would be used when operations were necessary. Brewer shuddered in spite of himself; he did not look forward to the day when he would find this place full of the wounded and dying.

He investigated the corner where he'd heard movement earlier, and it was there he found the doctor, stretched out on a pallet on the floor, fast asleep, his face turned away form the door. His uniform, such as it was, was rumpled. Brewer squatted down and turned his friend's head by the chin for a better look. Two things became immediately clear. The first was that the doctor was drunk. His breath reeked of whisky. Brewer rocked back onto his heels. He'd heard rumors aboard the *Defiant* about Spinelli's drinking, but he'd never found the doctor drunk. Obviously, something had changed within the past couple of weeks that he did not know about— yet. The second thing Brewer noticed was how pale the doctor looked in the candle light. He made a mental note to be sure to see the doctor on deck before the sun went down. He made his way quietly out of the sickbay, pausing only to blow out the candle and leave the lantern on the small desk.

Brewer wandered. His mind was so preoccupied with the questions surrounding the doctor that his body moved more or less of its own accord. He found himself up on deck and looked about in surprise, thankful that his body had already learned to keep his head low. He saw Mr. Tyler standing at the mainmast, directing a sail drill, so he clasped his hands behind his back and adopted his best just-passing-by attitude as he walked up to the acting-lieutenant.

"Captain," Tyler said as he saluted.

"Good day, Mr. Tyler," Brewer said. He gestured aloft with his chin. "How are the men adjusting to the smaller ship?"

Tyler grinned. "They like it right well, sir; not as much canvas to haul, so they are getting things done quickly."

Brewer nodded. "Keep them at it. We may need that speed one day. We don't have the firepower we had in *Defiant*, so that means we have to score more hits to do the same damage, and *that* means maneuvering fast enough to stay alive."

Brewer walked aft to where his first lieutenant and sailing master were conversing. Both men saluted as their captain approached, and he responded in kind.

"Ready to proceed, sir," Greene reported. "All personnel are present or accounted for, and supplies are aboard and secured."

"And the tides?"

"Three bells of the second dog watch, Captain."

"Very good," Brewer said. "Mr. Sweeney, will you please notify the harbor master we depart with the tide." He pulled a watch out of his pocket and studied it. "Mr. Greene, I believe it's time. Please excuse us, Mr. Sweeney. You have the deck until we return."

"Aye aye, sir."

Brewer led his first lieutenant below decks to his cabin, where Alfred had set the table for two. The two officers had barely taken their seats when the diminutive servant appeared with two goblets and a decanter on a silver tray. Brewer watched in bemusement, remembering dinners at his father's house when he was young.

His mother employed a cook by the name of Glynis, who had a son named Jeremy. A midwife's mistake during his birth left Jeremy lame in one leg, causing him to walk with a pronounced limp. Brewer's father had taken a liking to the lad as he struggled and grew, and took him under his wing as much as he could. At the age of eleven, Jeremy was hired to serve at the family table. Brewer remembered the sight of the small boy limping to the table with a platter or a bowl of vegetables in his arms, and the effort it took him to lift the platter as far onto the table as his arms would reach. One time Brewer had moved to help the lad, but a look from his father sufficed to keep him in his seat and allow Jeremy to complete his task on his own. After the meal, Brewer caught up to his father outside and asked him about it.

"William," he said, "that lad's already got a lot against him. He needs to learn that he can stand on his own two feet, so to speak. You helping him would only have told him he needs help."

His father had seen he did not understand, so he'd gently taken his son by the arm and steered him toward the barn. As the two strolled out into the sunshine, he'd continued.

"Son, a man—even a lad like Jeremy—is made up of two parts, the inside man and the outside man. Now, Jeremy's outside man will always hold him back due to his bad leg. That leaves the inside man to make up the difference. The inside man is where a man believes in himself as a man. The outside can be destroyed, or worse, permanently damaged. That is why the inside man is the stronger of the two, William. It cannot be damaged or destroyed unless the man allows it. The bad part is that if that happens, the man himself is destroyed. He may not be dead, but he will never consider himself a man again. A good inside can sustain a bad outside, but a good outside cannot sustain a crushed inside. Do you understand?"

"I think so, sir," William had said.

"Good. Now, the inside man, like a good sword, is forged through fire and tempering. Picking one's self up from a mistake, and so forth. I gave Jeremy a job to help him on the inside. He feels he is worth something now; he contributes to taking care of his mother. To him, it's what makes him a man."

They'd walked for a long time in silence, Brewer with his head down, studying the ground as he thought, his father watching the birds as they flew by. It took a while for Brewer to absorb what his father had told him, but when it finally made sense, he nodded to himself and looked up.

"I see now," he said. "I will remember that, father."

His father patted him on the shoulder. "That's all I ask."

Brewer waited until Alfred had left the cabin before raising his glass. Mr. Greene did the same, and the two men drank silently before turning their attentions to the meal before them. Brewer eyed the platter before them hungrily. It bore mutton chops trimmed with parsley and chives, and the aroma that filled the cabin was very enticing. A bowl of peas and another of young carrots looked equally delicious, and there was fresh-baked bread and a crock of butter to complete the feast. Both men dug in for all they were worth, the silence that filled the room speaking volumes of their opinion of Alfred's culinary abilities.

It wasn't until the last bite was swallowed that either man sat back and relaxed in his chair. As though on cue, Alfred appeared to clear the dishes.

"A wonderful meal!" the Captain said.

"Here, here!" Greene echoed.

"Thank you." Alfred acknowledged their compliments with a polite nod.

"I shall write Jenkins a letter and thank him for sending you to me," Brewer said. He was pleased to see Alfred smile.

Alfred removed the dishes and returned, carrying the silver tray with a pot of coffee and two cups, which he set on the table in front of Brewer before bowing and backing silently out of the cabin.

The Captain rose and poured coffee for them both, then handed one cup to Greene. Both men leaned back in their chairs and sipped the scalding brew.

"Mmm," Brewer said as he set the cup on the table. "Even his coffee is superb."

"Well," Greene said as he raised his coffee in salute, "at least we know he can cook!"

"No doubt about that. I'm afraid of what the Admiral will think when we come back from our cruise looking like two prize Christmas geese!"

They laughed together, but then Brewer saw his first lieutenant grow serious, obviously debating whether or not to say something. He leaned back in his seat, determined to wait his friend out.

Soon Greene stirred and spoke hesitatingly. "Speaking of the Admiral, I have never had the opportunity to ask you... about St. Helena."

Brewer looked at his cup on the table and said nothing.

Greene began to rise as he hurried on. "Sir, if I've offended in some way, allow me to apologize, and I shall withdraw!"

"Sit, Mr. Greene," Brewer said softly. "It is I who must apologize to you. You see, for several years, people have sought me out, but only to talk about Bonaparte. It got to the point where people would either argue with me or outright accuse me of treason for not making his punishment more severe." Brewer frowned at the memory. "Eventually, I just quit speaking about St. Helena altogether. I think Captain Norman rather resented the fact."

Brewer looked up and smiled, a bit embarrassed by the emotions the memories stirred. "Not what you wanted to hear, I'm sure." Brewer sighed. "You are, however, quite correct in pointing out that you have never asked me about St. Helena, and I appreciate that, Benjamin."

Greene was apparently making a mental note not to mention St. Helena again. Brewer smiled.

"I had no idea what to expect on the way to the island," he began, enjoying the surprise on his companion's face. "None of us did. We all knew that Bonaparte was making a fool out of the governor, and we were ferrying Lord Hornblower to replace him. Somehow, on the voyage down, I caught the new governor's eye—probably thanks to Captain Bush, but I'll never know for sure—and he asked for me to be his aide and run his office for him."

Brewer paused for a sip of coffee before continuing. "So I saw quite a bit of Bonaparte, as I was usually at my desk whenever he came to see the governor. At first he ignored me, but little by little, he changed."

"How so?" Greene asked.

"You must understand," Brewer explained, "that Bonaparte in 1817 on St. Helena was no longer the same man who was the victor at Austerlitz in 1805. He had been defeated militarily, and by the time I met him he had been exiled on St. Helena for nearly two years. I think it had begun to sink in just how far he had fallen. Boredom and depression were his ever-present enemies, and it was a battle for him simply to retain his sanity. He needed something he could focus his energies on, and he found it in the person of the British governor. Lord Hornblower was able to stand up to Bonaparte, not only man to man, but also soldier to soldier, which was far more important to Bonaparte."

"Do you mean he actually behaved? Or did he try to make a fool out of Hornblower, too? To outmaneuver him?"

Brewer considered. "Hornblower was a fresh challenge, and that alone was a tonic for a man half mad with the frustration of being a general without a campaign. But Hornblower would not react publicly as his predecessor did. But remember: Napoleon was famous for his attentiveness to soldiers. I believe he began noticing that I treated him with the respect an officer accords another officer, regardless of the state of politics between their countries. ."

Greene cocked his head.

"From my brief conversations with the man," Brewer explained, "it was obvious that the previous aide—a Foreign Office man named Wilson—considered Bonaparte a criminal who should have been shot by the King of France. I inferred he'd been most disrespectful, whereas I began standing when Bonaparte entered the room. When the governor discovered what I was doing, he approved and instructed me to continue. Next, I began announcing Bonaparte, if he would allow me, which he usually did. He started speaking to me as he passed through the office."

Brewer smiled. "Two incidents particularly come to mind. The first occurred after the governor had ordered a security crackdown around Longwood—that's the house where Bonaparte and his followers were quartered. Bonaparte burst into the office and demanded that I tell him the reason for the increased security. He leaned over my desk and positively demanded that I tell him." Brewer shook his head at the memory. "The only thought going through my mind was not to show fear in front of him. I stood face to face with Napoleon Bonaparte, Benjamin—practically nose to nose, in fact—and it was all I could do to lock my knees to keep them form knocking and stare into his eyes. Thank God, the governor walked in at that moment and dealt with Bonaparte's complaints."

Greene chuckled. "Not all wars are won on the battlefield."

"Indeed. The other incident occurred shortly before we left the island. The governor had been relieved, and we were waiting for his replacement to arrive. As I recall, we had not seen Bonaparte in some time, although I had been too occupied in preparing for the transition to really notice. I was so engrossed in my work that I paid no attention, one day, when I heard the door open, and I was not happy when the trail of footsteps stopped at my desk.

"'Just a moment,' I said. I was trying to finish a sentence in the report I was composing for Lord Hornblower. Let me tell you, Benjamin, my heart leapt into my throat when I heard Bonaparte say, 'Take your time, Mr. Brewer.'"

"Good lord. What did you do?"

"I jumped to my feet and tried to apologize for not acknowledging him when he came in, but he waved it off. I told him the governor was not in, but he said he had come to see me. I was astounded, Mr. Greene! Napoleon Bonaparte come to see *me*? He must have seen the uncertainty in my eyes, because he told me the governor knew of his mission and had approved in advance.

"We sat down together, and he gave me some sound advice about life. He said that luck occurs when opportunity is met with preparation. The most significant opportunity usually occurs only once in a lifetime, he told me, so you must be ready to seize it when it presents itself. He said that where most people go wrong is that they miss their chance. If they recognize the opportunity at all, they reach for it tentatively, as though they feared to take hold of it. Bonaparte told me you have to seize opportunity as soon as it presents itself. He likened it to a wolf taking its prey by the throat and hanging on until it is dead beneath him. That's what he did when he assumed the throne of France, and that was what he expected from his marshals."

Brewer looked out the stern window. "As he rose to leave, he put his hand on my shoulder, but he was looking out the window behind me. I shall never forget the look of incredible sadness that was on his face. It was as though the man was staring his doom in the face, powerless to prevent it. After a few moments, he blinked and sighed, and patted my shoulder.

" 'Mr. Brewer,' he said to me, 'remember what I have said. Your destiny will present itself, but you must be ready for it. When it appears, take it by the throat and make it surrender to you. Do not concern yourself with others; the best gift you can give them is your complete and total triumph. That is how you can change the world and make their lives better.' Then he smiled at me, and, taking me by both shoulders, he embraced me after the French manner, with a kiss on each cheek.

"'Farewell, Mr. Brewer,' he said. 'May the gods of destiny and victory be kinder to you than they were to me.'"

Brewer paused, trying not to allow the memory to overwhelm him. "When Bonaparte stepped back from me, I swear to you, Benjamin, I could not help myself; I came to attention and saluted him. I am no traitor, you understand; it was simply a gesture of respect from one military man to another. Bonaparte's face betrayed his surprise, but I caught the grin at the corner of his mouth. He, too, came to attention and returned my salute, after which he marched from the office without another word." Brewer looked down at the table and sighed. "I never saw him again. The Admiral told me he has received word that Bonaparte has died on St. Helena. Cancer of the stomach, I believe." He looked out the stern window again. "Well, at least he is free now."

Neither man said anything for several minutes. Finally, Brewer pushed his seat back and rose. Greene followed suit.

"Thank you for telling me," Greene said. "I shall keep your confidence."

A little later, Brewer ascended to the deck, once again without cracking his skull on a deck beam. He spied Dr. Spinelli standing alone on the lee rail, staring at Port Royal.

"Hello, Doctor," Brewer said as he joined his friend. "Did you benefit from your rest?"

Spinelli eyed his Captain suspiciously. "So, it was you, was it? I knew someone had been in the sick bay."

"Yes, well, I didn't want to disturb you. I'm sorry we haven't got together to play chess yet, Adam. Perhaps tomorrow, once we're at sea again?"

Spinelli shrugged. "Perhaps."

Brewer turned to study his friend more closely. That was not the reply he hoped to receive. He found the doctor sullen, his brow furled. Brewer sniffed discreetly but could not detect the smell of alcohol; but then, he was upwind. He should have stood to the other side, except the doctor had angled himself to the rail in just such a way to prevent that. Deliberately? Brewer stared out over the harbor's wave, hands clasped behind his back, wondering what to do. He looked at the deck and decided to go for the throat.

"Come with me," he said. He spun on his heel and headed for the companionway before the doctor had a chance to reply. "Mr. Reed, I shall be in my cabin."

"Aye aye, sir."

Brewer plunged below deck, leaving the good doctor to catch up. He threw open the cabin door and left it for Spinelli to shut.

"Alfred!" he called. The servant appeared in the doorway. "Coffee for two, if you please."

Alfred nodded and disappeared on his errand. The doctor arrived and closed the door behind him. He stood uncomfortably just inside the door, his hat in his hands, eyeing the deck.

Brewer took his coat off and hung it on a peg in the wall. His hat went on the peg next to it. He turned to see the doctor standing there and was struck by one thought—*this man looks lost!*

"Sit down, Adam, please," he said.

The two men took their seats at the table just as Alfred reentered the cabin, carrying his silver tray with the coffee on it.

"Thank you, Alfred. Doctor, have you met Alfred Thomas? He is here at the recommendation by our friend Jenkins."

"Yes," the doctor said. "We've met."

"Oh. Quite. Well, thank you, Alfred. That will be all."

"Yes, sir," the servant retreated from the room.

"So, Adam," Brewer said, startling his friend, "how have you been?"

"Well enough, Captain," Spinelli muttered.

Brewer said quietly, "I thought we were friends."

The doctor's head snapped up, a look of shock on his face. "What do you mean, sir?"

Brewer looked deeply into the doctor's eyes. "You are lying to me."

"Captain! I assure you—"

Brewer cut him off. "Adam, please! It is all too obvious. Anyone could tell by looking at you something is not right with you."

Spinelli stared at his hands, folded on the table in front of him. "I don't know what you mean."

The captain rested his chin between his thumb and forefinger and studied the man sitting across from him. The doctor looked crushed—there was no other word for it—and now he was dealing with the after effects of trying to drown his sorrows in drink.

"Adam," he said in what he hoped was a compassionate voice, "let me help you."

The doctor did not look up. "There is nothing you can do."

Brewer sighed and sat back in his chair. "I have to ask. Your duties, will you be able to—"

Spinelli's head came up. "I can do my job, Captain."

Brewer sat still, saying nothing, watching as the doctor went back to staring at his hands, a look of despair on his face. Brewer's mind was racing, trying to think of what he could say to ease his friend's burden and coming up empty. Well, perhaps the doctor would open up over a game of chess later. He leaned forward, resting his left forearm on the table.

"Very well," he said. "We'll let it stand for now. I have only one thing I must say to you, and I say it as your captain. You must watch your drinking. I cannot abide a surgeon who is drunk. Do you understand?"

"Yes, sir," the surgeon said sullenly.

Brewer rose. "My door is always open to you. Chess later?"

Spinelli rose and shrugged. Then he looked up and saw the naked concern on his captain's face. It broke his reserve a little, and he smiled wanly before he shuffled out of the cabin.

CHAPTER 3

Captain William Brewer felt a surge of pride well up as he ascended to the deck, ready to take his first command on its first voyage for His Majesty's navy. He inhaled deeply. He looked around the deck, feeling the movement of the ship. He was trying his best to look casual but feared that everyone could see how nervous he really was. The rigging and yards looked as though the admiral himself was expected aboard, and he nodded to himself at the quality of the work. He caught the eye of Mr. Snead, the bosun; a smile and a single nod sufficed to convey the Captain's appreciation to the standing officer, and a returning smile cracked the bosun's face as he saluted.

Brewer turned aft toward the quarterdeck, where he saw Lt. Greene standing, hands behind his back, feet spread, looking for all the world to Brewer like a sturdy oak, able to stand through the strongest hurricane winds that buffeted these waters several months of the year. The longer Brewer knew him, the more he liked the man, and he was coming to rely on him more and more. Mr. Sweeney was standing a short way off, his eyes scanning the sky and *Revenge's* sails.

Greene saluted as his captain approached. "Ready to proceed, sir. First of the ebb tide in about thirty minutes. Anchor's hove short."

"My compliments—*Revenge* looks very smart indeed. Shall we see if Mr. Tyler can take her out?"

"I believe he will do just fine, sir."

"Very well. Pass the word." Greene turned to give the order, and Brewer looked for the signals midshipman. "Mr. Short! Signal to the admiral! *'Revenge ready to proceed'.*"

"Aye aye, sir!"

Brewer turned back in time to see Tyler approach.

"You sent for me, Captain?"

"Yes, Mr. Tyler. Get the ship under way, if you please. Set your course due east for St. Kitts once we've cleared the harbor."

Tyler was surprised by the order, but he recovered quickly. "Aye aye, sir."

"Reply from the admiral, sir!" Mr. Short called from the fantail. "*'Good luck and good hunting.'*"

Mr. Tyler studied the tides for a few moments. "Stand by the capstan! Loose the heads'ls! Hands aloft to loose the tops'ls!"

Brewer stood off to the side of the quarterdeck, Mr. Greene at his side, and watched as Tyler got the ship moving. The anchor broke water and *Revenge* began her slow glide toward the harbor entrance and the open sea. Tyler guided the ship out of the harbor with more confidence than Brewer would have thought possible.

He turned toward his first lieutenant. "Rather well done, wouldn't you say?"

"Indeed, sir," Greene replied. "It appears that the rumors of Mr. Tyler's paying attention to Mr. Phillips' classes on *Defiant* may be true after all."

Brewer nodded his understanding. Mr. Phillips had received his commission at the tender age of sixteen after an extraordinary series of circumstances on his old ship, HMS *Retribution*. When HMS *Defiant* sailed to join the West Indies squadron, Captain Norman had ordered Brewer and the sailing master, Mr. Sweeney, to devise a program of instruction to teach Phillips everything he'd not had time to learn as a midshipman—in short, to prepare him for the commissioning board. Now that Brewer thought about it, he did recall seeing Tyler lurking within earshot whenever he or the sailing master was instructing Phillips in seamanship or ship handling.

Brewer stood over against the lee rail, watching silently as Tyler piloted *Revenge* out of Kingston harbor and settled her on her eastern course toward St. Kitts. It occurred to him how he had often seen Captain Bush strike the same pose, observing Brewer himself or another of the junior lieutenants performing just such a maneuver. He wondered —no, he was sure Bush had picked it up from Hornblower.

Tyler rejoined the captain and first lieutenant. Brewer patted him on the arm and said, "Keep this up, Jeremiah, and I'm afraid I shall have no choice but to put you in front of the first commissioning board I can find."

Tyler beamed at his captain's words.

Brewer stepped back. "Carry on, Mr. Tyler."

"Aye, sir." Tyler saluted and went forward.

Brewer turned to his first lieutenant. "A good beginning, Mr. Greene, and, let us hope, a good omen."

"Aye, sir," Greene agreed.

Brewer slept that night like a new king in his castle. His old hammock on HMS *Defiant* never seemed so comfortable. He found it impossible to sleep once the first rays of sunlight peeked into his cabin. He leaped to the deck and dressed. He stepped up onto the deck of HMS *Revenge* just as the dawn broke fully over his ship and crew.

Brewer walked over to the sailing master, who was standing beside the quartermaster at the wheel.

"Mr. Sweeney, tell me, what are your first impressions of *Revenge*? How does she sail?"

"Let me get a feel for her, Captain," he replied. "It's been a while since I've been in something this small. But so far," he added judiciously, "I think she'll do just fine."

Brewer looked around, joy in his heart. The ship—*his* ship —felt like an extension of his own body. He was no fool; he knew this sort of euphoria could not last, but he was determined to enjoy it while it did.

"Mr. Sweeney!" he called over his shoulder. "What say we see what our girl can do?"

Sweeney looked up at the sails with an appraising eye, then raised his eyebrows at his captain.

"Mr. Tyler! Call the hands, if you please. Make all sail! Let's see if *Revenge* can fly!"

"All hands! All hands! Make sail!"

Brewer stood between Sweeney and Greene, his hands behind his back, watching his men rush to carry out the orders. *Revenge* responded, leaping forward as her sails harnessed the power of the winds. He waited until all the canvas had shaken out and was drawing before he gave his next order.

"Mr. Reed, cast the log."

Reed went aft, taking Mr. Short with him. Brewer shared an expectant look with Greene as they waited as patiently as they could for the midshipman to report. The two young gentlemen moved to the fantail, Reed holding the triangular piece of wood strangely called the 'log' and Short manning the glass. Short watched the senior midshipman throw the log overboard, and as soon as he saw it, he turned the glass over and watched carefully as it ran through its 28-second cycle. The moment he saw the last grain of sand fall into the bottom of the glass, he call out, "Now!" Reed caught the line that had been running out after the log and quickly counted the number of knots.

Finally, Reed returned to the Captain and reported. "Thirteen knots, Captain!"

Brewer, Greene, and Sweeney all smiled at each other. Thirteen knots! And that was *before* they discovered *Revenge's* best point of sailing!

"All right, Sweeney," Brewer said, rubbing his hands in anticipation, "let's see what she can *really* do!"

For the next few hours, they put HMS *Revenge* through nearly every pace or maneuver any of them could think they might need. Hands were sent aloft to make or take in sail, brought down when the maneuver was completed, and then run back up again. Time and again, *Revenge* was pushed to her very limits, and every time she responded magnificently.

Brewer felt pleased at the way his ship performed. He looked over at his sailing master.

"Mr. Sweeney? Your verdict?"

Sweeney looked up at *Revenge's* canvas and pursed his lips. "Captain," he said, "I think she'll do just fine."

Tyler came up and saluted. "Ship on course for St. Kitts, sir."

"Thank you, Mr. Tyler," Brewer said. He turned to his first lieutenant. "You may dismiss the watch below, Mr. Greene. Hands to breakfast. Please join me in my cabin after you have seen to your duties."

"Very good, sir."

Brewer went below, listening to Greene bellowing orders and thinking once again how fortunate he was to have Benjamin Greene. He was still thinking about it when he entered his cabin. His eyes fell on the Bible lying on his desk. It reminded him to be thankful that Providence had put Greene on *Defiant*. That gave Brewer pause, and he sat at his desk and considered. Hornblower told him on St. Helena that he considered Bush indispensable as his first lieutenant.

Could he now have in Mr. Greene the first lieutenant to complement him? Could Greene be his Bush?

The knock at the door interrupted Brewer's meditations. He straightened his uniform.

"Enter," he called.

Greene entered, hat correctly held under his arm as he closed the door behind him.

"So," Brewer said, "how are things topside, Benjamin?"

"On course for St. Kitts, Captain. Mr. Tyler has the deck."

"Then will you join me for breakfast, Benjamin?"

The first lieutenant grinned. "Thank you, sir!"

"Alfred!" Brewer called over his shoulder. When the servant appeared, he said, "Another officer for breakfast."

"Yes, sir." He stepped out and returned a moment later carrying his silver tray, this time holding a decanter and two glasses. He set the tray on the table and departed without saying a word.

Greene watched him go, then turned to his captain and smiled. "It's going to take a while for me to get used to that."

Brewer grinned as he poured their drinks and handed Greene his glass. "I wonder what he'll say when he finally starts talking."

Breakfast was every bit as good as dinner the night before. When it was over, the two officers sat at the table sipping hot coffee and feeling satisfied.

Greene set his cup on the table. "With your permission, sir, I'd like to exercise my gun crews for an hour or so this afternoon."

"Good idea," Brewer said, as he refilled both their cups from the pot left by Alfred. "I want to be ready should we run into our friend again." He sat back, his eyes suddenly dark. "He made a fool of me once, and he escaped me the second time. It will be different when we meet again."

Greene lifted his cup in agreement. "Third time's the charm, sir."

The voyage to St. Kitts passed quickly for Brewer and his crew. The good weather they had enjoyed at Kingston did not abandon them, and the glassy surface of the sea was broken only by *Revenge's* wake as they sped on their way. The training was hard, but nobody seemed to mind. The entire crew went about their work purposefully. They, like their captain, had one thought in mind—to be ready when they finally ran into the French frigate again.

The ship slid into the harbor at St. Kitts early in the morning. After they rendered the appropriate honors, a pilot was sent to guide them to their berth. The sky looked suspiciously overcast, but Mr. Sweeney said that was normal for this time of year in the Caribbean.

Brewer appeared on deck dressed in his best uniform. He'd only just bought it in Jamaica, and this was the first occasion he'd had to wear it, and he could have sworn he'd seen in his mirror a smile tugging at the corner of Mac's mouth. He felt ill at ease, and he was sure it showed.

He looked around the deck. The routine in-harbor work was being done, and his men were careful not to appear to take special notice of him. Brewer turned aft and found Mr. Sweeney waiting for him.

The old sailing master saluted. "Captain."

Brewer straightened his coat for the third time since appearing on deck.

"Mr. Sweeney," he said, "I believe the tailor may have made a mistake. This coat just does not feel right."

Sweeney looked his captain over. "Do you know, I remember Captain Cook saying the same thing just before he went to meet the governor at St. Johns. He was wrong." He leaned in close. "Captain, you look fine. You are a credit to your ship."

Brewer stood erect, straightening his coat one last time.

Lieutenant Greene approached and saluted. "Boat's crew ready, sir."

"Very good, Greene. I will return as soon as I can."

Without further comment, the Captain strode to the entryway and descended to the boat. His coxswain stood to the side until his captain had taken his seat in the stern sheets. McCleary took his place and gave the order, and the boat moved toward the shore.

The first lieutenant and sailing master watched their captain row away. Greene took a deep breath and let it out forcefully, crossing his arms across his chest. He looked at his companion.

"The Captain seemed a little nervous, don't you think?"

Sweeney shrugged. "Maybe a little, but he'll be fine as soon as he realized that the governor depends on him, and not he on the governor. 'Tis *Revenge* and the rest of the squadron that bring the peace in these parts. The governor will surely have heard of the victory we had over the pirates, but he will also have heard about the frigate that escaped, and that will make him nervous. He'll be glad for *Revenge*, small as she is; and on land, William Brewer *is* HMS *Revenge*."

Upon arriving at the governor's residence, Brewer was shown into the library by a liveried servant who informed him that the governor would join him presently. Brewer stepped over to admire a large painting of HMS *Victory*, Nelson's flagship at Trafalgar. He was reminded of the late James Norman and the tragedy that plunged a nation into mourning and set a young lieutenant on the road to insanity. He shook his head at how senseless it all seemed now.

The door to the library opened, and a man entered. He was tall and thin, with a powdered wig on that hung down past his shoulders. His hawkish nose and pronounced cheekbones gave him an imposing look, which rumor had it he exaggerated by appearing to look down his nose at those before him.

"Commander Brewer?" he said as he stepped forward and extended his hand. "My name is Sir Henry Danforth, and I am the governor of St. Kitts. Welcome to our island."

Brewer bowed and shook the governor's hand, noting the way his speech, which was friendly, did not match his look. "Thank you, Governor," he said. "I bring you Admiral Lord Hornblower's greetings."

"Hmm." Danforth nodded to the picture. "Impressive, isn't she? The very embodiment of British sea power."

"Indeed," Brewer said.

"Yes," the Governor said. He stood next to Brewer for a moment and appeared to be looking down his nose at him, studying him closely. The Commander was momentarily unnerved by the experience, but he remembered standing before the Corsican and decided that the Governor fell short by comparison.

The Governor's head bobbed in a small nod, as though he had come to a decision, and he stepped to the side.

"Won't you join me in my office for a drink, Commander? There are matters I would like to discuss with you."

"A pleasure, sir."

The governor led the way out of the library and down the hallway toward the rear of the house. He opened a door at the end of the hall and showed Brewer into a large room, brightly lit by big windows, which gave the occupants a panoramic view of the interior of the island. The governor's ornamental oak desk was off to the left, and there was a large portrait of George IV on the wall behind it. Off to the right were two settees facing each other with a low table in between. In the corner was a table that held several varieties of wine and spirits, and it was there that the governor was bound.

"Port, Commander?" he asked.

"Thank you," Brewer said. He waited where he was until the governor returned and handed him one of the two glasses he carried. Brewer followed his host to two overstuffed leather chairs at the far end of the room. The governor stood behind the one on the right and indicated his guest should take the other. Both men faced each other, and the governor raised his glass in a toast.

"Your very good health, Commander," he said, "and a successful voyage."

Brewer raised his glass as well. "Thank you, Governor." Both men drank, then took their seats.

"HMS *Revenge* is a new ship, is she not?"

"She is indeed. She was a pirate sloop we took as a prize, and the Navy purchased her."

Governor Danforth smiled. "One less ship in the hands of pirates is always a good thing." He sipped his port. "I understand you were with the admiral when he fought the pirates north of Cuba. Tell me about that."

Brewer set his glass down on a small table next to his chair. "We carried out the admiral's plan, luring three pirate ships out of Cardenas on the north coast of Cuba. We sank one and took another, but the third unfortunately escaped in the confusion. I'm afraid I can tell you little more, as I was injured early in the battle and know only what I was told of what happened. The Americans played an important part, I understand; they arrived in time to seal the victory."

"So I heard," the governor said, playing with his half-empty glass. "I was wondering if you would mention that."

"It was in the admiral's plan for them to take part," Brewer said.

"Indeed," the governor said. Brewer could not tell if the man was being condescending or not. His host set his glass down and sat back in his chair. "Tell me, Commander, what is the admiral's plan for dealing with the pirate menace? The Americans have a squadron hunting them, and we have our own forces in the area, and yet the menace still exists."

Brewer leaned forward and met the governor's eye. "The admiral's plan is to find them and blow them out of the water."

"Yes, well," replied the governor, seemingly unimpressed, "let us hope he is as successful as he has been in his past endeavors."

Suddenly the door burst open, and a young woman swept into the room. Brewer and his host were instantly on their feet and gazing at the newcomer, Brewer in astonishment and the governor in resignation.

"Father, I wonder if... Oh! I'm sorry!" she stammered, as she realized what she had done. "I wasn't aware that you had company, Father."

"It's quite all right, my dear," the governor said. He turned to make the proper introductions. "Commander Brewer, may I present my daughter, Elizabeth. My dear, this is Commander William Brewer of HMS *Revenge*."

Brewer was instantly captivated by the vision that stood before him. Elizabeth Danforth was a tall beauty with long chestnut hair that hung down past her shoulders and framed a face that deserved to be in a masterpiece by one of the renaissance masters, with lips that could capture any man's attention and dark eyes in which a man might lose his soul.

Her mouth was generous, and her smile melted his heart. Her skin was tanned and reminded Brewer of the legends he had heard of the Caribbean beauties. To his embarrassment, he realized he was staring at her, a fact which seemed to amuse her.

Brewer bowed over her hand. "A pleasure, Miss Danforth."

She curtsied. "You are too kind, Commander."

Brewer caught a playful look in her eye as she turned to her father. "Father, have you invited our young Commander to dine with us? I believe the cook is working on some delicious mutton chops, Commander."

Brewer thought the governor appeared a bit frazzled by his daughter's actions but hid it well. "Yes, Commander, please do join us."

He bowed. "At your service, sir."

"Wonderful!" Elizabeth proclaimed. She moved swiftly to kiss her father on the cheek. Brewer was embarrassed to discover he felt a pang of envy. "I shall go inform the cook. See you both at dinner."

Governor Danforth drew a deep breath and expelled it loudly. "I hope you will forgive my daughter, Commander. Her mother died giving birth to her, and I sometimes think I have indulged her too much as a consequence. She tends to take advantage of me at the most awkward times for her own amusement."

Brewer shook his head. "You raised her yourself, Governor? You are to be commended, sir; she is an enchanting young woman."

"Thank you," his host said. "She is and always has been the light of my life. Now then, where were we? Oh, yes; we were discussing your admiral's plans to rid the seas of these pirates."

Elizabeth Danforth's eyes were dancing in her head as she walked to the kitchen on her mission to alert the cook. She had met many a King's officer in her father's study, but this Commander Brewer was different somehow. She was almost sure he knew just what she was up to when she'd maneuvered her father into a corner by inviting him to dinner as she did. It was a game she had played for some years now; she never tired of that exasperated, here-we-go-again look on her father's face as she burst into his study unannounced when he was in a meeting. She smiled at the thought, for she well knew that her father played the game every bit as well as she, and she loved him the more for it.

But this Commander Brewer interested her as no King's officer yet had. She had seen a knowing look in his eye as he watched her performance, and yet he had been content to allow her to have her game without any input from him. She paused as she reached the door to the kitchen to lean against the wall. Her hand went to her chest, and she was surprised to feel her heart racing. She suddenly wanted to know this Commander Brewer better, and she went into the kitchen looking forward to the meal—or more properly, the company.

The steward announced that dinner was served, and Governor Danforth led his guest to the dining room. The two men arrived before Elizabeth, so they stood and chatted amiably with his other guests until she arrived. Brewer watched as the others went to their natural places at the table, the governor at its head with his daughter on his right hand. Danforth indicated Brewer's place was at his left, and the Commander took his seat.

The meal that was placed before him lived up to Elizabeth's predictions. The chops were as savory as any that

44

Jenkins or Alfred had ever produced. Stewed potatoes and fresh cauliflower rounded out the fare, and everyone did the repast justice.

"Forgive me for asking, Commander," Elizabeth said as the meal was winding down, "but you seem young for command of a King's ship."

Brewer smiled. "How old does one have to be, Miss Danforth?"

She returned the smile, and very nearly succeeded in dazzling him. "It's only that I find that most of the commanders I meet in my father's study are older than you, some considerably older, and yet here you are."

"I was in temporary command of the frigate HMS *Defiant* after our captain was lost overboard in a hurricane. Admiral Hornblower accompanied us on patrol. The ship I now command was the first pirate vessel we encountered. We took it as a prize after a short battle. The Admiral arranged for the vessel to be purchased into the navy, and he appointed me as Master and Commander as a reward for my actions."

She had a playful grin on her face now. "Why did he not leave you in command of *Defiant*?"

"It seems there were too many senior officers for me to command such a large and important warship, my lady," he said in mock seriousness. "To put it plainly, it seems I was just *too young* for the job."

She whooped in laughter at his jest, only to cover her mouth with her napkin in embarrassment a moment later. The commander's eyes laughed at her, and she felt her heart melt inside her. She blushed and turned her attention to finishing her potatoes.

"Now, see there, Commander," the governor chastened him playfully, "you have committed the unpardonable sin of besting my daughter at her own game. Let me tell you, that is a feat rarely accomplished." He looked at the clock in the corner of the room, and rose from his place. "I have work to do. My dear, why don't you show the good Commander the gardens, that is, if you have the time, Commander?"

Brewer wiped his mouth and stood. "It would be my honor, Governor."

"Good," he said. "My dear, bring him back alive, won't you? And don't let her fool you, Commander; the only carnivorous thing in the garden will be my daughter."

Brewer followed his hostess out the French doors that led to the patio overlooking the grounds. She paused to let him catch up and admire the scenery. He looked out over a garden that would do justice to many a manor house anywhere in the English countryside.

"I'm impressed, Miss Danforth," he said.

"It's my favorite place to think. I often walk here in the cool of the evening. I'm almost sorry to have to show it to you now, in the heat of the afternoon."

"I assure you," he said with a smile, "the company more than makes up for any inconvenience brought on by the heat."

He thought her smile lacked sincerity, as though she had heard similar words from officers before, but her eyes said something different. He stood back and allowed her to lead him down the stairs and along one of the garden paths.

They walked on in silence. Brewer admired the sculpted, lush green plants and the manicured walkways. He understood why his hostess liked to come here to think; it must be peaceful when one was alone.

He turned to her as they walked. "This is a beautiful place. I can see why you come here."

"Yes," she said. He noticed she only turned to him for a moment before resuming her walk. "It is a peaceful place to reflect, to think, even to dream."

"What do you dream about?"

She laughed. "Not about dashing King's officers to come and rescue me, I assure you." She glanced at him to see if the barb had struck home and was surprised to see no reaction at all from her companion. "Only the things a simple girl would dream, Commander. Nothing as interesting as commanding a ship at sea, I wager."

He smiled, studying the ground ahead of the as they walked on. "Miss Danforth," he said, "I have only known you a short time, but I would say you are anything but simple."

She stopped and looked at him, and Brewer followed suit. Their eyes met, and he could tell from the intensity in hers that she was trying to see if there was anything to him, anything underneath the shell of the King's officer, and he understood why she was doing it. He had met so many in his time at sea who were nothing but an empty uniform and thought that a beautiful woman was a prize to be taken like a pirate sloop. Presently, and without a word to give him a hint as to the results of her search, she resumed their trek along the path.

"Tell me about your people, Commander," she said without preamble. "Where do you come from? How did you come to command a King's ship in the Caribbean?"

His eyebrow rose a fraction at her question. He glanced at her, but her eyes were focused on the pathway before them.

"My family comes from Kent," he said. "My father has a farm there. I decided I wanted to be a King's officer when I got my first look at the sea. I was six years old. My father was against the idea, I'm afraid. He wanted me to take over the farm from him, as he had from his father. I was fifteen when

I finally left home to join the service, and he was still against it."

"I'm sorry to hear that," she said. "Has he changed his mind, now that you are successful?"

"My father disowned me when I left home, Miss Danforth. I have not seen or heard from him since that day."

There was a sadness beneath his words that caught her attention. She had heard similar words from various officers before, of course, but the underlying tone behind them had always been one of resentment or bitterness. She stopped and turned to him.

"I am sorry," she said. "Please forgive me if my questions have caused pain."

"No need to apologise, Miss Danforth. It is an old wound. Please do not concern yourself."

They started off down the path again. She slipped her arm inside his, and she was surprised yet again when he did not react to this either. She smiled.

"Tell me, is the life of a commander as lonely as I have heard it to be?"

He smiled. "I will confess to you, Miss Danforth, that I am only now beginning to discover the truth of that for myself. I took command of our frigate HMS *Defiant* after Captain Norman was washed overboard in a hurricane, but with storm damage and pirate attacks, I was far too busy to be lonely before we reached Jamaica. Then, when we went out after the pirates, Admiral Hornblower was with us, so the burdens of command resided largely with him. I have only had command of HMS *Revenge* for the few days' voyage from Port Royal. I have seen it so, however, watching captains under whom I have served."

They walked on in silence. When they came round again to the house, she led him inside and bade him farewell.

"I hope you will call again when you next pass our little island," she said.

He bowed over her hand. "It will be my pleasure. Thank you for a lovely tour of the garden." He hesitated, still holding her hand.

"Miss Danforth, may I write to you?"

She did not meet his eyes, but he saw her smile. "Yes."

She curtsied and withdrew. He watched her disappear up the staircase and went to make his farewells to the governor.

Brewer elected to walk back to the wharf. He wanted time to think, and he wanted to think about Elizabeth Danforth. He had never met a woman who had so captured his attentions, and he found himself daring to hope that she might feel the same about him. He wished he could find an excuse to keep *Revenge* in port for several days while he got to know her better, but his orders were quite specific that he was to leave the following day, providing the winds cooperated. Unfortunately, according to Mr. Sweeney, St. Kitts was not known for contrary winds, so the odds of delay were remote.

It suddenly dawned on him how lonely his life was. He had never been what one might call a ladies' man, and up until now he had had no inclination for female companionship—not that he was bent the other way, as it were; he simply had never found a woman who could compare with the sea for his affections. Until now.

His mind naturally tended toward thoughts of marriage, and he wondered whether it would be fair to his wife to leave her for a year or two at a time and expect her to wait for him. He thought about his mentors, Hornblower and Bush. One had married, the other hadn't, yet both seemed happy enough. Still, Hornblower had been miserable in the days after his wife and son had to leave St. Helena and return to

England in order to save the boy's life. Then Brewer recalled the look on the admiral's face after HMS *Agamemnon* had docked at Plymouth: he could hardly wait to disembark and begin the long coach ride that would carry him back to Lady Barbara in Smallbridge. Brewer remembered that look well, and he envied the Admiral his happiness.

Captain Bush, however, was no less content in his bachelorhood. All through HMS *Lydia's* long commission fighting the Barbary pirates in the Mediterranean, Bush had written faithfully to his sister in England. Sometimes Bush would vent his outrage at something or other his sister bought, other times he would tell Brewer stories of his adventures with her when they were children. Brewer knew beyond doubt that his Captain loved and lived for his sister. There was never a hint of any other woman in William Bush's life, but Brewer never heard his captain speak against marriage either. Brewer shrugged; perhaps, for Bush, the right woman simply never came along.

Brewer turned the corner, and the road began its descent to the coastline. His eyes were on the pavement before him, but his mind was racing. He decided that, if the opportunity presented itself, he would ask the Admiral his thoughts on the matter. Yes, Brewer nodded to himself, that was the thing to do.

He had just quickened his pace when he heard a ruckus coming from a tavern ahead. Fearing one or more of his crew may be involved, he stepped inside. It took his eyes a moment to adjust to the dim lighting; when they did he was astonished to find Dr. Spinelli to be the one at the bar and in the midst of the uproar.

"Don't you talk that way to me, you little half-breed moron!" the doctor roared in a drunken rage. He picked up a tankard off the bar and hurled it against the wall. "I shall bring the might of King George down on your heads, mark me!"

The angry grumbling of the other patrons grew louder, and they began to close in around the doctor. Brewer pushed through the mob to stand beside his friend.

"What's going on here?" he demanded.

The sudden appearance of a King's officer, in uniform, caused the advancing mob to halt, but only for a moment. One man stepped forward and pointed a crooked finger at the doctor.

"This 'ere bloke thinks we're all peasants compared to 'im!" he accused. The crowd murmured agreement. Dr. Spinelli turned his back to them and leaned on the bar.

"Adam?" Brewer said. "What's going on?"

"Nothing," the doctor slurred. "Run along home. I'm no good to you now."

Now Brewer knew he had a problem on his hands. "Let me get you out of here," he said quietly.

The leader of the mob pushed in behind Brewer. "Let's get 'im, mates!"

Brewer's elbow shot backwards into the miscreant's ribs, and the same fist came up hard to the face. Brewer heard the satisfying crack of a nose breaking, and the fellow went backwards and downed those behind him. Before he could recover his senses, he found the point of Brewer's sword hovering menacingly one inch from his throat.

"Now, then," Brewer said slowly, "I hope we shall have no more of this... foolishness. Doctor!" he called over his shoulder. "Get out." The tip of the sword moved to touch his antagonist's throat, and he spoke in a voice that was pregnant with menace. "If anyone touches him, *you* die. Now, Doctor."

Spinelli knew better than to argue. He shuffled out of the tavern. Brewer didn't move until he was sure his surgeon was safe, then he followed him out.

The doctor was waiting for him in the street. He looked defeated and discouraged. Brewer took him by the arm and steered him toward the wharf. Spinelli tried to pull his arm free, but Brewer's grip was like iron. The doctor winced under its urging.

"Captain, please!" he cried.

Brewer stopped abruptly and faced his prisoner. "Not a word from you, sir, or I shall be glad to return you to the company of your friends." He let the arm go, and the doctor didn't move. Brewer nodded. "We're agreed then. To the ship, Doctor." Without another word, he turned and walked on, leaving his companion to catch up.

They rode the waves back to *Revenge* in silence. Spinelli looked haggard and defeated. When he stole a look at his captain, the face he saw was set in an unreadable mask with the eyes set looking ahead. When the doctor glanced at his captain's coxswain, he saw a very different face. This one had a look of near contempt; it was a face showing anger, the kind of anger that is brought about by a terrible waste, like one that happens because you did not take the help that was offered. Spinelli hung his head in shame and did not look up again until he went to board the ship.

Once on board, Brewer pulled his friend to the side and leaned in close.

"Go sleep it off, Adam."

Without another word, he left the doctor where he was standing and went below deck. Spinelli looked around, embarrassed and alone, and then went below himself to obey his captain's orders.

CHAPTER 4

Noah Simmons sat in the masthead, enjoying the cool evening breeze and the gentle sway of the ship while *Revenge* was in port. He leaned back against the mast and lamented the turn his life had taken; this miserable ship was a long way from the comfort of his father's mansion on Jamaica. He looked at the town in the distance, and his eyes narrowed with distain. He banged his head against the mast a couple times in self-recrimination.

The debacle of the previous evening had done nothing to improve his mood. Simmons had wrangled a spot of shore leave, hoping to look up an old acquaintance who Simmons had thought might be able to liberate him from his present, reduced circumstance and set him on his way to America. The plan had soured when Mr. Short presented himself just as Simmons was stepping ashore and announced he was going with him. As they'd walked through the town, Simmons had desperately tried to think of a way to get his of his unwanted shadow.

"Wouldn't you rather go find something to do on your own?" he'd said at last. "Do you know anyone here to visit?"

"Not a soul," Short had replied easily. "Besides, I'd rather stay with you."

Simmons had sighed in exasperation and quickened his step, but the smaller midshipman had kept up. Finally, he'd stopped at a corner to rest. Short had stopped as well, silently looking around at the town. Simmons had thought he saw the answer to his problems.

"Say, William, are you thirsty?"

Short looked up to him. "Reckon I am."

"Let's go." Simmons led his young companion down the road and into a tavern.

"I've never been in a place like this," Short said, as they made their way to a table in the back corner.

"I've no doubt," Simmons said as they sat. "It's about time you learned. Two pints." This last was to the waitress, who shot a glance at Short before going off to fill the order.

Short looked around and frowned at the smoky air and general stench of beer that filled the place. "I think I changed my mind. Can we go now?"

"No, we can't," Simmons said, a bit too quickly. "We've already ordered our drinks. We're not allowed to leave until we drink them and pay."

"Oh."

The drinks arrived, and Simmons dropped a couple of coins on the table. The waitress scooped them up and disappeared.

Simmons picked up one of the tankards and raised it in a toast. "Drink up, William!" He took a long pull and set the tankard down with a bang. He looked at Short with expectation.

Short picked up his drink and took a sip, and his face immediately wrinkled.

"What's wrong?" Simmons asked.

"It tastes terrible!" Short said.

Simmons laughed. "You'll get used to it."

Short set it down and pushed it away. "I don't think I want to."

Simmons could scarcely believe what he was hearing. "What? Why not? Don't you drink grog on the ship? Or beer?"

Short wiped his mouth on his sleeve and shook his head. "Grog? Never. Beer? Only when I absolutely have to."

"What! Why?"

"My daddy is a preacher in Bristol. He showed me what the Good Book says about the evils of drink, and he made me promise when I shipped out that I would stay as far away from it as possible. I told him I would, and I have kept my promise."

"That's great, William," Simmons said cheerlessly. So much for his plan of making the midshipman drunk and eluding him. He drained his drink, and Short's too, and they walked out into the evening, one of them stone sober, the other frustrated.

Simmons was roused from his memories by the sounds of someone climbing up the shrouds to join him. He was disagreeably surprised when Short's head appeared over the side.

"There you are," Short said as he climbed up. "I thought I'd find you here."

"And why was that?"

"Because you're weren't anywhere else."

Simmons looked at the boy, who was now looking out over the waves toward the town, and decided against asking what he meant by that. "Did you want something?"

"Oh, yes! Mr. Reed said he wants to see you in the mess right away."

Great, Simmons thought as he started over the side to make his way down. He stopped when he noticed that Short had not moved to come with him. "You're not coming?"

Short shook his head. "Mr. Reed said I should stay here."

Captain William Brewer was at that moment in his cabin, with Lieutenant Greene. Brewer had told him about finding the doctor and rescuing him from the tavern.

Greene shook his head. "Something is bothering him, Captain. We need to find out what it is before anything worse happens. A sailor may get drunk on leave and still perform his duties on board, but a doctor who gets drunk whenever he can is not a man to be trusted with the responsibilities of a surgeon on one of His Majesty's ships."

Brewer studied his clasped hands. "Quite right, Benjamin. Please send the good doctor to me when he awakes."

Greene got up. "Aye, sir."

Brewer spoke up just as his friend reached the door. "After the doctor arrives, I want you to search the sick bay and get rid of every drop of alcohol. Take possession of all of it; we can sort out the details later. Thank you, Benjamin."

Greene smiled and left. Brewer tried to prepare himself mentally for the trial that lay ahead. The doctor was in a delicate place, if Brewer was reading him correctly; the wrong push by the captain could send him over the edge.

A knock at the door brought him to the ready.

"Enter," he said.

The door opened slowly, and Dr. Spinelli crossed the threshold. He was still dressed in the same clothes he'd worn when Brewer brought him back on board the previous evening, and Brewer smelled the whiskey as soon as the doctor entered the cabin. Spinelli looked even more haggard then he had the previous day. The man looked lost.

"Come in, Adam," Brewer said. He indicated the seat the Mr. Greene had just vacated. "Sit down."

Spinelli shuffled to the seat and sat without a word. Brewer raised an eyebrow as he watched, but he said nothing.

"Alfred!"

The servant appeared. "Sir?"

"Coffee, if you please."

"Aye aye, sir." Alfred bowed and was gone. He reappeared with two cups and fresh coffee, which he set on the table. Brewer thanked him, and he left.

Brewer poured them each a cup and handed one to the doctor. Spinelli ignored it and stared at the table like a schoolboy about to be scolded by his headmaster.

"Adam," Brewer said, "what was that about? The tavern, I mean."

The doctor shrugged and muttered something. Brewer thought he caught the word "disagreement".

"Adam, I'm trying to help you. Why don't you tell me what's going on?"

The doctor remained transfixed. Brewer sighed and studied him for several minutes before rising and going to his sea chest. He opened it and removed a small box from inside. He resumed his seat, setting the box on the table in front of him. Spinelli paid no attention as he opened it and took out a small board covered with black and brown squares, each with a hole in the center. Next he began taking out the chess pieces, each of which had a small peg in the bottom which fit in the holes in the board. Brewer was very proud of his new chess set, which he'd bought in Port Royal before they set sail. This was the first occasion he had had to use it, and he hoped it would pique the doctor's interest.

He finished setting up the pieces, then made his opening move, advancing the king's pawn two spaces. He carefully inserted the pawn's peg into the hole in the board, then he sat back to wait.

It took several minutes for the doctor to stir.

"What are you doing?" Spinelli asked.

"Waiting for you to move," Brewer answered without taking his eyes from the board.

"I mean, what are we doing here?"

"Playing chess."

"Not me."

The doctor rose and moved to the door. Brewer did not say a word or move to stop him. Spinelli opened the door and ran headlong into McCleary, the captain's coxswain.

"Hello, Doctor," Mac said. He did not move from the doorway.

"Out of my way, sir!" The doctor tried to push past, but the coxswain was as immovable as the Rock of Gibraltar. The doctor staggered back a step and glared at the big Cornishman in outrage.

McCleary shook his head, as though he was dealing with a petulant child. He reached out, gently placing his hand in the middle of the doctor's chest, and moved him back a couple of steps into the room.

"Just following orders, Doctor," he said, then stepped out of the room and closed the door behind him.

Spinelli stared at the door in frustration. His breathing was heavy and ragged, and he was seriously considering committing suicide by opening the door and attacking the coxswain.

"Doctor," came a calm but commanding voice from behind him, "wouldn't you rather sit down and make your move?"

Spinelli's frustration reached such a pitch that he balled up his fists and wished he could hit something. A tear escaped his eye and slid down his cheek. He closed his eyes and drew a long, ragged breath, then let it out slowly and loudly. He turned and slumped back in his seat. With barely a look at the board he moved his queen's knight to bishop-three.

Brewer's eyes shot up, but the doctor's eyes were staring at the table in front of him, his face still a mask of defeat. Brewer pursed his lips, and his eyes narrowed in concentration, but still he could not see a way to break through and help his friend. He shrugged and decided to let the game continue. He reached out and moved his knight.

It took several more minutes before the doctor responded, and the captain moved his piece afterward, all without a word. As the game progressed, the doctor paid more and more attention. Brewer thought it was almost as if his mind was looking for something, anything, to reach out and latch on to in order to escape whatever thoughts were crushing it.

He allowed the game to play itself out in silence, not taking great care as to who was winning. His strategy bore fruit after three-quarters of an hour, when Spinelli took a rook that the captain carelessly left unguarded.

"Your mind does not seem to be on the game, Captain," Spinelli said.

Brewer sighed. "Yes, well, I suppose not. Actually, Adam, I've been concerned about you."

Spinelli looked up at that, but only for a moment before returning his attention to the board. "Thank you," he muttered quietly. "Nice set, by the way."

"Thank you. I bought it in Port Royal."

They played in silence for a while longer. Brewer noticed the doctor's moves, his gestures, became sharper, as though he were becoming frustrated again. He decided to push the issue now.

"Adam, won't you tell me what happened? What made you go back to the bottle?"

The doctor's hand paused in mid-move before placing the piece in its place. He sat back in his chair and, without taking his eyes from the board, asked, "If I try to leave again, will that gorilla you call a coxswain stop me?"

Brewer studied his friend for a moment before deciding to trust his instincts. "No."

The doctor studied the board for a minute before moving his knight. "Check."

Brewer moved his king and waited.

Spinelli moved a pawn. "I received a letter while we were at Jamaica," he said slowly, "from a doctor friend who lives outside London." He drew a ragged breath, and his eyes began to fill with tears. "He told me of a certain lady friend I knew. She... died... crossing a street in the fog... run down by a horse cab...." His voice trailed off and the tears rolled freely down his cheeks. Another ragged breath; his voice barely a whisper now. "Her name was Mary. I'd hoped to ask her... to marry me when we returned to England." At this, the doctor broke down completely. His chin hit his chest, and he wept openly.

"Adam, I'm so sorry," Brewer said, but the doctor wasn't listening. The Captain studied him for a minute, trying to decide if there was anything he could do or say that might ease his friend's pain. In the end, he rose, walked around the doctor to the door and opened it.

"Mac," he called softly, gesturing for the coxswain to follow him inside. They walked over to the still-weeping doctor. Mac took in the scene quickly and looked up silently, and Brewer was pleased to see compassion in his eyes.

Brewer touched the doctor on the shoulder. "Adam," he said quietly, "go with Mac." To the coxswain: "Take him back to the sickbay and make him comfortable. We'll let him sleep it off."

"Aye aye, sir," the big coxswain said. He put his hand under the doctor's arm to help him up. "Come along, doctor. I've got you." Spinelli obeyed without objection, proof to his captain that he was indeed insensible from grief and drunkenness. Mac maneuvered him out the door and pulled it closed behind him.

Brewer resumed his seat and stared at the closed door for several minutes. His heart ached for his friend, and he hoped that the doctor could deal with his grief and mourn in such a way so that he could still fulfill his duties. The Captain shook his head, wishing his friend had come to him sooner. *Well,* he thought, *I'll give him this voyage. If he's still like this when we return to Port Royal, I shall have to speak to the admiral.*

Alfred appeared at the table and placed the doctor's cup on his tray.

"Shall I bring more coffee, sir?" he asked.

Brewer was startled at his servant's voice. "No, thank you, Alfred." He began to put his chess set away.

Alfred put the pot and his captain's empty cup on the tray and made to retreat to his pantry. After a moment's hesitation, he turned.

"I hope the doctor will be alright, sir," he said.

"As do I. Only time will tell, I'm afraid."

The servant nodded sagely. "Please tell me if there's anything I can do to help him, won't you, sir?"

Brewer looked at his servant and smiled. "Of course, Alfred. Thank you."

"Not at all, sir."

Simmons walked into the midshipman's berth to find the senior midshipman reading at the table. "You wanted to see me?"

"Yes, Mr. Simmons," Reed said, closing the book and rising. "Did you enjoy you shore leave?"

"No, actually," Simmons sneered. "I wasn't able to do what I wanted. Couldn't make the right connections, you see."

Reed took another step closer. "Would that be due to Mr. Short tagging along?"

Simmons said nothing.

Another step brought Reed nearly nose-to-nose with Simmons. He looked up at the taller midshipman with open distain.

"What were you thinking, Mr. Simmons? Taking a kid like Short to a tavern and then buying him a drink? What were you planning to do? Get him drunk and then leave him there?"

Simmons was irritated to have the senior midshipman guess his intentions so accurately, but he was smart enough not to say anything that could be brought up before Mr. Greene or the Captain.

He shrugged. "He's in the navy, same as the rest of us. He'd have been okay."

"He's a kid!" Reed said forcefully. "And you, sir, need a strong lesson in how to look after your shipmates."

Simmons' eyes narrowed in rage. When he was in his father's house, no one dared to speak to him that way! He felt his fists clench involuntarily.

Reed recognized the look on the other's face and smiled. "Anytime you think you're ready, *Mr.* Simmons."

Without preamble, Simmons launched a right hook at the senior midshipman's head. Reed, expecting a move of this sort, ducked under the blow and stepped in to land three hard shots to Simmons' ribs, causing the taller man to double over and bring his head down to become a tempting target. Reed landed a combination to the other's head, dazing him, then finished him with a sharp uppercut that snapped the head back and put Simmons on the deck.

Reed stood over him. "Consider this a lesson. I expect you to start behaving like a midshipman of His Majesty's Navy. However it came to be, you are here now." He turned and walked away, but before he reached the companionway, he turned back.

"One more thing: Don't ever do something like that to Mr. Short again."

CHAPTER 5

HMS *Revenge* sailed from the island of St. Kitts with the morning tide, the winds being unexpectedly agreeable to the maneuver. Their course was south, their destination the French island of Martinique.

Captain William Brewer was on deck for most of that first day. He loved the feel of the sea air on his face, as *Revenge* made an easy six or seven knots gliding across the face of the waters.

Brewer walked over to the wheel, where Mr. Sweeney and Lt. Greene were talking.

"She's running well, Mr. Sweeney," Brewer said, joining them. "You have gunnery drill scheduled for the forenoon watch, Mr. Greene, do you not?"

"Aye, Captain, at six bells."

"Excellent!" Brewer exclaimed, rubbing his hands together in anticipation. "Let's make it a competition, shall we? Starboard battery versus larboard. Fastest reload time for the battery wins an extra ration of grog. In fact, we'll do one better! We'll time each individual gun crew, and the fastest reload wins extra liberty at our next English port of call. What do you think, Mr. Greene?"

"A fine idea, Captain."

The two men discussed details of the planned competition for a few minutes more, then Greene went forward, leaving Brewer standing with Sweeney, who hadn't said a word but was closely watching the captain.

Brewer noticed the covert attention of his sailing master. "Mr. Sweeney? Is there something you wanted to ask me?"

The sailing master shrugged. "Not really, Captain. You see, I've had the opportunity to observe many officers in my years of service, and after a while it gets easy to read them. Sure, people are different, but you'd be surprised how many react in similar ways to similar situations. Plus, I've always had pretty good instincts. So, well..."

Brewer was amused. "Well, what, Mr. Sweeney?"

Sweeney moved in closer for privacy. "Well, Captain, if I may be so bold, *what's her name?*"

The blush came too quickly for Brewer to hide it. He smiled at being discovered. "It shows that much, does it?"

Sweeney shook his head. "Not so's everyone would notice. But Captain Cook had a similar look in his eye after meeting the daughter of a chieftain in the South Seas."

Brewer chuckled. A side glance showed the master waiting expectantly, which made him smile again.

"Elizabeth," he said. "Elizabeth Danforth. She is the daughter of the governor of St. Kitts."

"Ah," Sweeney said.

"What?"

"Nothing, Captain. It's just that, throughout the voyage on the *Defiant*, I never heard you talk about any women other than your mother and sister. Now, after one day on the island, I see a young officer with all the signs of being overwhelmed by grace and beauty, although, knowing you as I do, I'm willing to bet there was a brain behind that beauty."

Brewer smiled. "And you'd be right. Will you walk with me?"

The master nodded once and fell into step beside his captain.

"Are you married, Mr. Sweeney? I hope I'm not being too forward."

"Not at all, Captain," the master said. Brewer noticed he was looking at the deck. "I was married once, but she died about ten years ago. I was at sea at the time; didn't find out about it for over a year when the ship paid off." He shook his head, as at a rueful memory. "I wondered why my letters went unanswered. She had no family, and neither had I, so there was no one to get me word. That took me a while to work through, let me tell you." He saw that the captain didn't understand. "I went ashore mad at her for not answering my letters, you see. And then to find out she'd been dead for over a year, well, I felt like a damned fool. I sat at her grave for nearly two days, talking to her, apologizing for letting her die alone, and weeping out of sheer helplessness."

"I'm sorry, Mr. Sweeney. I didn't know."

Sweeney waved off the apology. "No reason you should, Captain. As I said, it was a long time ago. I have lots of good memories. Why do you ask?"

Brewer sighed. "I've never met a lady that I would consider marrying, until meeting Miss Danforth. Ever since I left her side, I have been thinking about whether or not it would be fair for me to marry anyone, seeing as how I am at sea as much as I am." He shook his head. "To marry someone so dear, then leave her alone for so long..."

Sweeney nodded but said nothing, and the two men paced back and forth across the deck.

"What's special about her?" Sweeney asked. "Why do you want to marry her?"

Brewer's eyes narrowed as he considered the master's question, trying hard to deal in thought and logic rather than emotion. "Beyond the fact that she's beautiful, there's something about her that I have never encountered in any other woman. I cannot put it into words—at least, not yet. She's intelligent, humorous, playful, and yet caring all at the same time." He frowned. "I fear I shall soon sound like a lovesick schoolboy."

The sailing master chuckled.

Brewer appeared at the time appointed for the gunnery contest.

"Here are the rules!" he called to the hands manning the guns. "You will load and run out. Fire on command. You will be timed as to how long it takes you to reload and run out again. There will be a prize for the fastest gun crew as well as which battery is fastest as a whole. Lieutenant Tyler will keep the time. Are you ready?"

A cheer went up.

"Starboard battery!" Brewer called.

The starboard battery ran their guns out. The captains turned and looked to Brewer for the word. Brewer let them wait for a minute, taking in how the crews handled the delay. A few men fidgeted, most stayed focused on their captains, tense with anticipation.

"Fire!" he called. The entire battery—ten guns—went off, almost in unison. He watched as the crews rushed to get them reloaded and run back out, careful to notice which gun was the fastest. It was number seven. After the last gun was run out, he looked to Mr. Tyler.

"Mr. Tyler?"

"One minute and forty-seven seconds!" Tyler called.

"Not bad, men, not bad at all," Brewer said. "Larboard battery, let's see if you can do better!"

The guns were run out, and all eyes went to the Captain. Again he assessed the gun crews, then, "Fire!"

The men strained to do better than their comrades. Brewer noted the timing of the first gun run out, but he did not think it was faster than starboard battery's champion. As soon as the last gun was run out, he looked to his time keeper.

"Mr. Tyler?"

"One minute and thirty seconds!" Tyler said. "The winners!" he pointed to the larboard battery. Cheers went up all around.

"Mr. Greene, which gun would you say was the fastest?" Brewer asked.

"I would say number seven of the starboard battery, sir."

"That would be my judgment as well. Now for the prizes: An extra ration of grog tonight for the larboard battery!" A cheer rose. "And for the crew of the number seven gun, extra liberty at our next English port of call!" Three cheers rose for that, and the jubilant men of number seven slapped each other on the back and made merry.

Brewer, still smiling, turned and saw Spinelli make his way up on deck. He had seen nothing of the doctor since the previous evening. He seemed a little unsteady on his feet, but he made his way to the weather rail and inhaled deeply. Brewer excused himself and joined his friend.

"Hello, Doctor," he said.

Spinelli nodded a greeting. "Captain."

"You're looking better. Your color has improved, even since last night."

An embarrassed look swept over the doctor's face, and he hung his head briefly before raising it again. "Captain, about last night, I wish to apologize, not only for my behavior in the tavern, but also for the way I have acted since I came aboard in Port Royal."

This was new ground to Brewer—having a subordinate apologize to him—and he found it to be strangely unsettling. "Well, I'm glad you're doing better."

Spinelli turned to him, his fingers clenching and unclenching by his sides. "I also want to thank you for last night. I must confess, my memory is not completely clear as to the events, but I believe I told you about the letter."

"Yes."

Spinelli looked out over the waves, his eyes dark with grief and his mouth a thin line of pain. "I thought my life was over when I read those lines, William," he said softly. "All my hopes and dreams for the future, gone in an instant. I was... shattered, lost." He swallowed at the memory and shivered. "Like a fool, I sought solace, not from my friends, but from an old enemy. The bottle opened her arms, and I ran to her embrace!" He shook his head in chagrin. He turned to face his captain. "I know I should have come to you, but I didn't want to... bother you with my troubles. I tried to deal with it as best I could, on my own. I failed—abjectly. I'm sorry."

Brewer put his hand on the doctor's shoulder. "Adam, all that matters to me is that you are trying to move on. I understand that you cannot simply put her out of your memory, but I am willing to do all in my power to help you to live with the loss. We will get through this together."

The doctor lowered his head. Brewer had thought he could give his friend encouragement, but wasn't so sure he had succeeded. What would Hornblower do?

"Adam," he said, "you're going to be all right."

The doctor looked into his captain's eyes, and Brewer read fear and uncertainty there. But he also discerned a glimmer of hope. He held his friend's gaze with his own, and smiled. He was greatly relieved when the doctor smiled back.

"Thank you, Captain," he said. "If you will excuse me, I have some work to do in the sickbay."

"Of course. Chess later tonight?"

The doctor nodded and saluted before making his way below deck.

Through hooded eyes, Brewer watched his friend descend to the sickbay. The doctor's situation, and especially what he had said, struck a chord in the young captain that set his mind racing. He turned to stare out over the ocean, his eyes darting from wave cap to trough and back, as though searching for the tiniest fish in the sea. He caught himself beginning to fidget, and he knew that something had to be done. Fortunately, his time with Hornblower on St. Helena had taught him what he needed to do.

He turned away from the railing and walked briskly across the quarterdeck.

"Mr. Greene!" he called to his first lieutenant, standing at the wheel and speaking to Mr. Sweeney, "I need some time. See that I am not disturbed!"

"Aye aye, sir!" Greene called. He shot a questioning look at Sweeney, who merely shrugged and shook his head.

Brewer reached the far side of the quarterdeck and began to pace. Seven steps, turn, seven steps, turn, his chin down on his chest in his best Hornblower imitation. His eyes were focused on the deck in front of him, his mind clouded by questions.

He was thinking about Elizabeth, and he wondered if she thought about him. Normally, he would enjoy thoughts of her, but the combination of the sailing master's story and the doctor's descent into self-destruction gave him something decidedly unpleasant to consider. Could he bear to give his heart to her, only to have it crushed if she were not there when he came home? Or would it be worse, if she gave her heart to him and then the sea should claim him? Could he bear to leave *her* shattered, as the doctor had been?

Brewer frowned, realizing he was getting ahead of himself. After all, he had only met the lady once, and he wasn't even sure if she felt the same way about him. He stopped and put his hand to his chin, lost in thought. After a few minutes, it occurred to him that his crew might begin to stare at him standing there, so he began to pace again.

Was he jumping to conclusions? After all, he had only spoken to her for one afternoon. Granted, it was in a fairly romantic setting, but none of their conversation could be called intimate by any stretch of the imagination. Elizabeth had... entertained him, as he was sure she had many of the young officers whose duty made it necessary for them to call upon her father. She had neither said nor done anything improper; in fact, she was careful not to give any appearance or suggestion of it. She behaved like a proper hostess.

And yet he would swear on his life that there had been more to her manner than mere courtesy. He had looked into her eyes and seen something deeper, something he had never seen in the eyes of anyone else. And she had given him permission to write to her....

Brewer stopped his pacing and headed for the companionway ladder.

"Mr. Sweeney," he called over his shoulder, "I shall be in my cabin."

He made his way below. Once in his cabin, he quickly took his hat and coat off and got paper, pen and ink from his writing desk. He sat down and paused, pen suspended above the paper. How to begin? He closed his eyes for a second and took a deep breath, then he took the plunge.

Dear Miss Danforth,

I hope this note finds you in good health. I wished to thank you again for the afternoon stroll in the garden. Perhaps you might permit me to escort you again when I next visit St. Kitts?

You asked me about the loneliness of the captain's life. I have been pondering your question, and I am not sure that 'loneliness' describes it. 'Isolation' might be a more accurate word. I interact with the crew daily, but they cannot interact with me. They are forced by my position to treat me almost as royalty; in fact, while at sea, I am the embodiment of the King's authority. On most ships, the crew fear the Captain, afraid that a moment's hesitation or some accidental gesture will result in the cat showing herself at the end of the watch.

I was fortunate to learn my trade, as it were, under a man who thought differently. His name was William Bush, and he was my Captain aboard HMS Lydia. He taught me that to accept command of a King's ship is to accept a responsibility, part of which is to isolate one's self, to stand above and apart from the crew, and to use that perspective to regard them dispassionately and to treat them fairly. I suppose you could call it lonely at times, but it is what I was born to do.

Brewer set down his pen and reread what he had written. He frowned; it simply wasn't coming out as he'd thought it would. He was about to crumple the paper and start afresh when he noticed movement in the corner of his eye. He turned to see Alfred standing in the doorway.

"I beg your pardon, sir," the servant said with a slight bow, "but I was wondering if you had a preference for dinner today."

"No," Brewer said, still scowling at the disappointing letter. "Whatever you have will be fine, I'm sure, Alfred."

"Is there something I can help you with, sir?"

Brewer dropped the letter on the desk and shook his head. "Not unless you know how to write a better letter than this."

"I am sorry, sir." Alfred went into the pantry and returned with a pot of hot coffee. Brewer smiled; one of the benefits of being stationed in the West Indies was the availability of coffee. Alfred poured his captain a cup of steaming brew.

"I truly wish I could help you, sir, but my brother Stephen was the writer in our family. I was trained in the martial arts."

Brewer looked astounded. "Martial arts?"

"Yes, sir. I was trained extensively in sword fighting and the use of firearms. My father wanted me to be a soldier."

"Really?" Brewer asked, as he sat back in his chair.

"Yes, sir. My family were servants to the Duke of Northumberland's family for generations. My father was the second son and so became the gardener, but he wanted something more for his sons. We were five brothers, and we all completed primary school. Theodore was the eldest; he joined the merchant service and enjoys a life at sea. Nathaniel was next; he was apprenticed to a blacksmith in the next county. Arthur was third, and he was apprenticed to a printer. My brother Stephen, as I indicated earlier, is very bright, and a gift from one of the Duke's relatives enabled him to go to college and become a writer. I was the youngest child. My father wanted me to join the army, and to that end he arranged with the Duke for me to be instructed in swordplay and shooting."

"So how come you to be on a King's ship?"

Alfred smiled ruefully. "Well, sir, I went to Plymouth to see my brother when his ship returned from a voyage, and I was pressed into the frigate *Valiant,* en route to the South Seas. The captain discovered that my people served the

Duke, so he made me his servant. Turns out the family business, as it were, runs deep in my veins. By the time the ship made port again in England, I discovered I rather liked it. Captain Harris took me with him on his next ship. I was left behind in Port Royal six months ago when I was transferred ashore with fever. Jenkins and I knew each other professionally, and when I ran into him in Kingston, he told me about your situation and gave me the letter of introduction."

Brewer sat back a moment and took it all in. He wondered what else there was to discover about the man.

CHAPTER 6

HMS *Revenge* entered the French port of Martinique on a sunny morning. The bay was crowded with merchant shipping from several nations. Brewer noted a Dutch *fluyt*, a brigantine of unknown allegiance, three French ships of the type known as a *pinque*, two American schooners, and a Spanish *tartane*. He frowned when he saw six luggers that looked as though they were being prepared for sea.

Mr. Greene appeared beside him. "Quite a collection, Captain."

"Yes," Brewer answered. "What do you make of those luggers?"

Greene called for a glass and studied the ships for a moment. "French, I'd say, sir." He lowered the glass.

Brewer took the glass and studied the ships through it before handing it back to his first lieutenant. "During the wars, we fought many a lugger that looked just like those. I wonder if there is any truth to the rumors that the French are backing some of the pirate activity hereabouts." A few minutes' more study yielded nothing new.

"Mr. Greene, let us render appropriate honors for entering a friendly port. I imagine a pilot will be on his way out to us in short order. After we anchor, I shall go ashore to pay our respects to the governor. You have the deck; I shall be in my cabin."

"Aye aye, sir."

Brewer was lost in thought as he made his way below, composing in his mind the letter he had to write to the Admiral.

"Give way, all!"

Brewer kept his eyes straight ahead as he sat in the stern sheets of the gig. The waters were calm and the wind cool on this fine morning; it looked as though it was going to be a clear day.

Once ashore, he got directions to the governor's residence, which turned out to be a short walk from the waterfront. He took the opportunity to observe the town as he walked up the main road. He nodded greetings and tipped his hat to the ladies he passed; this was his first official call on a governor in a foreign port, and he was determined to show the best face of the Royal Navy. It did not take him long to notice differences in groups of people: the natives generally returned his greetings with a smile; the French also returned his greetings, but with much more reserve—it was almost as if the mere fact he wore a British uniform earned him their distain. And then there were the slaves, who did not return his greetings at all.

The town itself was not unlike Jamestown on St. Helena with its small seaside inns and sidewalk cafes catering to those come ashore. The streets were narrow, and he could see evidence of damage that had been repaired, probably from hurricanes like the one that took Captain Norman.

He arrived at the governor's residence and was shown into a parlor, where he awaited the governor's convenience. There was nothing special about the room; it looked like a typical room where visitors waited, except for an excellent bust of the late Emperor in one corner. Brewer appraised it with a critical eye and decided it was a very good likeness.

The sound of a clearing throat behind him made Brewer turn around to see a tall, older gentleman, graying at the temples and dressed in a splendid livery.

"If you will follow me, sir," he said, his English only slightly accented, "the governor will see you now."

Brewer followed the servant through the house to the governor's office. The servant knocked and opened the door, Brewer following him in. The governor was standing in the middle of the room. The servant led Brewer right up to him before standing off to the side, allowing the two men to face each other.

"Sir," he said, "may I present Commander William Brewer of His Britannic Majesty's ship *Revenge*?"

The governor nodded as the servant turned to Brewer.

"Commander, may I present to you Monsieur le Comte de Donzelot, Governor of Martinique."

Brewer bowed. "Governor, an honor to meet you."

The governor returned his bow. "The honor is mine, Commander. Tell me, to what do I owe the pleasure of this visit?"

"Purely social, I assure you. My ship and I are new to the Caribbean."

"Then I bid you welcome to Martinique. I trust that an additional British warship in the Caribbean means that your navy is going to redouble their efforts against the pirates that have plagued these seas of late?"

Brewer looked his host in the eye. "That is Admiral Lord Hornblower's intention, Monsieur le Comte. Would that also be the reason for those luggers I saw in the harbor being readied for sea?"

Donzelot moved gracefully to stand beside his ornate desk. "Those ships are merely a part of the general buildup of French naval forces in this area. I am expecting significant naval reinforcements from France very soon, to protect our growing interests in the region."

This was unexpected and unwelcomed news, to be sure. Brewer's eyes narrowed in suspicion, but the governor didn't seem to notice as he walked about the room, gesturing, obviously warming to a favorite theme.

"Martinique is ready for a tremendous commercial expansion, Commander, and I intend to see that neither pirates nor anyone else interferes with it."

"And what expansion may that be, M. le Comte?"

"Steamships, my dear Commander! Steam power will make France the dominant merchant power in the Caribbean. I am already in contact with companies in Bordeaux and Chaillot to create such a craft. I have engineers working on a steam engine that will produce power equal to twenty horses! You are perhaps familiar with the late American Fulton's experiments with steam-powered craft? No? Really, Commander, you must read up on it. I have even heard that he built a steam-powered warship."

Brewer's incredulity showed. *"A warship?"*

Donzelot frowned in concentration. "Yes. Let me see... a colleague saw the vessel in New York harbor. He described it as a floating battery powered by a steam engine. It was rumored to make five knots, steadily. Fulton designed and built it for your late war with the Americans, it seems, but it was not completed before the war ended. A sign of things to come, do you not think so?"

"Perhaps." Brewer looked around the room, his eyes settling on a portrait of the Emperor Napoleon on the wall. He walked over and studied it closely. "A fine likeness."

The Governor joined him. "I have always this portrait of the Emperor. I prefer it to portraits of him as Consul. He seems more... majestic."

Brewer nodded. "I agree."

The governor turned and considered him anew. "I am curious, Commander; you speak as though you have seen the Emperor. Is this so?"

"Yes, Monsieur le Comte, I had the honor on several occasions."

"Really? In what capacity?"

Brewer continued to admire the portrait. "You may have heard that Admiral Lord Hornblower was the governor of St. Helena? It was my privilege to be his secretary during that time."

The Governor looked at Brewer with a new appreciation. "Would you care for something to drink, Commander?"

"Yes, thank you, Governor."

The Comte rang for a servant and gave him the order. In a matter of moments, the servant returned with two small glasses on a silver tray. The Governor took them and thanked the servant.

"I hope you like Cognac, Commander," he said as he handed Brewer a glass. The Governor raised his in a toast. "To the Emperor, may the great God give him in death the peace he never had in life. Fond memories."

"Memories," Brewer echoed.

Both men savored their drinks and looked at the portrait for several minutes.

"Tell me, Governor," Brewer said, "did you ever meet the Emperor?"

"Yes," Donzelot replied, with an air of consequence. He turned and led Brewer to two easy chairs. "I was with him in Egypt and fought in the Battle of the Pyramids. I met him there when he would inspect our division. He made me a *General de Division* in December, 1806, and I had the honor to sit at his right hand when he made me a Baron of the Empire in 1808." The Comte stared out into space, momentarily lost in a memory. He blinked and looked at his guest.

"A question, Commander, if I may. A test, I will warn you."

"Very well."

"I also had the honor of fighting with the Emperor at Waterloo. Tell me, what did he tell you of the battle?"

Brewer's eyes narrowed, partly wondering how this was a test, and partly trying to remember if the Emperor ever mentioned the battle at all.

Brewer shook his head. "I don't believe he ever mentioned the battle. At least, not to me."

The Governor smiled. "You passed. To my knowledge, he has always refused to discuss the battle." Brewer saw him shiver. "Tell me, Commander, have you ever had a moment when you thought the world was literally going to end? A disaster so complete that life was over?" Brewer shook his head, and the Comte grunted, a rueful memory clouding his features.

"For me it was that moment, the end of the battle, there at Waterloo. I was with Ney; part of his force had finally taken La Haye Saint and opened the center of the British lines. He sent word back and begged the Emperor for more troops, that the British line was open before us, but the only troops available were the Old Guard. For some reason—I've never understood why—it took the Emperor over a half-hour to send them forward." Donzelot shook his head in regret. "Perhaps that is why he never discussed the battle. So. We watched the Guard advance, just as they had so many times before, but there was something different about the way they approached the British. I cannot say what, exactly, just that it was unlike any charge I had seen, even the one just days before when they broke the Prussians at Ligny."

"What happened?" Brewer asked.

The Comte looked at him, a bewildered look on his face. "They stopped, Commander. Always before, they plowed up to and through the enemy lines, like a farmer plowing a field, but this time they stopped short of the enemy. And then, the world came to an end. The Old Guard began to fall back." His voice broke at the memory. "Never had that happened before, Commander. If you were to speak to anyone in the *Grande Armee* during the Empire, and you were to ask him what is impossible, he would have told you two things: for God to lie, and for the Old Guard to fall back." Donzelot called to have their glasses refilled. Once the servant departed, he resumed.

"There I was, standing beside Marshal Ney, watching the Old Guard falter. The Marshal, he curses the Emperor for his hesitation in sending the Guard forward. I turn to look back at our lines, and through a quirk of fate, the winds clear the cannon smoke at that moment, and I have a clear view of the Emperor. He is sitting on his horse, and the look on his face! I shall never forget it, Commander, as long as I live. It was total shock and disbelief, and it was replaced by a look of recognition of doom. I have no other word to describe it. It was as though, at that instant, Napoleon Bonaparte knew all was lost. Then the army saw the Guard break, and the rout began. I fell back with Ney as far as Charleroi, where he abandoned the army in order to return to Paris. I never saw either him or the Emperor again."

Brewer studied the portrait. "It is my understanding that the Napoleon Bonaparte I knew was a very different man than the one who ruled the Empire."

"What was he like?" the Comte asked.

Brewer set his glass on the table and sat back in his chair. "If I had to describe him in one word, I would say he was bored."

The Governor was astonished. "Bored?"

"Yes. You must remember, on St. Helena he was isolated. On Elba, at least he could perform a semblance of the duties he had when he ruled not only France but also most of Europe—holding court, entertaining foreign dignitaries, administering Elba, and so forth—but on St. Helena he had absolutely nothing to do, and it was quite literally killing him. Until Lord Hornblower arrived on the island, he had nobody willing or able to stand up to him, intellectually or from a position of authority."

Brewer paused and took a sip of his Cognac. "I believe I was fortunate." The Comte regarded him with a quizzical expression and waited for him to elaborate. "I got the impression that I reminded him of his stepson, Eugene. I think he took a liking to me based on that."

Donzelot smiled. "That is understandable. The Emperor loved his stepson as if he were his very own. Before he divorced Josephine to marry Marie-Louise, I heard the Emperor say how he wished he could find some way to make Eugene his heir."

Brewer smiled over his glass and judged the time was right to change the topic. "Tell me, Governor, what do you know about French warships that defected from the Imperial Navy after the Emperor's second abdication and are now rumored to be, if not in the hands of pirates, then actively joining in acts of piracy in the Caribbean?"

Donzelot's eyes narrowed as he took a long swallow of Cognac. Brewer could tell from the man's body language that the topic was not unknown to him. The Comte set his glass on the table and sighed.

"I have, of course, heard these rumors, Commander. I tell you, officially, the policy of His Majesty's government is that these rumors are entirely false."

Brewer sat back in his chair. "With all due respect to His Majesty, I will tell you frankly, M. le Comte, that your information is flawed. I engaged one such ship not long ago. She was at one time a French frigate, and Lord Hornblower, who was with me during the battle, agreed with me that the actions of the crew in their ship handling, as well as their gunnery, were of a level much higher than ordinary pirates. They were nearly the equal to those of French warships I fought against during the wars. One might suspect that the ship was still manned by her French crew."

The Governor was not bothered at all by his guest's charges. "I do not wish to quarrel with you, Commander; I merely convey my government's official position on the question which you posed. Believe me when I say that I have nothing but respect for the honor of the Royal Navy. During the last stages of the Empire, I was in command of the garrison on the isle of Corfu. The British squadron intercepted several French merchant ships destined for us which contained only officers' personal property, including my personal library. The British commander, Captain Monbray, gallantly returned all our personal belongings intact. From that moment on, I made sure any British officers taken captive were well treated. They ate at my table and were given every privilege that honorable prisoners of war could be accorded."

"I am grateful to hear of your kindness, Monsieur," Brewer said, "and I assure you that Admiral Lord Hornblower insists that every member of his command uphold that same standard of honor. I trust that our two nations will be able to work together to eliminate the pirate threat from Caribbean waters to give merchantmen of all nations free passage."

"Indeed."

The Governor rose, signaling the end of the interview, and Brewer followed suit.

"Commander, I wish you success on your voyages. May you bring an end to the pirate scourge and also bring glory to your King and his Royal Navy." The Governor bowed formally.

Brewer returned the bow. "Thank you, Monsieur le Comte."

The governor escorted him to the door. Before opening it, he turned to his guest.

"Please convey to your admiral that I should very much enjoy the opportunity to share our reminisces of the Emperor."

"I shall be happy to inform the Admiral, Monsieur le Comte. Good day."

Brewer climbed back aboard HMS *Revenge* with his mind whirling. He barely acknowledged the salutes of his officers as he made his way directly to his cabin, leaving a thoroughly nonplussed first lieutenant and sailing master in his wake.

He burst through the door and shed his hat, coat and sword, setting them on the table before going to his desk and pulling out his writing utensils. He was just about to begin his report to the Admiral when he heard a throat being discreetly cleared, and he turned to find his attentive servant standing in the pantry doorway.

"May I get you anything, Captain?"

"No, thank you, Alfred. What do we have for supper tonight?"

Alfred smiled, the kind when someone realizes they know something you don't, and it intrigued Brewer. "Sir, have you spoken to Mr. Greene since you returned?"

"Mr. Greene? No, I didn't speak to him; I came straight here."

There was a knock at the door. "I imagine that will be Mr. Greene for you now, sir. Shall I get you coffee?"

Brewer sighed. "Yes, and for Mr. Greene as well. Enter!"

Sure enough, Mr. Greene entered the room.

"Good to see you back, Captain. How did your meeting go with the governor?"

Alfred appeared with the coffee. Brewer studied the smaller man's face as he poured their coffee, looking for any kind of a knowing look on it, but the servant was as innocent as could be.

"Thank you, Alfred," Brewer said when he had finished.

Alfred smiled. "My pleasure, Captain."

I daresay it was, Brewer thought as he watched his servant go.

He turned to Mr. Greene. "I understand you can tell me about our supper."

Greene was surprised, but he recovered quickly. "I don't know about that, but I can hand you this."

Greene passed him a folded sheet of good quality paper. He opened it to find an invitation from the captain of the French frigate for the English captain and his first lieutenant to have supper aboard his vessel. Brewer looked to Greene for an explanation.

"It arrived by boat not long after you went ashore, sir. I took the liberty of accepting on your behalf, sir; I hope you don't mind."

Brewer studied the invitation. "Not in this particular case, although I wouldn't make a habit of it."

Brewer pulled out his pocket watch. "We have just under three hours before we are due to arrive on our host's frigate." Brewer picked up his coffee. "Let me brief you on what the governor had to say."

Mr. Greene sat back in his chair with his coffee in hand and listened as his captain recounted the conversation between himself and the governor. He, too, was surprised by the report of an increased French naval presence in the Caribbean, though he privately thought they could use the help against the pirates.

"He had a portrait of the Emperor Napoleon in his office, and I commented on how good a likeness it was. Once he found out about my time on St. Helena, he wanted to know all about my time with Bonaparte." Brewer paused to look out the stern windows. "I wonder if all the French will treat me like that."

"Probably," Greene said. "At least, all those who loved the Emperor."

Brewer rose, and Greene followed suit. "Well, we need to get ready to dine on board the *Semillante*. Afterwards, I'm sure I shall have a massive report to compose for the Admiral."

Brewer met Greene on deck at the appointed hour. Mr. Sweeney saw them off. "Good luck, gentlemen," he said.

"Pass the word for Mr. Tyler," Brewer said to the midshipman of the watch.

Tyler arrived within minutes and saluted smartly. "You sent for me, sir?"

"Yes, Mr. Tyler. While we are visiting on the French frigate, you shall be in command of *Revenge*. If anything should go wrong, or if we are not back aboard by midnight, you are to take the ship out of the harbor at your first opportunity and return to Jamaica with all speed. Report to the Admiral for further orders. I have left you written orders in the desk in my cabin, should you need them. I advise you to seek out the counsel of Mr. Sweeney if you have any questions on your way."

Brewer could see the young lieutenant swallow hard. "Yes, sir," he said.

"I know I'm leaving my ship in good hands, Mr. Tyler," Brewer said calmly.

Brewer passed an appraising eye over the *Semillante* as McCleary nestled his gig under the frigate's entry port. She was a thirty-two gun ship; based on her small size, he guessed she was armed with 12-pounders. *Even so,* he thought as he led his first lieutenant up on to the deck, *she's huge compared to Revenge.*

The two British officers were welcomed by a full guard of honor. They acknowledged the guard, then presented themselves before the French Captain.

"I am Captain William Brewer, of His Majesty's Sloop *Revenge,*" Brewer said. "This is my first lieutenant, Benjamin Greene."

The French Captain stepped forward and offered his hand to Brewer.

"Thank you for accepting my invitation, Captain," he said, in well-enunciated English. "My name is Albin Roussin, and I am captain of the *Semillante.* Allow me to present my first officer, Augustin de Robespierre."

Introductions concluded, Roussin smiled. "If you gentlemen will follow me, we shall adjourn to the cabin."

They moved aft and entered the great cabin of the frigate. Brewer was impressed by how spacious it was, especially considering *Semillante's* size. The table was already set for four, and Brewer wondered why the setting would be so intimate. He hid his curiosity and forced himself to be patient.

A steward appeared, bearing four glasses on a silver tray. Roussin handed one to each of his guests before passing the third to his first lieutenant and taking the fourth for himself. He thanked the steward and turned toward the officers assembled.

"Gentlemen, a toast," he said as he raised his glass. "To our glorious king, Louis XVIII, long may he reign, and to his Britannic Majesty, George IV. Together, may they rule the world in peace."

They drank the toast in silence, but Brewer caught his first officer's eye and knew that Greene had also thought the toast strange.

Roussin moved to his seat at the head of the table. "Please, if you would, Captain Brewer, sit here on my right, and Mr. Greene beside you. Robespierre, on my left, if you please." The officers took their places, and Roussin clapped his hands. Immediately, stewards entered the room. Platters of meat were followed by bowls of vegetables and fresh baked bread, still piping hot. The last steward to set a plate on the table stepped back and bowed to his captain before making his exit.

"I hope you will forgive the apparent haste, gentlemen," Roussin said, "but in France we like to eat before we talk, and we have much to discuss."

"As you wish, sir," Brewer replied.

"Before us is the best this island has to offer, sir," Roussin continued, "and I hope it is to your liking. My chef can work miracles; those cutlets of pork before you, Mr. Greene, are his particular specialty. Please, gentlemen, let us not stand on ceremony, but let us eat like men who know how to do justice to a feast such as this."

The four men attacked the feast before them with gusto. The chops proved to be every bit as good as Captain Roussin predicted, and Brewer wondered if Alfred would be insulted if he brought back the recipe. Then he remembered the sword fighting lesson Alfred was supposed to give him, and decided not to make the request.

As the meal was winding down, the French captain leaned back expansively and addressed his guest.

"I must tell you, Captain Brewer," Roussin said, "that your reputation precedes you, even in this backwater corner of the Caribbean."

Brewer met his eyes. "My reputation?"

Roussin smiled. "We know about your time on St. Helena with the Emperor. I will tell you that several of my crew wished to ask you to speak of those days, but I told them that perhaps we could ask you another time. We have other topics that demand our time today."

Brewer and Greene shared a look; both British officers looked forward to getting to the real purpose of the evening.

Roussin waited while the stewards cleared the table and poured Cognac. Once they had retired, he addressed Brewer.

"Captain," he said carefully, "I know that you visited the Governor today. I can only imagine how little information he was willing or able to give you."

His guest said nothing, so Roussin continued.

"I imagine that the topic came up of pirates in possession of warships that once belonged to the Imperial Navy. Am I correct?"

Brewer nodded, but remained silent.

Roussin inclined his head as well. "I have also heard of your encounters with a pirate vessel that bore a strong resemblance to a frigate of the Emperor's navy."

Mr. Greene leaned his elbows on the table and steepled his fingers. "May I ask how you know this, Captain?"

Roussin shrugged. "I have sources beyond what many would call common knowledge. It is about these ships that I wished to speak."

"I'm listening," Brewer said.

The French captain swirled his drink, then brought it to his lips. Obviously, Brewer thought, he was in no hurry to say what was on his mind. He noticed the Lieutenant Robespierre shift in his chair ever so slightly; perhaps he wasn't the only one who thought Captain Roussin was dragging his feet. Brewer picked up his own glass, determined to wait his host out no matter how long it took.

Brewer watched Roussin carefully as the French captain set his empty glass on the table, staring at it as though trying to decide to cross the Rubicon. Finally, he sighed and looked up at his guests. "Gentlemen, I beg your indulgence. A part of myself does not wish to share this information, for reasons mainly concerning our status as recent enemies, but I believe it to be necessary.

"You are quite correct, Captain, in your belief that vessels formerly of the Imperial Navy defected from the fleet after the return of the Bourbon Louis XVIII and removed to the Caribbean. There were five ships that are known to have participated in the plot: one frigate and four corvettes, which are roughly equivalent to a British sloop-of-war. To my knowledge, your ship sank the last corvette remaining in the Caribbean in the action off Cuba. Of the other three, two were sunk by the Americans and the third sailed south toward Brazil and has not been heard from since."

Roussin paused to allow the steward to come in and refill their glasses. Once he left, Brewer seized his opportunity.

"I thank you for the information, Captain," he said softly, "but may I ask why you are telling me this?"

Roussin's smile looked infinitely sad to Brewer, and he could only imagine the anguish that was hidden beneath it.

"It is grievous, Captain, when one's duty to what is right outweighs one's loyalty to past comrades. I tell you this, because those officers and men of the rogue ships have betrayed their country, and any that are still alive must be brought to justice. When the Emperor was dethroned permanently, it was difficult for some of his officers to realize that we served *France* and not *Napoleon*. Those on the rogue ships could not make the transition, opting instead for a life of piracy, in order to not only take revenge on the world for the ousting of their Emperor, but also to pillage the weak for personal gain."

Brewer spoke up. "Why did the Governor not tell me this? You both serve Louis now, after all."

Brewer saw at once that this was the one question Roussin had hoped he would not have to answer.

"That is not easily explained, Captain," Roussin said, choosing his words carefully, "especially to one who did not live through Napoleon's first abdication in 1814." He paused, searching for a particular word and not finding it. "When that event took place, the Governor was in command of the garrison occupying the Greek island of Corfu. He refused to surrender the island to the British after the abdication; the King had to personally order General Donzelot to surrender and evacuate the island of all French forces. As a result, Monsieur le Comte Donzelot was not in favor at court and was not employed by King Louis."

"And you?" Brewer asked.

"I stayed loyal to my country," Roussin said, "as did Ney and many others, and served my King. When Bonaparte returned for the Hundred Days, I remained loyal to the King and was dismissed from the Navy until Louis XVIII was restored."

"I see," Brewer said. "Pray continue."

"Predictably, Donzelot jumped back to the Emperor's standard for the Hundred Days. After the Emperor's second abdication, he somehow escaped Ney's fate and was again left unemployed, until the King, in his clemency, offered him the governorship of Martinique in 1818.

"There are two factions in the French military, Captain, based on which side you were on during the Hundred Days. Yes, the rivalry persists to this day, for those of us who experienced those days, and the Governor and I were on different sides. Those who remained loyal to the King, such as Lieutenant Robespierre and myself, believe that those who deserted to the Emperor during the Hundred Days were traitors and should have shared Ney's fate."

Mr. Greene stirred. "I say, that's a bit harsh, don't you think?"

Roussin's face was a mask. "We are warriors, Monsieur Greene; what punishment for treason can there be but death?"

Greene sat back and said nothing, so Roussin continued his tale.

"I cannot be certain, of course, but I believe that the Governor said nothing to you regarding the renegade French warships because he, like them, was for the Emperor; he is in sympathy with them. I am not. I consider them deserters; again, there can only be one punishment."

"I see," Brewer said. This was the missing piece of information he had been seeking. Now much of the Governor's actions made sense.

Roussin studied his counterpart's features for a moment before nodding once. "I believe you do."

The men paused to drain their glasses. Brewer hoped that was not all his host had to say, and he was rewarded a moment later when Roussin made his announcement.

"The ship you are seeking is—*was,* I should say—the frigate *Pauline,* of forty guns. When she left France, she was armed with 28 18-pounders and 12 8-pounders. Her captain at that time was one Desaix. I do not know if this information is still accurate. Most likely it is not; the ships defected in late summer 1815. One bit of more current information I can give you: *Pauline's* current captain calls himself El Diabolito."

Brewer grunted. "I don't know about the rest of it, but I can tell you first-hand that she still carries the 18-pounders."

The two French officers smiled.

"Do you happen to know her whereabouts?" Greene asked.

Robespierre shook his head. "The *Pauline* hasn't been sighted since the battle with your squadron. Perhaps her captain has found a secluded anchorage on one of the more remote islands where he can make his repairs."

"Perhaps," Brewer said, disappointed at the news. Suddenly, something clicked inside his head. "Did you say El Diabolito? That's the second time I've heard that name. Who is he?"

Roussin shrugged. "No one knows his real name. It is said that he grew up in Cuba and frequently uses the island as his base of operations. I know that several times he has retreated there when pursued by the Americans, but he has been seen in other parts of the Caribbean. Just how he came into possession of the *Pauline* is a mystery, but since he assumed command, he has become much bolder."

"To the point of attempting to ambush a British frigate," Greene said.

"Exactly," Roussin nodded. "He must be tracked down and eliminated."

Brewer was silent during the short trip back to HMS *Revenge*. He was not looking forward to the report he had to compose tonight in order for it to go out with the next British ship bound for Port Royal. After they climbed to the deck, Brewer looked around and saw that the deck was deserted, aside from the watch. Satisfied that all was well, he said good night to Greene and made his way below. His body automatically bent to save his head from another bruising. He had no sooner closed the cabin door behind him and removed his hat and coat when he head a discreet clearing of the throat that he recognized as the faithful Alfred announcing his presence.

Brewer turned to the pantry door and saw the compact form filling the lower half of the doorway, feet spread, hands clasped behind his back.

He smiled. "Coffee, please, Alfred. I have a long report to write."

"Yes, sir."

Brewer broke out his writing supplies and arranged them on the desk, then sat down to compose the first major report of his career.

H. M. Sloop Revenge, Martinique Bay
November 11, 1821

Sir,
It is my honor to report the following information that I have learned during the course of my visit this afternoon to the Governor of Martinique and dining aboard the French frigate Semillante this evening.

When we arrived at Martinique, I saw six luggers being newly readied for sea. The Governor confided to me that this is part of a general buildup of French naval forces in the Caribbean. He is expecting reinforcements at any time, numbers unknown.

He went on to describe his visit to the French frigate. He was sure the Admiral would question him further when he returned to Port Royal, so he decided to make a copy for his own records in order to review it before the two met.

The coffee appeared on the corner of his desk silently, strong and hot and black. As "un-British" as it may seem, he had come to prefer it to the more traditional cup of tea.

Finally, he decided to add the following:

In closing, the Governor of Martinique asked me to pass on to Your Lordship his invitation to sit for an evening and share remembrances of the Emperor Napoleon, should you ever be in the area of the island of Martinique.

He read it over before finally adding the signature line: *Respectfully submitted by your ob'd't servant, William Brewer, Commander.* Then he went back and copied the pertinent facts he intended to review later. Once this was done, he folded the report carefully and sealed it, addressing it: *Lord Horatio Hornblower, Admiral Commanding, West Indies Squadron, Port Royal, Jamaica.*

A knock at his door caused him to automatically say "Enter", and his coxswain came in and closed the door behind him.

"Gig's squared away, sir," he reported, as he hung up his captain's coat and hat, then he set to generally tidying up the stateroom. "Anything else I can do for you before I turn in?"

"Yes, Mac, there is," Brewer said. "This report needs to go out on the first British ship heading to Port Royal." He hesitated, then pulled out the letter to Elizabeth that he had finished and sealed. "And see if you can post this to St. Kitts, if you please."

"Aye, sir." The coxswain took both missives and went to place them with the other dispatches and personal mail that would go out in the morning.

CHAPTER 7

Captain William Brewer stood on the deck of HMS *Revenge* watching as his crew made final preparations to go to sea.

"Mr. Greene," he said, "get the ship under way, if you please."

His lieutenant touched his hat and turned to his task. "Stand by the capstan. Loose the heads'ls. Hands aloft to loose the tops'ls."

The anchor broke out, and *Revenge* gained headway. The wheel was put hard over, and she brought her head around. Greene ordered hands to the braces, and *Revenge* began slipping through the water toward the open sea.

"Make your course for Curacao once we clear the bay," Brewer said.

"Curacao. Aye aye, sir!"

Brewer stood aside and observed as his first lieutenant transformed *Revenge* from a sleeping animal to a living, moving beast ready to belch fire and shot at her master's command. He'd learned early on in their time together on HMS *Defiant* that Greene's seamanship could be trusted in every circumstance, and the knowledge was no little comfort to him. In the open sea, he heard the commands and felt the bow swing around to the SSW and steady on.

"Well done, Mr. Greene," he said loudly.

"Thank you, sir."

Brewer stood silently for a few moments, feeling the movement of the deck under his feet and loving every minute of it. He raised his face to the sea breeze and drank it in. He walked over to the wheel.

"I relieve you, quartermaster," he said.

Seeing the man's fears in his eyes, he added, "You've done nothing wrong, Mallory; I just want to handle the wheel for this watch."

"Oh, aye, sir." Mallory stepped aside and allowed the Captain to take the wheel

Mr. Sweeney stepped up, his visage showing him to be as startled as the quartermaster.

"Sir?"

Brewer looked at him, the joy of the moment unmistakable on his face.

"Tell me, Mr. Sweeney," he said, shouting to be heard over the rushing wind, "don't you find that there are times when you just want to stand at the wheel and become one with the ship? Feel it obey your every signal and just be glad you're alive? My God, there's nowhere on earth I'd rather be just now than right here!"

"I know what you mean, Captain. And I'll confess to ye that I've felt that way myself a time or two."

Brewer rejoiced as he strained to hold the wheel against the wind. The exhilaration that flooded him was rare, and he cherished every second of it.

By the third day out of Martinique, Noah Simmons had decided that he had to jump ship at the first possible opportunity. The day before, he had begun bullying young Mr. Short into doing many of his duties while he spent his time trying to devise a way to disappear into a life of seclusion and debauchery. *Tortuga would be excellent,* he thought morosely, *if only the legends were still true. Too bad I don't see much chance of getting there to find out.*

He sat in the midshipman's mess, feeling sorry for himself and the horrible turn that had landed him in his present unsavory circumstances. He was not meant for this, Noah told himself for the umpteenth time, he deserved better. He still could not believe his father wanted to hold him accountable just because some Jamaican tart he was fooling around with got herself pregnant. Instead of protecting him, his father had said he had to get off the island, and on his own account, too, as he refused to fund his son's escape. The only thing he would do was arrange a place in a Navy ship. After that, he was on his own.

He looked up as Short wandered into the mess, probably heading to catch up on some sleep before he had to go back on watch again.

"Mr. Tyler's looking for you," Short told him. "It's almost time to cast the log."

Simmons closed his eyes and leaned his head back against the bulkhead. "Yeah? Well, you go take care of it for me."

Short took a step backward. "Mr. Tyler's looking for you to—"

"I don't bloody care who Mr. Tyler's looking for!" Simmons exploded as he leapt to his feet. Short stumbled back in terror, then bolted for the companionway ladder. Simmons caught him by the upper arm and squeezed hard. The boy cried out in pain.

"You listen to me, you little mama's boy," Simmons said in a low, menacing voice. "You just mind you do what you're told, so you don't get hurt. Understand?" He shook the boy hard until he cried out. "I said, do you understand?"

"Yes!" Short gasped.

"And don't even think about telling Mr. Reed or any of the officers, if you know what's good for you." He squeezed Short's arm harder.

"You're hurting me!"

"Understand?" Another squeeze.

"Yes!"

"Then get out of here and go cast the bloody log!" He flung the boy away nearly as easily as he would a rag doll.

Short picked himself up off the deck and hurried toward the ladder. He tried his best to stop crying and hide the pain in his left arm as he went on deck to cast the log. Lieutenant Tyler spotted him heading toward the fantail.

"Mr. Short?" he said. "Where's Mr. Simmons?"

"He's, uh, indisposed, sir. He asked me to take care of this for him."

"Indisposed? Very well. Carry on, Mr. Short."

Short completed his task with great effort; his arm made it difficult to move normally. After he recorded their speed, he wandered forward until he sat down on a coil of rope. He buried his head in his hands and began to weep softly.

It was that sound, that soft, pitiable wail, that attracted the attention of Jonathan Reed as he stood on the other side of the mainmast by the lee rail. He stepped slowly across the deck, following the sound to the sobbing figure on the coil of rope.

"William?" he asked. "William? What's wrong?" He reached out to touch the boy's arm, and the lad flinched in pain.

Reed squatted beside him. "William? What's happened to your arm?"

"It's nothing, sir," the boy whispered as he wiped his eyes on his sleeve.

Reed felt gently around the arm only to have the boy flinch again and recoil in pain. Reed's eyes narrowed in anger. He had seen this once before, on *Clorinda*.

"William," he said, softly but sternly, "take off your shirt and let me see your arm."

Short shook his head and curled up into a fetal position.

Reed sighed. "Look, William, you can show me here, now, or I will be forced to pick you up and carry you to Dr. Spinelli and have you take it off for him. You choose."

Short look sideways at him. Slowly, he undid his shirt and slid it off. Reed turned him gently to get a good view of a large, angry bruise around the boy's upper arm in the obvious shape of a man's hand. Reed's brow darkened.

"Who did this to you, William?"

The boy remained silent.

"Who, William?"

Still nothing.

"Was it Simmons?"

Short's eyes welled up with tears.

"He said he'll hurt me if I told you."

Reed's blood boiled. He'd been the victim of just such bullying when he first joined the fleet, and on *Clorinda* the victim had been nearly as young as Mr. Short; the torture had driven the lad to suicide. There was no way he would tolerate it now that he was Senior Midshipman.

"You stay here, William. I will ask Mr. Tyler to send you into the tops for the rest of this watch. You'll be safe there."

Short was clearly terrified. "What are you going to do?"

"Never you mind. You just go to the tops when Mr. Tyler tells you."

Reed went to Mr. Tyler with a made up story about some minor infraction he'd caught Short on and asked that he be put in the tops for the rest of the watch as punishment. Tyler agreed and gave the order.

Now that the boy was out of the way, Tyler went to speak to some friends. He could handle Simmons one of two ways —he could take it to the Captain or Mr. Greene, or he could use the justice of the lower deck. He considered this situation his responsibility to correct, so he opted for the latter course.

It was some little time later that Simmons decided he'd better put in an appearance on deck before the end of watch. He had just made to leave the mess when he noticed Reed standing in the doorway.

Reed looked around and took a step into the room. "Aren't you supposed to be on deck?"

Simmons shrugged. "Just stepped below for a minute. Headin' back up now."

Reed took another step forward. "Why bother? I'm sure Mr. Short has completed your duties for you."

Simmons stood very still and silent, his lips pressed into a thin, angry line.

"I don't suppose," Reed went on casually, "that you have any idea how Mr. Short got such a nasty bruise on his arm?"

"I couldn't say, really."

Reed nodded to himself. "That's what I thought you'd say." He raised his voice to be heard outside. "You can come in now."

Simmons' eyes grew wide when the boatswain's mate walked through the door and stood next to Reed. He carried a rattan in his hand. Worse, he was followed by four beefy tars, who stood silently behind Reed and the mate. All had dark looks in their eyes.

"These are some friends of the mate's," Reed said. "And do you have any idea what all of these gentlemen have in common, Mr. Simmons?"

"I can't imagine," Simmons said through lips that had suddenly gone dry.

"They're all rather fond of Mr. Short," Reed said. "You see, they all sailed with him on HMS *Defiant*, and they all sort of look after the lad."

Simmons remained silent.

"I bet if we put your hand up to that bruise on Short's arm, they'd match."

Simmons still said nothing, which brought some grumbling from the tars.

"It takes a special kind of scum," Reed said menacingly, "to terrorize a child. As senior midshipman, I will not tolerate such behavior. Take him, boys!"

The tars surged forward and overwhelmed Simmons almost before he could react. Two of them pinned his arms behind his back, and a third doubled him over with a hard shot to the stomach when he would not cease struggling.

"Here, now!" Reed said before the fourth could join in. "This is not a brawl."

"What are you going to do to me?" Simmons gasped.

The bosun's mate stepped forward and shook his rattan in front of Simmons' face. "We've all heard about the lad's arm; you really shouldn't have done that. You, sir, are going to kiss the gunner's daughter."

He took a step back. The four tars practically lifted Simmons off the deck as they brought him to the mess table.

"Properly, the lads here would bend you over a twelve pounder," the mate said, "but as we don't happen to have one handy, the mess table will have to do. Help Mr. Simmons assume the position, lads!"

The tars forced Simmons to bend over the table and held him there as the bosun's mate assumed his place and looked to Mr. Reed.

"Two dozen," Reed said.

The mate nodded and got to work. The *whoosh* as the rattan cut through the air ended with a sharp *crack!* on

Simmons' exposed backside. The midshipman's muscles spasmed in pain he had never imagined. The second blow caused him to begin to buck and fight for his freedom, but the hands that held him down were too strong. The third caused him to cry out in pain.

"Here, now!" It was one of those who held his hands who spoke. "You just shut yer mouth and take it like a man!"

"Bite down on this, mate," another said. "It'll help." A folded strap of leather was put between his teeth. Simmons bit down and somehow endured until the end.

With the twenty-fourth strike, the bosun's mate turned again to Reed.

"Punishment complete, sir."

"Very good," Reed said. "Mr. Simmons, any further conduct of this sort towards Mr. Short or any other member of this crew will be reported to the first lieutenant for more severe punishment. Dismissed."

The hands that held Simmons tight were released, but all he did was collapse on the table where he lay. It simply hurt too much to move, even to rise off the table surface. He was barely able to open his eyes enough to watch Mr. Reed and the bosun's mate leave. Right after that, his view was blocked by the face of one of those who had held him down. The brute was a particularly ugly fellow with missing teeth and very foul breath. Simmons could not recall his name.

"Let me clue you in on something, mate," he whispered. "The lad's our friend. You touch him again, and there won't be anything left of you for the first lieutenant to deal with."

Without another word, the four walked away without looking back.

Simmons spat out the leather strap and breathed deeply through his mouth. He squeezed his eyes shut against the tears and raged quietly inside. He knew some people in Port

Royal who might be persuaded to take care of the almighty Jonathan Reed, for the right price, of course.

Good weather favored HMS *Revenge* on her journey southwestward. The crew continued to accustom themselves to a ship less than half the size of the HMS *Defiant*. Their captain watched them with a pride swelling within his breast, one that he struggled to keep contained, lest its expression sap the ship's good order and discipline.

The passage from Martinique to Curacao took five days. On the afternoon of that fifth day, HMS *Revenge* was sailing due west, some twenty miles north of the island, under reefed topsails. The wind was lying comfortably one or two points on the larboard quarter; *Revenge's* pitch uncommonly gentle with hardly any roll at all.

"You know, Mr. Sweeney," Brewer said with a broad smile on his face, "I could get used to this sort of life."

The sailing master grinned and lifted his face to the sun and wind before answering.

"Not all passages are through cold seas."

Brewer looked skyward with a thrill; there was no doubt he was doing what he loved to do. But he also had paperwork to attend to. Reluctantly, he said, "You have the deck, Benjamin. Call me if anything needs my attention."

"Aye, sir."

"Sail ho!"

"Where away?" Greene cried as he reached for a glass.

"Three points off the starboard bow!"

"There she is, sir!" It was the high squeaky voice of Mr. Short that cried out. Greene located him in the mizzen shrouds, his legs and one arm securing his perch. "Not quite hull down and heading away from us!"

"Thank you, Mr. Short!" Greene said loudly. "Lookout! What can you tell me about her?"

"She looks like a brig, sir! Course roughly west of north, sir!"

"I agree, sir!" Short cried from the shrouds.

Greene lowered his glass and chuckled. "Mr. Short, my respects to the Captain; please inform him of the sighting and that we are moving to intercept."

"Aye, aye, Mr. Greene!" The lad untangled himself from the shrouds and was gone in a flash.

"Quartermaster, alter course to intercept."

Captain Brewer appeared on deck. "Report, Mr. Greene."

"We've sighted a brig, Captain, nearly hull down, running just west of north. I altered course to intercept, as per your standing orders. Course is presently NNW."

Brewer took a glass and studied the horizon for himself.

Greene leaned in closer. "Didn't Mr. Short give you a full briefing?"

Brewer smiled. "He did indeed. He was most conscientious. I sent him aloft to see if he could discern any more details."

Greene looked up, and sure enough, Mr. Short had resumed his station in the mizzen shrouds.

"Deck, there!" the lookout called. "She's seen us, sir!"

"She's making sail sir!" Short cried.

Both officers snapped their telescopes back to their eyes, confirming the sightings.

"Call the hands," the Captain said calmly. "Make all sail."

"All hands! All hands!" Greene bellowed. "Make sail!"

Brewer kept his eye on the small but growing white speck near the horizon as his crew exploded to their tasks. Canvas expanded overhead, and the deck seemed to leap forward under his feet.

"Mr. Greene!" Brewer called, "who has the best eyes in the ship we can send aloft?"

"That would be Mr. Presley."

"Then pass the word for Mr. Presley."

Duly summoned, Presley, a young hand in Tyler's division, presented himself.

"Mr. Presley," Brewer said, "I need you in the tops to keep an eye on our friend out there. Take Mr. Short with you to run messages."

"Aye aye, sir!" Presley saluted. "Short! You're with me!"

Short dropped from the shrouds and followed Presley up to the tops.

Greene watched the two youngsters scurry into the rigging and turned to his captain. "What would you give to bottle that energy so you could have it when you get old like us?"

Brewer feigned a look of indignation. "Speak for yourself, sir. Or perhaps speak to Mr. Sweeney!"

They both laughed. It was good, he thought, that his men were relaxed and eager going into an unknown situation.

Brewer made his way below deck to his cabin. Upon opening his door, he found his servant, Alfred, and his coxswain, McCleary, bent over together in a detailed inspection of his sword. His brace of pistols were also lying on the table.

Mac stood and looked a bit embarrassed. "Begging your pardon, Captain," he said, "but Alfred here was giving me some pointers on keeping your pistols and your sword in top condition."

"Is that so?" Brewer asked as he surveyed the scene.

Alfred was holding the Captain's sword, turning it over in his hands and admiring it with the eye and judgment of an expert. "A marvelous blade, Captain," he said. "The workmanship is exquisite. May I ask where you got it?"

"I was in command of a boarding party in the Med when we were fighting Barbary pirates. This was the pirate chief's sword. He presented it to me when he surrendered, and Captain Bush insisted that I keep it."

"Ah," Alfred said, "that explains it. I thought I detected the workmanship of the North African masters."

Brewer turned, curious, and inquired, "And how do you know the work of the North African masters, Alfred?"

The servant answered as he sighted down the length of the blade. "My father had several examples in his collection, sir. I trained on one very much like this."

He assumed the *en gardé* position, testing the blade's balance. McCleary chuckled. In a way, Brewer could understand the reaction: the sight of the diminutive manservant striking such a pose with a sword that was nearly as big as he was would seem comical to some, but Brewer knew better. He saw his servant's eyes dart in the coxswain's direction and he started to shout out a warning, but there simply was no time. Before he could even draw a breath to shout, the tip of the sword was lunging, its *swish* cutting the air, to come to a halt a quarter-inch from the coxswain's Adam's apple. Brewer stared, unable to speak now, as Mac backed up to the bulkhead and stood on his toes. The deathly quiet of the scene was cut by the hiss of McCleary's breath as the blade gently caressed the poor coxswain's neck.

"You were saying?" Alfred said quietly.

"Nothing," Mac gurgled. "Nothing at all. I swear."

"I thought not," the servant said. Another a *swish* brought the blade from the coxswain's neck to the servant's side, and both coxswain and captain breathed a sigh of relief.

A knock at the door interrupted the still tense situation.

"Enter!" Brewer said quickly.

The door opened and Midshipman Reed appeared. "Mr. Greene's respects, Captain; the enemy ship looks to be tacking."

Brewer was never more relieved to be called to the deck. McCleary hurried out the door even before the midshipman had finished speaking.

"Very well," Brewer said to Reed, "I'll attend."

Reed saluted, then followed the fleeing coxswain.

Brewer picked up his hat, but he checked himself in the doorway. He turned to see Alfred still turning the blade from side to side, his admiration undisturbed by the incident with the coxswain.

"Alfred?"

"Never fear, sir," the servant said, still without taking his attention away from Brewer's sword. "I shall put everything to rights."

Brewer headed up on deck.

He found Greene, Tyler, Sweeney, and Reed all in the bows looking at their quarry. They parted to allow their captain access to the rail. A glass was presented to him with his having to ask, and he focused in on the horizon.

"She appears to be tacking, sir," Lieutenant Greene said, "perhaps trying for a better point of sailing."

"Perhaps," Brewer agreed, "but her change in course should allow us to close the gap significantly. Let's see if we can improve the odds further. Benjamin, run up the signal, *'Flag to squadron, general chase'*."

Greene looked confused but did not question his captain. He turned and gave the order, and in moments the signal was flying for nobody to see. Nobody, that is, but their quarry.

Brewer saw the puzzled look on his first lieutenant's face, but for the moment his focus was on the enemy. After a moment, he lowered his glass.

"Mr. Reed, keep a sharp eye on that ship. I want to know any changes she makes."

"Aye aye, sir!"

"Gentlemen, I am trying, as we used to say when I was a boy, to 'spook' that ship out there. Judging from the way she is trying to avoid us, I'm betting they have a Royal Navy deserter or two on board who may be able to read our signals. They may react differently if they think we are leading a squadron instead of being alone. I'm hoping they will make a mistake in their haste to flee a squadron that will allow us to close on them quickly."

"There you are, Captain!" shouted Reed.

They rushed to the railing. Reed was looking through his glass and pointing.

"See, sir?" he cried. "She's in irons, Captain! She's all aback!"

"Then let's see if we can lay them by the heels! Gentlemen," Brewer said, "let us be about our business. You have the deck, Benjamin. Do all you can to close the gap."

"Aye, sir," Greene replied eagerly.

Brewer raised his glass again and studied the fleeing ship. Slaver? Could be; she was certainly running like one. He lowered his glass and pursed his lips as he thought. It was a race now, and *Revenge* could hold her own in one of those. He glanced aft, wondering if it would help if he took charge of the quarterdeck. *No,* he thought, *Let Greene and Sweeney do the job you gave them to do.*

He handed the glass to Mr. Short and instructed the young midshipman to deliver a message to the ship's doctor. He stood on the quarterdeck a while, observing the activity of the crew and the decisiveness of his lieutenant. Five hours to sundown; would that be enough time to overtake the fleeing ship?

Brewer returned below deck, moving automatically as his eyes adjusted to the gloom. He heard a throat being cleared ahead of him; the doctor was standing at his cabin door.

"Afternoon, Captain," he said. "For a moment I was afraid you might run me down."

"Doctor!" he said. "I can see Mr. Short is bucking for a promotion. Here I thought I would be able to take my hat off before you arrived."

Spinelli followed his captain inside and closed the door. "I was on my way to the deck; he found me just forward and directed me here."

Brewer took a deep breath. "I was hoping for a game of chess to pass the time while we close on that ship out there."

"Of course, Captain," the doctor said. He rubbed his hands together in anticipation.

"Ha! I see you are in a combative mood. Pour us each a drink, will you? Thanks. Your set or mine?"

The Doctor poured two glasses of Madeira. "Yours. It's better than mine."

"Fair enough." Brewer pulled the chess set out and set it on the table, and the two men went about the process of ordering the pieces. The Doctor drew white, and the game began. The first several moves were made in silence, until the Captain drew first blood by taking his opponent's bishop.

"Took you long enough," Spinelli muttered under his breath. Brewer ignored the remark.

"So, tell me, Captain," the doctor said, "what do you think we're chasing? A slaver?"

"That or a pirate," Brewer said as he moved his rook. "Check. Either one would run from a warship. The test will come when we catch up with them."

"How so?" Spinelli said, making a counter move.

"We shall fire a warning shot across their bow in an attempt to get them to heave to. That will tell us." His friend was still looking puzzled. "It's very simple, Adam; a pirate will turn and fight, but a slaver will surrender."

"Ah," the Doctor said with an exaggerated nod.

Belatedly, Brewer realized the questions had been a feint, distracting him from the game. Spinelli proceeded to unleash a flurry of moves that won him the game in short order and left his captain staring at the board in dismay.

"Adam, that was... extraordinary."

"Thank you, Captain," Spinelli said. He gallantly rose and refilled their glasses. By the time he returned, Brewer had set the board up for a rematch.

"Tell me," Spinelli said, "did you come across Lieutenant Roberts when you went to see the Admiral?"

"Yes. He seems to be doing well, and I believe his position as the admiral's aide is a good fit for him. He needed to have a purpose, and the Admiral has given him one."

"I am glad. I was afraid he would drop into a depression that would compromise his health. The loss of an arm is a traumatic event; many do not recover from it."

"Well," Brewer said, as he picked up his knight, "I cannot say for certain what will happen in the future, but for now, and I think for as long as he is working with the Admiral, he will be fine." He put the knight down between the Doctor's white bishop and a pawn, and then he looked up with a smile. "Checkmate."

Spinelli stared at the board with a scowl on his face. A knock at the door spared his Captain any recriminations. Lieutenant Greene entered the room.

"Sir," he said, "it looks like we will overtake the brig before dark, as long as the wind holds."

Brewer slapped his hand on the table. "As I hoped! Don't just sit there, Doctor; get the good Lieutenant a drink."

The Doctor silently threw a 'later for you' look at his captain before rising to fulfill his task. Greene wondered what he had missed. Dr. Spinelli returned with a glass for him, mumbled a reply to Green's thanks, and resumed his seat, scowling as before at the board.

"When we go on deck, Benjamin," Brewer said, "I want you to get one gun in position to fire on the enemy. It might induce them to heave to before we actually overhaul them. If that doesn't work, I intend to have Mr. Sweeney lay me by pistol shot and run the guns out."

"Aye aye, sir. I wonder, if it is a slaver, how much head money will there be?"

Brewer shrugged. "Depends on the number of Africans aboard."

Greene's eyebrows rose in hopeful anticipation. Brewer could not blame him for thinking about it. He knew of many fellow officers who were able to retire quite comfortably off head money.

Two hours later, with approximately two hours of sunlight left, they had closed the gap by more than half. Brewer, frustrated, gauged the distance. If he had one of the old long nines, he could open fire with it and possibly bring the enemy to heel. As it was, they still had a ways to go before he could consider opening up with a 12-pounder. He cast a wary eye at the sun.

"I want every stitch of sail on *Revenge* right now. I know, Mr. Sweeney; it's not wise in this wind, but we're only going to do it for a short run to catch that ship and take her before dark."

"Aye, sir," Greene said. He headed aft, bellowing orders as he went. Within minutes, *Revenge's* speed increased, as did her heel.

"Stand by, Mr. Sweeney," Brewer said. "We just need to hold long enough to get in range..." He leaned against the rail and brought the glass to his eye again briefly. "Just a little more..." He turned to his sailing master. "Run to the quarterdeck, and send Mr. Greene to me. I want you to alter our course two points to the starboard. Two points only, now, Mr. Sweeney! If the enemy does not heave to after our warning shots, I will come to the quarterdeck and direct the action from there. Understand? Go, then!"

The sailing master went aft and Brewer focused his attention on his quarry. Mr. Greene appeared almost immediately.

"Benjamin," he said, as he felt the ship alter course, "as soon as our change allows the forward 12-pounders to bear, I want you to put a warning shot across her bows. Send word by runner when you are ready to open fire. I will answer by a wave of my hat."

"Yes, sir," Greene replied, and sped off.

Brewer made his way to the quarterdeck. He found Mr. Tyler conversing with Mr. Sweeney.

"Gentlemen," he said hurriedly, "here is what I plan to do. Lieutenant Greene is going to send a runner when he is ready to open fire. At that time, Mr. Tyler, we will take in sail and reduce *Revenge's* heel. That will give Mr. Greene a steady platform to put a warning shot off their bow. If that ship does not surrender, we'll turn hard to port and put a broadside in her stern as we pass."

Not long after, Mr. Short came to the quarterdeck and saluted.

"Mr. Greene's respects, sir, and he says he's ready."

"Then now, Mr. Tyler."

Tyler grabbed a speaking trumpet and began shouting orders. Hands ran aloft to take in sail, and *Revenge* leveled off. Brewer removed his hat and waved it. Seconds later, the sounds of a 12-pounder shattered the calm. Brewer got a glass to his eye but failed to see where the shot fell.

"Did anyone see the shot?" he called.

"About thirty yards off their starboard bow, sir," Lieutenant Tyler said.

"Mr. Short," Brewer called, "Inform Mr. Greene I want another warning shot, close enough that they can't miss it."

The midshipman took to his heels.

In less than a minute, the 12-pounder's report was heard again. This time the geyser of water rose ten feet off the other ship's starboard beam. Brewer immediately saw action on the brig's quarterdeck. Two minutes later, a white flag was run up, and he could see hands going aloft and taking in sail.

"That's done it!" he exclaimed. "Mr. Sweeney, heave to. Mr. Tyler, I want the larboard battery loaded and run out, then pass the word for Mr. Greene."

Once he was sure the surrender was authentic and not a ploy to lure an overconfident Captain in close, Brewer addressed his lieutenant. "Good work, Benjamin," Brewer said. "Take a boarding party and see what we have here. Take Mr. Reed with you, you can send him back with your report."

"Aye, sir," Greene replied, and he went forward, bellowing orders for a boat's crew and boarding party.

The captain stood at his lee rail along with the sailing master, quartermaster, and second lieutenant and watched *Revenge's* boat pull its way over to the chase. They watched their comrades climb up onto their adversary's deck. Greene, Reed, and three hands, all of them armed, headed for the quarterdeck, while other parties fanned out forward. It took several minutes before Lieutenant Greene was able to step to the rail with a speaking trumpet.

"She's a slaver, sir!" he shouted. "I will send Mr. Reed back with a report within the hour."

"Very well!" Brewer shouted back.

"Well, well," he said as he stepped away from the rail. "A slaver, indeed! That means head money, gentlemen." He looked around and saw smiles on every face. "Mr. Tyler, you have the deck. I shall be in my cabin, working on a report for the admiral. Call me if our prize so much as twitches, and have Mr. Reed report to me directly when he comes aboard."

"Aye aye, sir," Tyler said.

Brewer went below. He was barely a paragraph into his report when there was a knock at his door and Dr. Spinelli entered.

"Well, Adam," Brewer said, "what can I do for you?"

Spinelli rubbed his hands together. "I hear we're all going to be rich."

Brewer set his pen down carefully; it was a right-handed quill, and he wanted it to last. He indicated a seat for his friend, but the doctor was too excited to sit. "That's the word in the fo'c'sle. We're going to divide a king's ransom in head money!"

Brewer chuckled. "I'm afraid they're in for a bit of a disappointment. There will be head money, yes, but I haven't received a count from Lieutenant Greene yet, and it is unlikely to worth a king's ransom!"

The doctor looked downcast. "Adam, if you want, you can have a seat, and we shall await Mr. Reed's report together."

"Thank you," the doctor said as he sat.

Brewer went back to his writing. He was nearly finished detailing the pursuit when there was a knock at the door and Mr. Short entered.

"Mr. Tyler's respects, sir, and he says to tell you that Mr. Reed is on his way back," Short said breathlessly.

"Thank you, Mr. Short. My compliments to Mr. Tyler; Mr. Reed is to report to me when he comes on board."

"Aye aye, sir," Short withdrew.

Brewer grinned at the doctor. "Not long now, Adam."

It was barely twenty minutes later when Mr. Reed stood before his captain.

"The ship is called the *Kingfish*, Captain," Reed said. "American, home port of Charleston, South Carolina. She has 105 negroes on board. They had an outbreak of fever some time back, and nearly half their number died as a result. Sir, several of those still alive are barely hanging on."

Spinelli didn't hesitate. "Shall I go, sir?" he said, rising to his feet and looking as if he were prepared to swim to the other ship, if need be.

Brewer thought it over for a second, then nodded. "Yes, Adam, I think you should."

"I'd like to take Julius, as well," the doctor said, naming his mate, "and I'll need a few minutes to gather some medicines."

"Of course," Brewer said. Spinelli left the cabin in a hurry.

The Captain turned his attention back to Reed. "Continue, Mr. Reed."

"Aye, sir. There's a minimum of crew on board, sir; I believe some of them were carried away by the fever too. Sir?" Reed seemed shaken somehow. "Below deck's a shambles, sir. The negroes are chained up, and the filth, sir! I don't..."

"Hush, I know it's bad," Brewer said. "Alfred! Something strong for this officer. Sit, Mr. Reed."

Alfred returned with a glass of wine, and Reed thanked him before drinking. He closed his eyes for a moment to compose himself. He shuddered, and the eyes opened.

"Sorry, sir," he said.

"No need, Mr. Reed. I know of many officers who have seen what you have seen and lost their lunch over it."

Reed grinned sheepishly. "I lost mine on the slaver, sir."

"Where were they heading?"

"Captain said they were making for a Spanish port: Cuba, maybe, or Puerto Rico. Before he sighted us, he was heading for Charleston."

Brewer rose, and Reed followed suit. "Very good, Mr. Reed. See that Spinelli gets all the help he needs to save those people. Get the brig ready to sail to Port Royal. Send Mr. Greene back for orders."

Reed came to attention. "Aye aye, Captain."

After his senior midshipman had gone, Brewer amended his report to include all the information that Reed had told him. Alfred brought him a glass of wine, and he sat back to consider. No one could retire on the head money from 105 negroes, but the crew would appreciate the bounty nonetheless. He thought about what the midshipman had said about the appalling conditions that existed below decks on the slaver. Brewer had been fortunate to have never been aboard such a ship, and he was not particularly anxious for that to change. Conditions like those were worse than how the animals on his father's farm lived; he could not conceive of a human being, even a convicted murderer, being forced to endure such an environment.

Mr. Greene arrived within the hour.

"How bad is it, really, Benjamin?" Brewer asked.

"It's worse than anything I've ever seen, but I've never been on a slaver before, so I have no idea it what I saw was the norm or not."

Brewer pulled out a fresh sheet of paper and began writing. "How are they fixed for supplies?"

"No shortage there, sir, although I have no idea what it is that they've been feeding the negroes. Some kind of porridge, I think, but it looks like slop."

Brewer shook his head. "A diet like that couldn't have helped them fight off the fever."

Greene stood silent, shaking his head in agreement.

"Who was the captain?"

"Jonathan Burchell, an American from Connecticut." Greene looked baffled. "That's in the *northern* United States, isn't it? That's not a slave state, is it?"

"No. After the money, I suppose. We'll see if the admiral wants to turn him over to the Americans."

Brewer set the pen down and sealed the orders. "*Kingfish* will accompany *Revenge* back to Port Royal. You will be in command. I suggest Mr. Reed will be valuable to you, but that is your decision. Choose a prize crew, and perhaps an extra hand or two to assist the doctor if you feel it's necessary." He stood and handed the packet to Greene. "Your orders, *Captain*, in case we get separated."

Greene accepted the packet with great humility. In truth, he was surprised by how much he was affected by the responsibility.

"You'll do fine, Benjamin," Brewer said. "Make sure you keep order. That crew are prisoners, not passengers. Watch for treachery."

"Yes, sir," Greene said. The two men shook hands, and Greene left.

Brewer walked from the Port Royal wharf to the Admiral's house. He had decided to make a habit of it, as it gave him a chance to calm his mind and order his thoughts. The morning was bright and pleasant, and the sea breeze felt cool as it brushed by his ears and cheeks. They'd had no trouble during the voyage, both ships entering the harbor shortly after dawn.

It was Lieutenant Phillips who answered the door.

"Welcome, Commander," he said. "Please come in. The Admiral is occupied at the moment and asks that you would be so kind as to wait."

"Of course," Brewer said. He stepped inside and removed his hat, placing it under his left arm out of habit. He nodded to Phillips' pinned sleeve. "How have you been, Lieutenant? The arm giving you any trouble?"

"Not a bit, sir," Phillips said as he led his former captain to the library door. "Oh, every once in a while I remember that it's not there anymore, but otherwise I'm learning to get along without it. The stewards are kind enough to help me with my coat sometimes." They reached the door. "Please wait here. May I take your reports to give to the Admiral? Thank you. There are refreshments on the table, if you desire, and I shall be back as quickly as I can."

"Thank you, Mr. Phillips."

Phillips closed the door, leaving Brewer alone. He poured himself a lemonade and passed the time perusing the bookshelves. He noticed a book about the American Revolution, and it reminded him of meeting John Adams in the bookstore in Boston during HMS *Defiant's* stopover in that port.

It was not very long at all before Mr. Phillips returned to take him to the Admiral.

"Oh, I almost forgot, Commander," Phillips said in the hall. "Have you heard that Lieutenant Gerard was promoted?"

"What? Gerard's a commander now?"

"Yes, sir!"

Brewer beamed. "It's about time."

Mr. Phillips could only agree with the sentiment.

CHAPTER 8

Lieutenant Phillips opened the door and announced, "Commander Brewer, sir." He stepped aside and let Brewer enter.

Hornblower rose and came around his desk with his hand extended. Brewer grasped it heartily.

"It's good to see you again, Commander." Hornblower led his protégé to two overstuffed leather chairs that faced each other over a low table. "I read your report of your meetings in Martinique and immediately forwarded it to the Admiralty in London, with a request for any information they may have on collusion between French expatriates and pirates. We'll see what they send us; in the meantime, we shall have to keep a closer watch on the island. Tell me, what was your impression of the Governor?"

"Bonapartist through and through, my lord," Brewer said. "He only warmed to me after he found out about St. Helena."

Hornblower sat back in his chair, his brows furled in deep thought. "That fits with other reports I've heard. I was interested to read of his affinity for steam power." The Admiral shook his head. "We all know that steam power is the coming means for powering not only commercial ships but also warships, but I shall tell you, William, that I am not at all convinced that in this case progress is a good thing. It frightens me to think that soon captains will be at the mercy of an exhaustible fuel supply. Bad enough that we are limited by food and water, but now to be constrained by the supply of coal as well?" He grunted. "Not yet, anyway. My information is that the technology won't meet our needs for several years yet."

"They are making great strides in stretching the water supply by means of those metal tanks that are being installed in the new ships and refits."

Hornblower shrugged. "That will make everyone happy, except perhaps the cooper and his mates."

Brewer laughed. "We could always make topmen out of them."

The Admiral chuckled and then leaned forward. "Now, on to the important matters. I have forwarded to the Americans the confirmation that El Diabolito is in command of the *Pauline*. Commodore Porter has fought him more than we have, and he is more familiar with the pirate's likely moves." He shook his head in frustration. "We have been trying to lay our hands on that pirate for nearly ten years now, and the Americans for longer than that. We have no description of him, and none of his acquaintances we have captured have been willing to give us one."

"Should I take *Revenge* and begin a sweep of the outer islands?" Brewer asked.

Hornblower looked up at him. "Whatever for?"

Brewer was suddenly unsure of himself in the face of his mentor's reaction. "To try to find the *Pauline* before she can be fully repaired, my lord."

Hornblower waved his hand dismissively. "Since we know the pirate's gunnery is very nearly at French wartime standards, we can safely assume he will still have the services of their carpenter as well. If that is indeed the case, I am sure the *Pauline* has been repaired and moved to a safe anchorage by now. No, our best chance at laying our hands on this devil lies in determining where he is most likely to strike next and to be ready for him."

"Yes, my lord."

The Admiral picked up Brewer's report from his desk. "I have here your report on the prize you brought in, but I would like to hear it from you."

Brewer spent the next twenty minutes describing the pursuit and how they were able to cut the slaver off after they became hung in the stays. Hornblower listened attentively, nodding his head from time to time.

"Whew," Hornblower said when his protégé was finished. "105 negroes rescued! That was a good day's work."

"Indeed," Brewer said. "And I think I have reason to be personally grateful for the occasion. Tending to the survivors gave our good doctor a focus and purpose. He was in need of both."

The Admiral rose and went to pull the bell cord to summon a servant.

"Dinner will be served soon," he said as he resumed his seat. "I hope it will be convenient for you to dine with me?"

"It would be a pleasure," Brewer said.

When a servant announced the meal, the two officers adjourned to the dining room and partook. Brewer found himself missing Alfred's fare, but after what had happened to Jenkins, he wasn't about to mention Alfred to the Admiral.

Afterwards, they returned to the sitting room, where coffee was served. Admiral Lord Horatio Hornblower was suddenly caught up in a memory. The sight of his protégé, sitting here, reporting to him after the first cruise of his first independent command, reminded the Admiral of how he himself felt when he took command of HMS *Hotspur*. He wondered if the same warm feeling he was now experiencing had flooded Cornwallis's breast or Pellew's as they watched Hornblower so many years ago.

The Admiral studied his young captain, looking for indicators of what sort of commander he would become. He felt entirely justified in giving Brewer command of *Revenge*, despite his youth, and something told him that he need not worry about how Brewer would turn out.

He smiled, remembering a conversation on St. Helena with the Corsican on this very topic.

"May I compliment you, Governor," Bonaparte had said one afternoon, not long before they left the island, "on your choice of M. Brewer as your aide?"

"Thank you," Hornblower had replied. "He has exceeded all my expectations."

"May I ask how he came to your service?"

"He was pointed out to me by Captain William Bush. You may remember him from the dinner soon after my arrival."

Bonaparte thought for a moment. "He escaped captivity with you."

"Correct. Mr. Brewer was one of his officers. I watched him on the voyage to St. Helena and judged him to be competent. Once I assumed office as governor, I realized very quickly that the former governor's aide would not work out."

Bonaparte had smiled. "He considered me evil incarnate."

"Precisely. Once I decided that a new aide was necessary, Mr. Brewer naturally came to mind. And, as I said, he has exceeded all my expectations."

"Mine as well, *mon ami*," the Corsican had agreed.

Now, years later in his office at Port Royal, Hornblower felt pleased that his instincts had been justified. He was sure that, were he here, Bonaparte would also be pleased with how the young lieutenant had turned out.

And yet, Hornblower became aware that all was not quite right with his protégé. He could not put his finger on what it was. Brewer seemed... not upset, possibly anxious? Yes, perhaps; but it seemed more of an uncertainty, almost as he himself had felt during the long voyage back from the Pacific in HMS *Lydia* when he brought Barbara back....

And suddenly, he knew, and the knowledge made him smile again and relax.

"Tell me, William," he said, "have you heard from Bush lately?"

"No, my lord," the Captain replied, "but I haven't had a chance to check the mail here as yet."

"Yes, of course," Hornblower said; it was hard, trying to draw Brewer out without being crass about it. Still, there was no time like the present.

"William, is there something you wish to ask me?"

The young captain reacted as though he had received a jolt of electricity. His head snapped up with eyes open wide and his mouth agape. It was all the confirmation the Admiral needed.

"Excuse me, my lord?"

"William, there is that in your manner that puts me very much in mind of my own state on the return journey of the *Lydia* from the Pacific, when we were transporting a certain passenger back to England. I infer that there is now... a lady in your life."

Brewer seemed unsure whether or not to be embarrassed. At last he said, "How can you tell?"

The Admiral chuckled. "As I said, I recognize the symptoms." He paused to sip his wine.

"So," Hornblower asked coyly, "who is she?"

The younger man smiled shyly. "Her name is Elizabeth Danforth, my lord, and she is the daughter of the governor of St. Kitts."

"Ah," Hornblower said with an nod and another swallow. "Beautiful, I suppose?"

Brewer blushed. "I think so, my lord. She just - I'm not sure how to put it, exactly. It was as though she was the only one in the room to me." He stared into space, picturing her and remembering the moment. "I never met anyone like her before."

"I felt the same way on that voyage with Barbara. Your young lady is not betrothed, I trust?"

Brewer frowned, as though the thought had never occurred to him until that moment. "Not to my knowledge, my lord."

Hornblower chuckled. "Let us hope not, William; it certainly complicates things."

A little silence settled on the room, and Brewer looked out the window at the view of the bay. Hornblower could almost see the exertion of his friend's ordering of his thoughts. He was certain that Brewer had something particular on his mind to ask, but he decided not to force the issue. He would wait and let Brewer bring it to light himself.

In the end, he didn't have long to wait. He soon saw his guest's eyes come into focus, and a look of determination come upon his face, and he knew that the crucial decision had been made. Brewer turned back toward his mentor and leaned forward, placing his elbows on his knees.

"A question, if I may, my lord?"

The Admiral nodded.

Brewer chose his words with care.

"Ever since I met Elizabeth, I have thought of asking her to be my wife. I have never felt drawn to a woman like this before. But the more I thought on it, the more I became aware of the amount of time she would be condemned to spend alone, waiting for me to return. Then I thought about you and Captain Bush, the one married with someone waiting at home, the other content to be a bachelor. I guess I am just having trouble deciding which I should be. Do I have the right to force such isolation upon Elizabeth?"

Hornblower listened silently, surprised at how each word brought him back to that first voyage with Barbara. Of course, the situation was not quite the same; Hornblower had also been dealing with feelings that he had betrayed Maria, but the sensation of meeting a woman you felt unworthy of, and then torturing yourself over your chances to be with her forever, these were feelings the Admiral understood all too well.

"Do you believe the lady shares your affections?" he asked.

Brewer hung his head for a moment before answering. "I don't know. I mailed her a letter before we left Martinique, but I've not received one in return as yet. Although," he said quietly, "I am in hopes there is one waiting for me."

The Admiral chuckled. "Well, perhaps fortune may yet smile upon you." He took a drink from his cup. The liquid had gone tepid, but Hornblower took no notice. No one had ever asked him this before, not even Bush, although Hornblower privately was sure the oceans would run dry before William Bush had a woman in his life who was not related to him.

And now young Brewer sat before him, wondering if his life or hers would be ruined if he allowed himself to be happy with this young woman. Hornblower remembered feeling that way himself, first with Maria, then with Barbara.

He shook his head in self-recrimination and looked out the window. He still felt a pang of regret at the way he had treated Maria. To this day he could not state with absolute certainty why he had married her. He would have said he loved her, but not in same way he loved Barbara. With Maria, he always felt as though he was being pushed along by an invisible, inexorable Hand of Fate which he was powerless to resist, mainly because he could not bring himself to break her heart. And yet, it was Maria who given him his son, the true joy of his life.

Hornblower scowled as he always did when he remembered that it was also Maria who'd sat helplessly in Southsea watching their two babies fade away while he escaped to sea. He felt the old, familiar, aching shame. Now he looked at his young friend and wondered what to say to him. Hornblower shuddered inside; he hated the thought of exposing himself. Not even Bush had ever been able to draw him out completely. Barbara was the only one he had ever let inside.

That thought gave him pause—what would Barbara advise him to say to young Brewer? Here was a man falling in love, or at least *hoping* to fall in love, but afraid of the loneliness or pain the separation could cause. What would Barbara say, were she here?

In his mind, he saw her face, and she smiled at him, that knowing kind of smile she would get when he asked a silly question to which he already knew the answer. *Horatio*, the vision said, *I love you, and the long separations only make our reunions all the more joyous. My husband, you are worth waiting for, and I shall be waiting for you to come home to me. Tell Mr. Brewer to be happy. He must speak to the young lady, and hopefully he will find she considers him worth the wait as well.*

"William," Hornblower said, "for myself, all I can tell you is to be happy. It's not a curse, or something that only comes true for others. Both Captain Bush and myself have been happy in the life we have chosen, and so shall you be. Speak to Miss Danforth, William, and the two of you decide what sort of life you will build together. The question you must answer is whether this young woman is intended by the Almighty to be part of your happiness or not."

Brewer nodded slowly as he considered all that his mentor had said. He swallowed hard. "I just hope the answer won't be 'No'."

It was time to go. Brewer bade his friend and mentor farewell. Outside in the hallway, he was intercepted by Lieutenant Phillips.

"I'm glad I caught you, Commander," he said. "I took the liberty of inquiring for you, and I have the mail bag for HMS *Revenge* in my office."

Brewer followed the lieutenant to his office, while he retrieved the bag. Phillips handed it to him, and Brewer searched its contents until he found what he had hoped for, a letter addressed to him in a woman's hand that was unfamiliar to him. There were also letters from his sister and mother, but these he returned to the bag with the others. "Thank you, Mr. Phillips. Please see that this is sent out to *Revenge* as soon as possible."

The lieutenant smiled. "The mail boat's waiting for it to leave, sir."

Brewer nodded. "Good man."

He put the letter in his coat pocket and walked out into the hot afternoon Caribbean sun and started down the street. He turned in to the first coffee house he came to and ordered a cool drink while he worked up the nerve to open the letter.

He took it out of his coat pocket and set it on the table in front of him. His waiter returned and set his drink on the table, but Brewer never knew he had come or gone. His focus was on the letter, as though he could somehow divine its contents without having to actually open it. He saw no seal imprinted on the wax, but he could understand her not wishing to start tongues wagging.

Brewer frowned and felt slightly ridiculous; he knew he was stalling. The only way to know for sure was to open the letter and read it.

He picked up the letter and broke the seal. He hesitated just for a moment before unfolding the note and scanning the first few lines.

My Dear Captain,

I hope this note finds you well and happy in your new command. I received your very kind letter only this morning, and as I had a few minutes to myself, I wanted to assure you that I, too, enjoyed our walk in the garden. It is my favorite place to wander, and I should very much enjoy having you escort me there again, should you find yourself in the vicinity of St. Kitts.

Thank you for telling me about Captain Bush. I am glad you were able to have such a teacher in your life. I have discovered that not everyone has the opportunity to learn from someone who is very good at what he does. Cherish that, and make sure you pass it one to someone who will cherish it as much as you do.

I also congratulate you on finding that thing you were born to do. That is a rare accomplishment. I hope you will continue to enjoy success and fulfillment in all that you do. I do have a question, however, and I pray you will not think me too forward for the asking, but I shall put it forth in any case. My question is, since you have found what you were born to do, does that mean that there is no room left in your life for anything—or anyone—else?

BREWER'S REVENGE

*I hope your duties will allow you to write a few
lines to me. I look forward to your reply.*

Sincerely,
Elizabeth

Brewer read the letter twice through before setting it
down. His heart was racing and his hands were sweating,
both for reasons that had nothing to do with the heat of the
Caribbean afternoon. He closed his eyes, forcing himself to
take deep breaths and calm down. Then he opened his eyes
again and looked down at the letter. The handwriting was
beautiful and delicate, and the paper was expensive. He
brushed the words with the back of his fingers and somehow
felt closer to the author. He blushed at the thought of acting
thus in a public place, like some adolescent schoolboy.

He smiled and refolded the letter before putting it inside
his coat pocket. He stood and pulled some coins from his
pocket, dropping them on the table to pay for his drink
before stepping out onto the sidewalk. He hadn't taken two
steps before he heard his name. He turned to see Gerard.

"Commander!" Brewer greeted his old friend.
"Congratulations on your promotion! It is long overdue!"

"Thank you," Gerard said breathlessly. "I'm sorry to have
to chase you down like this, but you managed to get out of
the Admiral's house before I could give you your orders."

"And what do these say?" Brewer asked as the two
officers began to walk down the street.

"You are to take *Revenge* back to sea in two days' time
and sail due east. You are to patrol the waters off Puerto Rico
as long as your supplies hold out."

"And what am I looking for?"

"Pirates."

Brewer looked at his friend. "El Diabolito?"

"No," Gerard said. "Roberto Cofresi."

Brewer stopped and turned so he could speak in a low voice.

"He's not the one I want, Gerard."

Gerard placed his hand on his friend's arm. "I know, William, believe me. But right now, Cofresi is the biggest threat to shipping from the Bahamas to the Windward Islands. The latest dispatches from London mention him by name, and Admiral Hornblower wants him dealt with as soon as possible."

Brewer frowned in frustration. Before Gerard arrived, he was just beginning to formulate a plan to put to the Admiral to allow him to take *Revenge* back to Martinique to try to pick up El Diabolito's trail. Now, to be pulled off the hunt like this...

"Gerard," he said slowly, "can't you convince the Admiral to allow me to take *Revenge* to search for El Diabolito? Surely there are other ships to send."

"William!" Gerard said, in a tone that got his friend's attention. "There is no one else to send. *Defiant* was ordered to Bermuda. *Clorinda* is at this moment on her way to the Bahamas, *Phoebe* is cruising off Nicaragua, and *Roebuck* is still off Curacao, watching the arms trade with Venezuela. The rest of the sloops or schooners are all occupied as well."

"But surely—"

"Commander, the Admiral has given you your orders. What answer shall I take back to him?"

Brewer's eyes snapped up, but it was clear from the look on Gerard's face that the Admiral's aide would brook no further debate on the topic.

"You may tell Admiral Hornblower that I will carry out my orders to the best of my ability."

"Thank you," Gerard said, and his expression softened. "I am sorry, William. But take heart; if there's one thing I've learned about pirates, it's this: you never know who you might run into."

Gerard bade his friend farewell, and Brewer watched him walk back toward the Admiral's house. He looked at the packet he held in his hand and resigned himself to following his orders. His day would come; he was sure of it. All he had to do was wait and be ready, just like the Corsican had said.

CHAPTER 9

Dr. Spinelli climbed up on deck and was immediately glad that he had. He enjoyed the sea air and the Caribbean sun warm on his face. He had slept most of the last two days out of sheer exhaustion after his round-the-clock service on the slaver. Despite the deplorable conditions below deck when he'd boarded the ship, he had lost only two of the rescued Negroes on the voyage back to Jamaica. He had been particularly touched at the way several of them paused to thank him for his kindness as they were removed from the ship. The thanks had been not in any language he knew, but the clasped hands and the looks of gratitude had spoken eloquently.

An hour ago, he had been sitting in the sick bay, rereading the letter that told him of poor Mary's death. What a horrible way to die! Run over by a horse with some drunken cabbie at the reins! He set the letter down and stared at the bulkhead. Part of him felt as though he should have been there, that if he had been, perhaps he could have saved her. They had been so right together! She had known he was a sailor, had known what that meant. She had been fine with it; in fact, she'd told him before he boarded *Defiant* that for her, he was the one man in England worth waiting for.

He knew what was happening and was trying desperately to stop it. He was becoming morose and depressed; the old craving for the bottle was trying to reassert itself.

That was really what drove him up onto the deck. He hoped the air would clear his mind as well as his lungs. He was even glad now that Mr. Greene had confiscated all his caches of whiskey. Not that he'd felt that way when he got back to the sick bay and found it all gone! He had marched right back to the Captain's cabin and complained mightily, only to be told that all sick bay spirits were under the direct control of the first lieutenant for the duration.

He was very thankful to have a friend like William Brewer. He could think of captains who would have been done with him after the incident in the pub, one or two who would have left him there at the mercy of the mob. Not Brewer.

The Doctor took an easy turn around the deck and considered his captain. Brewer had come aboard HMS *Defiant* at the same time as himself, along with the rest of the junior officers, all of them potential targets for that insane maniac James Norman. Young Phillips bore the brunt of Norman's torture, and it had fallen to Brewer to defend him as best he could.

Spinelli stopped and looked absently at a twelve-pounder. Yes, that hurricane they'd encountered west of Bermuda definitely saved Brewer's career, if not his life. Norman would have either shot Brewer or written a report that would have put the young lieutenant on the beach permanently. Personally, he thought Norman would indeed have murdered Brewer in cold blood that day, had the wave not come along and swept the captain to his final reward. It was just like the hand of God Himself was protecting Brewer. Spinelli remembered the Bible held a prominent place on the Captain's bookshelf, and he knew that Brewer read from it every day. Maybe there was something to all that stuff, after all? He shrugged and continued his walk.

He had taken to Brewer as he had to few men in his life, certainly since he'd joined the Navy. He was an easy man to follow, as though leading were as natural to him as breathing. He wore the mantle of authority as easily as some men wore a fine silk shirt. With some captains he had encountered, their authority was a flag they constantly waved to remind the crew who was in charge. Not so with Brewer.

Spinelli smiled as he stepped over a coil of rope. He had known officers who would simply have ridden the patronage of a man like Hornblower to a post-rank and then retired to their country estates, but Brewer worked and refined his craft; that much was obvious from watching the man perform his duties. Spinelli firmly believed Brewer had earned command of HMS *Revenge*, and now he was going to make the most of his opportunity.

The Doctor paused as he came up on the first lieutenant speaking with Mr. Sweeney. The two men greeted him cordially.

"Feeling better today, Doctor?" Sweeney asked.

"Yes, thank you, Mr. Sweeney. Just taking a walk around deck to clear my head." Spinelli brought a kerchief out to mop his brow, but his hand was shaking so much that he had a difficult time of it.

"Are you sure you're okay, Doctor?" Greene asked. "Do you need a drink? For medicinal purposes, of course."

Spinelli looked hard at the first lieutenant to see if his words were intended to be a knife, but he saw only concern on the other's face and rebuked himself for his thoughts.

"No, thank you," he said, then he smiled. "But I shall remember your offer."

Spinelli excused himself and walked slowly around the deck for another hour, alone with his thoughts. By the time he was done, he felt much better about his situation, and by extension, himself.

Noah Simmons walked less than a mile from the wharf along Port Royal's main street before turning off into a seedy neighborhood. He knew that Mr. Reed had meant to keep him on the ship, but he'd managed to get away, and without a tail this time. Now it was time to see about making Mr. Reed disappear.

He entered a tavern he remembered from his days before the Navy. It was a dark hole, the kind of place where a man could arrange anything that was needful—if the price was right. He paused inside the door to allow his eyes to adjust to the poor lighting, then made his way to the bar and ordered a pint.

"Tell me," he said to the barkeep as he plunked the foaming tankard before him, "have you seen Bobo around?"

"Who wants to know?" the barkeep asked.

"A paying customer," Simmons replied. "Now, have you seen him or not?"

A voice spoke from a dark region at the end of the bar.

"Hello, Noah."

Simmons picked up his tankard and made his way over. He slip into the empty seat.

"Bobo. Just like you to be lurking in a dark corner."

Bobo shrugged. "It lets me see who's coming. And I hears things no one knows I hears. I heard *you* have to leave town rather sudden-like."

Simmons tried to brush it off. "It's nothing. Just a bit of bad luck."

Bobo sneered. "That's not what I heard. I warned you that sooner or later you'd mess with the wrong wench who had the wrong daddy, and now you have. I heard your Pa had to save your life by getting you posted to a Navy ship!"

Simmons' face grew hard. "You know, you really ought to shut your trap."

Bobo laughed in his face. "And who's going to make me? You? Don't make me laugh, little governor's son."

Simmons wisely decided to hold his tongue. He needed Bobo's particular services.

"Look, Bobo, I didn't come here to argue with you."

"I bet you didn't! So why did you look me up?"

"I've got a job for you."

"You! A job for me? And just how do you expect to pay for this job?"

"I'm good for it."

"Sure you are!" Bobo paused to take a great gulp from the pint in front of him before leaning in close. The mercenary had on a black knit cap, from under which hung thick black hair past his eyebrows. He was unshaven, which gave him a menacing look in the darkness, but it was his breath that made Simmons recoil.

"Just for laughs, Noah, tell me what this job is."

"I want you to take care of someone."

Bobo started to snicker into his beer. Simmons sat back in his chair and felt ridiculous.

Bobo finally stopped chortling and smiled at his guest. "And just who is this person that you need me to make him disappear?" His eyes went wide. "Or is it a woman? Don't tell me! You got yerself in in trouble with *another* wench, and if she don't disappear, yer old man is going to make you join the army this time, is that it?"

Bobo laughed again, pounding the table in glee. Simmons sat there, helpless and boiling.

"No, it's not a woman, Bobo. It's someone from my ship. His name is Jonathan Reed."

"Oh, now I understand!" Bobo crowed. "You tried your usual ways on that ship of yours, didn't you?"

"What ways?"

"Come, now, Noah, old governor's son. You tried to walk in and take over, get the weaker ones to do your work for you, maybe bullied 'em to make 'em do it, and this Reed taught you a lesson right proper, didn't he?"

Simmons stewed, and Bobo had another laughing fit at his expense.

"Will you do it?" Simmons asked.

Bobo drained his tankard in one long pull. He slammed it down on the table and looked Simmons in the eye.

"No."

Simmons was stunned. "What? Why? Bobo, I can pay!"

Bobo's left arm moved in a flash, and before Simmons could blink a very nasty looking dirk was imbedded in the table top less than an inch from his forearm.

"Listen to me, little governor's son," Bobo's voice was low now, and menacing. Simmons held very still as he went on. "'Tis time you learned a lesson in life, Noah boy, and that is that you should never get yourself into situations you can't get yourself out of. Cowards like you always have to go and get someone else to finish your dirty work, while you sit in yer daddy's mansion and drink his whiskey. Well, it sounds like you're moving in a different world now, little man, and you need to learn to look after yourself."

"What? Bobo, don't you know what I could do for you?"

"You can't do nothing for me! Those days are long gone now, Noah. I promise you one thing: nobody in this town is going to help you with this little job of yours, neither."

Simmons became desperate. "But, Bobo!"

Bobo leaned in again and pulled the dirk from the table.

"Noah, you're on your own. Don't come back here again."

Simmons sat there, stunned.

Bobo began to clean his dirty nails with the point of his knife. He glowered at the midshipman from under his drawn brows. "You have two ways you can leave this establishment: immediately or dead. Choose now."

Simmons silently got up from his chair and made his way to the door, the sounds of laughter slowly receding in the background.

William Brewer sat in his cabin and stared at his orders. They were just as Gerard said; HMS *Revenge* was ordered to patrol the waters off Puerto Rico in search of any information that would lead to the capture or death of the pirate Roberto Cofresi. His orders gave him one day to finish provisioning his ship; *Revenge* was expected to sail with the morning tide on the following day. Brewer read the orders for the third time and was strangely disappointed when they did not change.

He sighed and rose from his desk. He opened the door and called, "Pass the word for Mr. Greene!" He closed the door and sat down again.

"Alfred!"

The servant appeared. "Sir?"

"Coffee for two, please."

"Yes, sir."

A knock on the door announced the first lieutenant's arrival.

"Enter!"

Greene entered the room. "You sent for me, sir?"

Brewer handed him the appropriate papers. "Our orders."

Greene sat down and read the documents, and Alfred arrived with their coffees.

"Thank you, Alfred," Brewer said.

"Yes, thanks," Greene added.

Alfred bowed and left the room. Brewer sipped his coffee and waited until Greene finished and set the pages down.

"Not exactly what we were hoping for, is it, sir?" Greene said.

Brewer grunted. "I should say not." Brewer took a drink of his coffee and set the cup down rather hard on the desk, a move he regretted instantly and hoped Alfred did not hear. Satisfied that the servant was not going to come charging back into the cabin, he leaned back in his chair.

"I want El Diabolito. That pirate ambushed my ship, Benjamin, killed my men before I could even get them to Jamaica. I owe him for that, and I intend to repay that debt in full."

Greene nodded, his eyes hooded in rage at the memory. "I quite agree, sir."

Brewer stood. "Well! That's not going to happen any time soon, is it? I suppose all we can do is to carry out our orders and hope for the best. Alert the purser and the cooper about our unexpected departure. I'm sure Alfred will want to make a trip ashore as well." He paused a moment to think. "Oh! I shall make a call for mail at the turn of the first dog watch tomorrow. Any officer or man wishing to post mail before we sail can do it then."

"I'll spread the word, sir." Greene picked up his hat and left the room.

"Alfred! More coffee!"

"Aye, sir."

Brewer pulled out his writing desk and took out a sheet of paper, pen, ink, and blotter. He took Elizabeth's letter out of his pocket and unfolded it. He read it again, and his heart leapt. He was considering how to answer when Alfred arrived to refill his cup.

"Tell me, Alfred," he said, "you said your brother was the writer in the family?"

"That's right, sir."

"Did he have any rules regarding letters to young ladies?"

The servant set the coffee pot down. His eyes briefly searched Brewers face. "I believe I heard him speak on the subject once, sir. He said that honesty was always the best policy, but if that didn't work, stick to the weather."

Brewer laughed. "Thank you; I'll keep that in mind."

"A pleasure to be of service."

Brewer picked up his pen, was still for a moment, then wrote.

My Dearest Elizabeth,

I pray this letter finds you well and happy. I just have time to write you before my duty takes me to sea again. I am to hunt pirates in the waters off Puerto Rico. I cannot tell whether this will allow me to visit you; I can only trust that the good Lord will have mercy on me and allow me a moment in your company.

You asked if there was any room in my life, now that I have found what I was born to do. Let me tell you that there is. Since I met you, I have become conscious of a void, an emptiness, that I never knew was there before. I wish to know all about you. Tell me your likes and dislikes, tell me what your favorite things are, and tell me what you want out of life.

I will tell you a secret: until now, the only women in my life have been my mother and sister. I say this so you will understand if I should seem, shall we say, not as suave or 'worldly-wise' as some other officers with whom you may have corresponded. I can only promise you that I will share my heart honestly with you, which is another thing I have never done with anyone else.

Your Ob'd't Servant,
William

He read the letter over twice before deciding that he did not know how he could improve upon it, so he sealed it and addressed the outside for mailing. He dashed off longer letters to his mother and his sister, telling them all about *Revenge's* first cruise and the capture of the slave ship. He smiled at that; he knew they would get the *Gazette* and look for Admiral Hornblower's report. He could just imagine how they would tell everyone in the village of his exploits. In fact, the only one who would not congratulate them would probably be his father, but that was a cross he just had to bear. He decided not to mention Elizabeth to them; he was none too sure himself where he stood in that regard, and did not want o have to answer questions.

"Alfred!" he called.

The servant appeared, poised and awaiting for orders.

"How are we fixed to have a party?" he asked.

Alfred considered for a moment. "How many, sir?"

"Five. Six, including me."

"It can be done, sir."

"For tonight?" Brewer asked.

A quick moment's thought. "Yes, sir."

"End of the first dog watch?"

"That will be fine, sir."

"Excellent!" Brewer said. "Make it so. Draft whomever you need to help you."

"Thank you, sir," Alfred said.

Brewer wondered about the smile that was creeping onto his face, and had an idea for whom it boded trouble.

Brewer sat under the stern windows of the cabin and watched as Alfred transformed the cabin for his first dinner party on HMS *Revenge*. In truth, Brewer felt badly that he had not entertained his wardroom before now, but with Alfred's help he would make it up to them.

Alfred reminded him of a conductor leading an orchestra. There was no wasted movement, every action had a specific purpose, and every purpose added to the transformation of the cabin. And if Alfred was the conductor, then the brass section—indeed, the entire orchestra—was the captain's coxswain, McCleary. Oh, there were a couple hands who were acting as stewards, but the main part of the work fell to Mac.

The cabin was ready as the ship's bell tolled the end of the first dog watch, the appointed time Brewer had set for the gathering. The tolling of the bell was followed soon after by a knock on his cabin door. He opened it to admit his guests: Mr. Greene and Mr. Tyler, Mr. Sweeney and Dr. Spinelli, and finally Mr. Reed, all mingling in the stern cabin.

As Alfred saw to it that everyone was offered a drink, Brewer addressed the gathering. "Gentlemen! I want to thank you one and all for making the maiden voyage of HMS *Revenge* not only successful but a profitable one as well!"

Cheers and "Here! Here!" echoed though the cabin. Brewer held up his hand for silence.

"A ship is only as good as her officers, and men take their leads and measures from the examples you set. If we have performed well, it is a just reflection of your good works, and I thank you all!" Sweeney's faint nod acknowledged the truth of this; Greene and Tyler both looked almost overwhelmed by the compliment; the doctor looked half-ashamed at first, then settled his shoulders, as if resolving to be fully worthy of the praise he had only partly earned. The midshipman seemed to be weighing his captain's words, and Brewer briefly wondered what Reed was considering.

"I know you are as anxious as I am to see what Alfred has prepared for us, so gentlemen, if you will follow me?"

He led them to the table and took his place at its head. Mr. Greene took his place to his captain's right, and was joined by Mr. Tyler and Mr. Reed. The good doctor took his place on his captain's left, with the sailing master next to him. McCleary was pressed by Alfred into service to carry a huge beef and kidney pie to the table. The pie crust was a golden brown, and the aroma reminded Brewer of a great inn in London, renowned for its cuisine. It was joined on the table by a ragout of pork, bowls of carrots and peas, and a fat roasted chicken.

"Help yourselves, gentlemen," Brewer said. "We'll not stand on ceremony tonight. Give your attentions to that pie, Mr. Greene! Mr. Reed, that chicken is positively begging to be eaten!"

The men needed no further encouragement. Soon every plate was filled, and the stewards were keeping busy making sure the glasses were not allowed to stay empty. Alfred was called into the room and loudly applauded, a compliment Brewer would have thought him accustomed to, but which in fact made him appear uncomfortable, and he made a mental note of that.

When the food was devoured and the dishes cleared away, the stewards filled the company's glasses and withdrew. A solemnness descended upon the party.

All eyes turned to Mr. Reed, who as the junior officer present was responsible for carrying out the ritual of the royal toast.

Reed rose to his feet and lifted his glass. "Gentlemen, the King!"

"The King!" everyone echoed, and they all drank.

"Now that we are all comfortable," Brewer said as Reed resumed his seat, "let me inform you of our orders. We are to patrol the waters east and south of Puerto Rico, hunting for the pirate Roberto Cofresi. We are to stay on station until recalled; we are only allowed to leave in order to replenish supplies or water. We leave on the morning tide."

There was silence around the table. Mr. Greene was the first to break it when he asked the question that was on everyone's mind.

"And what of El Diabolito, Captain?"

Brewer put on his best 'I-don't-like-this-either' expression and said, "El Diabolito will just have to wait, I'm afraid. Admiral Lord Hornblower considers Cofresi a more immediate threat to shipping in the Caribbean."

"Sir," Mr. Tyler spoke up, "isn't it possible that Cofresi will be able to lead us to El Diabolito?"

Brewer smiled. "That may prove so, Mr. Tyler. Never fear, gentlemen, I intend to do all in my power to see that pirate on the gallows and to ensure that HMS *Revenge* puts him there."

He was pleased to see that there was grim agreement on every face at the table.

The Captain of HMS *Revenge* stepped on deck at six bells of the morning watch. The sun was well above the horizon, on its way to dominating the Caribbean sky. His practiced eye swept over the deck, rigging, and sails and saw that all was ready for sea. He turned toward the quarterdeck, where he saw Lieutenant Greene talking to Mr. Sweeney and Mr. Simmons.

146

"Good morning, gentlemen," Brewer said as he approached them. A part of his brain was reading the waters' movements from the deck's motions. It was as if his legs received and relayed signals that came from the beyond the harbor, from the very depths of the ocean, as well as the wind-blown surface.

"Good morning, Captain," Greene said as all three saluted. "Slack water now, sir. Ebb in ten minutes, and the anchor's hove short."

"Very good, Mr. Greene," Brewer said. "You may get the ship under way. Set your course due east after we've made open waters."

"Aye, sir!" Greene picked up a speaking trumpet and issued the appropriate orders, and soon *Revenge* was making her way slowly toward the harbor entrance. Brewer stood in his usual place on the lee rail, silently but assuredly watching the work and pleased by what he saw. As the ship broke out into the open waters of the Caribbean and the bow swung around to the east, he wondered what the future held, professionally as well as personally.

Brewer watched the waves glide past, *Revenge* having no trouble with the gentle swells, and allowed his mind to run free. He envied Hornblower and Bush; their generation rose through the ranks during the wars, when the combination of a much larger fleet and vacancies created by battle casualties meant promotion was fairly rapid for those who managed to stay alive and do their duty. Promotion in the peacetime Royal Navy was mainly a matter of influence and political connections. He had Lord Hornblower as his patron, but his failure to be confirmed as captain of HMS *Defiant* had made it plain that influence had its limits, as more than one patron jostled to get a prime posting for a junior officer. His lips compressed into a thin, angry line at the memory of that loss, although logically he understood the admiral's reasons for giving the ship to someone else. Paradoxically, he was also stung by a sense of shame, remembering that it was the admiral who was responsible for his present command. Had he truly earned the posting? He was truly grateful for his good fortune in having *Revenge,* and he knew that there were many who would take his place if they could. It was his feelings for Elizabeth that brought on this concern for the future.

Brewer chided himself for worrying. Whatever the future held, he would deal with it as it came. He just hoped he wouldn't have to deal with it alone.

Training began again in earnest to make HMS *Revenge* the ultimate fighting ship of her size in the Caribbean. It was also during this time that *Revenge* suffered her first casualty.

It happened on their third day at sea. The ship's bell had just tolled six bells in the afternoon watch. The men were being exercised aloft that afternoon. Brewer watched from the quarterdeck and was not particularly pleased with what he saw. He walked over to where Mr. Greene and Mr. Tyler were directing the exercise.

"Well, Mr. Greene?" he said. "What do you think?"

"I can't say I'm satisfied, Captain. The men seemed to take too long to complete the simplest maneuvers. I apologize. I will work them harder tomorrow."

Brewer's eyes narrowed. "You'll work them harder now, Mr. Greene," he said. "Another hour."

Greene and Tyler shared a concerned look, and Greene spoke to his captain.

"Sir, the wind's picking up. Wouldn't it be safer for the men--"

Brewer cut him off. "We may need to fight in *any* wind, Mr. Greene. Another hour."

"Aye, sir," Greene said. Both he and Tyler saluted and ordered the hands back up the shrouds to the yards.

Brewer retreated to the quarterdeck. He chided himself for being so short with his officers, but his mood was growing dark at the wasting of their time spent out here, rather than searching for El Diabolito. He looked at the sky and realized Greene was right about the wind. Part of him, the angry part, did not care; the men deserved the extra work, it said. But the larger part of him had compassion for them, and he knew it was wrong to take his frustration and anger out on his men. He sighed, mainly because he hated having to correct a mistake made out of frustration. He was just about to turn around when a sudden gust of wind shook the ship, and he heard two voices.

The first uttered a terrified scream, followed quickly by a desperate cry for help.

The second was the cry, "Look out below!" It was followed by a sickening thud.

Brewer ran toward the crowd gathering on the starboard side of the mainmast. "Make way!" he cried as he approached, and the crowd parted like the Red Sea before Moses. He arrived to see a hand (he was suddenly ashamed that he couldn't recall the man's name) sprawled on the deck, Greene and Tyler kneeling over him.

"I've sent for the surgeon, sir," Greene said.

Brewer nodded dumbly. The doctor would come quickly, he was sure, but there was little to be done for the poor fellow. Looking at the body, Brewer thought he had a broken leg, at least one broken arm, God knows how many internal injuries, and a broken neck, judging from the way the man's head was lying against his chest. He looked up the mainmast and saw many hands still up there, all looking down at the tragedy.

"Mr. Tyler," he said, "let's get the men down to the deck before someone else.... Make sure they come down the larboard side, if you please."

"Aye aye, Captain." Tyler's voice was subdued. He looked at the hand on the deck one last time, then rose to direct the others down.

The crowd parted again, and Dr. Spinelli appeared. He ran a quick, appraising eye over the man on the deck, then he looked at his captain, his face a mask of hopelessness. He knelt beside the man and did a quick but thorough examination before standing again and sighing.

"I'm sorry, Captain," he said. "There's nothing I can do. He's dead."

The full force of responsibility and consequences hit Brewer like a broadside. He was stunned into silence as though by a physical blow. Mr. Greene noticed his captain's condition, and when he did not speak, stepped up.

"Thompson, Jenkins," he said, "take this man below. After the doctor is done, sew him up. We'll bury him at sea when the captain says so."

The crowd broke up slowly. The man was taken below. Greene saw that the Captain had not moved; he was still standing there as though in shock.

"Captain," he said to get Brewer's attention, "I need to speak to you in private, sir. May we speak in your cabin?"

Brewer's eyes came back into focus. Greene stepped back to allow his captain to lead the way, and in doing so, he saw Mr. Sweeney standing at the back of the dissipating crowd. He motioned for the sailing master to follow.

"Mr. Reed," Greene said over his shoulder, "get this deck cleaned up. Mr. Tyler has the deck. I shall be in with the captain."

Greene heard the two men reply "Aye, sir" to his retreating back as he followed Captain Brewer and Mr. Sweeney below and into the captain's cabin. McCleary was there, ready to take the captain's coat and hat and stow them properly. He had not been on deck, so he was shocked by Brewer's ghastly expression when he entered the cabin. Greene looked to Mr. Sweeney and motioned for him to fill in the coxswain.

"Alfred!" Greene called. "Claret!"

The silhouetted figure appeared in the doorway for a split second before disappearing in response to Lieutenant Greene's command. Greene and Sweeney steered their captain to the seats below the stern window and sat him down. Alfred brought a goblet of dark liquid, which Greene pressed into Brewer's hand.

"Drink this, sir," he said, as Alfred set the carafe on the table and silently retreated, but he did not leave the room.

Brewer obeyed, taking the glass and drinking deeply. He closed his eyes. They watched his body shudder, and his eyes opened slowly. He seemed bewildered to find that he was now in his cabin, and somewhat embarrassed to find four faces looking at him in raw concern.

"Gentlemen," he said slowly, "I apologize for my... weakness. Who was the seaman?"

"Grant, sir," Greene answered. "Able seaman, main topman."

Brewer groaned in guilt. His chin dropped to his breast, and he found he had to squeeze his eyes shut to prevent a tear from escaping and rolling down his cheek. It took him several moments to regain control of his emotions. Finally, he took a deep breath.

"Mac," he said, raising his head, "find out if you can whether he had any family."

"I will, sir," the coxswain assured him.

"Captain," Greene said, "I can write the letter to his family. I was in command of the—"

"No!" Brewer said, a little too strongly, he realized, and shook his head slowly. "No, thank you, Benjamin; I will write the letter."

"Yes, sir," Greene said. His captain was looking down at the deck again; Greene caught Mr. Sweeney's eye and saw the concern on his face. Greene silently motioned toward the door with his head, and Sweeney nodded.

Brewer looked up. "Gentlemen," he said softly, "if you will excuse me, I have a report for the admiral to write. Mac, I want that information about Grant's family as soon as you can get it, please."

"Right away, sir," the coxswain said.

"Are you sure you're all right, sir?" Greene asked.

"Yes, Mr. Greene," Brewer's voice was a mixture of embarrassment and irritation, but Greene knew better. "I'm fine. You may return to your duties. Thank you all."

Brewer rose to his feet, and all realized the meeting was over. They filed out of the office. At the base of the companionway, Greene stopped to talk to Sweeney while Mac departed on his mission.

"What do you think?" Greene asked quietly.

"Of the Captain?" Sweeney shrugged. "He's taking Grant's death hard, that's for sure. Like he considers it his fault."

"He probably does." Greene told Sweeney how the captain had ordered the extra hour of drill aloft, despite the warnings about the wind.

"So, the Captain blames himself for Grant's death," Sweeney said. "I think we need to bring in help."

Greene looked his question.

Sweeney said firmly, "We need to see the surgeon."

CHAPTER 10

The good doctor was at that moment just completing his examination of the body that had been brought to his sickbay. Some of his findings agreed with the quick examination he had performed on deck—for example, he confirmed that the cause of death was a broken neck—but some findings were truly surprising. He was just cleaning his hands preparatory to writing his report for the captain when Lieutenant Greene and Mr. Sweeney entered.

"Can you spare a moment, Doctor?" Greene asked.

"Of course," Spinelli said. "I was just finishing up my examination of Grant's body." He turned to the seamen who had brought the body down. "Okay, you men, you can sew her up now."

Greene and Sweeney both stared.

"Her?" Greene asked.

"Yes," the good Doctor said heavily. "Seaman Grant was a woman."

"Are you sure, Doctor?" Sweeney said without thinking.

Spinelli turned to him with his eyebrows raised. "Do you want to check for yourself?"

Sweeney blushed. "Ah, no, thank you."

Spinelli eyed the master. "I didn't think so. Yes, it seems that our Seaman Grant was indeed a woman. Records show that she joined the ship in Jamaica, and I'm afraid that, being in the state that I was at that time, I performed nowhere near the usual examinations for new enlistees." He shook his head in self-recrimination. "What did you want to see me for?"

Greene leaned against the surgeon's desk and crossed his arms across his chest. "Did you see the captain on deck?"

"Yes," Spinelli said. "He looked as though the death was hitting him pretty hard."

"More than that, Doctor," Greene said. "The Captain personally ordered the extra hour of drill aloft over the objections of myself and Lieutenant Tyler."

Spinelli considered what Mr. Greene had said, his eyes darting from place to place. Finally, both eyebrows rose, and he expelled a breath the other two did not realize he had been holding.

"Poor William," the Doctor said.

"Doctor," Greene said, "I think today would be a very good time for you to play chess with the Captain. Perhaps when you deliver your report? Say, in an hour's time or so?"

Spinelli stared out into empty space from hooded eyes as he considered the request. He nodded, more to himself than to the others; it sounded like a reasonable plan. The Captain might not even suspect that the suggestion was anything other than a spontaneous idea after the delivery of a report.

"Very well," he said, "I'll do it. Perhaps the Captain will feel like talking by that time."

The two visitors arose and thanked the surgeon. As they made their way out of the sickbay, they saw Thompson come back in with Grant's hammock and two round shot to be sewn up at Grant's feet. Greene shook his head at the loss. Able seamen, especially topmen, were hard to replace.

Jonathan Reed stood on the deck of HMS *Revenge*, directing a party charged with cleaning up the deck. There was not a lot of blood; most of what there was had come from an open wound when a broken bone in one of Grant's forearms broke through the skin. There was also a fair-sized puddle under the dead man's head. The seamen under Reed's direction swabbed the deck and rinsed the residual mess into the bilges; now they were holystoning the deck to make sure no stain remained.

Mr. Greene came on deck and gave orders to reduce sail. Reed looked up and watched the men out on the yards reefing the tops'ls. He turned back to the men he was supervising on the deck. He was about to say something to one of them about his stoning when he heard a *whoosh* go right past his head, followed immediately by a *thunk*. A heavy dirk was sticking out of the deck less than a foot from him, vibrating. He looked up at once, but he saw nothing suspicious from the men still in the yards.

"Kelly, Jones," Reed said, "Look at this. You're both witnesses."

"I saw it come out of nowhere," one of the tars said.

Reed went over and pulled the dirk from the deck planking. It was one of the long, midshipmen's dirks. Anyone could have obtained one in the midshipman's berth. *Could it have been an accident?* he wondered. *No. There was no shout of warning, and no seaman could lose one of these aloft and not know it. This had to be a deliberate attempt on my life. But who ...?*

"Kelly," he said. The man got to his feet and stood before the Senior Midshipman. "Go find Mr. Simmons. Say nothing to him, I just want to know where he is."

"Aye, Mr. Reed."

The deck was almost back to normal when Kelly returned, a bare ten minutes after he had left. He found Reed standing out by the railing.

"Mr. Simmons has been in the midshipmen's berth since he came off watch, Mr. Reed," Kelly said privately. "I found three hands who'll swear to it."

"Thank you, Kelly," Reed said. "Make sure you keep this between us. Help Jones finish this deck now."

"Aye, Mr. Reed."

Captain William Brewer was trying to write a report of the death of the seaman Grant for Admiral Lord Hornblower, and he was having a very difficult time doing so. The guilt and responsibility for Grant's death were hitting him hard. He'd had crewmen die in battle under his command, but Grant's death was different. It was unnecessary. Grant would not have been up there but for his orders—orders given for the sole reason (when he was honest with himself, he knew it was true) that he didn't like the orders he had been given by the admiral!

He had heard older and more senior officers talk about the loneliness of command, but he had never felt it himself until right now. He remembered Captain Bush telling him how Captain Hornblower would stand off alone and brood over problems before announcing his decision, and he remembered Bush himself doing the same thing countless times on *Lydia*. Thus far, Brewer himself had been more consultative in him command style, seeking and taking advice from Hornblower (understandable, as a senior officer), Mr. Greene, Mr. Sweeney, and others. But now he knew why his mentors had done as they had. Now he knew what it really meant to be *responsible* for the lives of your crew.

He put the quill down and rose from his desk. He poured himself another glass of claret, emptying the carafe, and stood before the stern windows, watching *Revenge's* wake and wishing his troubles would recede just as easily. The glass was nearly drained when he heard a knock at his door.

"Enter."

The door opened to admit Dr. Spinelli.

"Something I can do for you, Doctor?" the Captain asked.

"Ah, no, Captain," Spinelli said. "I have finished my examination of Grant's body, and I wanted to submit my report to you on the incident." He handed over the report and took advantage of his chance to look around the cabin while Brewer read it. He eyed carafe, and his eyes darted to the Captain, hunched over his report. He was studying it, or trying to, when he stopped and his head came up in surprise.

"Grant was a woman?" he demanded.

"Afraid so, Captain," the Doctor answered.

"And nobody knew? None of his—her—mess mates?"

Spinelli shrugged. "If they did, they kept the secret very well."

Brewer shook his head in disbelief. *"Mazel tov."*

Spinelli's eyes narrowed. "What's that, Captain?"

Brewer dropped the Doctor's report on his desk and sat back in exasperation.

"Mazel tov, Doctor. It's a Jewish phrase I learned in the Mediterranean. It means 'congratulations,' or 'good luck'. Not only did I make a mistake, and one of my crew died for it, it turned out to be a woman."

Spinelli considered his friend's words as he watched the Captain stare blankly at the desk, looking sick. Just how much of that carafe had he consumed? He grabbed a chair, sat down opposite the Captain and tried to make eye contact with him, but it was impossible.

"William," he said, "look at me."

Brewer ignored him.

Spinelli slapped the desktop hard and loud with the palm of his hand.

"Look at me!" he yelled.

That did it. Brewer raised his head. Out of the corner of his eye, Adam noticed Alfred appear in the doorway, whether out of curiosity at the noise or to be ready to defend his captain, he did not know. Whatever the reason, the servant retreated without coming any closer.

"William," the Doctor said in a calmer voice, "Grant's death was not your doing."

The Captain's eyes were bitter, dismissive, disbelieving.

"It was not your fault," Spinelli insisted.

"I gave the order," Brewer said quietly, coldly. "*I* sent them back aloft. Greene and Tyler, they asked me not to, warned me about the wind, but I *wouldn't listen...*"

Spinelli felt terrible for his friend's suffering. If anything, he thought this must be worse than what he suffered over Mary's passing. The difference was, the Captain *was* responsible, at least indirectly, for Grant's death.

"Look, William," he said slowly, "accidents happen to every captain, sooner or later. Every captain has lost men who fell from the tops, with or without high winds. Grant knew the danger when she went up there. Whoever she was, she was not a novice. She was rated Able Seaman. She knew what she was doing up there. There's nothing anyone can do when God says it's your time."

Brewer's face was devoid of emotion, staring at the surgeon through hooded eyes that actually frightened the Doctor with their coldness.

"Not quite, Doctor," he said in a voice that was ice cold. "You see, there is something you don't know, something that makes all the true things you just said absolutely null and void in my case. What you don't know, Doctor, is that the only reason I ordered the extra drill aloft—the *only* reason I overruled two of my officers—is that I was upset that

Revenge has been ordered to waste our time off Puerto Rico, looking for God-could-care-less Roberto Cofresi, instead of being allowed to do what I wanted, which was tracking down El Diabolito."

His eyes blinked once, then turned to gaze out the stern window again.

Adam stared wide-eyed at his friend. *So,* he thought, *at last we come to the truth. The worst part is, I can see where he's coming from! Grant did not die during normal training; she died during a training that should never have been ordered, especially in peace time.* He swallowed hard in sympathy. *Poor William! Now what do I do? Well... It's best to be truthful and blunt, I suppose.*

"I see," Spinelli said. "In that case, Captain, I'd say you learned a very important lesson, and I'd even say you learned it cheap."

Brewer's head snapped back. His eyes narrowed in suspicion, maybe even anger, but Spinelli didn't care right now.

"What do you mean by that?"

Spinelli sat back upright, his backbone ramrod straight an inch away from the chair's back.

"I mean, Captain," he said in a voice that was totally devoid of pity, "that you learned the lesson that captains cannot permit their emotions to get the best of them, because when they do, innocent people—usually their own crew—die because of it." He pushed the chair back and rose. "And I say you learned it cheap, because only one person died because of it." He turned and left the cabin without another word.

Brewer sat there, considering all that the doctor had said. He did not move or make a sound, only his eyes darted from place to place, seeing nothing, as he strove to come to terms with his guilt. Eventually, a soft voice from somewhere in the back of his mind broke through the turmoil and told him that the Doctor was right. He had allowed his emotions to master him, and they had prompted the fatal orders. Now the question he had to answer was, where do I go from here? *You learn from it,* the voice told him, *and you do whatever is necessary to make sure it never happens again. No-one else dies because you are not in control of yourself. You must be an unfeeling rock, at least at sea, and not allow emotions to provoke you into any more bad decisions. What was it Bush used to say? He learned from Hornblower that the Captain is inevitably responsible for everything that happens on his ship. He alone bears all responsibility. He alone... Alone. A captain cannot have friends, because one day he may have to order that friend to his death in order to save his ship and crew. Worse, he cannot be blinded into putting his ship and crew into danger, seeking vengeance for the friend's loss. THAT is the loneliness of being a captain of a King's ship. Now go and do it.*

Brewer blinked and looked out the stern windows. Dusk was falling, and the ship's wake looked strange in the failing light. He rose from his desk and went to sit under the stern windows, turned so he could study where he'd been, and try to figure out a way so that it didn't happen again.

The remainder of his watch was the most stressful time of Jonathon Reed's life. He was forever looking over his shoulder or scanning aloft, looking for anyone who might have a mind to drop something else on him. His nerves got to such a raw edge that he exploded at an innocent question from Mr. Short. He quickly apologized to the boy, and, seeing there was less than an hour left in their watch, allowed him to take his favorite place in the mizzen shrouds, acting as an additional lookout.

Reed realized there was no way he was going to be able to keep this thing quiet while he investigated it himself. He finally decided he would have to report the incident. When he heard the ship's bell ring eight bells, he headed aft toward the quarterdeck, where he found Lieutenant Greene speaking to Mr. Sweeney.

"Begging your pardon, Lieutenant," he said as he saluted, "might I have a private word with you, sir?"

"Of course, Reed," Greene replied. He passed command to Mr. Sweeney and preceded the midshipman to the gunroom. When they entered, he directed the steward to bring them both a glass of wine.

"Now, Mr. Reed," he said, after the steward had brought their drinks and departed, "what can I do for you?"

"Well, sir, I'm not quite sure how to put it."

Greene looked somewhat amused. "Just say it plainly then."

The senior midshipman looked ill at ease. "Very well, sir. I believe someone tried to kill me during the last watch."

The look of surprise on Greene's face turned to one of sober intensity when he realized that Reed wasn't kidding. "Come with me," he said. He led the midshipman into his cabin and closed the door. He sat at his desk and indicated that Reed should sit on his sea chest.

"Now," he said, "tell me what happened."

Reed launched into his tale. He told it slowly, careful not to omit anything, including how he sent Kelly to find Simmons.

"Why Mr. Simmons?" Greene inquired.

"I've had trouble with him almost from the day he joined the ship, sir. I had the boatswain's mate give him two dozen for terrorizing young Mr. Short. Sir, Simmons left bruises on the boy! Anyway, I've been waiting for him to try to get even with me, but I never thought he would go so far!"

"I see," Greene said. He had never been one for the so-called "justice of the lower deck", but if Simmons had brutalized the boy, perhaps he'd deserved it. "Continue, Mr. Reed."

"Not much more to tell, sir. I was going to keep it quiet and try to investigate myself, but it was distracting me something awful, sir. I decided to come and tell you."

"Quite right," Greene said. "You'd have been in serious trouble yourself if you hadn't reported it. Where is the dirk now?"

"Mr. Jones has it hidden, sir."

"Go get it."

Reed left the cabin on his mission. Greene sat back and considered. Could it have been an accident? *No, nobody had any reason to have such a weapon aloft. It has to have been intentional—and planned.*

Reed returned and handed the weapon over to Greene. Greene turned it over in his hands and looked at it. The blade was discolored slightly where it had been imbedded in the deck planking. Greene pursed his lips; the weapon could definitely have done for Reed, had the aim been a little better. He set the dirk on his desk and stood.

"Sit here, Reed. I want you to write a report of this incident for the captain, just as you told it to me, including the parts about Mr. Simmons. If you finish before I return, you are to wait right here for me."

"Yes, sir."

Reed moved to the desk and picked up the quill from the desktop and began to write. Greene made his way back up on deck. He found Mr. Sweeney and briefly explained what was going on, and the two men went to examine the scene of the incident. They found Kelly on deck, and he showed them the exact spot where the dirk struck the deck and where Reed had been standing. Both men looked aloft. Greene wondered for a moment if it would be worth it to go aloft and see if he could determine where the would-be assassin had stood, but he decided to first see how Reed's report was coming along.

He found the midshipman just finishing. Greene read it and was pleased to find it a neat, tight, well-written document that wasted no words.

"Where did you go to school, Reed?" he asked.

"Never been inside of one, sir," Reed answered. "My mother taught me to read and write, and when I was on *Clorinda*, the captain's wife taught all the midshipmen the social graces, including how to write a proper letter."

"Well," Greene said as he folded the report in his hands, "I'd say you learned your lessons well. Let's go see the captain."

A matter of minutes found the two men in the Captain's cabin.

"What's all this, Mr. Greene?" Brewer asked.

"Well, sir, it seems that someone tried to kill our Mr. Reed today."

"What?" Brewer said. "When? Where?"

For the second time, Reed told the story, careful not to leave anything out. He saw the Captain react a bit when he got to the part about Mr. Simmons, but he did not interrupt. Reed finished his tale; Greene handed over the report Reed had prepared.

"Thank you." Brewer set the report on his desk. "Mr. Greene, don't we have a spare cabin in the gunroom?"

"Yes, sir," Greene replied.

"Until we get this mystery solved, Mr. Reed sleeps there. At least he can lock the door after a fashion so he can sleep. And tomorrow morning I want you to question every man who was aloft when the attack took place."

"Aye, sir."

"And so, good night, gentlemen. We shall pick up the investigation in the morning."

News flies on a small ship, and despite all attempts to keep things quiet, by morning the whole ship was whispering about the attempt on Reed's life. Reed's sleeping in the cabin in the gunroom probably started the questions running around the ship, and it was likely that Kelly and Jones provided the answers. Brewer and Greene knew better than to try to find out who was doing the talking; they would rather listen to see if they heard anything to help solve the mystery.

Greene spent most of the morning questioning those who had gone aloft to shorten sail the day before, but nobody reported anything incriminating. Several stated that, in light of what happened to Grant, they were taking care for their own safety and not looking around to see what anyone else was doing.

He reported as much to the captain at the turn of the watch. The two men stepped over to the privacy of the lee rail.

"Nobody saw anything, or at least not that they're willing to admit. What do we do now, sir?"

Brewer considered for a moment. "I hate to admit it, Mr. Greene, but if they tried once, they will most likely try again. Make Mr. Reed's sleeping arrangements permanent for the duration of this voyage, and assign him a seaman to act as a bodyguard. At the very least, it will mean an extra pair of eyes to watch for any more falling dirks."

That night, Noah Simmons was aloft, sitting in the foretop, high above the deck. He was enjoying the cool breeze and the stars when he became aware of someone behind him.

"I wants me money," a voice said.

Simmons did not turn around. "For what? He's still alive."

"'E won't be for long. Give me what you owes me."

Simmons shook his head. "The deal was that you would be paid when you finished the job. Not before."

The other leaned in closer until Simmons could feel his putrid breath on his ear when he spoke. "Don't play games with me, boy, or you might end up like the other one."

"What other one?"

"Grant."

Simmons stiffened slightly. "What did you do?"

" 'E saw the dirk on me hip and started asking questions. Wouldn't stop, so when that wind hit, so did I."

Simmons felt a hand on his shoulder and shivered at the implication. He tried to put up a brave front.

"Finish the job, and you'll be paid."

It took a couple minutes of silence for Simmons to realize the other had gone just as quietly as he had come. He rested his head back against the mast and blew out a breath to try to calm himself. That jack he hired would finish the job. He had to.

He closed his eyes and enjoyed a fresh breath of wind. His thoughts turned again to leaving *Revenge*. He knew he couldn't go back to Jamaica; his father would never allow it, and besides, there was the little matter of the wench and her father to consider. No, he would have to cast his eyes elsewhere to make his fortune, but where?

Then it hit him. The United States was a new nation booming with opportunity. In a port like New York, he would have no trouble disappearing and finding a niche where he could make his fortune.

Simmons opened his eyes and smiled. Yes, New York.

Now, all he had to do was to watch for his opportunity.

CHAPTER II

HMS *Revenge* reached her patrol area the next day and set about making her presence known. Ten ships were stopped or hailed in the first week, but none had any knowledge of the whereabouts of the pirate Cofresi or El Diabolito. Brewer took another ten days to conduct a detailed inspection of the Puerto Rican coastline for inlets that could hide pirate vessels—or at least as detailed as one could make from offshore. His orders made it clear that under no circumstances was he allowed to violate Spanish possessions, save for the certainty of capturing Cofresi himself. His search resulted in the mapping of numerous places that could shelter a schooner or cutter with no problem, several of which were located east of San Juan.

But weeks of patrolling the waters around the island resulted in nothing else. No new information regarding the locations of either Cofresi or El Diabolito was gleaned. Brewer was smart enough to realize that his voyage had not been completely in vain—there had been no pirate attacks in these waters since HMS *Revenge* arrived on station.

It was at six bells of the forenoon watch, and the captain, first lieutenant, and sailing master were in conference on the quarterdeck.

"Weeks of searching," Brewer lamented, "and nothing to show for it."

"We have apparently stopped the attacks in this area, sir," Greene pointed out.

"Or they're just waiting for us to use up our supplies and be forced to go," Sweeney said.

"Either way," Brewer cut in, "we've got nothing, and the Admiral's order not to set foot on the island prevents us from kicking the anthill over and seeing what comes out. I just wish—"

"Sail ho!"

The three officers looked up at the lookout and he pointed to the southeast. *Revenge* had just turned east to run along the southern coast of Puerto Rico, so that meant the strange sail was approaching the island from the south. They moved to the railing and raised glasses to their eyes. Sweeney called to the lookout.

"What do you make of her?"

"Looks like a small brig, sir!" the lookout replied. "No flag that I can see!"

Brewer lowered his glass. "Call the hands, Mr. Greene. Make all sail. I want to intercept that ship. Mr. Sweeney, give me a course to do so."

Both men moved off to complete their respective tasks with alacrity. Brewer kept his eye on the speck of white on the horizon as it slowly became larger. The question was, what would the other captain do when he sighted *Revenge*?

He felt the deck beneath him leap ahead. For the moment, the strange sail continued on her course. She was hull up now, and still no flag.

"Mr. Greene," he said, "post extra lookouts. I want to know the moment that ship does something."

"Deck ho!" cried the lookout, pointing WSW. "Squall approaching!"

Brewer turned and saw a violent storm being carried by the wind much faster than *Revenge* was, and it was heading straight at them, or rather, straight at where they anticipated intercepting the strange sail.

"Captain!" It was Mr. Short, in his favorite place midway up the mizzen shrouds. He was pointing at their chase. Brewer turned immediately and put his glass back to his eye. The ship had either seen them or the storm, or both. For whatever reason, it was crowding on sail and turning to the northeast, trying to stay ahead of the storm.

Brewer lowered his glass and looked aloft. The increase in the wind that was bringing the storm was also increasing *Revenge's* roll, and he knew that very soon he would have to reduce sail. He looked back to the chase and saw that they were barely closing now. He checked on the squall and spent an anxious minute looking back and forth between the two before he decided that the squall would overtake them before they could close.

"Mr. Reed," he said, "make sure the guns are secure enough to ride out this storm. And anything else that might break away!"

"Aye aye, sir!"

"Mr. Tyler! Make sure the stores are secure!"

"Yes, sir!"

"Mr. Greene! Reduce sail! I want single-reefed tops'ls only, if you please!"

Greene promptly began calling the orders, his voice pitched to carry over the sound of the rising wind.

Brewer cast a rueful eye toward the chase he had been forced to abandon. She was far enough away that it seemed probable she would find shelter before the storm caught up with her, possibly in one of the very coves he had mapped. *There will be another time,* he promised himself.

"Mr. Short! Get the pumps set up! I suspect we'll need them soon enough!"

"Aye aye, sir!"

Revenge began to roll alarmingly as the storm neared. Brewer stood it as long as he could before having to anchor himself. He was pleased to look down the deck and see not one gun broke free from its lashings. He prayed that Mr. Tyler had been as successful at his work with the stores below. The ship's motion worried him, and he went to find Greene.

"Mr. Greene!" he said. He had to practically shout in Greene's ear in order to be heard over the wind. "I think you'd best make up a hawser. Use spars or whatever you need to act as water-stops. And take in all sail."

Greene barely had time to carry out his instructions when a rogue wave hit at the same moment as a gust of wind rolled HMS *Revenge* over on her beam ends. The stress was too much: her fore topmast snapped off. It was only Greene's quick action in getting the hawser over the side that saved the ship so that only four or five feet of deck were under water on the lee side.

Brewer found himself on the deck at the base of the mizzenmast. He had lost his grip on the rail as the ship rolled over and was heading across the deck for the open sea when someone tackled him and drove him to where he now lay. As soon as the hawser lines went taut, his assailant rose cautiously.

"Are you alright, Captain?"

"Mac!" Brewer said as the Cornishman helped him rise. "Where did you come from? Never mind! We need to get every hand we can on that rope and right the ship! Mr. Tyler! Take some hands and cut away that wreckage before it pulls us under!"

Brewer slid down the deck and started helping hands out of the sea and back up the deck, one of the first of whom was Mr. Short, who had been below deck with the pumps.

"Mr. Short!" Brewer exclaimed. "How did you get out there?"

Short clung to his captain for dear life. He wiped the water from his eyes and looked around. There was terror in his eyes until he saw Brewer hanging on to him.

"Captain!" he said. "I have no idea! I was below with the pumps when the ship rolled over. The water rose sudden-like, pushed me up to and off the deck, and the next thing I know, you're pulling me out of the water!"

"Are you hurt?"

Short moved his arms and legs. "Don't seem so, sir."

"Good. Stay here by me. You shall take charge of the injured."

He slid back down the deck into the edge of the water, grabbing everyone he could lay a hand on and passing them to Short. Those who were uninjured he sent to the hawser rope, and those who could do no more than survive he ordered Mr. Short and his party to make as comfortable as possible further up the deck. Kelly had arrived and was bracing the wounded men so they wouldn't slide down the deck again.

Tyler showed up at his captain's side.

"Wreckage cut away, sir," he said. "I've got three of the lads helping shipmates back aboard forward, sir."

"Good. Send all the men you can to help Greene on the hawser rope, and send one man below to check on the doctor, if you please."

"Aye, sir."

Short slid back down the deck to him.

"Sir! The wind!"

"I can't do anything about the wind, Mr. Short!"

"But sir! It's gone!"

Brewer stopped and looked around. Short was right; the storm had moved on past them. He had been so busy, he hadn't even noticed.

He saw now that Mr. Greene and his party were making headway; the deck was slowly flattening out. *Revenge* was lying low in the water, a testament to how much water she had taken on when she rolled.

"Mr. Tyler! Get below deck and see about the pumps. Take McCleary with you. Do whatever you must, but get those pumps running. Form bucket brigades in the short term if you have to, but we must get that water out of the ship!"

"Aye aye, sir!"

Brewer walked over to Mr. Greene's party. They looked exhausted and bedraggled, but most of them looked exhilarated as well. "Well done, men! Tie off the hawser for now, and we'll bring it back aboard later." He looked around. "Mr. Greene, get the rest of our people out of the water and see how many we lost. I also need a damage report. Tyler is below, seeing about getting the pumps working."

"I'll see to it, sir."

"I'm going to survey below deck."

Brewer went below and met Mr. Ringold, the carpenter, coming up from below.

"I was just coming to find you, sir," he said. "Captain, there's more than six feet of water in the hold."

"Mr. Tyler is working on getting the pumps operational. Go and see if he needs help. After they are operational, report to the first lieutenant."

"Aye, sir."

Brewer moved forward in search of the doctor. He finally found him up on deck, tending to the men who had been pulled from the water.

"There you are, Doctor," he said.

"Oh, hullo, Captain. When the sickbay rolled over, I thought it would be a good idea to make my way up. Fortunately, I'd heard the warnings about the storm and had locked down all the cabinets of medicines. I have a mess to clean up, but hopefully we didn't lose too many medical supplies."

Brewer looked around. "Any idea yet what the score is up here?"

Spinelli shook his head. "No. I'm afraid it will be some time yet before we can account for everyone and report those we assume are lost overboard. As for these, many seem to have swallowed a bellyful of water, but otherwise most of them should be set to rights soon enough. Two men sustained broken bones when the fore topmast went over; I have them over there, laying up against a gun for now." He looked out over the water and pointed to the few bodies floating a distance from the ship. "William, look."

Brewer surveyed the sight. He tried to say something, but the words caught in his throat.

"There was nothing you could have done," Spinelli told him. "From what I understand, it was on us too quickly to take evasive action, and you did what you could. It might have been much worse."

"I know," Brewer said quietly. "But I don't think I'll ever get used to losing even a single crewman."

Spinelli turned his attention back to the wounded.

Brewer saw Mr. Greene talking with Mr. Snead, the boatswain. From their gestures, he could tell they were discussing jury-rigging a new topmast. Both of them nodded their heads in agreement, and Snead moved off to put their plans into motion. Just then, Brewer heard the familiar clanking of the pumps going into operation and silently thanked God that Mr. Tyler knew what he was doing.

Greene walked over and saluted.

"Damage report, Mr. Greene."

"The pumps are operational, sir, and Mr. Snead will begin jury-rigging the new fore topmast shortly. I have the purser checking on the stores below, but with as much water as we have in the hold, it's a good bet we lost a lot of provisions."

"No doubt," Brewer said. "The pumps have priority as far as manpower goes, then the stores. For now, we stay hove to while we make repairs. I'm going below to see what my cabin looks like. Call me if I'm needed."

"Aye, sir."

Brewer went below and found Alfred and Mac hard at work straightening things.

"How bad?" Brewer asked.

"We were fortunate, sir," Mac said. "Nothing we can't fix good as new."

Brewer was thankful for that. "Mac, do you know how the galley made out?"

"Some damage when the ship rolled, sir. Lucky the cook was able to put the fires out. I think they're working to repair the damage, and then they'll try to relight the fires."

Brewer nodded and looked around his cabin. He was glad to see that his library had survived; it was on the opposite side and so had stayed high and dry, the books so snugly pressed together that they had not fallen. His portable writing desk, tucked away safely in his sea chest, had also stayed dry. He breathed a silent thanks to God for protecting them.

A knock on the door heralded the arrival of the purser. He did not look happy.

"I'm sorry I took so long to report, Captain, but I wanted to check everything before I spoke to you. I estimate 85% of our foodstuffs and water are now fouled."

Brewer kept his face impassive.

"Thank you. Let me know when you have a detailed report, with a list of what we will most urgently need."

"Yes, sir." The purser left the cabin.

"Captain?" Alfred said as he approached. "Would you like something to eat? I have some leftover ham and ship's biscuit, and there's wine for you to drink."

Brewer was about to refuse, but his stomach rumbled loudly, so he accepted his steward's offer. Alfred brought the cold fare, and to Brewer it was every bit as good as one of the steward's feasts.

After he ate, Brewer went back on deck and found Mr. Greene and Mr. Sweeney in conversation on the quarterdeck.

"Do we have any idea just how far the storm blew us off course?" he asked the sailing master.

"Yes, sir. I make our position as just southeast of Puerto Rico. The storm hit us hard, but it blew by very quickly."

"Mr. Greene, how is the jury-rigged mast holding up?"

"It will serve for now, Captain, until we can get back to Port Royal for a new one."

Brewer nodded. "Have you heard the purser's report?"

"Yes, sir."

Brewer frowned and tapped his fingers on the rail. "Five days back to Port Royal. More, if we allow for strain on the mast."

"If I may, sir," Greene said, "I believe St. Kitts is only two days from our present position. We could get provisions there, and possibly a new topmast as well."

Brewer turned to the sailing master. "Mr. Sweeney?"

Sweeney thought for a moment before agreeing with the first lieutenant. "Aye, she'll make it all right. We can move now, Captain, and she'll sail better as we get the water out of her."

"Very well. Make course for St. Kitts."

It occurred to Brewer that returning to St. Kitts might afford him an unlooked-for occasion to see Miss Danforth again, and for the first time in days, he felt his heart lift.

CHAPTER 12

HMS *Revenge* slid almost unnoticed into the harbor of St. Kitts. Most of the damage they'd suffered in the squall southeast of Puerto Rico had been repaired, under the direction of Mr. Ringold the carpenter; a day or so in port would be sufficient to complete repairs and see to provisioning. Brewer's mind was running in a hundred different directions regarding the needs of his ship; his fear was that he would forget something important. He shook his head in amazement and wondered, *How did they do it? Hornblower, Pellew, Hardy, how did they do it? A thousand details to attend to, all of them ultimately the captain's responsibility. It's almost overwhelming!* He took a deep breath to steady his self-control. *No,* he thought calmly, *I can do this.*

He turned to his first lieutenant. "Mr. Greene, I shall be going ashore to pay my respects to the governor and ask for any help he can give us. If at all possible, I want to be under way with the morning tide."

"Aye, sir," Greene said. "What about shore leave?"

Brewer considered. "If the repairs are completed, then you may authorize shore leave as you see fit."

"Thank you, sir."

"And pass the word—any officer or hand who has mail to send should bring it on deck. I will take it when I go."

It was less than thirty minutes later when Brewer found himself in the stern sheets of his gig, with McCleary guiding it toward the pier. The mail was on the floorboards between his feet, but he hardly felt it. So much had changed over the last few weeks, with Grant's death after his orders, the damage to the ship, the lost men and the injuries sustained in the storm. He had been forced to acknowledge and accept the loneliness of command, although he would admit to no-one that it was the most bitter of dregs he had ever been forced to swallow.

The Governor received Brewer in a large room on the second floor of his residence that appeared to the Commander to be a combination library and conservatory. The Governor was actually playing on the old-style harpsichord when Brewer entered the room, and he was pleased to wait for the Governor to finish.

"Welcome, Commander," said as he rose and strode across the room to shake Brewer's hand. "Is this a social call?"

"No, Governor," Brewer said. "My ship was damaged during a storm off Puerto Rico while we were hunting pirates. The storm blew us east, so I made the decision to put in here and make the necessary repairs. We also need water and provisions. I hope to set sail tomorrow or the day after."

"I see," Danforth said, as he led his guest to comfortable chairs before the fireplace. "And, if I may ask, were you looking for any particular pirate?"

Brewer nodded as he sat. "Roberto Cofresi. I am under orders to apprehend him if at all possible."

"Well, if there is anything I can do to assist you, Commander, please let me know." The Governor arose and looked at his pocket-watch. Brewer arose as well.

"Is something wrong, sir?" he asked.

The Governor's eyebrows raised. "Wrong? Good heavens, no, Commander. I'm wondering what's keeping my daughter."

Brewer's brow furled. "I'm sorry, sir; I don't understand."

The Governor smiled. "It's very simple. Your ship arrived this morning, and you yourself have been in private conversation with me in my house for eleven minutes now. It may interest you to know, Commander, that my daughter spends a good deal of time now watching which ships arrive in our harbor, and when she is absent, she has spies who keep watch for her. And the staff within the house keep her informed of every visitor I receive."

At the moment, the door of the library burst open, and Elizabeth Danforth swept into the room. She was obviously playing one of her games with her father, but her smile at seeing Brewer was genuine.

The Governor looked again at his watch. "Twelve minutes," he said. "Something happen to your spies, my dear?"

"Good morning to you, too, Father," she said with a kiss on his cheek. She turned to Brewer. "Commander, how pleasant to see you again."

Brewer bowed and kissed her hand. "The pleasure is mine, I assure you."

The Governor made a show of snapping the cover of his pocket-watch shut and replacing it in his waistcoat pocket. "Commander, I think that concludes our business. As I said, if I can help in any way, please feel free to contact me."

Brewer shook hands with him. "Thank you, sir, for everything."

The old man nodded once, in a sagely sort of way, and Brewer noticed the twinkle in his eye. He smiled at his daughter as he left the room.

Brewer turned his attention to his hostess. Elizabeth was if anything more beautiful than he remembered; he wondered if that was a case of absence making the heart grow fonder, or had she done something different especially for him?

"Thank you for writing to me," Brewer said.

"It is I who should thank you," she replied warmly. She stepped over toward him and held out her hands, which he took in his own. "I have never looked forward to a man's visit before. I assure you, my father may have spoken in jest, but I have indeed kept an eager eye on the harbor, and asked the servants to keep me informed if any naval officer arrives. How long can you stay?"

"I wish I could stay as long as you like, but that is not possible," Brewer replied, touched by the young lady's frankness. "I must sail as soon as repairs are completed, on the morning tide, if possible."

"I feared as much," she said. Brewer heard a sadness in her voice that cut him like a knife to his heart. "Can we walk in the garden?"

"I would like that very much," he said.

Soon they were strolling among the flowers and plants, enjoying the fragrances on the air and the bright colors of the blossoms. Brewer looked around and smiled.

"What is it?" Elizabeth asked him.

"Oh," he said, looking into her eyes. "I was just remembering the warning your father gave me on my last visit, about carnivores in the garden."

He watched her eyes as she searched for the memory and laughed when it came to her. Her brow rose, whether in reproof or play, he did not yet know.

"You would do well to remember that warning, Commander," she said.

"I promise you, I shall." He offered her his arm. She accepted it with a nod and a smile, and they continued their walk around the garden, speaking of anything that came to mind, enjoying each other's company.

She noticed that something was troubling him. "What is it, Commander? You can tell me."

He glanced down at her and saw only honesty and care in her eyes, and he smiled. He placed his free hand on hers that had his arm.

"There are things I must tell you," he said slowly, "I just don't know how."

She walked by his side in silence, content to wait for him to find the words.

"I have no family, Elizabeth," he said. "My father disowned me when I chose the Royal Navy over our family's farm. I have neither seen nor heard from him since that day. I correspond with my mother and sister, but I am dead to my father. I have no home, aside from my cabin on *Revenge*. I have very little money..."

"William," she stopped and turned toward him. It was the first time she had spoken his name, and the sound somehow filled him with hope. She reached up and touched his cheek with her free hand. "I could not imagine anything better than a man who is free. We can build our own life together."

He looked into her eyes and wished for all the world that they were man and wife. As it was, he drew her to him and embraced her. He was pleased when she did not resist. For her part, Elizabeth buried her face in his chest and put her arms around him.

"I wish I could take you with me," he said. "But our mission would endanger you."

She did not move. "I'm in no hurry."

He pulled away so he could look in her eyes. "I've searched my whole life for you."

"I don't know why," she smiled. "I've been here the whole time."

He laughed at that, and they started down the path, her arm again in his. They wandered around the garden, lost in their own conversation. To Brewer, it was heaven.

"I told you about myself," he said, "but I know almost nothing about you."

"Well," she said, "I do know how to cook and keep a fire."

She almost laughed at the look on his face.

"You seem surprised," she said. "I'll have you know, sir, that before my father accepted this posting three years ago, we lived alone, he and I, in a small cottage outside Oxford. We had no servants, so I grew accustomed at an early age to daily chores. I ran the entire household myself before I was ten." She looked at flower as they passed by. "Sometimes, I wish I could go back to that."

"What?" Brewer said. "You mean you would actually prefer to live *without* servants?"

"Well," she said, her cheeks reddening, "perhaps not *without*, but there was a certain intimacy I felt with my father in those days, a feeling of togetherness, that has faded as the distances between us have increased in the great house. And now I have nothing to do to show my father that I love him, for all the work is done for us."

"I see," Brewer said, a look of mock consternation on his face. "So, am I to understand that you want me to be rich, but not *too* rich? Perhaps I should only look for the *small* pirate ships to take as prizes?"

She stopped walking, and that drew his attention to her face. Her brows were furled and her eyes hooded; Brewer found it took all his control not to burst out laughing at the sight.

"Sir," she said quietly, "I remind you of my father's warning."

"Ah," he nodded. "Thank you." He offered her his arm and they resumed their walk.

"May I ask a question?" she said. He nodded, and she looked up at him. "My father said you knew Napoleon Bonaparte. Is that true?"

He nodded. "I'm afraid it is."

She shook her head in wonder. "That must have been extraordinary. How did you meet him?"

"When Admiral Lord Hornblower was Governor of St. Helena, I was his aide and confidential secretary, so I saw him every time he came to see the Governor. He spoke to me several times."

"Were you frightened?"

Brewer smiled. "No. You must remember that by the time I knew Bonaparte, he was no longer the monster who terrorized Europe and conquered its nations at will. The Bonaparte I knew, his worst enemy was boredom. He needed mental stimulation, so to speak, and I think that he came to complain to the Governor in part for the purpose of engaging him in conversation."

"Did you ever get to speak to him?"

"Occasionally." He smiled at the memory.

"What did he say to you?"

"He warned me to always be ready for opportunity to arise. He said that when it did, I should reach out, grab it by the throat, and take it for my own."

She looked up at him. "That sounds like good advice."

He wondered if she meant what he thought she meant, that he had an opportunity here, with her. His mind started racing, but he stopped it with a decision to be bold.

"Elizabeth," he said softly, "may I ask you a question without appearing forward?"

"Of course."

He stopped and looked into her eyes. "You know your father better than I; is it too early for me to speak to him?"

She looked up at his eyes, and then buried her face in his chest. He felt her sigh, and when she looked up at him again, he got the distinct impression that she was trying to decide the best way to deliver bad news.

"William... yes, I believe it is," she said, "at least from his point of view." She frowned and shook her head, as though she feared she was not making herself clear. "My mother died when I was born. Ever since then, my father has been very protective of me, even more so since officers have wanted to court me. Don't misunderstand, William; my father likes you very much. He just needs time to come to terms with the inevitable outcome. The next time you are in port, plan on dining with us. Hopefully, by then he will be ready. Don't worry, I'll be working on him in the meantime." She looked up at him and smiled. "Consider yourself a prize that has been captured, sir."

He chuckled. "I see your father was right."

CHAPTER 13

HMS *Revenge* warped out of the harbor at St. Kitts bright and early the following morning. Brewer stood on the quarterdeck, watching as the diligent Lieutenant Greene piloted the ship toward the open sea. On a whim—or perhaps as a hope—Brewer asked for a glass and went to the fantail to lift it to his eye. His faith was rewarded as the image of Elizabeth Danforth came into focus. She was standing at the end of the pier, waving her handkerchief at the departing ship. He lowered the glass and raised his hat to her. He did not know if she could see it or not, but he felt better for having made the attempt.

They passed into the open sea, and Brewer ordered a course set for Puerto Rico. He wanted to resume his search in the area where they had been chasing the brig. He intended to make his ship known to Vieques and Flamenco, off Puerto Rico's eastern tip, which is where he figured their chase had been blown by the storm winds. *If that fails to stir any interest,* he thought, *then we'll have to find a way to shake trees and see what kind of fruit we can get to fall.*

Lieutenant Greene came up and reported. "We are on course for Puerto Rico, Captain. Currently, we are on the larboard tack, running under all plain sail to the royals."

"Thank you, Mr. Greene," Brewer said. "I want an hour's exercise at the guns today. I also want the crew drilled in boarding and repelling boarders." He grimaced. "Best to be prepared when dealing with pirates."

"Agreed, sir," Greene replied.

Brewer frowned, as an idea struck him. Acting on it, he went below and entered his cabin. Mac was there to take his hat and coat and hang them up properly. As he was divesting himself of his coat, Alfred appeared in the doorway.

"Would you like your breakfast now, sir?"

"Yes, thank you."

Brewer stared at the pantry door and rubbed his chin. "Mac," he said, "I want you to take Alfred down to the armory and give him his choice of sword and brace of pistols. We may need him if we get boarded by pirates."

Alfred arrived then with a platter, which he set on the table. He placed the captain's plate in front of him, and Brewer could hardly believe his eyes. Two eggs, fried, with the yolks still soft! A huge slice of ham! Potatoes, sliced and fried, covered with butter! Toast and marmalade! And, to top it off, piping hot coffee! Brewer stared at his servant in amazement.

"As you requested, sir," Alfred said, "I took advantage of our stop in St. Kitts to lay up some cabin stores. Per your orders, I purchased two large hams and sent them to the gunroom with your compliments."

"Excellent!" Brewer said. He rubbed his hands in anticipation before picking up his knife and fork and digging in to the fare. Alfred took the silence as the compliment it was meant to be and retreated with a smile on his face.

HMS *Revenge* was moving smartly under all plain sail. The sun was high in the sky and the seas were calm. The primary work at hand was getting the crew ready to fight pirates when the time came. At Brewer's request, Alfred agreed to give lessons in using a sword to Lieutenant Tyler and the midshipmen on the quarterdeck. The exhibitions drew quite an audience, and, to Brewer's quiet satisfaction, Alfred patiently answered all questions put to him by the crew. Only one of the crowd dared to argue with him, upon which Alfred invited him to step out, take a sword, and prove his point. The seaman stepped forward and accepted Mr. Tyler's blade. Alfred parried his attacks while the seaman attempted to lecture him, then went on the offensive. Within seconds, the seaman's blade was on the deck, and he felt the point of Alfred's saber on his chest. The watchers cheered, and the seaman spent the next half-hour learning the proper way from his new master.

The days proceeded, as did the training. Although Brewer would not admit it to anyone—except perhaps to Elizabeth—he felt a lump in the pit of his stomach every time he saw the hands go aloft for sail drill. He made a supreme effort to school his features to calmness. He was The Captain. He could not show fear.

One Sunday, Brewer was particularly pleased with his weekly inspection, so he declared a mending day for the crew, to give them a well-earned day of rest. In very short order, the men settled down to various projects and hobbies. Some did indeed mend articles of clothing; others carved pieces of wood or bone; a few read or composed letters; and one sailor brought out an oboe and began to play.

Out of the corner of his eye, Brewer noticed Mr. Short, in his usual place in the mizzen shrouds, start suddenly and turn to look over his shoulder out to sea. He walked over.

"Is something wrong, Mr. Short?" he asked.

"Dunno, sir," the midshipman said uncertainly. "I thought I heard something."

"Aren't you a little young to hear the call of the sirens, Mr. Short?" Brewer joked. "I mean, you're not even Greek—"

Just then, a gust of wind brought the faintest whiff of a distant sound to the captain's ears.

"There it is again, sir," Short said.

"I heard it too," Brewer said. "My apologies. Get me a glass, please. One for yourself as well."

Short jumped down to the deck. "Aye aye, sir."

"Pass the word for Mr. Greene!"

Short was back within moments. He handed his captain one glass and carried his own back to his perch in the shrouds.

Greene arrived. "You sent for me, sir?"

"Yes, Benjamin," Brewer said. He was pleased to see his first officer already had a glass. "Mr. Short and I heard a sound carried by the wind from the north. It may be cannon fire. What would you say, Mr. Short?"

"Could be, sir!"

"Deck ho!" came the cry from the lookout. "Sail on the horizon! At least two ships, maybe three. Too many sail for one!"

Brewer lowered his glass. "Mr. Greene, let's investigate. Call all hands to make sail. Helm! Hard to starboard! New course due north! I want to close on that sail!"

Hands sprang to the shrouds as *Revenge* came around to her new course. The ship picked up speed. Mr. Short changed his place for a better view in the larboard shrouds.

"I've got the sails, sir!" Short called from his perch. "Still hull down, two points off the larboard bow!"

"Lookout!" Brewer called. "What do you see?"

"Two ships, Captain! One is a flute, and it looks like she's trying to run away from a cutter maybe, or a schooner, sir! Could be a pirate run out from the shore trying to board, sir!"

"Beat to quarters!" Brewer cried. "Mr. Greene, load the guns, but don't run them out just yet!"

"Aye, sir!"

"Mr. Sweeney, steer straight for them!"

"Straight for them! Aye, sir!"

"Excuse me, sir," a voice behind him said.

He turned and saw Mac standing there with his hanger in one hand and his pistols in the other. Brewer nodded his thanks and armed himself, then went forward for a better look at the situation. The flute was making all sail, but there was no way she could escape the smaller, faster pursuing ship, which he could see now see was a schooner of about 10 guns. It might have been warning shots that he and Mr. Short heard, for the flute did not look damaged. If the schooner was indeed manned by pirates, it was possible they wanted to capture the ship intact and add it to their fleet.

Brewer looked around at *Revenge*'s 12-pounders, loaded and ready to be run out at his command, and silently fumed. *As soon as I get back to Port Royal,* he promised himself, *the first thing I'm going to do is trade two of these guns for long nines!*

He put his glass back to his eye and saw activity on the pirate's deck, indicating they had spotted *Revenge's* approach. Now the question was, what would they do next? He waited as patiently as he could for the answer, because their actions would dictate his own. He didn't have to wait long, for it became clear as the pirates closed on the flute that they intended to grapple and board the merchantman. Brewer snapped his glass shut and headed aft. He knew what he had to do now.

"Mr. Sweeney," he said when he arrived on the quarterdeck, "I want you to lay me within pistol shot of that schooner. After we fire a broadside, dump sails and swing us round for a shot down the stern. Mr. Greene, run out the larboard battery. We need to make every shot tell against their hull. Keep the shots low; I don't want to damage the flute if we can avoid it!"

His order acknowledged, Brewer stood on his quarterdeck and watched as his ship approached the enemy. He saw the pirates grapple the flute and a wave of men swarm over the merchantman's side and on to her deck. He hoped the flute's crew could hold out long enough for his plan to be implemented.

The pirate's bow was against the flute's side. This had the effect of turning the schooner's broadside toward the approaching *Revenge*. The pirate got off two broadsides as *Revenge* approached, but their shooting was ragged. Most of the crew was probably part of the boarding action. Brewer and Greene felt the ship shudder slightly when a couple of the shots struck home in their bow.

"6-pounders, sir?" Greene asked.

"So it would appear," Brewer replied. "Get ready. When I give the word, you may fire as your guns bear. One broadside, then reload for a second through her stern. After that, secure the larboard guns as quick as you can. I will bring *Revenge* around and let you know if I want you to run out the starboard battery."

Greene saluted and went to his guns, pausing to give each gun captain his instructions.

Brewer stood at the larboard rail now, concentrating on the closing gap between *Revenge* and the other two ships. The flute's crew must be holding their own, because he saw a second group of men board from the pirate ship. He considered the closing gap again and turned to his sailing master.

"Mr. Sweeney," he said, "when I give the word, I want you to put the helm over hard to starboard and back the main and mizzen topsails. That should slow us down enough for Mr. Greene to put a broadside into the schooner. As soon as we clear her, I want to put the helm over to port to give Mr. Greene a shot at her stern. Understand?"

"Aye aye, Captain!"

Brewer stepped away. "Stand by, Mr. Greene!"

"Stand by, men!" Greene called to his crews.

All eyes were on Brewer. He ignored it as best he could and concentrated on not missing the right moment to act. *Just a few moments more...*

"Mr. Sweeney," he said. "Now! Hard to starboard!"

Sweeney barked orders to the helmsmen and the hands who would back the sails. Brewer felt the ship swing sharply to the right. He looked down at Greene and nodded.

"Fire as your guns bear!" Greene yelled.

Brewer watched as *Revenge's* guns went off one or two at a time. Greene was jumping down the line from gun to gun to make sure no one fired too early. The effect of the schooner was a wonder to behold—at least for the British. Brewer guessed that Greene had loaded the guns with canister over round shot, which, when added to the blast from the two 18-pounder carronades, turned the enemy ship into a slaughterhouse. He looked down again at the battery and saw Greene and Tyler urging the men to load quickly with round shot. He turned to Sweeney again.

"Now, Mr. Sweeney!" he called. "Hard to port!"

The ship swung around again. Almost immediately Brewer heard guns begin to go off. He looked forward, thinking some captain had fired early, but he saw again Mr. Greene jumping from gun to gun, personally directing their fire. He turned back to the schooner in time to see its stern disintegrate under the concentrated fire of Greene's broadside.

"Well done, lads!" Greene cried. "Now, secure your guns!"

"Excellent!" Brewer said to himself. "Mr. Sweeney! Bring us around!"

Brewer ran to the opposite rail to get a good look as *Revenge* came around. The breeze was just enough to clear the smoke from the broadsides away. He saw the damage was even greater than he'd hoped it would be.

"Mr. Greene! We shall board her!"

"All hands! Prepare to board!"

Blades, pikes, and axes now appeared in the crewmen's hands as *Revenge* closed in on her quarry.

"Benjamin, you take a group forward and board as soon as we make contact. I will try to draw their fire from here, and then my group will follow you. If you secure the schooner, move on to help the flute! Don't wait!"

"Aye, sir! You men!" Greene said, pointing to a couple of groups who had gathered behind him. "Follow me!"

A cheer went up as the men fell in behind Greene, who led them forward. Brewer turned and saw Mac standing three feet away, Alfred beside him. The servant had his saber in one hand and a pistol in the other. Brewer also noticed two additional pistols in his belt.

"Glad to have you with us," he said.

"My pleasure, sir," Alfred replied.

"You men!" Brewer called to those who were left. "With me!"

Lieutenant Greene waited impatiently as Mr. Sweeney guided *Revenge* up against the schooner. When the captain drew the pirates' attention aft, he led his men over the rail and down onto the deck of the schooner. They were confronted by dozen pirates as soon as they touched the deck, and Greene saw more of them coming forward. He parried a blow from the nearest pirate, sidestepped a second blow and brought his saber down on the man's neck. He pulled a pistol from his belt and shot a second pirate in the chest and used the empty gun to hit a third attacker in the face. The man went down, and Greene ran him through before stepping over the body and pressing forward.

Reed was quick to follow his lieutenant. He used his pistol almost immediately to take one pirate down. He ducked under another pirate's slashing attack and slashed across his stomach with his saber. The man doubled over with a gasp that tuned into a scream, dropped his weapon and clutched at his entrails. Reed parried another attack and momentarily trapped the pirate's sword long enough for Kelly to step around them and stab the man in the chest with his pike. Kelly picked up the dead pirate's pistol and, finding it was loaded, promptly used it to shoot another pirate who was giving Jones a very bad time in the back. Reed lit a grenade and sent it down the deck to explode under approaching three pirates, while Kelly tossed another one down the forward hatch.

Lieutenant Greene and his twenty-five men secured the forward part of the ship as Brewer and his force of twenty came over the rails as well. The remaining dozen or so pirates on the schooner deck threw down their swords and axes and surrendered.

Brewer made his way over to Greene. "Keep fifteen men with you and secure this ship. Look below, to make sure there are no surprises for us down there. I am taking the rest on to the flute. Tyler has a force of thirty who will be coming over the rail in about five minutes. If you don't need them, send them on after me."

Green, who was still catching his breath, nodded.

"Let's go, men!" Brewer cried. He led his tars up and over the flute's railings with a great war cry and launched into the fray. He swung his saber at anything that looked like it might be a pirate, once feeling a jarring pain that ran all the way up his arm to his shoulder when his blade bit into a pirate's thigh all the way to the bone.

Mac was never far from his captain's side, his eyes scanning the rigging for anyone who might want to target his captain. He shot two pirates off the yardarms and brought another one down by throwing a hatchet at him. Alfred protected Brewer's back, using his skills as never before. The first pirate that he came up against actually laughed at his size, until Alfred shot him in the middle of his forehead. He picked up the dead man's saber and took on two pirates at once, ducking under one man's thrust and running his blade through the pirate's stomach. He sidestepped the second man's downward thrust just in time, allowing the pirate's blade to get stuck in the deck. Alfred dodged around and reached up to carve the man's throat open. He kicked another pirate's knee in, causing the man to fall to the deck, where upon he jumped on the man's stomach and brought both sabers down on the pirate's chest and left them buried there. He pulled two more pistols out of his belt and shot two more pirates, then reclaimed his sabers. Looking about, he realized the tide of battle had separated him from the captain.

Brewer and Mac were fighting back to back when Alfred found them. Brewer had estimated there were possibly as many as 100 pirates on the deck of the flute, with more probably below. At the moment, however, he was too busy to think about his estimate, other than to hope he'd guessed high. He was fighting for his life, his saber in his right hand, his empty pistol in his left hand; he was holding it by the barrel and using it like a black jack. He ducked and parried without conscious thought, his body reacting to keep him alive. Every so often he felt Mac's back against his, and the feeling gave him a confidence to keep fighting, even as his arm grew heavy and his boots slipped on blood on the deck.

He saw a few men whom he took to be those still alive from the flute's crew. They seemed to be fighting well, taking their stand on the quarterdeck.

Suddenly he found himself beset. Three pirates, each coming from a different point of the compass, had singled him out as an officer. Brewer ducked to avoid a high slash by the one in front of him. At the same time, he brought the butt of his pistol down as hard as he could on the inside of the knee of the one to his left while he stabbed out before him, taking the charging pirate under his rib and up into his heart. The one to his left fell to the deck in a cry of pain, and Brewer wasted no time in twisting hard, bringing his blade down on his enemy's neck, nearly taking his head off.

That left the third man, the one he had caught a glimpse of on his right. He turned quickly, raising his saber, in time to see Alfred pulling his blade out of the pirate's chest. He nodded his thanks, and his servant saluted with his weapon before jumping to help Mac.

Brewer now found himself fighting an older pirate who was content to stand off and duel with him, having seen what happened to his comrades who charged in. Brewer realized that this one had lived to such an old age because he possessed good sense and skills, which he demonstrated when he dodged a blow from the butt end of Brewer's pistol and sliced open his upper arm, causing Brewer to drop the pistol to the deck. Brewer barely managed to parry two more thrusts before it began to dawn on him that he was out of his depth. His arm was aching and useless, hanging dead at his side, blood soaking his uniform sleeve and dripping down his arm. His opponent charged and made a hard thrust; parrying it pushed Brewer back against Mac and almost caused them both to fall to the deck.

Just when Brewer thought the next blow from his opponent might be the last, he noticed a quick movement to his right. Alfred came around from behind and threw himself between his captain and the pirate, pivoting to engage the swordsman twice his height. Gasping for breath, Brewer had a moment to watch the two engage in a masterful display of swordsmanship. A premonition caused him to turn in time to see another pirate coming at him. Desperately he parried the other's thrust and twisted his wrist as he brought his arm up and around to strike a slashing blow to the man's neck. He looked back to see how Alfred fared but was unable to catch sight of him before another pirate imposed himself on his attentions.

Alfred had returned just in time to save his Captain's life. He stepped in and parried the killing blow, then attacked to draw the pirate's attention from the captain to himself.

He advanced and retreated, made thrust and parry as the two joined in a dance of death. The light in the pirate's eye at facing so small an opponent quickly faded as he realized Alfred's skill, and the amused look was replace with one of determination not to die. They maneuvered for advantage, or as much as was possible on the crowded deck, the pirate using his advantage of superior reach and Alfred ducking inside to strike at his opponent at every opportunity.

The pirate soon realized that he was dealing with a far better swordsman than his previous opponent, and he decided to try a different tactic.

"I compliment you on your skill, small one," he said. "Why not throw in your lot with me? I can make you rich beyond your wildest dreams!"

Alfred said nothing. He parried a blow and dodged right, making a slash which the pirate parried.

"What?" the pirate said. "No interest in treasure? That is too bad, since you, as small as you are, cannot expect to escape me with your life."

Alfred took a step back and waved the tip of his sword before his foe. "I find the blade to be the great equalizer."

The dance resumed with a renewed ferocity. Gradually Alfred detected a weakness in his opponent's technique and began to exploit it. He landed a glancing blow that drew blood from the pirate's forearm and another that drew blood from his thigh.

The pirate knew from the two wounds that the tide of battle was beginning to turn against him. Never had he seen such skill in a foe. One more wound in the right place, or a deeper cut instead of a slice, and the little one would not hesitate to take full advantage of his misfortune. The only two assets he had were his reach and his strength, but he courted death every time he tried to get close enough to use his strength.

His opportunity came when his smaller foe parried a blow, and he was able to lean in and slide his saber down so the two weapons were hilt to hilt. He struck at his foe's head with his injured arm, but the smaller man dodged it. However, his dodge was just enough to put him a little off balance, which was enough for the pirate to give a mighty shove and lift his opponent into the air and send him back almost ten feet! He was disappointed to see the little demon land on his feet and crouch to keep his balance on the treacherous deck. Rather than charge, he retreated below deck. His foe pursued, and the battle resumed in the more confined spaces.

Alfred had never been a religious man, but he'd seen the captain read his Bible often enough that it seemed appropriate to thank God when he landed and kept his footing. He prepared himself for his enemy to charge at him like a bull, and he was surprised when he disappeared below deck instead.

It never occurred to him *not* to follow the pirate below; his only thought was not to allow the blackguard to escape. He caught up with him quickly, and the two crossed swords again.

He never suspected a trap until his foe stepped back and lowered his sword. He turned just in time to catch a glimpse of something moving before a pain erupted in the side of his head and everything went black.

The pirate who'd knocked the little swordsman unconscious smiled.

"Shall I kill him, Captain?" he asked.

Roberto Cofresi looked down at his foe. "No," he said. "This one has earned his life. He has great skill."

His eyes were drawn to the deck above them by a great cry. A pirate ran down to them.

"What is it?" Cofresi asked him.

"A new group has boarded from the British ship."

"How many?"

"Too many," the man said. "Perhaps fifty."

Cofresi shook his head. "Time to go. There's no profit here. This will teach me to sail with so few men. Everybody up on deck and over the side. Swim for land."

One pirate looked uneasy. "What about the men who cannot swim?"

Cofresi shrugged. "They are welcome to remain here and hang. You choose, but it's time to go."

Brewer felt his strength ebbing with every thrust and parry. He could feel the blood from his wound dripping from his fingers now. It had to end soon....

Just then, he heard a shout coming from aft. He turned to steal a look aft and saw Greene and Tyler coming over the rail at the head of what had to be fifty men! The pirate fighting him saw it, too, and made one last slash at Brewer, which he just managed to parry, before turning and running.

Brewer looked aft again. The group that came over the railing appeared to be splitting in two, Greene taking one group to secure the quarterdeck while Tyler lead the second group and began fighting his way forward. The lieutenant was searching as he came, and when he saw Brewer standing beside McCleary, he pointed to him with his saber and headed his way.

"Thank God you're alive, sir!" Tyler shouted over the din of battle.

"Thank you, Mr. Tyler, for your timely arrival!" Brewer said. "Leave five men here with Mr. McCleary to help us secure the deck. Take the remainder and search below for any pirates who may be lurking down there. Free any prisoners of the flute's crew you may find."

"Aye, sir!" Tyler turned to his men. "You five!" He pointed with his saber. "Stay with Mr. McCleary and guard the Captain! The rest follow me below! Let's go!"

Tyler led his men down below deck. Brewer didn't immediately hear any pistols firing or cold steel crossing, which encouraged him a little. He turned to Mac.

"Situation?" he asked.

Mac looked around, assessing. "Looks like the fo'c'sle is secure, sir. Recommend we head aft and squeeze the bloody buggers between us and Mr. Greene."

"Do you see Alfred?"

Mac shook his head. "No sign of him, sir."

Brewer grimaced wearily, and Mac looked at him with concern, noticing the bloody sleeve.

"Captain, you're hurt! Sit down here, sir. You men! Form a ring!"

"Mac, I'm fine," Brewer tried to say. Mac cut him off before he could finish.

"Captain, either sit down and let me look at it, or I take you back to Dr. Spinelli over my shoulder."

Brewer saw the compassion and worry in his coxswain's face and decided to submit.

Mac cut the sleeves of the coat and the shirt away, then used the shirt sleeve to make a bandage. He helped Brewer to his feet.

"Can you go on, Captain?" he asked.

"I'm not dead yet, Mac," Brewer replied somewhat testily. "Let's get to Mr. Greene and secure this ship."

The group made their way aft, careful to skirt wounded pirates who might take a stab at passing enemies. Several were running to throw themselves overboard to swim to shore, which was just visible on the horizon. When they encountered wounded sailors from *Revenge*, they helped them forward. At last they came upon Mr. Greene, standing on the quarterdeck beside a tall member of the flute's crew with a very bloody saber in his hand.

"Captain," Greene said, "may I present Mr. Van Dyke, first mate of the Dutch cargo ship *Amsterdam*?"

Brewer nodded his greeting, his strength beginning to wane again.

"Our heartfelt thanks, Captain Brewer," the mate said. "Your timely intervention and the valor of your men have saved our ship and our cargo."

"And what of your captain?" Brewer asked, looking around.

The mate looked stricken. "Regrettably, Captain Yoost was killed attempting to repel the pirate attack."

"I regret we were not able to come to your aid sooner." A thought struck him, and he turned to his coxswain. "Mac, go below and check on Mr. Tyler. See if you can find Alfred."

Seeing him hesitate, Greene spoke up. "I'll stay with the captain," he said.

Reassured, the coxswain saluted and was gone.

"Mr. Greene," Brewer asked, "if you are here, who is on the schooner?"

"Nobody, sir," Greene said. "I inspected below decks. Captain, that ship is settling in the water, and there's nothing we can do to save it. I sent word back to Mr. Sweeney to back *Revenge* away from her and send boats. *Revenge* should tow the schooner away from the flute and allow it to sink undisturbed."

"A sound plan," Brewer said. "Let's get the wounded back to *Revenge* so the doctor can have a look at them. Have you a doctor on board, Mr. Van Dyke?"

"Yes, Captain."

"That is well." The blood loss from his wound was making it hard to think.

"Captain," Greene said, "you should return to *Revenge* and have the doctor sew up that arm."

Brewer tried to shrug him off. "I'm fine, Mr. Greene."

"With all due respect, Captain, I insist. I can look after things here and then come to you and report."

Greene looked around. "Mr. Simmons! Take four hands and see to the moving of the wounded back to the ship when *Revenge* sends boats. Make sure the Captain goes on the first boat."

"Yes, Mr. Greene!"

"And Mr. Simmons," Greene added somberly, "after the wounded have been taken care of, prepare our honored dead for burial at sea."

"Pardon me a moment, gentlemen," Van Dyke said. He turned and spoke to one of his seamen in Dutch. The man bobbed his head and scurried away. "I have sent for additional bandages for your arm, Captain. And, as for the burial, I would consider it an honor if we could bury them from here, the *Amsterdam*, which they gave their lives to save from the pirates."

Brewer looked at Greene and then at their host.

"That would be very kind, sir. Thank you."

Chapter 14

Captain Brewer was taken to the captain's cabin of the *Amsterdam* and made to sit down while their doctor applied additional bandages to his injured arm and put it into a sling. He was also given a fortifying glass of wine. McCleary arrived and made sure his master stayed seated until it was time to return to HMS *Revenge*. He'd found Alfred below decks, unconscious from a blow to the head, but otherwise uninjured. The *Amsterdam's* doctor looked at him and said he should be recovered in a day or two.

Mr. Greene reported an hour later that the pirate schooner had finally slipped beneath the waves. He also said that two boats were on their way from *Revenge* to transport the wounded. When Brewer asked about the butcher's bill, Greene said that he counted the bodies of seventeen of *Revenge's* crew, along with twenty-five from *Amsterdam*. Captain Van Dyke was even now assessing whether he has sufficient crew left to get the ship to the nearest Dutch port. Greene estimated that more than a hundred pirates had perished as a result of their two broadsides and the boarding action. On *Amsterdam*, Greene said he'd counted seventy-five pirate dead. He also reported that they'd taken twenty-seven prisoners.

Brewer thought the ride back to HMS *Revenge* was miserable. Mac was beside him in the stern sheets, conning the boat, as he did whenever the Captain was aboard, but looking at the injured in the boat tore at Brewer's heart. He told the men he was proud of them, that they had fought well and saved a valuable ship from the clutches of the pirates. He was pleased to see several of them smile at his words.

Brewer felt relieved to sit down in his own cabin. Mac had had to help him board *Revenge*, but he'd walked to his cabin on his own. He was just about to drink a glass of wine that Mac brought him when the door burst open and Dr. Spinelli surged into the room. At the sight of his captain sitting quietly with a drink in hand, he pulled up short.

"I beg your pardon," he said, as he set his medical bag on the desk. "I was led to believe you were dying."

"Sorry to disappoint you," Brewer said wearily.

Spinelli pulled up a chair beside his captain's wounded arm and began removing the dressings. When he was able to see the wound, the bleeding still had not stopped completely. He examined the arm carefully before sighing.

"Saber wound?" he asked, receiving a nod for his answer. "I'm going to sew this up. We need to watch for infection closely. I'd rather not have to take the arm off, if it's all the same to you."

"Oh, I assure you, I like the arm right where it is."

The doctor asked for brandy, not to drink, but to wash the arm and his instruments. It burned abominably, and Brewer gritted his teeth, then he flinched as the needle bit into his skin.

"I suggest you hold still." Spinelli bent to his work, and soon he was able to apply a clean bandage and put his captain's arm back in the sling.

"Now," the doctor said as he repacked his bag, "I want you to rest for a while."

"I have to return to the *Amsterdam* for the burial of our dead."

"I'll leave word with Mr. Sweeney to call you when they are ready. In the meantime, rest. You lost a lot of blood, and your body needs to recuperate."

The doctor watched as Brewer stretched out on the settee under the stern windows of the cabin. He could see his patient was moving gingerly, but that was to be expected. As the Captain settled in, Spinelli turned to Mac.

"You know the signs to look for?"

"Indeed I do."

"Good. Call me immediately if you see any of them, no matter what he says." He motioned with his head toward the Captain, who was already falling asleep in spite of the throbbing pain in his arm.

It seemed to Brewer that he had just fallen asleep when Mac touched his shoulder to wake him.

"Sir," he said, "they're ready over on the Dutch ship."

"What?" Brewer said wearily. "How long have I been asleep? Ow!"

"Easy with that arm, sir," Mac said as he helped his captain sit up. "You've been sleeping for nearly three hours."

God! My arm hurts!

"Okay, Mac," he said, lurching to his feet. "Let's figure out how to get a coat over this bandage without tearing the wound open." Ruefully, he wondered if a tailor would be able to repair the damage to his slashed, bloodied, and dismembered coat.

Captain William Brewer stood at attention on the deck of the *Amsterdam*, listening to Captain Van Dyke address the *Amsterdam*'s crew in Dutch, presumably praising those of HMS *Revenge*'s crew along with his own who'd given their lives to fight off the pirates. He talked for several minutes, and Brewer was startled when he suddenly switched to English.

"We thank the great God," Van Dyke said loudly, "for sending our rescuers from HMS *Revenge* to help us defeat those who sought to kill us all and take our ship and cargo. May God receive their souls in mercy, and may He comfort the family of each who gave their lives to keep us safe. Their sacrifice will not soon be forgotten. We shall now recite the Lord's Prayer. Captain Brewer, if it please you, your men shall recite the prayer in English while my men and I say it in our Dutch."

"Thank you, Greene," Brewer said. He led off.

"Our Father, which art in Heaven,"

Captain Van Dyke and the Dutch crew echoed the British lead.

"Onze vader die in de hemel zijt,"

"Hallowed be Thy name."

"Uw naam worde geheiligd."

"Thy kingdom come,"

"Uw rijk kome,"

"Thy will be done on earth as it is in Heaven."

"Uw wil geschiede op aarde zoals in de hemel."

"Give us this day our daily bread,"

"Geef ons heden ons dagelijks brood,"

"And forgive us our trespasses,"

"En vergeef ons onze schuld,"

"As we forgive those who trespass against us."

"Zoals wij ook aan anderen hun schuld vergeven."

"And lead us not into temptation,"

"En lei dons niet in bekoring,"

"But deliver us from evil."

" Mar verlos ons van het kwade."

"Amen."

"Amen."

The Dutch *"Amen"* struck Brewer hard. He turned his head to look at his men. There was Mr. Greene, standing at attention, a rock Brewer knew he could rely upon; Mr. Reed, who had helped lead the first wave against the pirates; Mac, who had saved his life once again. Behind him were a dozen of the crew, all of whom did him proud this day. He looked over at *Revenge*, standing alongside at pistol shot, and saw Mr. Tyler on the quarterdeck, someone he could invest in as Captain Bush had invested in him, and Mr. Sweeney beside him. He'd never felt so proud in his life, to be able to lead such men, and to fight with them.

"Captain Brewer," Van Dyke said, "do you wish to say a few words?"

"Yes," Brewer said. "Will you please translate for me? Thank you. We are proud to be able to fight alongside the gallant crew of the *Amsterdam*." He paused to allow Van Dyke to translate. "Your honored dead, and ours, will long be remembered." Another pause. "We now honor the memories of our fallen comrades." A pause. "We commend their bodies and their souls to God Almighty, who shall judge the living and the dead at the coming of his Son, Jesus Christ. We therefore commit their bodies to the deep."

Van Dyke translated Brewer's last words before signaling to his crewmen standing at the grates. They lifted the grates one at a time, each lift sending two bodies to the water. Each was bound in identical sailcloth, so there was no way to tell British from Dutch. Brewer thought it was somehow better that way—equal honor for equal death.

When the last grate had discharged its burden, Van Dyke barked a command in Dutch, and his men were dismissed. He turned to his guests.

"I thank you again. Without your intervention, it is unlikely that any of us would have lived to see the setting of the sun as free men, if we lived at all. I am sorry for your losses, as I mourn for my countrymen."

"You honored the fallen well," Brewer said. "But can you make the nearest Dutch port?"

"Yes. We will sail for St. Eustatius."

"Well, may you reach harbor safely," Brewer said. The two men shook hands, and Brewer and his party returned to HMS *Revenge*.

Captain Brewer raised his glass in a toast. "To fallen comrades," he said. Echoes of "Fallen comrades" filled the gunroom. Brewer drank somberly. Lieutenant Greene, who as ranking lieutenant in charge of the mess had extended the invitation to the captain to dine at the gunroom table, sat at the head of the table with Brewer on his right. Beside the captain sat Dr. Spinelli, with Mr. Reed next to him. On Greene's left sat Lieutenant Tyler with Mr. Sweeney on his left.

This was their first chance to relax since parting company with the Dutch ship some thirty hours earlier. Yesterday had been busy, with the doctor tending the wounded, and the captain overseeing the cleaning of weapons and gear and the readying of the ship for getting underway. And then there had been the difficult duty of burying the men who did of their injuries. Mr. Greene, seeing that the Captain was still weak from his wound and feverish, begged Brewer that he be permitted to carry out the ceremony so the captain could rest, but Brewer insisted on seeing it through. He watched as each of the seven bodies slid from the grate to its watery grave, Spinelli and Mac beside him.

"Captain," Spinelli had said, "you should be in bed."

"Soon enough, Doctor," Brewer had replied wearily. "What's the score down there?"

"One or two are touch and go; the rest should pull through." The doctor hesitated a moment before stepping closer for a private word. "William, you *must* rest! Listen to me! If you go to bed now, you may wake up with two arms. If you *don't* go to bed, if you allow this fever to get worse, it may cost you the arm, or even your life."

Brewer shot a hard look at his friend. He felt weak and irritable, but he saw the concern in the doctor's eyes and gave in.

He turned to his coxswain. "I suppose you're on his side in this?"

"Yes, sir," Mac replied laconically.

Brewer shook his head in mock disbelief. "Where did I get such a mutinous crew?" he said. "Very well, Doctor. You win."

"Thank you, Captain." Spinelli turned to Mac. "Take him below and give him a stiff glass of Madeira before he goes to bed. And stay with him; you know what to watch for."

"Aye, sir."

And so Brewer had gone to bed. He'd slept nearly sixteen hours, and when he awoke, the fever had broken. The doctor was pleased, though he warned the captain that he was not out of danger yet.

"We still need to watch for infection," Spinelli had said. "Infection can turn to gangrene, and gangrene will cost you your arm at a minimum, and possibly your life."

Now, in the gunroom, all that seemed like a long time ago. His arm still ached like the devil, and it screamed bloody murder if he moved it wrong or bumped it. Still, the comradery and laughter around the gunroom table was infectious and seemed like a good medicine.

Greene rose to his feet. "Gentlemen! We are honored to have the captain join us tonight, especially since we have him to thank for the feast we are about to enjoy!"

Old Smoot, the gunroom steward, led the procession, carrying a tray with one of the huge hams Alfred had purchased for the gunroom on Brewer's orders. His mates followed, bearing trays loaded with a ragout of beef, stewed potatoes, carrots, peas, fresh baked bread with butter, and pudding. Applause and shouts of approbation resounded as the feast was placed on the table before them. Brewer looked back toward the door and saw Alfred standing in the background. He had directed Alfred to rest for a couple days to allow the ache in his head to subside, but apparently to no avail. Still, Brewer could not be angry with him; he knew how it felt to need to do something.

Greene claimed the honor of carving the ham, and he placed a huge slab on Brewer's plate. Brewer protested gently, but Greene just as gently reminded him that he was a guest in his officers' gunroom.

"I hear and obey, then!" Brewer said. He held out his plate. "Doctor, would you be so kind as to scoop me out a helping of those stewed potatoes? Thank you. And you, Mr. Sweeney, may I trouble you for some of those lovely peas? Thank you. To your good health, gentlemen!" He set his plate down and dug in.

After the party was over, Brewer met privately in his cabin with Greene, Tyler, and the Doctor. Mac was also there, still acting as the doctor's watchdog.

The four took their seats around the table, with Mac taking up his usual position just inside the cabin door.

"Gentlemen," Brewer said, bringing the meeting to order, "what have we learned from our captives?"

Greene leaned forward and began. "The schooner we sank was indeed commanded by Roberto Cofresi, Captain. Several of our prisoners claimed he was one of the pirates who jumped over the side and swam for shore. They also gave us a physical description of Cofresi, which matched the pirate Alfred was last seen fighting."

"Ah!" Brewer remembered vividly the self-possession and skill of the man; so that had been Cofresi! He felt embarrassed at how poorly he had fought against the pirate chieftain. *One thing's for sure,* he promised himself, *the moment I'm recovered from this arm wound, I'm going to ask Alfred for private tutorials!*

"Captain," Greene said, "we do have some good news. One of the prisoners mentioned a communication from El Diabolito."

Brewer reacted without thinking, leaning towards the speaker, and winced at the stabbing pain in his arm. Mac took a step from the door, but Dr. Spinelli stopped him with a raised hand. The Captain adjusted slightly in his seat, his breathing slowly returning to normal.

"I must remember," he said slowly, "not to do *that* again. Now then, Mr. Greene, tell me about the communication."

"One of the prisoners claimed they received a letter from El Diabolito," Greene said, "promising a huge payday."

"When? Where?" Brewer demanded.

"He refused to say, Captain."

Brewer frowned and looked at the table as he digested this latest intelligence.

"He might be making the whole thing up, sir," Tyler said, "hoping to buy some leniency from you and mislead you at the same time."

Brewer looked at the young lieutenant and considered his words. Finally he spoke. "You may be quite correct, Mr.

Tyler. However, it is too good a lead to pass up. We shall have to judge his words carefully. Mr. Greene, send for the prisoner."

Within minutes the cabin door opened, and a short, stocky pirate in shackles was led in and settled in a chair opposite the captain, with Mac behind him. Brewer was surprised to see none of the characteristics of a native of the Caribbean about him; this man had fair skin and blonde hair.

"I am Captain Brewer," he said. "What is your name?"

"Why do you wish to know my name?" the pirate asked.

"I usually like to know who it is I am taking to their hanging."

The pirate smiled. "If that were the only reason, I should not be here. What is it you want?"

"For starters, you can tell me your name."

The pirate studied Brewer for a moment, then shrugged.

"My name is Charles Gibbs."

"And where are you from, Mr. Gibbs?"

The pirate's eyes narrowed. "And why do you wish to know that, Captain?"

"For one, you don't look like you're from around here. There is also an accent to your speech that reminds me of a man I once met."

"And who would that be, Captain?"

"An American by the name of John Adams."

Gibbs stared at the captain. "A great hero of our revolution, Captain, who was also our president."

"Our?"

"I am from Connecticut."

"Is that one of the United States?"

Gibbs nodded. "It is in the region of the country known as New England."

"Indeed, I met Adams in Boston."

"Now then," Gibbs said, "what can I do for you, Captain?"

"You can tell me about the letter from El Diabolito."

Gibbs' eyes sparkled as though he thought he had a bargaining chip in his hands. "Why should I do that?"

Brewer shrugged. "You probably shouldn't. Mr. Greene, take this pirate back to the rest of his ilk. We make Port Royal in three days, Mr. Gibbs. You die in four."

Mac grabbed the pirate from behind and lifted him out of the chair.

"Here now!" Gibbs protested. "Just a minute, Captain!"

Brewer signaled for Mac to wait. "Yes, Mr. Gibbs?"

"I might know something about the letter, Captain, but you have to let me go free."

"I cannot do that, but I will tell the admiral everything you tell me came from you."

Gibbs thought it over and jerked his head. "Okay. You win."

"Put him down, Mac," Brewer said. Mac planted the pirate back in the chair. "Now, Mr. Gibbs, this is your one chance to tell me *everything* about that letter."

Gibbs looked around at the grim faces, then began. "Not quite a week ago now, a ship pulled in with a letter addressed to our captain. He took it into his rooms to read it privately. Later, he called a council. He announced that news had come from El Diabolito of a huge treasure ripe for the taking, the likes of which has not been seen since the Spanish treasure convoys of a hundred years ago."

"Yes?" Brewer said. "And how was this treasure to be taken?"

The pirate hesitated, and Mac kicked the back of his chair. Gibbs glared over his shoulder before addressing Brewer again.

"I don't know, and that's the truth. The letter said that we should sail for port within a week or ten days to receive instructions on the location and timing of the attack." Gibbs paused to see if that was sufficient; the hard looks he received made it clear it was not. He took a deep breath before continuing. "Cofresi told us we had two days to consider the offer. He said to weigh the gain against the cost. Anyway, we met together again at the appointed time and voted to go. The trouble was space; our schooner was very fast but also quite small. You caught us trying to get a larger ship."

Brewer shared a quick glance with Greene and Tyler. There was still one piece of information missing. Brewer nodded to Greene.

"What port were you to sail to?" Greene said.

The pirate just looked at him.

"The port!" Greene raised his voice in demand.

Gibbs looked around with hooded eyes and sighed in defeat.

"Caracas."

Brewer had Mac return Gibbs to the prisoners.

"Well," he said, "now we have something to go on."

Greene shook his head in disgust. "El Diabolito is in Caracas, waiting to give detailed information on this attack to Cofresi and whoever else he asked for help, while here we are, nearly 500 miles north and heading in the wrong direction."

"Not for long," Brewer said. "Not if I can help it. Mr. Tyler, call the hands to put on all sail. I want to be in Port Royal as soon as possible."

"Aye, sir," Tyler said, and left the cabin in a hurry.

"But, sir," Greene asked, "won't Admiral Hornblower send us right back to Puerto Rico, especially since Cofresi escaped back to the island?"

Brewer smiled. "What makes you think Cofresi will still be on Puerto Rico? Don't you see, Benjamin? Look, if you were Cofresi, what would you be doing right now?"

Greene considered. "I suppose I'd be trying to put together another crew."

Brewer nodded agreement. "And you'd be looking for another ship, right? For what purpose?"

Brewer sat back and watched the concentration and conflicting emotions cross his friend's face, one hard on the other, and he smiled when at last he saw realization dawn.

"To get to Caracas so I don't miss out on the big attack!"

"Yes!" Brewer cried. "And *that* is why the admiral will let us go to Caracas."

CHAPTER 15

HMS *Revenge* entered the harbor at Port Royal at two bells of the forenoon watch and made her way slowly to her berth. No sooner had she dropped anchor than orders were heard to ready the captain's gig. The boat was quickly lowered, and Brewer was on his way ashore. He stepped quickly up the street to the admiral's house, driven by a sense of urgency fed by his desire not to allow El Diabolito to escape him again. He winced inwardly when he realized that his knock on the door was more pound than knock, but it got the desired result when Lieutenant Phillips opened the door.

"Commander!" he said. "We've just now received word that HMS *Revenge* was in port. To what do we owe the honor?"

"I must see the admiral, Lieutenant," Brewer said.

"He is currently away, sir, meeting the governor. He may not return for hours."

"I shall wait. My business with the admiral is urgent, Mr. Phillips; I must see him at his earliest opportunity."

"Very well, Commander," Phillips said. "Would you care to wait in the admiral's study?"

"Thank you." Brewer handed Phillips the reports he had brought with him and followed the lieutenant to a room rather smaller and more personal than the office where he had previously met with the admiral. The rectangular room's opposite wall was dominated by three large windows of twenty panes each. The wall to the right had a small fireplace off-center with a small desk beside it, and on the wall over the desk was a large portrait of Lady Barbara Hornblower. On the opposite side of the room was a small settee and a painting of a seventy-four gun ship of the line under full sail.

"I shall have some refreshment brought to you, Commander," Phillips said, and he closed the door behind him.

Brewer looked around, then strolled over to admire the portrait of Lady Barbara. He judged it a very good likeness of her; the pose was of her standing in a garden in a beautiful pink gown and matching bonnet. It made him wish to have a portrait done of Elizabeth one day.

That was when the bust in the corner beside the desk caught his eye.

It was the bust of Bonaparte that Brewer had seen and admired in the admiral's office. He wondered for a moment what made Hornblower move the bust in here, out of sight of those whose official duties brought them to his office. Was Hornblower like him, reluctant to talk about the Corsican?

Brewer studied the bust. He was struck again how alive the eyes seemed, how full of his spirit, almost like the man himself; a man might almost expect the marble mouth to open and speak.

A knock at the door heralded the arrival of the steward with the refreshments. The door opened and closed, and a tray was set down on the table. Brewer ignored it all.

"You really miss the old boy, don't you?"

Brewer spun at the unexpected voice.

"Gerard!" Brewer said. "Good to see you, old fellow!"

Brewer came over and shook his friend's hand heartily. He noted that Gerard had brought a decanter of what looked to be Madeira and three glasses. "Doubling as a steward now, are you?"

Gerard flashed one of his fabulous smiles as he poured them each a drink. That smile reminded Brewer of the first time he'd met Gerard—when he came aboard *Agamemnon* with Captain Bush just prior to their departure for St. Helena. Gerard had walked up to him that night in the wardroom and shook his hand warmly with that same dazzling smile.

Gerard handed him his drink and nodded toward the bust.

"Miss him?"

Brewer shrugged. "I suppose so, at times. You don't meet a personality like that and then just forget him."

Gerard eyed the bust with a knowing look and nodded his agreement.

"Did you ever get to meet him?" Brewer asked.

"Once," Gerard said. "Do you remember when the admiral allowed Boney to accompany him on an inspection of *Agamemnon*? Word flew around the ship after Boney was spotted approaching with the admiral; how could you miss him in that hat? He came on board and followed the admiral around on his inspection, and then we went out to sea for drills. Boney got to see our men drill aloft and also gunnery practice. Were you aware, William, that Boney started out as an artillery officer?"

Brewer shook his head. "I did not know that."

"Nor did I, until he told me. That explained why our gun drills were of special interest to him. The admiral translated for me, and Boney asked question after question about our guns and how we use them. Good questions, too. I realized right away that this man knew what he was talking about. He told me that one of his army 'broadsides', as it were, was equal to about ten *Agamemnons* lined up end to end! I asked him which he preferred, army artillery or navy. He laughed and said army, without question—the targets were not moving!"

Both officers laughed, then they stood silently, staring at the bust, each lost in his own thoughts, feeling fortunate to have known such a person as Napoleon Bonaparte.

"I took the liberty of sending a note to the admiral stating that he must return immediately for urgent business. No, no, don't worry, William; believe me, the admiral will be thankful when he arrives," Gerard said. He paused to refill their drinks. "Now, what brings you home, and in such a hurry?"

Brewer briefly described the sinking of the pirate schooner and the retaking of the *Amsterdam*. He had just begun to tell Gerard about the interrogation when the door opened and the admiral came in.

"You will pardon my interruption, gentlemen, I'm sure," Hornblower said. "Mr. Gerard, thank you for your timely note. Mr. Brewer, what do you have for me? I saw Mr. Phillips when I came in. He showed me your reports, but I want to hear it from you. I understand you fought a battle against some pirates. Why don't you start there?" He settled himself comfortably.

"Very well, my lord," Brewer said, and he retold the story he had related to Gerard only minutes before of the sinking of the pirate schooner and the retaking of the Dutch flute. Then he told of his interrogation of the pirate Gibbs and the revelation of the letter from El Diabolito.

"And what of Cofresi himself?" Hornblower asked.

"Witnesses say he was one of those who escaped the flute by jumping over the side and swimming ashore, my lord."

The Admiral nodded. "As soon as *Revenge* is provisioned, your orders are to sail back to Puerto Rico and resume your search. Cofresi must be captured or killed."

Brewer lowered his eyes while his mind raced. He thought perhaps that the admiral would take this position; now he had to choose his words with great care if he did not want to be sitting on his heels off Puerto Rico while Diabolito and Cofresi were meeting in Caracas.

"Excuse me, my lord?" he said.

Hornblower looked up, surprised. "Well?" he growled.

"Begging your pardon, my lord, but Gibbs told us that Cofresi was on his way to Caracas. His men had voted to go, so he has no choice. I believe he will get a ship for his depleted ranks and head south to get in on that big attack. Sir, I request permission to sail for Caracas to look for Cofresi there."

Hornblower opened his mouth and closed it again without saying anything beyond a muffled "Ha-hm!" He rose and began to pace. Both men knew enough to sit quietly and allow their chief the uninterrupted time he needed to convince himself that Brewer's request had merit.

Back and forth, back and forth paced Hornblower, his chin planted on his breast and his brows furled in concentration as his mind processed scenario after scenario. Should he allow Brewer to head south? Or should he send Brewer back on patrol and send *Clorinda* to Caracas? He thought about his available forces and how they were currently deployed, and he frowned. He gazed at the clock, acutely aware that time was of the essence, or whomever he sent to Caracas would find the nest empty and the vultures flown. *Decide! You must decide!*

Hornblower ceased his pacing and made his way back to his desk. He paused to gaze at his wife's portrait, wishing not for the first time that she were here. He sat at his desk and asked Mr. Gerard to refill their glasses and pour one for him. He made a note at his desk before turning to his two officers.

"Mr. Brewer," he said, "I have considered your request, and I believe someone must go to Caracas to investigate your information. My problem is, whom do I send? *Clorinda* is just completing some repairs, and we would have to move heaven and earth to have her ready to sail within two or three days. As you know, time is of the essence. Can *Revenge* be ready to sail on the morning tide?"

"Yes, my lord."

"Very good. Your orders are to sail for Caracas. Once there, you are ordered to capture or kill the pirate Roberto Cofresi. You are also ordered to discover all you can regarding the pirate El Diabolito."

"Thank you, my lord," Brewer said.

"Mr. Gerard will have your orders to you before you sail," Hornblower said, sitting back in his chair and tasting his drink for the first time. "I will of course be reading your reports over the next few days, but is there anything else you wished to discuss with me?"

"There is one matter I would like your advice on, my lord," Brewer said as he set his glass down. "It seems someone on board my ship tried to murder my senior midshipman."

"What?!?"

Both Hornblower and Gerard were shocked by Brewer's revelation.

"We had a seaman killed by a fall from aloft during high winds," Brewer explained. "Mr. Reed, the senior midshipman, was supervising two men who were cleaning the deck afterward when a midshipman's dirk struck the decking not twelve inches behind him. He called the two hands he was supervising as witnesses that it was still vibrating from impacting the deck. Nobody aloft admitted the dirk was theirs. He spoke to Mr. Greene, who had him write out a report of the incident. That report, my lord, has been forwarded to you along with my own."

"If the knife had been dropped by accident, it would have been claimed, " Gerard said. "What have you learned in your investigation? Have you apprehended the scoundrel yet?"

"No," Brewer said. "Mr. Greene has interviewed everyone who was aloft at the time, but nobody saw what happened. For now, Mr. Reed is sleeping in a spare cabin in the gunroom, and I have assigned a hand to stay with him at all times—a second set of eyes to watch out for any more attempts on Reed's life. So far, nothing else has happened, but we are no closer to finding who did this than the day it happened."

Hornblower looked thoughtful as he leaned back in his chair. "So, you've had a death and a near death. William, I have to ask: are you sure the two events are not related?"

Brewer frowned. "My lord, to my knowledge there is nothing to connect these two deaths. It is true that the time between them is rather close, but I have no reason to believe they are related. The hand who fell was rated as able seaman and an experienced topman, but there was a sudden and sharp gust of wind right before she fell."

Brewer hoped they wouldn't catch the pronoun, but they did. Both officers' heads snapped up at it. Gerard spoke first.

"Excuse me, Commander, but did you say *she?*"

"Aye," Brewer said with a sigh. "Seaman Grant was indeed a woman. I have submitted the doctor's report as well, my lord."

Hornblower did not pursue the issue, and Brewer breathed a silent sigh of relief.

"The normal procedure in a case like this," the Admiral said, "is to transfer Reed off *Revenge* for his own safety. But, if I do that, it will leave you with only the youngster Short and the malcontent Simmons, if I recall correctly."

"That is so, my lord."

Hornblower shook his head ruefully. "I have no one available of comparable skill to give you to replace him, Mr. Brewer. Mr. Reed will have to stay aboard *Revenge*. I want you to redouble your efforts to catch the perpetrator. Perhaps we can throw a rock in the waters, so to speak, and see what the ripples reveal. Well, as soon as you have your orders, you may proceed. Report as you are able."

Hornblower picked up his glass and drank, and Brewer realized the meeting was over. Gerard rose.

"If you'll excuse me, my lord, I'll get the Commander's orders ready for your signature." He turned to his friend. "Good to see you again, William. Come home safely."

Brewer watched his friend go before turning back to see the Admiral gazing at his wife's portrait on the wall.

"A fine likeness, my lord," he said.

"Yes," Hornblower agreed. "She sent it to me for Christmas last year. I am hoping to talk her into coming out here, but so far she has resisted my suggestions." Hornblower turned to him and smiled. "She reminded me that the last time she was on a boat to the Caribbean, she was captured by the Spanish and held captive for a year. She says she doesn't want to go through that again."

Brewer chuckled and nodded at the bust. "I see you've moved him."

"Yes." Hornblower sighed and looked at the bust. "When it was in my office, it naturally generated a great many questions, not to mention the occasional remark about my rumored friendship with the French Tyrant. I will confess to you privately, William, that it was very difficult for me to hold my tongue on more than one occasion."

Brewer sighed. "I know what you mean, my lord."

Hornblower reflected that Brewer was the one man besides the Corsican himself who would understand his reasoning, and the floodgates opened. "I consider my friendship with Napoleon Bonaparte to be a private matter, something I cherish and don't like to share with anyone. You and I may speak of it sometimes, because you were there and experienced it with me, as Barbara and Bush did, though not to your extent. I know what was involved in that friendship, and I will not have my patriotism over it called into question by those who have no idea what went on." Hornblower closed his mouth, embarrassed by his own garrulity.

"I couldn't have said it better, my lord," Brewer said.

The Admiral looked at him warmly. "Thank you, William," he said quietly, then he sat straight and said "Ha-hm!" Brewer realized the Admiral was back in charge.

"Mr. Gerard will have your orders, Commander. Good luck."

"Thank you, my lord." Brewer stood to attention and left the room.

He made his way to Gerard's office and found him putting the finishing touches on the orders.

"Wait here while I get the Admiral to sign these," he said. Brewer sat in the small office until his friend returned. "Here," Gerard said as he handed Brewer his packet of orders. "They say exactly what the admiral told you. You are to take *Revenge* to Caracas and see what you can find. Report when you can."

"Thank-you, Gerard," Brewer said. The two men shook hands.

"Good hunting," Gerard said, as his friend walked out of the office.

Captain William Brewer sat in his sea cabin on board HMS *Revenge*, sipping Alfred's good coffee and thinking about his mission. His ship was sailing roughly SSE, on course for Caracas. He estimated a week at the outside for the journey; he only hoped he would not be too late.

Brewer smiled with a touch of pride as he thought of how quickly Lieutenant Greene and the crew had made *Revenge* ready for sea. Gibbs and the rest of the pirates had been transferred ashore before he returned. Part of him wished he could have stayed to watch the pirates hung, but his present mission was far too important for him to delay even one day. He thought over Hornblower's parting words at Port Royal.

"Commander," the Admiral had said, "I am taking a great risk in sending you. Columbia has declared its independence from Spain, and there are rumors that the Spanish will fight to retain the territory. Don't do anything that would cause an incident."

Brewer again made a mental note not to accuse the new nation of being a haven for pirates. He rose from his seat and walked to his cabin door. He opened it and stuck his head out.

"Pass the word for the doctor!" he called.

"Aye, sir!" came the anonymous reply.

"Alfred!"

The quiet-moving servant presented himself. "Sir?"

"The Doctor will be arriving momentarily. Another cup for coffee, if you please."

"Very good, sir."

Brewer got out his chess set and began setting up the pieces, reflecting how fortunate he was to have Dr. Spinelli aboard. The good doctor gave him a sounding board, an independent ear, as it were, to talk to when he needed to talk. Chess was an additional benefit, and one he hoped to exploit to pass the time on their journey south.

The doctor arrived and sat at his place. Alfred brought the coffee, and the two men went to battle once again.

"What?" the doctor said. "No witty comment? No welcome? No 'How have you been, my dear Doctor?' You just expect me to sit down and move?"

"I gave you coffee," Brewer said as he moved his queen's knight out. "What more do you want?"

"A little appreciation would be nice," the doctor said as he countered with a pawn. "I'm beginning to feel abused."

Brewer advanced a pawn of his own. "I wouldn't doubt it, after the way you've been playing lately."

"Very funny," Spinelli said. He took his captain's knight with a bishop. "So, Captain, to what do I owe the honor?"

Brewer ignored the question as he moved his other knight.

"I see," Spinelli muttered. He moved another pawn. "One of those, is it?"

"One of what, Doctor?" Pawn advances.

"You're bored again, Captain, is that it?" Pawn takes pawn.

"What makes you say that?" Knight takes pawn.

"Am I wrong?" Bishop takes knight. "Check."

Brewer sighed. "No," he said as he moved his king, "you are not."

"Ah," Spinelli moved his knight. "Check. I thought that might be the case."

Brewer moved his king again. "I am having trouble with the waiting, Adam. I fear that by the time we get to Caracas, all we shall find will be an empty harbor."

Spinelli moved his queen. "I take it the admiral was not entirely sanguine about sending his newest commander south to a new nation looking for pirates?"

Brewer's hesitation told the doctor he was right on target. "I wouldn't worry about it, William. If Hornblower didn't think you were ready for the mission, we'd be heading for Puerto Rico at this very moment. Did the admiral mention anything else?"

Brewer moved a rook. "We talked about the attempt on Mr. Reed. The admiral wanted to transfer him off *Revenge*, but he had no one available to replace him. Have you kept your eye on Reed?"

"Yes," Spinelli moved his queen again. "There have been no other actions against him, and he is seeing to his duties with his customary competence. What did the admiral have to say?"

"He wanted me to step up the investigation." Brewer's rook moved almost the length of the board and took a pawn. "He likened it to tossing a stone into a lake and seeing what the ripples turned up."

"An apt metaphor," Spinelli observed. He moved a pawn. "And just what—or who—is the rock you are going to throw into our pleasant little pond?"

"My 'rock,' Doctor, as you so astutely put it, is Lieutenant Greene," Brewer moved his queen across the board and looked up with a smile. "Checkmate."

Lieutenant Greene was at that moment sitting at the table in the gunroom with various papers filled with his notes on the investigation spread out in front of him. He was waiting for his appointment to arrive, and he filled the time by refreshing his memory on the facts and assumptions. Whoever had thrown the knife had to have been almost directly above Reed, because all reports stated the dirk had pierced the deck at a nearly perpendicular angle. The ship was rolling at the time, but only very slightly. But was the knife meant to do for Reed, or to warn him off of some action?

A knock interrupted his thinking.

"Excuse me, sir," a hand said, standing in the doorway. "You wanted to see me, sir?"

"Yes, come in. I'm sorry; you appear to be listed in the ship's books simply as "Scar". Do you have another name?"

Scar's fingers went to the scar on his face. "Well, if I did, sir, I've long forgotten it."

"Well," said Greene, "I'm looking into the attempt to kill Mr. Reed, and I'm looking at who was above him on the yardarms that day. I understand you were stationed on the starboard side that day, is that correct?"

"That's correct, sir. On the mainsail yardarm."

"I see. And you were also in the tops when seaman Grant fell, weren't you?"

Scar was surprised by this question. "Why, yes, sir," he answered slowly. "Right next to 'im, in fact."

Now Greene looked surprised. "Really? Right next to Grant? Did you see him fall?"

"Well, no, sir," Scar tried to look sheepish. "I was trying not to fall meself."

"Of course," Greene said. "Did you notice anything unusual about Grant before he fell?"

"Unusual? What do you mean, sir?"

"Did Grant seem normal? Distracted? Upset?"

"Ah, nothing unusual, Lieutenant. Just regular Grant."

Greene picked up one of his notes and searched for something. Scar found it quite disconcerting.

"And did you see Grant fall?" Greene asked without looking up.

"No, sir. As I said, I was busy at the moment, trying not to fall meself."

"Yes, that's right. Very well, Scar, you are dismissed. If you think of anything else, report it to me immediately."

"Aye, sir." Scar got up to go. He stopped at the doorway and turned.

"Sir, may I ask why we're going over all this again?"

Greene sighed and picked up another paper.

"The admiral thinks the two occurrences, on the same ship and so close together, make quite a coincidence," Greene said, again without looking up from his papers. "He wants us to investigate whether the two may be related somehow."

"I see. Thank you, sir." Scar said and left.

Mr. Greene looked at the empty doorway long and hard.

Scar was not in a happy mood as he made his way forward. He'd thought he had matters well in hand with this Reed business. True, the job was not technically completed yet, but it was only a matter of time until the right moment arrived and opportunity presented itself, even with all the extra precautions the captain had initiated. But now, the whole thing could be put through the ringer, and him with it! Scar silently cursed his luck. Why did Grant have to notice the dirk hanging at his side in the first place? After that, there was no way he could have Grant around afterward to say what he had seen, was there? That gust of wind had simply been too good an opportunity to pass up.

He sat down at his mess table to think. He got up and got his ration of grog and brought it back to the table while he went over his options. He could stay silent; just sit back and see where the first lieutenant's investigation led him. He could always create a little diversion later to blow smoke in the good lieutenant's eyes. Then he could finish the job, collect his pay and quit the ship the first chance he got. Not a bad idea, that, only Reed had been on his guard since his first try, and with that Kelly watching his back all the time, chances were hard to come by.

Scar took a gulp and wiped his mouth on his sleeve. So what if they ask questions? Let them ask till they use up all the wind from the sails, for all the good it will do them. There was no way they could ever connect what happened to Grant with—*Wait a minute,* he thought suddenly. *Wait just a bloomin' minute!*

Simmons! That skunk Simmons! Scar drained the remainder of his grog in one long swallow and slammed his tankard down on the table. His eyes were hooded in a simmering rage as he mulled over the implications.

Everything depended on what Simmons would do when he heard that the first lieutenant was looking to connect Grant's death to the attack on Reed. The skunk might run to turn him in for both crimes, hoping to have his part in the Reed incident either overlooked or forgiven. Or he might try to force Scar to finish the job on Reed by threatening to tell Mr. Greene who had killed Grant. The easiest way to shut Simmons up would be to kill him, but then Scar would not get paid. No, he needed Simmons alive, at least for now. Scar arose and headed for the deck. He would watch Simmons until he saw the chance to get him alone, then he would make that skunk understand that he was no one to be trifled with.

Scar mounted the deck and went forward to lean quietly against the railing. Dusk was falling, and if Mr. Simmons followed his usual routine, he should come up on deck and climb into the foretop to dream away the evening hours in relative solitude. Well, Scar decided, tonight he won't be so alone.

Scar squatted behind the shelter of a 12-pounder and waited. Simmons was dangerous to him now, and he had to be put in his place quickly. One word from Simmons to Greene about Grant might be enough to put Scar's head in the noose. Of course, Scar could take Simmons with him; all he had to do was spill the beans about Simmons hiring him to kill Reed. Scar grunted. It would be small consolation for getting his neck stretched.

He looked down the deck through the fading light and saw Mr. Reed directing some hands who were working with rope. He sighed, thinking of what he could do with the amount of money Simmons had put on the boy's head. Scar's eyes narrowed at the thought of it. It was only dumb luck that had saved him that first time, and, quite honestly, a second opportunity had simply never presented itself. The biggest reason for that was easy to identify—Kelly. Even now, the tar stood behind Reed, his eyes scanning the deck and the rigging above for threats. Kelly was at his job every moment Reed was on deck. Scar felt a grudging admiration for the man's devotion and skills, even if he was proving to be a major pain in the backside.

Scar was about to give up his vigil for the night when he suddenly found his patience rewarded. Simmons emerged from the forecastle stairs. He stepped up on the deck and paused. Scar followed his eyes and saw Simmons staring at Reed. Scar smiled. *Good,* he thought. *He still wants Reed dead. That helps me.*

Simmons shook his head in disgust before making his way to the shrouds and beginning his ascent. Scar waited until he was long gone before coming out of his hiding place. He gazed at the shrouds for several moments before following skyward. He would come at Simmons from behind, as he had before.

Noah Simmons settled into his spot in the tops and tried to enjoy the wind on his face. This was the only place where he could relax just a little and try to order his thoughts. Right now, the main consideration was getting off this ship at the first foreign port they encountered. He was convinced now that Scar would never finish his job and quite possibly might turn on him to demand payment anyway. The murdering swine had already proved himself by killing Grant in cold blood to hide his tracks. Simmons had no doubt he would not hesitate to do so again.

An all too familiar voice told him he was no longer alone.

"Evenin'," it said. "Where's me money?"

"For what? Like I said before, he's not dead yet."

"Yea, well, things have changed all of a sudden, and I decided that you're going to pay me anyways."

Simmons chuckled. "Of course things have changed, you idiot. And that is exactly why you *won't* be getting paid."

"You know about that, then?"

"Of course. Do you think you're the only one Mr. Greene questioned? News travels fast on a ship this size, mate. From now on, you're going to mind your manners. If you manage to finish the job, we can talk."

Simmons felt a knife against his throat.

"Don't get so high-and-mighty with me, chum. I can easily slit your throat and toss you overboard. From this height, dark like it is, they might not even hear you fall."

Simmons was a coward, but his terror gave him speed and strength. He grabbed Scar's wrist and twisted the blade away from his throat. He ducked and got his throat out of the way, then smashed the seaman's wrist into the mast. Scar screamed but managed to hold on to the knife. Both men got on their feet, and Simmons tried to keep the mast between them. Scar switched the knife to his right hand and move to his right to get at his foe. Simmons followed suit quickly just as Scar made a lunge at him and missed by a hair's breadth.

Just as Simmons dodged the strike, a strong gust of wind came out of nowhere and threw him right at his attacker. Fortunately, Simmons strategy came to his rescue: he slammed into the mast and clung for dear life. Scar, however, was not so lucky. The strong gust caught him off balance after his attack, blowing the seaman right off the top and into a freefall to the deck below. He landed on the forward 12-pounder starboard, breaking his back and several ribs on impact before bouncing off and landing on the deck.

Simmons pushed himself off the mast and back onto the foretop. He made it to the rail and looked below. His legs turned to rubber and he sank onto the foretop.

Scar's scream, followed by the loud crack of his back breaking on the gun, was heard all over the deck. Mr. Reed was first on the scene and quickly ascertained that the fallen man was indeed dead. He moved to prevent anyone from touching the body. He looked up and saw Simmons looking down from the foretop with a terrified look on his face. Reed was officer of the watch, so he took control.

"Pass the word for the captain," he said. "Also Mr. Greene and the doctor. Nobody touches anything until they get the okay." He looked around. "Kelly! Mr. Simmons is in the foretop. Take Doby and bring him and anyone else you find up there down, and keep them secluded until we can question them."

"Yes, Mr. Reed."

Within moments, the Captain and Lieutenant Greene arrived. Mr. Reed briefed them. Just then, Kelly and Doby returned to the deck with Mr. Simmons. Simmons went straight to the captain and pointed at the body on the deck.

"It were him, sir!" Simmons said. "He told me the whole thing in the tops, sir! It were him the whole time!"

"Whoa, there, Mr. Simmons!" Brewer said. Mac stepped forward to protect his captain, but Brewer motioned him back. "What are you talking about?"

Simmons pointed to the knife on the deck by the dead man's hand. "He came up behind me in the foretop, sir, and laid that knife to my throat. Said he killed Grant and tried to kill Mr. Reed! Said he'd pin the whole thing on me if I didn't pay him off and help him get off the ship!"

"Mr. Greene," Brewer said, "please take Mr. Simmons to the gunroom and hold him in isolation for the time being. Mac, take him." After they were gone, Brewer surveyed the situation.

Reed looked at Kelly and Doby. "Anyone else up top?"

"No, sir."

Dr. Spinelli arrived and went to the body immediately, checking for a pulse. Finding none, he performed a quick examination. Brewer watched his hands expertly feeling down the spine and then the rib cage before checking the skull and then the arms and legs. He rose and stood with a grim look on his face.

"What happened?" he asked.

Mr. Reed repeated what he'd heard and seen. Spinelli listened without comment and nodded when Reed was through.

"That account is consistent with my preliminary examination, Captain," he said. "The seaman apparently landed on the gun. The spine seems to be not only crushed, but severed, with several ribs driven into the lungs."

Brewer nodded. "Mr. Reed, have the body taken to the sickbay. Have him sewn into his hammock when you are through with him, Adam. Let me know when we can dispose of the body." The two men stepped aside as three men ordered by Reed moved in to lift the body. After they backed away, Brewer spoke softly. "We have one man saying that this was the fellow who killed Grant and tried to kill Reed."

Spinelli sucked in his breath. "Really? Who?"

"Simmons."

The Doctor looked doubtful. "Not exactly who I would call the most reliable witness."

Brewer shrugged. "We'll see where it leads. Right now, Mr. Greene has him in the gunroom until we can question him. I'd like you to be there, Adam."

"I'll be glad to lend an ear. Do you want me to tend to the dead seaman first?"

Brewer thought it over. "Will it make a difference?"

Spinelli shook his head. "A couple of hours won't matter."

"Good," the Captain said, "then let's take care of Simmons first."

"Mr. Short," the Captain called, "follow me. Mr. Reed has the deck."

"Aye aye, sir."

When the threesome arrived at Brewer's cabin, the Captain turned to Mr. Short.

"My compliments to Mr. Greene," he said, "and will he please escort Mr. Simmons to my cabin. You will find him in the gunroom."

"Aye aye, sir!" The midshipman saluted and headed forward.

"Couldn't you have sent him to do that while we were on deck?" the Doctor asked.

Brewer grinned. "If I had, Simmons would have been here waiting for us when we arrived."

"Ah!"

The two men sat down and awaited the arrival of their guest. Spinelli was just about to voice an opinion when the awaited knock was heard at the door.

"Enter!" Brewer said.

The door opened slowly, and Mr. Greene entered, followed by Simmons and McCleary, who closed the door behind him and assumed his usual position of guard. Simmons appeared supremely confident as he took the indicated seat in front of the Captain.

"Mr. Simmons," Brewer began, "I would like you to tell me what happened on the foretop. I know you already gave your report, but I want to hear it firsthand."

"Of course, sir," Simmons said. "I was sitting in the foretop, as I often do when I am off watch in the evening, when this seaman Scar comes up behind me. I didn't even know he was there until he spoke in my ear. He told me he wanted money from me, and he wanted my help getting off this ship."

"And why would he come to you?" Brewer asked.

"I guess he thought I was still on good terms with my father, sir," Simmons said, "and would be able to appeal to him the next time we were in Port Royal."

"I see," Brewer said. "Please continue."

"I told him to go away and leave me alone, sir. That's when I felt the knife on my throat. He tells me to reconsider, if I don't want to end up like Grant. I asked him what happened to Grant, and he says, 'Let's just say that fall wasn't an accident.' I tell him again to go away. That's when he says that maybe I'll believe him after he does Mr. Reed proper this time. I asked him what happened with Reed, and he says that the boy got lucky. I asked again about Grant, and he says that Grant saw the dirk on his hip and wouldn't quit asking questions about it, so when that gust of wind hit, he gave Grant a little shove, as it were."

Simmons sat back in his chair, looking very satisfied with himself. Brewer looked from Greene to Spinelli before looking out the stern windows. Finally, he turned back to Simmons.

"Please continue, Mr. Simmons."

"Well, sir, something made his knife move away from my neck a bit—I don't know if the ship rolled or what, but I took advantage of it and got to my feet. I maneuvered to my right to keep the mast between us. Then the wind blew hard; it threw me up against the mast and knocked Scar off balance."

"I see," Brewer said. "Very well. Mr. Simmons, you will return to the gunroom and write out a report of what you have just told me. *Exactly* what you have just told me, Mr. Simmons. You are dismissed."

Simmons rose, looking a little disappointed at the reception his tale received. He mumbled, "Aye, sir" and knuckled his head before turning to head out the door. Mr. Greene and Mac followed him out.

Brewer turned to the Doctor, still seated and looking intently at his hands.

"Well, Adam? What do you think?"

Spinelli looked up. "Sounds plausible."

"It sounds highly convenient."

"Convenient for whom?"

"Convenient for Simmons."

Brewer related Simmons' abuse of young Mr. Short and the discipline that Mr. Reed had applied. The Doctor's eyebrows rose, but he nodded in agreement.

"Sounds like the blackguard got what he deserved."

Brewer shrugged. "Perhaps, but it gives Simmons a solid motive to want to take revenge on Reed."

"So," Spinelli thought out loud, "you think Simmons hired Scar to kill Reed? What about Grant?"

Brewer frowned. "That part of Simmons' story is probably true. I imagine Scar did tell him about killing Grant, if only to frighten him into paying up. Mr. Greene says that Scar admitted being right next to Grant on the yardarm right before he fell—*she* fell, I mean."

"Hum," Spinelli shook his head. "If you're right, this isn't over yet."

"Oh, I think Reed is safe enough, for now anyway. Simmons is not the type to do his own dirty work. In any case, I'll make sure that Kelly continues his current assignment until we know for sure."

Spinelli rose. "Well, I shall leave that to you. I will go do my exam on the dead seaman and write you a report. You should be able to have the burial by the end of the next watch. I'll let you know for sure."

"Thank you, Doctor."

"Chess later?"

"Of course."

CHAPTER 16

"Let go," Tyler called. The anchor dropped into the waters of the harbor at Caracas a second later.

"Well done, Mr. Tyler," Brewer said.

"Thank you, sir!"

"So, Mr. Greene," Brewer said softly, "now we get to see if our information is correct."

"If we're wrong, Captain," Greene shook his head ruefully, "after all that you went through to convince Admiral Hornblower to allow you to pursue ...."

Brewer grimaced. "Don't remind me." He clenched and unclenched his hands behind his back. "No, Benjamin; the information is correct. It has to be."

The two men walked to the railing and surveyed the harbor. Various fishing boats rocked on the water, but what attracted their attention was a powerful 44-gun frigate at anchor. Brewer called for a glass and studied the ship, then lowered the glass and passed it to Greene.

"What do you think, Benjamin?"

Greene studied the ship for a few moments. "Spanish built, I'd say, sir, but she's not flying any flag. Her gun ports are closed, but I'd venture a guess that a ship that size would carry 18-pounders."

Brewer's face was grim. "I agree. The question is, what's she doing here?"

"Activity on her quarterdeck, sir," Greene added. "We're being studied."

Brewer took the glass back and put it to his eye. He saw a group of officers studying *Revenge.*

"Mr. Reed," he called out, "run up the colors."

"Aye, sir!"

He turned back to Greene. "Maybe they'll be so kind in return."

"Let's hope so, sir."

The answer was not long in coming, but it was not the one they thought they would get. Mr. Short was in his usual place in the mizzen shrouds when he made the announcement.

"Frigate's sending a boat, Captain!"

Brewer turned from where he was in conversation with Mr. Sweeney and Lieutenant Tyler and headed for the rail.

"Have they shown their colors yet, Mr. Short?" Brewer called.

"No colors, sir!"

Brewer put the glass to his eye. "One officer. Looks like an invitation of some sort, I'd say." He handed the glass back to Simmons. "Mr. Greene, make ready to receive our guest."

The young officer came aboard, and Mr. Greene greeted him and brought him over to where his Captain was standing with Mr. Sweeney. Brewer saw the young man was South American, but when he spoke, he had a Spanish accent.

Lieutenant Greene made the introductions. "Captain, may I present Lieutenant Escobar of the Chilean frigate *Valdivia.* Lieutenant, this is Captain William Brewer of His Majesty's Ship *Revenge.*"

Escobar bowed. "It is an honor, *Capitan.* I come with a note to give you." With a flourish he brought a folded paper out from his coat pocket.

Brewer unfolded the note and was surprised to see that it was written in good English. "It seems that Captain Turrado of the *Valdivia* is inviting me to lunch with him and his admiral. They request I come right away with Lieutenant Escobar." He handed the note to Lieutenant Greene and looked back toward Escobar. "Lieutenant, would you please excuse us for a moment?"

Escobar bowed again. "But of course, *Capitan*."

Brewer crossed the quarterdeck with Greene and Sweeney.

"Chilean," Brewer said. He pointed to the note in Greene's hand. "What do you think, Benjamin?"

Greene considered for a moment. "I think they didn't waste any time before wanting to speak to you," he said softly. He handed the note back to Brewer. "I wonder who this unnamed admiral is?"

Brewer shook his head and looked to his sailing master. "Mr. Sweeney?"

Sweeney considered their options, his eyes darting from the Chilean lieutenant to their frigate to the note in his captain's hand. "I think it's usually a bad idea to insult the captain of a 44-gun frigate."

Brewer smiled. He looked at Greene, who nodded his assent as well.

"Very well," Brewer said softly, "it's decided. Benjamin, keep everyone on the ship until I return. If you've not heard from me by the first dog watch, leave immediately and head for Port Royal."

Greene looked distinctly unhappy, but only said, "Your orders will be obeyed, sir."

"One more thing," Brewer said. "Any note from me will have the word 'lieutenant' misspelled in the heading. If you receive anything else, disregard it and head for Port Royal."

Greene met his master's eyes, not liking the need to take such precautions, but he bowed in acknowledgment of his captain's unspoken reasoning. "Aye, sir."

Brewer led the officers back to the waiting Lieutenant Escobar.

"Forgive the delay, Lieutenant," Brewer said. "I shall be delighted to accept your captain's kind invitation. We can leave immediately."

"*Excellente!*" Escobar said. "Shall we go, *Capitan?*"

They rode to the Chilean ship in silence, Brewer seated beside Escobar in the stern sheets. He climbed up to the deck of the frigate and was met immediately by a distinguished-looking officer who looked to be nearly as old as Admiral Hornblower. He bowed to Brewer before offering his hand.

"I am Captain Turrado of the frigate *Valdivia*," he said.

Brewer saluted before accepting the offered hand. "Commander William Brewer, captain of His Majesty's Sloop *Revenge.*"

"It was very kind of you to accept such an abrupt invitation, Commander," Turrado said. "I must apologize for my forwardness, but the Admiral insisted. If you will follow me, I will take you to him."

"Thank you, Captain." Brewer followed the Chilean captain to the door of the great cabin. The guard at the door nodded at the captain's approach and knocked on the door.

"Enter" was heard from inside, and the guard opened the door and stood back, closing it again behind them.

Brewer stepped in and handed his hat to the steward. The admiral stood with his back to them, looking out the stern windows of the frigate. Brewer thought the set of the shoulders looked familiar.

"Sir," Captain Turrado said, "may I present Commander Brewer of the Royal Navy ship *Revenge.*"

The Admiral turned and smiled. "I believe the Commander and I have met."

Brewer nodded. "Lord Cochrane. A pleasure to see you again."

The Chilean captain's eyebrows rose inquiringly, and Cochrane smiled. "The Commander and I met on the island of St. Helena several years ago," he explained, then turned back to Brewer. "Did you know why I visited the island?"

"No, my lord."

"I went there to offer the throne of a united South America to Bonaparte," Cochrane said. He saw the look of shock and disbelief on the Englishman's face and chuckled aloud. "That's the same look old Boney had on his face when I told him of my offer. In fact, he thought me quite mad."

Brewer grinned. "I can well imagine."

"In my own defense, I must say it was not entirely my idea, Commander. It was first suggested to me by Bernardo O'Higgins, then Supreme Director of Chile, when we were fighting for Chilean independence from Spain. We were dining one evening when O'Higgins said he feared for the future of not only Chile but also the other republics that were attempting to break away from the yoke of Spain. Even if they all succeeded in gaining their freedom, what was to stop Spain from returning in a few years with all of its European might and attacking just one of the newly-independent and still weak nations? He feared that if Spain managed to regain a foothold in the continent, many of its former colonies would either collapse from fear of reconquest or else ally themselves with Spain as a vassal state, similar to the arrangement Bonaparte had with the German states during his rule. O'Higgins said what was needed was for every South American state from Chile to Venezuela to unite under a single throne. A single nation of that size and resources would be unassailable by nearly any European nation, and, once organized, would be an economic power that could one day eclipse England. I asked him whom he had in mind to ascend to this throne; the organizational skills alone that would be needed at the outset would be well beyond those of most men. He shrugged and said that perhaps he would see about rescuing Bonaparte from his prison when the time was right. We laughed it off as some sort of pipe dream. Then I had the opportunity to visit St. Helena while I was awaiting a connection to Argentina, so I took the opportunity to speak to Bonaparte about the scheme. He, too, considered it a nothing more than a flight of fancy, but he did say that he had learned not to predict the future. He told me that if circumstances warranted another visit from me in five or ten years, he would receive me."

The men paused as a steward knocked and entered the cabin carrying a tray of refreshments. Each took a glass of wine, and the steward withdrew.

"That sounds like something very much to Bonaparte's liking, my lord," Brewer said sadly. "Too bad we'll never know now how it would have turned out."

Cochrane's hand stopped halfway to his lips. "What do you mean?"

Brewer looked surprised. "Forgive me, my lord, I did not know you were unaware. Bonaparte died last spring. May, I think."

Cochrane hung his head in a moment of mourning. "Do you know the cause?"

"Cancer, I believe, my lord."

Cochrane nodded and raised his glass in a silent toast to their departed adversary. Brewer and Turrado joined him, and then all three drank. The steward entered the room again and whispered something into his admiral's ear.

"Good," Cochrane said, and the servant departed.

"I am told that our meal will be ready momentarily," he said. "In the meantime, Commander, let me say that I was surprised to see a British man-o-war show up in Caracas just now."

"Really?" Brewer said. "Why should that surprise you, my lord?"

"Come now, Commander, there are few reasons which may explain your presence here. You have either heard something or are looking for someone. Which is it?"

"Very well, my lord, I am looking for someone."

"Who, may I ask?"

"The pirate El Diabolito."

"Ah," the Admiral said. "I thought as much."

"Has he been here, my lord?"

"Yes, Commander. In fact, he sailed just yesterday."

Brewer could not believe it! They had missed their quarry by only twenty-four hours!

"Do you know where he has gone, my lord?"

The steward opened the door at that moment and made an announcement in Spanish. Brewer looked to Cochrane for a translation.

"He says our feast is ready," the Admiral said. To Brewer's frustration, Cochrane led the way to the table, all talk of the pirate's whereabouts seemingly forgotten for the moment.

The three men sat down to a meal mostly consisting of dishes Brewer had never seen before. Much of the food was spicy after the Spanish manner, which he was pleasantly surprised to discover was very much to his liking. He noticed that the Admiral had no hesitation in feasting on this 'foreign' fare.

The meal was taken mostly in silence. Brewer could not tell if this was due to some Chilean custom or his questions regarding El Diabolito's whereabouts. When the last of the meal had been consumed, Cochrane sat back in his chair as the stewards cleared the table and brought cigars and brandy for the officers. The Admiral saw Brewer's surprise at the drink and laughed.

"I have not gone totally South American in my tastes, Commander," he said. He waited until the cigars were lit and the brandy poured before he continued.

"Commander, you asked if I knew where your pirate had gone. I must say I do, although I fear I cannot tell you."

Brewer was astounded at this and did nothing to hide his feelings.

"Excuse me, my lord?" he said, his voice betraying his incredulity. "May I ask why in Heaven's name not?"

Cochrane looked at him coolly over his glass. "I advise you not to forget to whom you speak, Commander. But to answer your question, I cannot tell you because El Diabolito is working for me at the moment."

Brewer stared at the Admiral in undisguised shock. "I beg your pardon, my lord?"

Cochrane blew a cloud of smoke at the deck above. "I believe you heard me, Commander. He has been hired to do a job, and to that end, he has been granted a Letter of Marque by my government."

Brewer sat back in his chair. He used the time to consider this new information and also to puff on his excellent cigar. He, too, blew a cloud heavenward before looking at his host.

"With all due respect, Admiral," Brewer said, noting that Cochrane noticed the different term of address, "that hardly matters to His Majesty's government or to its navy. El Diabolito is wanted for piracy, and I intend to take him back to Port Royal for trial and hanging, but that would only happen in the event that I cannot sink him when I find him."

Cochrane waved his cigar. "And you expect to bring him to heels with your one little sloop?"

Brewer smiled. "I seem to recall you did more with less."

Cochrane spread his arms and did a graceful half-bow of surrender.

"Touché, Mr. Brewer," he said. "Still, I must ask you to let it go for now."

Brewer sat forward and shook his head. "That pirate ambushed my ship and killed my men. I will not let that go."

"Very well, Commander." Cochrane rose and pulled a watch from his pocket. He read it, did some calculations in his head, and returned it. "Nearly three hours to sundown; yes, I think we can make it. Commander, if you will please send a note back to your ship, I would like you to join me on a quick trip ashore."

Brewer rose. "And where would we be going, sir?"

Cochrane smiled. "To see if we can find you some answers, Commander."

Brewer was intrigued enough to write the note to Mr. Greene. He remembered to use the code word, and he instructed Greene to sail for Jamaica if he was not back on board by midnight. He signed the note and handed it to Cochrane, who passed it on to Captain Turrado without reading it.

"Captain," he said, "see that this is sent to the British ship at once."

"Yes, Admiral," Turrado nodded to Brewer and left on his errand.

Cochrane gathered his cloak and hat. "If you are ready, Commander?"

The ride to shore was conducted in silence, the only voice being the commands of the coxswain. When they stepped on to the pier, a carriage was waiting for them. Cochrane remained silent as he climbed up into the tram, and Brewer could only follow him and contain his curiosity. Cochrane had said they were going to get him some answers, so Brewer had to sit back and enjoy the ride until they got to the end of the line.

The end of the line turned out to be a mansion on the outskirts of Caracas. The driver pulled up to the front door and Cochrane alit without any preamble. Brewer followed him to the ornate door and waited while the Admiral knocked. A servant appeared, and Cochrane spoke to him in Spanish. The servant stepped back to allow the officers entrance, and Cochrane signaled for Brewer to follow. They were led to what appeared to be a small parlor.

Cochrane turned to Brewer. "I must ask you to remain here for a few minutes. It is necessary to prepare the way. I shall return for you shortly."

Brewer met his gaze. "As you say, my lord."

The door was closed behind him, and Brewer surveyed the room. It was not a big one, but one wall was covered floor to ceiling with books on either side of a fireplace and chimney. Two overstuffed leather chairs stood before the empty fireplace, and the wall opposite was dominated by a large landscape of a lush valley, probably in Spain, Brewer supposed. He stood before it several minutes and admired the artistry.

Soon the door opened, and Admiral Cochrane appeared and motioned him to follow. Brewer picked up his hat and followed his host into the hallway and up a marble staircase to a door at the end of the hall. Cochrane knocked once and opened the door without waiting for a reply. He led the way in, and Brewer followed.

Inside, Brewer noticed the third man in the room standing in front of a large desk. He was small, a full six or eight inches shorter than Brewer's six feet, two inches, and he was thin. He had an intelligent face with a high forehead and dark eyes, and he was dressed in a military full-dress uniform. Brewer nodded a greeting to the man and turned to Cochrane for an explanation.

"Commander," the Admiral said, "allow me to introduce to you Simon Bolivar, President of Gran Columbia."

Brewer saluted the President, who returned the gesture.

"Welcome, Commander Brewer," Bolivar said, in English, to Brewer's great relief. "Admiral Cochrane tells me that you are seeking the man called El Diabolito."

Brewer nodded. "That is correct, Mr. President."

Bolivar indicated his guests should sit on the settee while he took the chair opposite.

"And he also tells me he has asked you to cease your pursuit, at least for the time being, and you have refused."

"That is also correct, Mr. President."

"May I ask you why?"

"He is wanted by the British government for piracy."

"I see," Bolivar said. "Is it also true, as Admiral Cochrane tells me, that he ambushed your ship and killed some of your men?"

Brewer's expression hardened. "Yes, that is true."

"So it is fair to say that you want him more than your government does?"

Brewer remained silent.

Bolivar continued. "Commander, I must join Admiral Cochrane in asking you to forego your pursuit of this criminal."

This was what Brewer had come all this way to hear. "And why should I do that, Mr. President?"

Bolivar looked at Cochrane, who nodded. Bolivar drummed his fingers on the desk, then turned back to Brewer.

"Commander," he said, "I ask that what I am about to tell you be kept in the strictest confidence. I know that you will need to report it to your Admiral Hornblower, but other than that, please tell no one."

"Very well," Brewer said.

"We have received information from our spies in Panama that the Spanish are going to attempt to send one more treasure galleon, perhaps the last one ever, to Spain. It is scheduled to leave Portobello within the next few months. The gold and silver from Manila has already landed at Panama City and is being transported overland by mule train. Our information is that the galleon will carry upwards of five million pesos, Commander, and perhaps many times that. It will also be heavily guarded. The only significant naval forces I have are those belonging to Admiral Cochrane's squadron. So, I have been forced to seek—how shall I put it?—additional aid."

"El Diabolito and his frigate?" Brewer asked.

"Precisely," Bolivar said.

Brewer added slowly, "Along with any help he could bring along."

"Yes."

Cochrane leaned forward, placing his elbows on his knees and his fingertips together. "Commander Brewer, the seizure of this galleon will not only cripple Spain, it will finance revolutions for independence throughout South America for years to come. In any case, El Diabolito and his associates will be operating under a letter of marque issued by President Bolivar. You cannot interfere, not now."

"I have no intention of interfering with your seizure of the galleon, Admiral," Brewer said, as calmly as he could, "but I do intend to track this pirate down and bring him to justice at the earliest possible moment."

"I see," Bolivar said. "Tell me, Commander, would you consent to carry a letter to your Admiral Hornblower for me?"

"Of course, Mr. President."

"Thank you, Commander," Bolivar nodded graciously. "You shall have it before you leave this house." He paused as a servant came in with three glasses of tequila. "Commander, the Admiral here tells me you knew Bonaparte on St. Helena. Is this true?"

"Yes, Mr. President."

"We have something in common, then. In 1804, while I was living in Paris, I attended his coronation at Notre Dame. It was a life-changing event, Commander, let me tell you that. The spectacle, the grandeur, they made an indelible impression. At that moment, I would have given anything to be him. He was my inspiration from that moment forward. His life would be my life. I have dedicated my life to bringing liberty, fraternity, and brotherhood to South America."

Brewer smiled. "I can well understand what you mean when you say that seeing him was a life-changing event. In my capacity as secretary to Governor Hornblower, I was fortunate enough to get to speak to him on several occasions. I would not trade his words or those memories for all the wealth in that galleon you're hunting."

Bolivar rose. "We are of one mind in this, Commander. Now, if you will excuse me, I have a letter to write."

Cochrane and Brewer rose. Bolivar stepped up to the Englishman and shook his hand by way of a personal farewell, and then the admiral led him out of the room and back to the small parlor where Brewer had waited when he first arrived. Cochrane closed the door behind them.

"Admiral," Brewer said, "you might have told me who it was we were coming to see."

"Perhaps," Cochrane replied as he took a seat by the fireplace, "but had you known, you might have refused to come. The President was the only one who might have been able to persuade you to give up your chase, at least for a time."

Brewer said nothing; instead he perused the bookcases, which proved a fruitless and frustrating exercise, as all the titles were in Spanish. Cochrane, too, remained silent, and Brewer decided it was better that way. Eventually the door opened; a servant entered and presented Brewer with a sealed letter address to Admiral Hornblower.

"The President asks that you sail at once for Jamaica with that letter, Commander," Cochrane said as they left the house. "The contents are extremely time-sensitive. Your admiral must receive it at the earliest possible moment."

"I quite understand," Brewer replied. He was silent during the ride back to the pier, as well as on the boat back to *Revenge*. All the while, he could neither escape nor silence a voice in the back of his mind warning him that something was not right.

Brewer went straight to his cabin after returning to his ship. He laid his hat and coat across his bed. He took the letter from President Bolivar from his pocket and put it on his desk, then he sat and slumped backward, staring at the letter, disgusted with himself and the situation. He could not get away from the feeling that he was being played, that this "time-sensitive letter" was nothing more than a ploy to keep him from closing in on El Diabolito. And yet, as a commander, and a new one at that, it was not within his authority to refuse a request from a head of state, and he was sure that Cochrane had made that plain to Bolivar.

He angrily pushed himself to his feet and went to the door of his cabin.

"Pass the word for Mr. Greene!" he called.

He closed the door again and made his way back to the desk and stared at the letter until Mr. Greene arrived.

"Benjamin," Brewer said sourly, "we sail with the morning tide. We will stop at Curacao to take on any water or provisions we need, and then we are to make course for Port Royal."

Greene's brows furled at this unexpected turn of events, even as the obligatory "Yes, sir" sprang from his lips. The tone of his answer roused his captain from his brown study. Brewer said nothing, instead merely pointing at the letter on the desk. Greene picked it up and read the address.

"Admiral Hornblower?" Greene said. "Who is it from?"

Brewer closed his eyes as he massaged the bridge of his nose. "Simon Bolivar, President of Gran Columbia. He has asked that we deliver it to Admiral Hornblower immediately."

"At once,? But what about El Diabolito?"

Brewer frowned. "I am being forced to give up the pursuit, at least for now."

Brewer could see the anger coming over his first lieutenant's face and imagined his own must have looked similar in Bolivar's office. His eyes went from Greene's face to the letter and back again, and he decided his first lieutenant had a right to know the truth.

He rose and went to the stern windows and sat on the couch that ran under them.

"Benjamin, come and sit here, next to me. I have something to tell you that is private in the extreme." Greene sat next to him, shoulder to shoulder, and the two men leaned their heads close together as Brewer related, in as quiet a whisper as he could manage, his adventures since he left *Revenge*. Right up to Bolivar's explanation of the supposed treasure galleon preparing to sail from Portobello in Panama, of the plans to intercept the galleon at sea and use the money to finance revolution throughout South America, and of the fact that they hired the pirate and his frigate to help with the dirty work!

"It was only after I refused Bolivar's request to put off my pursuit of the pirate that the President asked if I would carry a letter to Admiral Hornblower, Benjamin," Brewer said sourly. "I knew I was being manipulated, but there was nothing I could do about it. I pray the Admiral will allow us to go straight for Portobello after we drop off this letter."

"Well," Greene said as the two men stood, "*Revenge* will be ready to sail with the morning tide, sir, whatever the destination."

Brewer smiled and placed his hand on his friend's arm. "I'd never do with you, Benjamin. I could not ask for more in a first lieutenant."

"Thank you, Captain," Greene said. "If you will excuse me, I will begin the preparations for getting under way in the morning."

The Caribbean sun had barely cleared the horizon when Captain Brewer stepped on to the deck of his ship to find his officers already assembled. Salutes were exchanged, and they got down to business. The grim look on their captain's face set the tone.

"Ship is ready to proceed, Captain," Greene said. "All notifications have been made, and the anchor is hove short."

"Well and good," Brewer said. "The sooner we are away from here, the better I like it." He stepped away from the group to cast an eye over the deck and the upper works.

Satisfied that all was indeed in readiness, he said, "Take her out, Mr. Greene."

Greene began bellowing orders into his speaking trumpet. HMS *Revenge* exploded like an overturned anthill. The ship gained steerage way, the bow came around, and the ship began to glide toward the open sea.

HMS *Revenge* cleared the harbor. Once she was in open waters, Lieutenant Greene set her course for Curacao. Sweeney estimated that, maintaining a speed of five to seven knots, they would sight Curacao shortly after sunrise.

Brewer inquired after the water supply.

"We have enough to reach Curacao," Greene said with a dubious look on his face, "but just barely."

"Good enough. Mr. Greene, will you join me for breakfast?"

"Delighted, Captain," Greene said.

"Then let's go. Mr. Tyler, call me if there's anything that needs my attention."

The two men entered the cabin to find the table already set for two.

Brewer pointed to the table. "I did not say you were coming."

Greene looked over the setting and smiled. "It would appear that Alfred knows you better than you think he might, sir."

As the officers were taking their seats, Alfred brought out two steaming platters, each with fried eggs, slabs of ham, and toast on them, and set one before each officer. He went back to the pantry and returned with his familiar silver tray containing two cups of hot coffee and the crock of butter.

"This is the last of the eggs and the butter, sir," Alfred said.

"Good thing we make port in Curacao tomorrow," Brewer said.

Alfred smiled. "Yes, sir."

The two officers dug into their repast with relish.

"You, know, Captain," Greene said between mouthfuls, "all we need to do is to invite the Admiral aboard for dinner. One taste of Alfred's cooking, and he will give you any mission you want!"

"Not on your life!" Brewer said firmly. "The last time I allowed the Admiral anywhere near my prize servant, I lost him! I hope to hang on to Alfred for a long time."

"Oh, quite," Greene said. "I see what you mean."

When the meal was over, and Alfred had cleared the table and poured coffee, Brewer considered his options.

"Benjamin, I don't want to spend one minute more than necessary at Curacao. As soon as possible, arrange for enough stores to get us to Jamaica. See to it that the purser, Alfred, and the wardroom steward, if he needs to, go ashore to do their shopping."

"I shall see to it."

Brewer stood. "The sooner we can deliver our mail, the sooner we can get to Panama. I hope."

CHAPTER 17

The following day, Brewer stepped up onto the windswept deck of HMS *Revenge* just as six bells sounded in the morning watch. The sun was barely over the horizon in the east. The first lieutenant and sailing master were conferring next to the wheel, so he walked over to join them.

"Good morning, gentlemen," he said. The others returned his greetings and Greene said, "We are approaching Willemstad."

Brewer nodded. "Proceed, Mr. Greene."

Greene picked up his speaking trumpet, and tars were sent scurrying to set the correct sails for entering the harbor. Brewer stood back beside Mr. Sweeney and watched as his second-in-command took *Revenge* into the port. He crossed his arms across his chest and nodded in silent approval.

Mr. Sweeney leaned in close. "You've got a good one there, Captain."

Brewer smiled. "And well I know it, Mr. Sweeney."

The purser was sent ashore to arrange for such supplies as they needed to get them back to Jamaica. Brewer himself went ashore briefly to pay his respects to the governor, who turned out to be a thoroughly disagreeable man who seemed to want nothing better than for the British to be off his island.

His men met with more cooperation, and the revictualing of HMS *Revenge* proceeded at a good pace.

But when resupply effort was complete, unexpectedly contrary winds kept them in port for another forty-eight hours. It was a frustrating time for everyone. Shore leave was denied, as Brewer wanted to be ready to sail at the first opportunity, and to prevent unauthorized visits ashore he ordered double watches, instructing Mr. Greene to assign the most vigilant of the sailors.

Midshipman Noah Simmons had not been especially anxious to leave *Revenge* in his personal wake in Curacao. He had not been questioned about Scar or Reed since that last uncomfortable interview with the captain; this meant, he assured himself, that he was well and truly in the clear and could afford to pick the best port in which to disappear. He still wanted to do for the insufferable first midshipman, but not if it meant jeopardizing his own freedom. Still, the completely unreasonable confinement of all hands to the ship annoyed him. Several times he'd made his stealthy way up from the orlop to see if he could arrange a little unauthorized liberty, only to find dauntingly alert hands patrolling the deck.

It was early in the forenoon watch of the third day when they were finally able to make their way to open water.

Hoping to make up as much time as possible, Brewer directed Sweeney to lay on as much sail as possible.

Curacao was only a few hours behind them when a call came from the lookouts.

"Sail ho!"

Lieutenant Tyler was the officer of the deck. "Where away?" he cried as he reached for a glass.

"Two points off the larboard quarter!"

Tyler trained his glass along the indicated bearing, and a small mound of white came into view.

"I've got 'em, Mr. Tyler!" a familiar voice cried from the mizzen shrouds. Tyler looked up to see young Mr. Short with a glass to his eye. "Still hull down!"

"I see that," Tyler called back. "Keep your eye on them." He looked around and spotted the tall midshipmen. "Mr. Simmons! My respects to the captain; please tell him we've sighted a sail off the larboard quarter."

"Mr. Tyler!" It was the lookout again. "I think it's that frigate from Caracas!"

The strange ship was now hull up but didn't seem to be drawing noticeably closer.

"Whoever she is," Tyler murmured, "they don't seem too intent on catching up." He lowered his glass in thought. "He's tailing us."

Brewer appeared on deck and headed straight for Tyler, accepting a glass from the quartermaster along the way. "Report, Mr. Tyler," Brewer said as he put the glass to his eye.

"We sighted that sail just before I called you, sir. Lookout thinks it might be our friend from Caracas."

"The *Valdivia?*" Brewer considered the significance of that. Abruptly, he called for Mr. Sweeney and the first lieutenant, then he directed Tyler to send Mr. Short to the tops as an additional lookout.

When Greene and Sweeney joined him, he announced, "We have a shadow. The lookout thinks it might be the Chilean frigate from Caracas. They're pacing us, making no attempt to overtake us. That leads me to believe that President Bolivar has sent Admiral Cochrane to make sure to take his letter to Jamaica and nowhere else."

"So, what do we do, sir?" Greene asked.

Brewer lowered his glass and snapped it shut in disgust.

"We go to Port Royal, Mr. Greene," he said.

As he turned to go, the lieutenant spoke up again. "Captain? If you've got a minute, there's something I need to discuss with you."

"Very well, Mr. Greene. Is this a conversation we can have here, or do we need to do this in my cabin?"

Greene looked around. "This should be fine, Captain. Perhaps if we stood at lee rail?"

Brewer nodded curtly and lead the way until they were standing apart from all the others.

"Well, Mr. Greene, what is it?"

Greene looked over to where Tyler was watching the other sail, and then he looked back at his captain. "It's about Mr. Tyler, sir. Captain, I think we need to intensify his training somewhat."

Brewer locked eyes with his premier while he considered the request, then he said, "I'd like you and Mr. Sweeney to join me in my cabin."

"Yes, sir."

Brewer left the deck feeling ashamed that he may have overlooked something, but holding in his mind the beginnings of a plan that would set it right. He entered his cabin, and Mac helped him out of his coat and put away his captain's coat and hat.

"Will there be anything else, sir?" the coxswain asked.

"No, Mac, that will be all. Thank you. Alfred!"

The servant appeared. "Sir?"

"Refreshments for three officers, please."

The servant nodded, and silently vanished.

Greene and Sweeney arrived minutes later, and Brewer directed them to the settee under the stern windows. Alfred handed each man a glass of wine and withdrew.

"Mr. Greene," Brewer said, "tell Mr. Sweeney what you told me on deck."

Greene relayed his observations and concerns regarding Mr. Tyler. Sweeney sat back in his seat, sipping his wine and listening without interrupting. When Greene finished, the sailing master looked to his captain.

"Your opinion, Mr. Sweeney?" Brewer asked.

"I agree with the lieutenant," Sweeney said. He leaned forward and rested his elbows on his knees. "Mr. Tyler does well in simple ship maneuvers. I think he needs more work."

Brewer took this all in. "How would you rate Mr. Tyler's navigational abilities?"

"Sir?"

"If I were to walk up to Tyler right now and ask him to figure out our position, could he do it? Would he put us in the Caribbean or the Mediterranean?"

Sweeney chuckled a bit. "I believe he would come up with an answer, Captain, beyond that I am not willing to vouch."

Brewer rose, put down his empty glass, and lead the way back to the deck. There he sent Greene to relieve the second lieutenant and send him along.

"Yes, Mr. Tyler," Brewer said, when he came before him, "I have decided to intensify your training. You've done well on what has been asked of you thus far, but I want you to be able to take command of this ship with confidence, should that become necessary. Don't think it cannot happen! As a second lieutenant in the Med, I was force to take command of my frigate when the captain and first lieutenant were both wounded in a battle with Barbary pirates. Mr. Sweeney will be working with you on your ship handling and navigation. Do you understand?"

"Yes, sir."

"Good." Brewer pulled a watch from his pocket. "It will be noon in less than an hour, Mr. Tyler. I want you to take the noon sighting, and then use that to figure our exact position."

"Our position, sir?"

"Yes, Mr. Tyler. Never fear, Mr. Sweeney will be right beside you if you need some help." Brewer could see the unease in his young lieutenant, and he smiled reassuringly. "Don't worry, Jeremiah, you will not get in trouble if you fail. In fact, you will probably fail many of the first tasks you are given. It's not to mark you a failure, believe me; we do it because we need to know how much you already know. That way, we know what you still need to learn. Do you understand?"

Tyler nodded, obviously still unsure of himself. "I think so, sir."

"Good lad," Brewer said. "Off with you, then. Report to me when you have our position marked."

Tyler saluted and left, Mr. Sweeney hard on his heels. Brewer watched them go, then he walked over to stand by Greene.

"How has Mr. Tyler done on his watches?"

Greene considered for a moment. "Fine, as far as I know. I have never relieved him and found the ship in anything less than pristine order."

"Good," Brewer said. "Hopefully, he'll pick things up as fast as Mr. Phillips did."

The ship's bell had just tolled three bells of the afternoon watch when Captain Brewer saw Lieutenant Tyler and Mr. Sweeney standing by the wheel in deep conversation. He avoided them, so as not to disrupt the lesson. He looked up at Mr. Short in his usual perch in the mizzen shrouds, a glass to his eye, keeping a watch on their pursuer.

"Report, Midshipman," he said as he approached. "Any relative movement from our friend?"

"Not one bit, Captain," the midshipman reported. "He's just sitting out there, keeping station on us."

I bet he is, Brewer thought sourly, *making sure we do just as we're told, and nothing more.* He lowered the glass. *If I had* Defiant, *things might be different; they wouldn't be so cocksure that I would remain subservient.* Revenge *just doesn't have the firepower to take her on.*

Brewer sighed in frustration, his lips compressed in a firm, angry line.

"Carry on, Mr. Short," he said as he turned and walked aft.

Brewer marched aft, still thinking about the *Valdivia.* His eyes were on the deck, and with his mind so occupied, he accidentally walked straight to where Sweeney and Tyler were working out their problem. The two men stepped back, startled; they hadn't noticed their captain approaching. They quickly saluted and muttered greetings.

Brewer apologized. "I'm sorry, gentlemen; I wasn't watching where I was going."

Tyler stepped up. "I was just about to come and find you, sir. I've finished working out our position."

"Yes?" Brewer looked past Tyler to the sailing master and received a nod of confirmation. "So, where are we, Mr. Tyler?"

"I place us just about here, Captain," the Lieutenant said, pointing to a spot just southeast of Jamaica, "dead on course for Port Royal, as ordered. I estimate we'll sight the harbor entrance shortly after dawn tomorrow."

"Well done, Mr. Tyler," Brewer said. "You may carry on."

"Aye, sir," Tyler saluted and was gone.

Sweeney stepped up beside his captain.

"How did he do, Mr. Sweeney?" Brewer asked.

"Captain," the sailing master said, "do you remember a certain conversation on this subject we once had aboard *Defiant*?"

Brewer thought for a moment, and then his eyes snapped to Sweeney's.

"Yes, I believe I do."

Sweeney smiled. "Well, the lad put us to shame."

Brewer's eyebrows rose. "Really? And just how did he do that, pray tell?"

Sweeney leaned in close and lowered his voice. "He had us in the right *hemisphere*."

The Captain flinched. "Ouch. Point taken." Both men laughed.

"Seriously," Sweeney said, "his first effort was pretty good. He forgot to make one correction, so his position was off by about 300 miles to the east. Once we went over it again, he found the mistake on his own and corrected it nicely."

Brewer was impressed. He hadn't known what to expect from Tyler's first effort, but he had not looked for this level of proficiency. He would have to keep a closer eye on his second lieutenant.

The evening breeze was cool and delicious when Brewer stepped up on deck. Dusk had fallen, and many of the crew who were off watch were up on deck to take advantage. He strolled forward and saw Bean, a new hand who joined at Port Royal, sitting by the foremast and playing a sprightly tune on his fiddle. Two of the crew got up and began to dance a jig, much to the enjoyment of those who gathered around to watch. When that was done, Brewer saw another hand called Masterson pull a fife from inside his shirt and play for the next group of dancers.

Brewer hung back from the crowds and envied them their happiness. He could not share it. His life now revolved around one obsession: finding and killing the pirate El Diabolito.

Brewer walked back to the quarterdeck. He was smart enough to know that he had to be careful—obsessions could be overwhelming, and he'd already seen the consequences of obsession taking control of a mind. Brewer considered the matter again as he began to pace. He *owed* those who had died on *Defiant*. He as captain should have known to stay farther away from the fog bank, should have known an enemy could be hiding there. He'd failed, and his crew paid the price. Now it was up to him to avenge them. Revenge was all that mattered.

Brewer stopped pacing and looked out over the moonlit ocean. The admiral had to let them go to Panama. He *had* to. El Diabolito would be there, and then all would be made right.

The sun was barely above the horizon the next morning when the lookout was heard.

"Land ho!"

Lieutenant Greene went to the rail and grinned at the sight of the strip of brown and green that divided the blue sky from the ocean. He turned and searched for only a moment before spying the midshipman of the watch.

"Mr. Simmons!" he called. "My respects to the captain; tell him we have sighted land, and I am about to take in sail."

"Aye, sir!"

Captain Brewer appeared on deck within minutes. He went to the starboard rail and surveyed the island that was rapidly approaching, and then he turned to his first lieutenant.

"All right, Benjamin," he said, "let's take in sail."

Greene picked up his speaking trumpet and began bellowing commands. Hands appeared seemingly from nowhere and scurried up the shrouds to carry out his orders. Within minutes, *Revenge* was gliding across the waves under her topsails. The drop in speed was immediate, and suddenly it seemed as though the ship was tired after its long run from the South American continent.

"Bring us around to the west, Mr. Greene," Brewer said, "until we get to Port Royal."

The ship began to swing around when the sound of the lookout's cry shattered the calm.

"Deck there! The frigate's closing!"

Brewer, Greene, and Sweeney all spun to watch the *Valdivia* close rapidly. She had not reduced sail, and she was now on a course parallel with *Revenge*. Well within broadside range, Brewer noted, if they had a mind to start a war.

As the big frigate overtook them, Brewer made out the form of Captain Turrado waving a mock salute before he turned his frigate SSE.

Toward Panama, Brewer thought coldly. His rage boiled as he watched the frigate sail away. He had to take several deep breaths, in and out slowly, before he could trust himself to turn and deal with his crew.

"Mr. Greene," he said, "take us straight in when we get there."

One more glance at the fast-dwindling tower of sail.

"I need to see the Admiral as quickly as possible."

Brewer was shown in to the Admiral's study. Hornblower looked up from the letter he was composing to the Lady Barbara and greeted his friend. He rose from his desk and shook his protégé's hand warmly. "To what do I owe the honor?"

"I have been asked by no less than Simon Bolivar to deliver this letter to you," Brewer said, handing over the letter. "He insisted we sail straight from Caracas to give it to you, and he even sent Lord Cochrane's Chilean frigate along as a shadow to see that we did just that."

Hornblower took the letter with a wary look on his face and set it down on his desk unopened. "Bolivar, eh? It sounds as though your search for your pirate has led you through some deep waters—if not the ones you intended to sound."

"Indeed, my lord," Brewer agreed. "I have written you a full report; Mr. Phillips has it. I apologize for not waiting to see you until you had read it."

The admiral resumed his seat and waved Brewer towards the nearby chair. He picked up the letter, broke the seal, read it quickly, then he stared off into space for a few moments. Finally, he looked back at Brewer.

"Can you read Spanish?" he asked.

"No, my lord."

He tossed the letter on the desk. "Then this will do you no good. It merely states that the government of Gran Columbia wishes nothing but good will to exist between our two nations, and that he is fighting for freedom on land just as we are fighting for freedom on the seas."

Brewer grunted. "Just as I thought. It's meaningless. Only intended to keep me from finding El Diabolito."

Hornblower sat back in his chair. "Captain, I think you should tell me about your visit to Caracas."

Brewer took a deep breath and did so, concluding with the news that that Bolivar had hired El Diabolito as a privateer to help capture the Spanish galleon.

"This is obviously the big attack that Gibbs referred to in the letter addressed to Cofresi. According to Cochrane, we missed the pirate by less than a day, but I couldn't break away to pursue." Brewer's tone was bitter. "Perhaps if I'd been a post captain with a 44-gun frigate, I might have refused their 'request' and set out for Panama, but, as it was..."

"Stop, William," the Admiral said sternly. "I doubt that Cochrane himself or Pellew in their heydays would act as you described. You did the only thing you could do." The Admiral stared out into space for a few moments, his brows knit in concentration. Suddenly he turned back to Brewer.

"Tell me again about the treasure."

Brewer repeated all he could remember of what Lord Cochrane said about what would likely be the final Spanish treasure galleon to sail from the new world for home port. When he finished, his mentor had a wistful look in his eye that puzzled the young captain. Hornblower noticed and smiled.

"I was just thinking, William," Hornblower said longingly, "that I wished Elizabeth were queen again, and we had the same unofficial sanction as Drake and Hawkins! We would live like kings off that galleon."

"Wishful thinking, my lord," Brewer said, "but what are we to do about El Diabolito? I'm sure he's recruited Cofresi to aid him. If we go after them immediately, we could have much of South America angry with us, but if we wait and allow them to help Cochrane take the galleon, we may lose them altogether."

Hornblower rose suddenly and began to pace the length of the study. Brewer could tell from the set of his shoulders and the determination in his stride that his admiral was not be interrupted before a decision had been made, so he settled back in his seat and sipped his drink. Back and forth, four long steps and turn, his chief paced the room, his chin firmly planted on his chest, unseeing eyes staring at the floorboards, that magnificent mind racing, oblivious to all around him.

Brewer smiled at the sight, remembering how many times he had heard the familiar footfall pattern coming from within the governor's office, and how he had written Captain Bush after seeing the admiral pacing on HMS *Defiant's* quarterdeck. Bush had written back and congratulated him on surviving the experience, saying that he had witnessed many midshipmen and even a few lieutenants filleted for interrupting the admiral's pacing. Bush had likened it to watching a smoldering volcano, waiting to see whether or not it would erupt.

Brewer turned his head and caught sight of the bust standing silently in the corner. *Well, my friend,* he thought, *what would you do, were you us? Even though this is at sea and not on land, that would not stop you from having your opinion. In fact, I am almost certain what that opinion would be.*

"What do you think he would say, William?"

Brewer was startled at the sound of the Admiral's voice coming from right behind him. Brewer chided himself for being so lost in the past that he'd neglected to notice his admiral had ceased pacing.

Brewer turned in his seat. "I can only see our friend offering but one piece of advice, my lord. *Hit them as hard as you can with everything you've got.*"

The Admiral nodded as he resumed his seat. "That definitely sounds like something our friend would say, but consider this, William: Who is it we are to hit? The Spanish? We are not at war with them, and unfortunately, it is no longer the times of Elizabeth, so we cannot seize their treasure galleon. And despite his association with pirates, we cannot attack Admiral Cochrane; he is an admiral of a newly-independent sovereign power, whether it be Chile or Gran Columbia matters not. Even El Diabolito and his pirates may be thought of as under Bolivar's protection."

Brewer could hardly believe his ears. "What does that leave us, my lord? Are you saying we can do nothing?"

"Why, no, Commander," Hornblower said, slowly and deliberately, "I am saying nothing of the kind. We are in possession of creditable evidence regarding the probably location of at least one and possibly more criminals wanted for crimes against the British Empire. I intend to hit them with everything I've got."

Brewer relaxed and smiled, silently kicking himself for doubting his mentor.

"You will take *Revenge* and sail for Panama as soon as you are ready for sea," Hornblower said. "*Crab* will accompany you; use her for scouting and sending messages. I shall follow you within the week with *Clorinda* and *Phoebe*. Your orders are to probe the coast until you find the galleon."

"But, my lord, Bolivar said it was leaving from Portobello."

Hornblower smiled. "You will forgive me, I'm sure, Commander, if I have my doubts of the president's probity on that particular point. *You* will probe until you find it and report its location to me. We will wait out to sea for the pirates to appear, then we shall attack them in turn."

Brewer grinned. "And what of Cochrane and Bolivar, my lord?"

The Admiral shrugged. "President Bolivar can write his next letter to the Admiralty in London, and Admiral Cochrane can hand-deliver it."

HMS *Revenge* and HMS *Crab* sailed south from Port Royal with the morning tide. As was becoming his habit, Brewer briefed his senior officers over dinner on their first night out of port.

Alfred and the steward cleared the dishes, and the King's health was drunk. Glasses were refilled and cigars passed out and lit. It occurred to Brewer that he was beginning to feel that the men in this room with him were almost like family to him. He wasn't sure if this were a good thing or not; he certainly could see good points and bad that could come out of it. He resolved to write a long letter to Captain Bush and ask his opinion.

When Alfred had withdrawn, Brewer raised his voice above the din in the room.

"Gentlemen!" he said. "Now that you've been properly wined and dined, let us get down to business, shall we? Our orders and to sail for Panama and find a Spanish galleon that is preparing to sail for Spain. What is so special about this particular galleon, you ask? Let me tell you! This particular galleon is the last and by far the greatest of the Spanish *treasure* galleons. And before you ask, *No,* Elizabeth is not on the throne of England again."

Mr. Sweeney grinned and shook his head. "Too bad."

"We have information," Brewer continued before anyone else could chime in, "that the galleon is supposed to leave from Portobello, but the admiral has doubts about that information's reliability. Hence, we are to look for it and then send *Crab* to the admiral with its location. We will begin at the western end of Panama and work our way eastward along the coast."

Lieutenant Greene sat forward. "Then what are *we* here for, sir?"

"Pirates. The admiral agrees that if we find the galleon, we shall also find El Diabolito along with Cofresi, and who knows how many others. Our orders are to stand off out to sea from the galleon and attack the pirates in turn as they show up. Admiral Lord Hornblower will be joining us with two frigates, so we should have the firepower to handle not only *Pauline* but also the *Valdivia,* should Admiral Cochrane object to us attacking his help."

"But what about the galleon, Captain?" Mr. Tyler asked.

"It sails to Spain, if Cochrane doesn't take it with *Valdivia.* Our interest is only in the pirates who are already wanted for crimes against the British Empire." Brewer quickly read the disappointment in the room. "Gentlemen, I assure you I am not in love with the idea either, but we have our orders. Of course, if anyone manages to swim to London, resurrect Elizabeth and put her back on the throne before dawn, I'm sure we would all be greatly in your debt."

There was a muted laugh that made its way around the room. Brewer could understand how they felt. They saw only the treasure, while he saw a totally different objective.

"Thank you for your company, gentlemen," he said. They rose and bid their captain a good night. Only Dr. Spinelli kept his seat. As the door closed behind the last man out, Brewer looked over at his friend.

"I'm afraid I'm not in the mood for chess tonight, Adam," he said.

"Good," Spinelli replied. "Neither am I. I just want to make sure you're okay."

"I'm fine."

The Doctor rose. "If you say so. If you want me, just pass the word. Good night." And he left the cabin.

He did not look back to see his captain staring out into space, his thoughts visible on his face.

Revenge.

Outside the Captain's cabin, Mr. Reed waited for Lieutenant Greene.

"Pardon me, sir," he said quietly. "Is there someplace I can speak to you privately?"

Greene had thought to go to his cabin and get some sleep before heading up on deck, but he could see that something was troubling the lad.

"Very well, Mr. Reed. Follow me."

Reed was surprised when the first lieutenant led him below to the sick bay. Greene knocked on the door before entering

"Mr. Greene," the Doctor said, "and Mr. Reed! I've only just arrived myself. Is there something I can do for you gentlemen?"

"For the moment, just sit and listen, Doctor," Greene said. "Reed wanted to speak to me in private, and I can't think of a more private place in the ship, outside of the captain's cabin." Turning to the midshipman, he said, "I know this may not be what you had in mind, but believe me when I say that you can trust the doctor. I do, and so does the captain. You may speak freely in front of him."

"As you say, sir," Reed said. The doctor offered him a seat on a chest, and Reed gratefully accepted. He took a deep breath to steady his nerves. "It's just this, sir. I've been thinking about Mr. Simmons' testimony on what happened in the foretop. Am I correct in thinking he said that Scar *admitted* that he killed Grant and tried to kill me, and *then* tried to get money from Simmons and his help in getting off the ship?"

"Yes, that's what he said."

Reed frowned. "No, that's wrong."

Greene and the Doctor studied him intently. "Excuse me?" Greene said.

"Beg your pardon, sir. It's just that Scar was in my division, so I got to know him pretty well. Not a bad sailor, but not a good man to be sure. He'd slit his own mother's throat for a shilling, but he'd never do it for free."

The Doctor leaned forward now, his elbows on his knees and his forefingers steepled before him. "What are you getting at, Reed?"

"Mr. Simmons told the First Lieutenant that Scar admitting to killing Grant and trying to kill me *before* anyone gave him money. Scar wasn't like that, sir; he'd never do something like that unless he had money in the bank."

Greene leaned back against the bulkhead and blew out a great breath. "So what you're saying is you think someone paid Scar to kill Grant and yourself?"

"Yes, sir," Reed said.

"Who do you think is responsible, Mr. Reed?" Spinelli asked.

"Mr. Simmons," Reed said.

"To pay you back for the 'discipline' you imposed on him?" Greene asked.

"I suppose so, sir."

Greene considered for a moment before looking to the doctor. "What do you think, Doctor?"

Spinelli shrugged. "I agree with young Mr. Reed here. I think we need to go see the captain."

Greene considered a moment longer before nodding. "So do I. Let's go, Mr. Reed. You come, too, Doctor."

The three men made their way aft. Greene turned to the midshipman before he knocked at the captain's door.

"You're sure about this, Mr. Reed?"

Reed swallowed hard. "Aye, sir."

"Good enough for me," Greene said. He knocked at the captain's door and opened it after hearing the cry to enter.

They entered, and Reed shut the door behind them. Mr. Greene turned to his captain.

"Pardon me, sir, but Mr. Reed has—"

"I'm sorry to interrupt, Mr. Greene," Spinelli said. He turned to the captain. "Sir, do you remember what we spoke about earlier, just before I left? Mr. Reed has had similar thoughts."

"Really?" Brewer looked to Reed.

Spinelli turned to Greene. "When we spoke earlier, the Captain deduced a very similar scenario to what Mr. Reed said in the sickbay."

Greene looked miffed. "You might have told me, Doctor."

Brewer looked at Reed. "Sit down, Mr. Reed. Now, tell me what you think. You may speak freely."

"Well, sir," Reed said, "I think Simmons paid—or was supposed to pay—Scar to kill me. Scar missed, but knowing him as I do, I imagine he still wanted to be paid, and I'd bet that's what he was saying in the foretop before he fell."

"Do you have any proof, Mr. Reed?" Brewer asked.

"None, sir," Reed answered. He looked chastised for voicing his conjectures. "But it all *fits* somehow."

"Don't feel bad, Mr. Reed," Brewer said. "I'm inclined to agree with you, but without solid evidence to back us up, we can't take Simmons to court martial."

"Isn't there something we can do, sir?" Greene asked.

The Doctor, who had been listening intently, spoke up. "I have an idea, Captain."

Mr. Reed walked into the midshipman's berth and found Mr. Simmons relaxing there. He got himself a drink and sat down on a sea chest to take a sip.

"You know," he said conversationally to Simmons, "you were pretty lucky that night in the foretop."

"Really?" Simmons asked. His voice was casual, but Reed saw how the other midshipman's shoulders tended.

Reed nodded his head vigorously. "Most definitely. Scar was in my division, you see, so I got to know him pretty well. Not a bad sailor, but no morals in the man at all. He'd slit his own mother's throat if someone promised him a shilling to do it."

"What's your point, Reed?" Simmons drawled, his eyes shuttered.

"Just this. As I said, I knew Scar well. He'd slit his mother's throat for a shilling, as I said, but he'd never do it for nothing. His most basic motivation was profit. You said he killed Grant and tried to kill me *before* he approached you for money and help getting off the ship. That means he killed one person and tried to kill me for nothing, *and Scar would never do that.*"

Simmons looked bored. "So?"

"So," Reed rose to his feet, "if Scar tried to kill me, someone must have paid him for it."

"Really? Any idea who?"

"Actually, yes. I think you did it."

Simmons rose to his feet and faced Reed. "Prove it."

"Well, that's just it," Reed said as he stepped toward the junior midshipman. "I can't. Not yet, anyway. But don't worry, Mr. Simmons; I'm not done with you yet. I intend to keep asking questions and looking into things here and there, and one day it will all fall together, and I shall get to see you at the end of a rope where you belong."

Simmons' eyes narrowed. The two men stood inches away from each other now, and any spark would be sufficient to make the tense situation explode. Reed stood silently, ready to fight, his eyes doing the accusing now. Simmons remembered what had happened the last time he'd challenged Reed, and he wasn't anxious for a rematch. Choosing the better part of valor, he stepped back and smiled.

"That will be the day," he said. "Let me know when you think you have some actual evidence, old boy. Until then, have a good evening. I'm going to the foretop. Should be much nicer now, don't you think?"

Simmons walked out of the midshipman's berth feeling pretty good. He didn't see the smile that crept onto the corner of Jonathan Reed's mouth.

CHAPTER 18

HMS *Revenge* slid into the harbor at the island of San Andres just as dusk was beginning to fall. Brewer hoped to pick up some local intelligence that might help him narrow his search a bit for the Spanish galleon. Only one ship in the harbor attracted their attention.

"Our old friend from Martinique," Brewer observed. "The *Semillante*, I believe."

"Looks to be," Greene agreed.

"Let's beat them to the punch this time," Brewer said. "Have a boat lowered. Send Mr. Tyler over with an invitation for their captain and first lieutenant to dine aboard *Revenge* tonight at the turn of the second dog watch. I think Alfred will be up for the challenge, don't you?"

Greene grinned. "Indeed, sir."

"Good. I shall go and write out the invitation. Send Mr. Tyler to my cabin, if you please."

Brewer went below and wrote out a nicely-worded invitation for the dinner and handed it to the second lieutenant when he arrived. Then he informed Alfred of the change in his plans.

"I should think there will be seven for supper," Brewer said. He counted on his fingers. "Myself, Mr. Greene, Mr. Tyler, Mr. Sweeney, the doctor, and the two French officers. Can you be ready to serve by the end of the second dog watch?"

The servant closed his eyes for a moment, a gesture that Brewer knew to mean that he was calculating times and recipes in his mind. The eyes opened again with no change in his expression.

"Yes, sir."

Brewer was tempted to pry regarding the menu but decided against it. "Thank you, Alfred. I'll have some coffee, please."

Brewer returned to his writing desk to write some more letters. The first was to Elizabeth. It astonished him to realize that this was the first letter he had sat down to write her since leaving St. Kitts before the battle with Cofresi. He could not believe he had been so busy as to have her pushed so far back in his mind, and he determined to make up for it.

My Dearest Elizabeth,

Please forgive me for being so late in writing you. I have been in a battle against the men of the pirate Roberto Cofresi, my first action as captain. I am pleased to report to you that we sank his schooner and retook a Dutch merchantman he was trying to capture. I was injured in the action, a flesh wound in the arm, but the doctor was more than equal to the task and I am as good as new.

We took our prisoners back to Port Royal to be turned over to the Admiral. On the way, one of the pirates divulged a piece of information that caused the Admiral to send us to the coast of Panama. I do not know when we shall be together again. I pray when I do see you again, the time will be right for me to speak to your father. I cannot picture a greater happiness than coming home to you.

I wonder if I may prevail upon you for a small request. I would like to have a small picture of you, something to gaze upon when I am missing you so. Can you have a miniature painted? The artist must be of a good quality. I shall forward the cost to you as soon as I return to Jamaica.

I hope this letter finds you in good health and longing for me as I am for you. Know that you possess my heart and always will. As I have been, I shall always be,

Your Ob'd't Servant,
William Brewer
Captain, HMS Revenge

Brewer carefully folded, sealed, and addressed the letter. It was followed in quick succession by letters to his mother, sister, and Captain Bush. In Bush's letter, he went into greater detail regarding the battle and his wound. It felt strangely good to be able to speak plainly about it to someone who had been through something similar and would understand what he was saying as well as what he could not put into words.

Mr. Tyler returned with a note from Captain Roussin of the *Semillante* stating that he and Lieutenant de Robespierre would be honored to attend. *Good,* thought Brewer. *Let's just hope he's as forthcoming with information as he was the last time we met.*

Alfred outdid himself with the feast, so much so that Captain Roussin insisted on thanking him personally and offering him a commission in the French navy to come and cook for him. Brewer laughed and said that such a thing would lead to war between the French navy and himself.

Brewer watched as the French captain lit his cigar and took a deep, appreciative drag before blowing a cloud of rich, blue smoke toward the deck above. Roussin held the cigar in front of him and admired it.

"An excellent cigar," he said. "May I ask where you got them?"

Brewer smiled. "My source is Admiral Lord Hornblower, Captain. I can ask him where he gets them, or you can ask him yourself, if you happen to put in at Port Royal."

Roussin looked at his first lieutenant. "I believe that can be arranged. Do you not agree, Robespierre?"

"Oui, Capitan."

"There is a saying in English," Brewer said. "*'Fancy meeting you here.'* Are you familiar with it? No? Well, it means that we did not expect to find your vessel in these waters."

"Nor we yours, Captain. It is a day for surprises, is it not?"

Brewer grinned and looked at Mr. Sweeney. The master shook his head and smiled back. He was not going to get involved this time. Brewer was on his own.

"Captain," Brewer asked, "how is my friend, the Governor of Martinique these days?"

"A little out of favor, I'm afraid. Do you remember those six luggars that were nearing completion in the harbor there the last time we met? It seems that some pirates visited the harbor a few days after my ship sailed and stole all six of them."

Brewer's brows flew skyward at the revelation. He looked to Greene and Sweeney and found them equally surprised.

"I'm astounded, Captain! How were they able to do this so easily?"

Roussin shrugged. "The usual way, Captain; the governor was paid off. I believe now that those luggars were always intended for those pirates. It would be interesting to put the governor to the sword point and ask him how much they paid him." He took another drag of his cigar and blew the cloud skyward, then shook his head ruefully. "A shame it will never happen."

Brewer shared a knowing look with Greene.

"Captain, what do you think those six ships were for? I mean, do you have any idea what the pirates will do with them?"

"None at all, Captain."

Brewer looked again at Greene, who nodded this time.

"Captain," Brewer said, "I think I might know where you might find those ships. We are out here looking for a Spanish treasure galleon."

Now it was the Frenchmen's turn to share a knowing look and a nod.

"So," Roussin said, "the rumors are true."

Brewer inclined his head. "We found out from one of Roberto Cofresi's men, whom we captured." He told Roussin and de Robespierre what Gibbs had said about the letter from El Diabolito, and their trip to Caracas, only to miss the pirate by one day. The two French officers listened without interrupting and shared a worried look when Brewer finished.

"So, Captain," Roussin recapped, "you are saying that El Diabolito has added these six luggars to the *Pauline* and any other ships he may have in order to capture this treasure ship from the Spanish. Where would he get the cannon for them?"

Brewer sighed. "While we were in Caracas, we met someone else. Do you know the name of Admiral Cochrane?"

Roussin thought it familiar, but de Robespierre remembered Cochrane's exploits in the Mediterranean during the wars.

"That's him," Brewer said, "only now he is an admiral in the Chilean navy, and he is helping Simon Bolivar seal the independence of Gran Columbia by arranging for the pirates to steal the galleon so the bullion does not make it to Spain. The pirates will get cannon for their luggars from Cochrane or Bolivar."

Roussin understood it all now. "Spain cannot afford to make war in the New World without that gold. How much is on that galleon?"

"I'm not sure," Brewer admitted, "but rumor has it that it is to be the last—and the largest—shipment of new world wealth."

Roussin considered this while taking several puffs from his cigar. Alfred took advantage of the momentary lull in the conversation to refill everyone's glass. After he left, Roussin looked at Brewer.

"Captain," he said, "as you must know, we are not in these waters by accident. We have heard rumors that the *Pauline* is or soon will be in this area, obviously to go after the galleon. We are after our ship."

"Why now? After all these years?"

"Rumors of her misdeeds have finally made their way to Paris. The King himself charged me to recapture or sink each ship that went rogue. *Pauline* is the last remaining vessel."

"So we have a common enemy."

"So it would seem. What will you do about the galleon?"

"Our orders are to attack the pirates. We are not to attack the galleon."

Roussin shrugged. "Too bad. So you are content to let Bolivar have the gold?"

Brewer made a dismissive gesture. "Bolivar says he wants the gold to finance wars of independence from Spain, but the bottom line is he doesn't want Spain to get it. Hence, the pirates."

"I see," Roussin said. "Bolivar entices the pirates to attack the galleon by telling them whatever they take is theirs. He loses nothing in the bargain, not even political ground. Brilliant!"

Brewer found it hard to disagree with the sentiment.

Roussin leaned forward. "Captain, I propose we work together to find the *Pauline* and El Diabolito."

"Two ships would give us a wide search area, Captain," Greene interjected.

"Agreed," Brewer said. "But with one proviso. I get El Diabolito. You can have the *Pauline*."

"Done," Roussin said. The two captains shook on it and sealed the deal.

"I hate to admit this," Brewer said, "but there is one small problem."

"And that is?"

"I don't know what the pirate looks like."

Roussin laughed. "You've never seen him?"

Brewer shook his head. "I just know he commanded the *Pauline* when she ambushed my ship."

"You will have no problem recognizing El Diabolito, *Capitan*," de Robespierre said. "He lacks an ear."

Brewer was sure he misunderstood the Frenchman. "Excuse me?"

"No ear here, Captain," Roussin said, touching his own right ear. "Apparently, at some time in the past, the Spanish thought he had betrayed them, so they gave him the same punishment that the Apostle Peter gave to the servant who came to take away his Lord in the garden. They cut off his ear."

"Well," Brewer said, "he shouldn't be hard to find."

"Except for one thing," Roussin said. "The last time El Diabolito attacked a ship, he took ten of his crew before the battle and cut off their ears to make it harder to identify him."

Brewer frowned. Lieutenant Greene, sitting next to him, barely heard what he muttered under his breath.

"Sadistic brute."

The two ships sailed the next day. Brewer sent *Crab* back to Hornblower with the news that the pirates now had six luggars allegedly stolen from the governor of Martinique and probably armed by Bolivar. He also sent word that he was starting his search in concert with the French frigate *Semillante* at the eastern end of Panama; they would work their way west.

Brewer stood on the quarterdeck of HMS *Revenge* and studied the *Semillante* through his glass. Captain Roussin and he had agreed that the ships should be just close enough that signals could be clearly read, in order that each ship might go to the other's aid, should the *Pauline* be sighted.

They sailed ESE toward the Gran Columbian port of Cartagena. *Revenge* ventured close enough to the harbor mouth to make a quick survey of the ships inside. There was no sign of either Cochrane's *Valdivia* or the *Pauline*. The two ships moved southwest along the coast until they reached Panama. *Revenge* worked inshore, checking each inlet or harbor, searching diligently for the luggars or the *Pauline*. *Semillante* stood out to sea, at the extreme edge of signal-range, so as not to cause any undue commotion. Every night, *Revenge* would move out to sea and get ready for the next day's search.

This worked well for the first couple of nights. Each ship flew its night signal during the hours of darkness, and all was orderly. Brewer discovered something different on the third night, when Mac awakened him shortly after 2:00 am.

"Begging your pardon, Captain," the big coxswain said. "Mr. Tyler sends word that we've lost *Semillante's* night signal."

Brewer was instantly awake. "Very well. I'll come."

He arrived on deck and received Mr. Tyler's report.

"He was there when we came on watch, sir," Tyler said as he handed Brewer a glass. "We've been checking every half hour, as you ordered, and when we went to check at four bells, it was gone. I took a quick run up to the mizzen top myself, Captain, but I didn't see any sign of *Semillante's* night signal. I came down to the deck and sent for you."

"Thank you. I have the deck! Quartermaster! Hard to starboard! Course due north!"

"Due north! Aye, Captain!"

"Mr. Tyler! Take in sail! One reef only! I don't want to run into anything unknown in the dark! And I want silence on deck. Everyone is to watch and listen. Pass the word, quietly now!"

"Yes, sir!"

Brewer looked skyward and was glad for a good moon.

"I want extra lookouts aloft, Mr. Tyler," Brewer said. "Give each man a glass."

Brewer began to pace the quarterdeck to hide his excitement. *Revenge* slowly made her way north in the darkness, looking for her consort. He was still pacing when he heard eight bells ring out and saw Mr. Greene come on deck to take over the morning watch. Brewer briefed his first lieutenant on what had happened during the night.

"It will be light in less than two hours," the Captain said. "Perhaps then we can conduct a more effective search."

"But what could have happened, sir?" Greene asked. "*Semillante* was in good shape. There was no explosion, and I can't see anyone being able to sneak up on a man of war and simply steal her."

"I agree," Brewer said. "Walk with me, Benjamin." He began pacing again. "I agree with your reasoning. I've spent the last several hours running through every possibility I can think of, and none of them make sense. That means one thing: *Semillante* doused her night signal on purpose."

"You think she saw something in the moonlight."

"It's the only explanation that makes sense."

"The *Pauline*?"

Brewer shrugged. "Possibly. Or one of those stolen luggars."

"And you think Roussin went dark in order to try to stay close until daylight?"

The Captain nodded.

"In that case, Captain, she shouldn't be hard to find."

Brewer stopped pacing. "What do you mean?"

"All we need to do is to wait for daylight and listen for the gunfire."

Brewer grinned. "I see what you mean, Benjamin."

"With all due respect, sir, why don't you turn in for an hour or so? I will call you if we find something before daylight."

Brewer surrendered gracefully. "Perhaps you're right. Very well. You have the deck, Mr. Greene."

It seemed to Brewer as though he had barely closed his eyes before Mac was at his side.

"Begging your pardon, sir," he said, "but lookout's sighted sails on the horizon, and we might be hearing gunfire, sir."

Brewer sat up and shook the cobwebs out of his head. *"Might?"*

"It's a long way off, Captain. The sound is very faint."

"I'll come."

Mac fetched his captain's coat and hat and helped him with his hanger. Brewer nodded his thanks and made his way out the door.

He arrived on deck and made his way straight to his premier. Greene handed him a glass, pointing out the speck of sail on the horizon.

"Mr. Tyler volunteered for the tops, sir," said Greene. "He's the one who identified them."

Brewer lowered his glass. "Them?"

"Tyler thinks there's two ships out there."

Just at that moment, the breeze brought the slightest sound to their ears.

"Did you hear that, sir?" Greene asked.

"I did indeed," Brewer said as he lowered his glass. "Gunfire." He turned to the quartermaster standing at the wheel. "I have the deck. Quartermaster, hard to larboard! Straight at those two ships! All hands to make sail, Mr. Greene! Beat to quarters!"

The deck of HMS *Revenge* exploded with activity. Brewer moved forward in order to get a better view. Through the glass at his eye, he saw the growing dot of white seem to separate a bit and then come back together, as though a ship made a pass and then turned to come around again. He nodded to himself. Tyler had been right; there were definitely two ships out there. Now he had to determine how to bring *Revenge* into the action.

Greene joined him at the bow as the ship picked up speed. Both men watched the growing white field with anticipation.

"Deck there!" Tyler called when the ships were hull up. "I can make one ship out! It's the *Semillante*!"

Brewer looked at Greene and said, "Do you want to wager on who it is they're fighting?"

Greene shook his head.

"Pass the word for Mr. Short," Brewer said.

The young midshipman arrived quickly.

"Mr. Short, right now Mr. Tyler in the foretop is our best eyes on the fight before us. I want you to be the runner between him and me. Go ask him if the *Semillante* is the near ship or the far."

"Aye, sir!" The lad saluted and was gone in the wink of an eye, making his way up the shrouds like a monkey. He came back even faster.

"Mr. Tyler says that now the far ship is *Semillante*, Captain! He also says he thinks the other ship is *Pauline*!"

"I hoped as much!" Brewer said. "Stand by, Mr. Short!"

"Aye, sir!" The boy leaned back against the breach of a gun, bent over, his hands on his knees and breathing hard.

Brewer put the glass back to his eye to assess the rapidly changing situation. The two ships ahead of him were now running parallel courses away from him; it looked like the fight had turned into a straight out slugfest, like two fighters standing in the center of a ring trading blows. No maneuver, no technique, just trying to hit the other guy harder than he hit you. *Revenge* was approaching from *Pauline's* larboard quarter. Brewer hoped El Diabolito's attention was firmly on the *Semillante* and so would not see him approaching almost from behind.

"Benjamin," he said, "load the guns, but do not run them out yet. I intend to rake the pirate's stern with the larboard battery and then turn as sharply as we can and give them a second dose with the starboard battery. Mr. Short, tell Mr.

Tyler to come down and report to me." Brewer waited until the lad was gone and said to Greene, "We're close enough now that we don't need him up there anymore. I need him at his guns."

Greene agreed.

"I'm returning to the quarterdeck. Report to your guns, Mr. Greene. Wait for my command, then run out your guns and fire as they bear. Make sure your captains are true, Benjamin; we want to rip the insides out of the pirate, but only the pirate."

"Yes, sir. It would be distinctly embarrassing to shoot up our allies, not to mention counter-productive. We need their help."

Mr. Tyler approached, and Brewer congratulated him on his work in the tops, then sent him on to Mr. Greene and his guns. By the time Brewer arrived on the quarterdeck, Mr. Sweeney was making ready to carry out his captain's maneuver.

A petty officer came up and saluted. "Something happening on *Semillante*, sir!"

Brewer and Sweeney went to the starboard rail just in time to see the Frenchman's mizzen top fall over. It broke clean away from the mast and appeared to hang from the main top for a minute before crashing to the deck below, taking the main top down with it. The French frigate seemed to stagger away from the pirate.

"Sir," Sweeney asked, "do we still wait for pistol range?"

Brewer shook his head and raised a hand. "Mr. Greene! You may fire as your guns bear!"

Greene waved his acknowledgement. Brewer saw him bark an order, and the guns were run out as one.

Brewer looked around and spotted Simmons. "Mr. Simmons! Hoist the colors!"

"Aye, sir!"

"Now, Mr. Sweeney! Hard to starboard!"

"Aye, Captain!"

HMS *Revenge* swung around and righted herself. Brewer waited impatiently for Greene to give the command to fire, but he knew better than to interfere. Greene knew his business, and Brewer stayed out of his way. Even now, he could see his first lieutenant moving from gun to gun, making sure their captains knew their orders and what he expected of them.

They were getting close enough to *Pauline* that Brewer and Sweeney could occasionally see the quarterdeck when the obscuring smoke from firing guns wafted away. Nobody on the pirate ship seemed to be the least bit aware of their presence yet. *Good,* thought Brewer. *Mr. Greene will announce our arrival any minute.*

But then *Pauline*'s lookout raised the alarm, and some of the crew began to react. Brewer saw Mr. Greene's raised arm, sword in hand, fall and the word "Fire!" pierced the air.

Double grape from the forward carronade swept the pirate's quarterdeck while double-shotted 12-pounders made a shambles of the stern, deadly splinters erupting from the woodwork to aid the attackers. Brewer heard the roar of the guns going off singly or in pairs, the gun captains being careful to make sure of their targets. The carronade on the quarterdeck delivered a parting shot of grape to take care of any stragglers or those who were too dazed to take cover.

Brewer and Sweeney crossed to the larboard rail and waited for the smoke to clear so they could survey the damage. It turned out to be better than Brewer could have hoped. The dead lay scattered on the quarterdeck, and the 12-pounders had destroyed the stern and part of the enemy's upper works. As they swept on past the *Semillante*, Brewer saw Roussin at the fantail waving his hat in recognition before turning back to attend to the needs of his ship. Brewer waved his hat in reply, not knowing if his ally had seen it or not.

"Sweeney, bring us about. Hard to starboard." He raised the speaking trumpet. "Stand by, Mr. Tyler!"

Tyler waved his hand to show he understood. Brewer saw him talking quickly with Greene before going back to his gun captains individually, as Greene had done earlier. Finally, he took a step back and raised his sword. He looked for word from the quarterdeck.

Revenge came around, although with a loss of speed. Brewer stood beside Sweeney on the quarterdeck as the time became right for action. Brewer caught Tyler's eye and nodded once. Tyler's arm came down, and his voice broke as he shouted the command to fire.

There were a few pirates on their quarterdeck with muskets, but grape from the forward carronade eliminated them as a threat. Again the 12-pounders barked in ones and twos, belching smoke and fire and sending storms of deadly splinters down the length of the pirate's gun deck. As the smoke cleared, Brewer saw to his chagrin that the pirate's rudder remained intact, allowing them to maneuver. He also saw what every captain feared most. The ship had turned away from *Semillante*, training her larboard battery squarely on HMS *Revenge*. Brewer could see their 18-pounders ready to wreak carnage on his ship.

Brewer turned to Sweeney standing beside him. "As an old friend used to say, 'For what we are about to receive, may we be truly thankful.'"

Sweeney leaned in. "Did the old friend survive?"

Brewer nodded, and Sweeney grunted.

That was when *Pauline*'s captain let loose his broadside. Brewer felt the heat from the muzzle blasts as the deck beneath him shuddered and writhed in pain. The worst part was the screams of his crew. He saw his men felled by the enemy shot or splinters. A few were dismembered before his eyes, body parts being taken away by enemy balls, and one man even disintegrating into a cloud of flesh and bloody mist, as though the body had exploded. He saw Mr. Short dive to the deck moments before an 18-pound ball scraped the mizzenmast right where his head had been. Thankful to see the lad rise, Brewer turned back to the pirate ship just as someone on the enemy's deck pointed a musket at him and fired. He felt a searing pain in his head, and all went black.

Lieutenant Greene became aware of the captain's condition when Mr. Short came running down the deck bellowing his name. The lad skidded to a stop on the bloody deck and saluted.

"Mr. Greene! The Captain's been wounded! Mr. Sweeney begs you to come to the quarterdeck at once!"

"I'll come!" Greene looked around for Tyler, only to find him on the deck with two grape holes in his chest and another in his head. It was all he could do to keep his composure as he looked around and spotted Mr. Reed.

"Mr. Reed! I must go to the quarterdeck. Lieutenant Tyler is dead. You are in charge of the guns for now. Get every gun into service that you can, loaded and run out."

"Aye, sir!" Reed stepped into his new responsibilities without a question. Greene made a mental note to mention it to someone, if they survived the battle, that is.

Greene arrived on the quarterdeck a moment later to find Brewer on the deck with McCleary tending to a bloody head wound and Mr. Sweeney standing over them, blood on the side of his head and his shoulder.

"Mr. Sweeney, are you hurt?"

"Nay, Mr. Greene, the blood belongs to the Captain."

Just then, the last of the pirate's guns went off together. The balls were aimed high this time to target masts and sails, and debris from the rigging crashed to the deck. Greene and McCleary shielded the captain's body.

"We need to move him," Mac said, and before anyone could object, he lifted Brewer's body off the deck, careful to cradle the head, and carried him back toward the fantail. He gently lowered him to the deck and went back to work on the Captain's wound.

"Mr. Sweeney!" Greene said. "Turn us away from *Pauline*! Try not to give her a clean shot at our stern, if you can help it!"

"Aye, sir!"

Fortunately, the wheel had survived the massive shockwave of destruction, and Sweeney and the quartermaster were able to steer the ship away and out of the battle for now. Greene and Sweeney watched helplessly as the *Pauline* took advantage of a shift in the wind that allowed her to cross *Semillante's* stern and rake it, the broadside taking the Frenchman's mizzen down altogether. Surprisingly, the *Pauline* did not pursue either of her damaged foes, but instead turned south and tried to limp away. Greene was puzzled at this for a moment, then he remembered that the pirate's immediate goal was nothing less than the Spanish galleon.

Unfortunately, neither *Revenge* nor *Semillante* was in any shape to pursue the enemy frigate. Both ships were still clearing away wreckage and restoring guns to action. Greene went aft to the fantail to check on the Captain. He found McCleary, bare chested, holding his shirt like a bandage against Brewer's head to stop the bleeding.

"How is he?" Greene asked.

"I think he just got nicked," Mac said. "Bloody, but head wounds are like that. Wouldn't hurt to get the doctor up here for a look see."

"Agreed." Greene turned. "Mr. Short! Run below and tell the Doctor to come up on deck at once!"

"Aye, sir!"

The Doctor brought a small bag with him that had bandages in it. Mac reluctantly moved to allow Spinelli access to the wound. The Doctor gently peeled back Mac's shirt until it was completely off and handed it back to the coxswain (who promptly threw it overboard). Spinelli leaned in close to look and probe gently with his fingertips. Finally, he straightened up and reached for the bag. He pulled out a dressing and pressed it against the wound before retrieving a bandage to secure it to the side of his head.

"He should be alright," the Doctor said, "although he'll have a devil of a headache when he wakes up."

"That's what McCleary said," said Mr. Greene.

"In that case, don't call me again unless his nurse gets shot!" Spinelli said. He hurried back below to his wounded charges before anyone could comment.

Satisfied that the captain was in no immediate danger, Greene turned his attention to the ship. The wreckage was almost cleared away, and it looked like Mr. Reed and his men had every available gun back in action again. Greene cast an eye at the retreating *Pauline*. She was making her way slowly despite carrying a good deal of sail, evidence in Greene's eyes that French gunnery doctrine still favored taking out the enemy's rigging.

"All right, Mr. Sweeney," he said, "let's get after them."

Brewer's first conscious thought was how badly his head was hurting. He opened his eyes, and Mac's face came slowly into focus. The gentle rise and fall of his body told him that his ship was moving.

"Mac?" he said softly. He tried to sit up, only to get a lancing pain in his head that nearly made him cry out.

"Captain?" Mac said. "Lay back, sir, please! Mr. Greene! The Captain's awake, sir!"

"Captain?" Greene said as he stooped nearby.

"Benjamin? What happened?"

"You were grazed in the head by a musket ball, sir. We took damage from the broadside after you were hit, and the *Pauline* limped away from the battle. Neither *Semillante* nor ourselves were able to pursue right away. We've cleared the wreckage away and are under way again. *Semillante* is about two or three hours behind us, at least that's my estimate, judging from the damage she took."

"Very well," Brewer said. "Get me on my feet."

"Gently, Mac," Greene said, as the coxswain slowly assisted his captain to his feet. Brewer staggered a little with the motion of the ship, so McCleary held on to his arm for the time being. Brewer bent over slightly and held his head with both hands as he struggled to master the pain. They heard him inhale, a long, slow hiss as he straightened up. Mac moved to stand before him.

"How are your eyes, Captain?" he asked. "How many fingers?"

"Only one," Brewer said, "but that's a thumb."

Mac smiled. Brewer nodded slightly and instantly regretted it. "Stay close for now, Mac," he said quietly.

"Aye, sir."

Brewer held on to the Cornishman's strong arm as he walked forward to the wheel. Every step was agony due to the throbbing pain in his head. Nevertheless, he was lucky to be alive, and he knew it. How many of his crew, he wondered, had not been so fortunate?

"What is our course, Mr. Greene?" he asked.

"Due south, sir," Greene said. "We are currently in pursuit of the *Pauline*."

"Was she badly damaged? From your description, she doesn't seem to be sailing very well."

"I think we can thank the French doctrine of firing at the upper works for that, sir. *Semillante* did some real damage, even if she didn't take a mast down. Combined with our two broadsides to the stern, I'd say *Pauline* is in sad shape at the moment. The big question—and the one we cannot answer— is, how many men does she have left?"

"Can we overtake her?"

Greene looked at Sweeney before answering. "Even if this wind holds, sir, I'm not sure we can overtake her before dark."

Brewer stepped away from McCleary and surveyed the deck. "Run in the guns, Mr. Greene, and let's get every stitch of sail on that she'll carry. We must overtake that ship!"

"Aye, sir," Greene said. He saluted and moved off, barking orders to Mr. Reed regarding the guns and calling the hands to make sail.

When Greene was finished, Brewer called him over. "Mr. Reed is in charge of the guns? Where is Mr. Tyler?"

"Dead, sir. He was killed in *Pauline's* broadside."

Brewer's face was grim. "I see. Carry on, Mr. Greene."

Greene saluted. "Aye, sir." He hesitated a moment, then leaned in and spoke softly to his captain. "Sir, perhaps you'd like to lie down for a while and rest your head? It may be hours before we can close the gap enough to open fire."

Brewer shook his head, albeit very tenderly. "No, thank you. I feel that if I lie down right now, I don't think I would be able to get back up again. No, there will be plenty of time to rest when El Diabolito is dead, Benjamin."

Mr. Short came up and saluted. "Begging your pardon, sir, but the doctor sends his respects and would you be so kind as to report to sickbay so he can check up on you, sir?"

"Very well, Mr. Short. You may tell the good doctor I am on my way. Benjamin, you have the deck."

"Aye aye, sir."

Brewer made his way below, carefully at first, until he decided that walking normally was not causing his head to hurt any more than it was already hurting. He entered the tiny sickbay to see it literally brimming with injured. Dr. Spinelli approached him, still in his bloody apron.

"What's the butcher's bill thus far?" Brewer asked.

"Twelve dead, seventeen wounded." Spinelli saw the relief on Brewer's face at the low number of wounded. "There are two or three of the wounded who are in danger, but the rest should recover. William, I am sorry about Mr. Tyler."

Brewer nodded and grimaced. He'd had the makings of a first rate officer, and the loss was a severe blow.

"Sit down over here," Spinelli said, taking the captain by the arm. When Brewer was seated, the doctor began tenderly untying the bandages around his head. When the wound was exposed, Spinelli looked around it carefully and gently probed the wound, drawing a sharp hiss from his patient.

"Sorry." The doctor moved away for a moment and came back with a glass. "Drink this."

"What's in it?"

"Just drink it. Sir."

Brewer did so and made a face. "Gawd! What was that stuff?"

"Laudanum. It should help with your headache. Now, hold still while I put a new bandage on your head."

Brewer sat still and suffered the doctor's ministrations.

"There!" Spinelli said when he'd finished. "You should be fine in a few days, Captain. I think you may want to consider parting your hair on the other side from now on, sir."

"I shall take it under advisement," Brewer said as he left the sickbay.

When he got back on deck, he got a glass and headed for the bow. It was obvious as soon as he got there that *Revenge* was indeed narrowing the gap on *Pauline*, but the question still remained as to whether they would close it before the darkness descended and offered the pirates an excellent opportunity to escape. Brewer looked skyward, trying to judge the light, but he had to admit it was going to be close.

With less than an hour of daylight left, Brewer and Greene met at the bow again and measured the distance.

"If we had a long nine, I bet we could reach them," Greene said.

"But we don't," replied Brewer. "Just get me within range, Benjamin. We'll put another broadside in her stern and then board her."

"Board her, sir?" Greene said. "We don't have the manpower."

"We can't trade broadsides with her 18-pounders, and we don't want to wait for her to complete her repairs and outsail us! We have no idea when Admiral Hornblower or Captain Roussin will arrive, so we have no choice but to hit them hard and board!"

"Aye aye, sir."

Suddenly, Mr. Reed ran up to them, glass still in hand. "Sir, look!"

Brewer turned in time to see something go very wrong on the pirate frigate. All three men snapped glass to their eyes to get a closer look, and it soon became evident that some hastily done repairs made to the *Pauline's* upper works had

come undone, the immediate result of which was a drastic
drop in the frigate's speed.

"Quickly, Benjamin!" Brewer said. "Go aft and have Mr.
Sweeney alter course two points to larboard. Tell him to be
ready to put the wheel hard over to starboard so we can cut
across her stern and rake her. If the wind allows, we shall
come around to starboard for another pass before going in to
board her. Have the hands prepare to board on my
command."

"Aye, sir!" Greene saluted and hurried aft.

"Mr. Reed!" Brewer turned to his senior midshipman.
"Ready the larboard battery first, then the starboard after we
come around!"

"Aye aye, sir!"

Brewer took one last look at the confusion on *Pauline*,
watching men begin to cut away the wreckage as the two
ships came closer and closer. He noted the slight movement
caused by Mr. Sweeney's alteration of *Revenge's* course, and
he turned to hurry back to the quarterdeck to direct the
attack from there.

He arrived to find Mac and Alfred standing off to the side,
both outfitted for boarding with cutlasses and two braces of
pistols each. Mac handed over a brace of pistols for his
captain, and Brewer thanked him.

"Mac, do we have any grenades we could throw in just
before we board?" Brewer asked.

The coxswain grinned. "I'll take care of it, sir."

CHAPTER 19

"Good man. Now, Mr. Sweeney, stand by. Hold, hold... Now! Hard to starboard! Mr. Reed! Fire as your guns bear!"

HMS *Revenge* swung around, and Brewer counted six guns going off as they swept past the pirate's stern. Now she came around again, and he watched Reed and his men move to the starboard battery and run it out. Reed looked to the quarterdeck, and Brewer nodded at him. The *Pauline* was turning to larboard, trying to get a shot at *Revenge*.

"Fire, Mr. Reed!" he cried. "She's turning! Fire now!"

Reed barked his command, and the starboard battery rang out. Unfortunately, Brewer counted only five guns that went off, a testimony to the power of the pirate's single broadside earlier.

"Right at him, Mr. Sweeney!" Brewer ordered. "Take us right into her stern! That's it!"

He watched as Sweeney ordered the hands to back the main topsail. *Revenge's* speed dropped instantly, making her impact with *Pauline* nothing more than a good bump.

"Mr. Greene! Boarding parties ready? Right! Now, Mac!"

The coxswain had five or six men with him, all armed with grenades, which they tossed into the pirate stern and up onto her quarterdeck. As soon as they went off, Brewer put his sword in the air.

"Board!" he shouted.

Mac helped several hands jump through the frigate's shattered stern windows. Some of the men threw grapples and climbed up onto the quarterdeck. Mac himself waited for Brewer and Alfred. Mr. Sweeney and Mr. Short would stay on board *Revenge*, along with a few hands for sail-keeping duties.

They climbed over the rail amidst the chaos of destruction. Dead bodies and tackle wreckage made an obstacle course of the bloody deck, and those who were alive and fighting for their lives now had a hard time not stumbling over the corpses. To Brewer's consternation, Alfred disappeared almost immediately.

"Mac! Where did Alfred go?"

"Dunno, sir! Look out!"

They were already in the thick of the fight, there between the wheel (or what was left of it) and the fantail. Mac dodged to the right and shot a pirate who was rushing toward Brewer, sabre raised for a killing strike. The Captain in turn pulled out a pistol and put a ball in the head of a pirate who was about to run Mac through from behind. Both men had their cutlasses out now and went to work. Mac picked up a second one from the deck and used both to run a pirate through.

Brewer fought his way out on to the deck. He brought his blade down on one man's neck and then lunged past him to bury it in the chest of the man behind him. He pulled the blade out just in time to duck under a slashing attack. He pulled out his other pistol and shot that pirate in the gut. The man grabbed his stomach and dropped to the deck, the amount of blood flowing past his fingers testifying that the wound was mortal.

As he fought, Brewer's eye searched the pirates still standing for a man with a missing ear. Once it almost cost him his life, but the pirate's pistol misfired. Brewer ran him through and pushed him to the deck. Finally, he spotted his quarry forward and to larboard. The pirate was not a big man, but he was fighting well and carried himself with an air of command, so Brewer thought he was fairly safe in thinking this was not a decoy. He spotted a gun on the deck and picked it up, using it to shoot the pirate immediately to El Diabolito's left. The pirate chief turned to face him. At that moment there came one of those lulls in battle that made conversation briefly possible.

"El Diabolito?" Brewer demanded. The pirate nodded. "I am Captain Brewer. You ambushed my last ship, and I am here to repay you for it."

The pirate grinned. "Go ahead and try, Englishman. Come to your death, if you dare."

The two men crossed sabers and went at each other ferociously. The pirate was smaller than Brewer, but muscular and quick, and the Captain was thankful now for all his practice against Alfred. Brewer slashed at the neck, only to have the pirate duck under it and make a thrust, which Brewer sidestepped. He brought down his blade hard, but the pirate parried it with such force that it jarred Brewer's shoulder. The two men stepped back to size each other up again.

Alfred was at the moment rushing to the forecastle. Across the ship, he had recognized the one man he wanted to meet again, and it looked like he was again going to jump over the railing and try to escape. On the way forward, Alfred picked up an axe, and now he threw it so it landed in the railing right beside the pirate. Roberto Cofresi turned and grinned.

"So, my little friend," he said, "we meet again."

"I don't believe we finished our engagement the last time," Alfred said.

"No," the pirate replied. "I was merciful to you. Not a mistake I will make this time, I assure you."

"Don't worry," Alfred said as he charged. "You won't have the chance."

Noah Simmons was a part of Mr. Greene's group that went in through the frigate's stern windows and what was left of the captain's cabin. He was armed, as many of his group were, with a pike and a pistol. He made sure he was not in the front as the group probed their way down the ship's gun deck. The scene was of the most horrific carnage he had ever witnessed. He finally made his way by keeping his eyes on the back of the head of the man in front of him so he didn't have to look at the guns that were overturned, crushing the bodies of men and boys beneath them. He tried his best not to look at the piles of raw, bloody meat that had been human beings until they met with British or French shot. He stepped in one such pile and slipped, causing him to double over and come face-to-face with a man's skull, or rather the left side of one, lying on top of another such pile. He managed to stagger off to the side before retching the contents of his stomach all over the bloody deck.

Simmons rejoined his group, and together they fought their way forward. He used his pike to run pirates through at a distance or to help a shipmate, although more than once he used it to finish off a pirate who was down on the deck. Simmons cared not at all for chivalry or any of the so-called "rules" of warfare, and he was not about to let some wounded pirate stab him in the back, or the leg, in passing. Now that Scar was dead and his own misdeeds safely hidden, his whole focus was on surviving long enough to get off *Revenge* at his first opportunity and making it to the United States to start a new life. One thing that was definitely not included in those plans was fighting on board a pirate frigate. His only mission was to make it out alive.

On the frigate's deck, Mac had settled down to his usual job, which was guarding his captain's back. He could plainly see that the captain had found El Diabolito himself, and the two men were engaged in a duel in which no quarter would be asked for, nor would any be given. Mac took up station behind the captain and a few feet away. He was still holding a saber in each hand; he was getting pretty good at tying up a pirate's cutlass with one saber before disemboweling him with the other. At one point, he ducked under a high slash and a buried his right-hand saber in the man's chest, then he let go of the blade so he could pull a pistol from his belt and shoot another pirate. He yanked his blade from the dead man and fought on.

Brewer soon realized that his head was giving him more trouble than he originally thought. The pounding had increased, and he was afraid that the wound had begun to bleed again. Twice he had to back off to blink clouds out of his eyes, the second time barely clearing his vision in time to parry a thrust at his neck. Alfred's admonitions during their training to keep moving and thereby keep control of the engagement rang in his ears. Diabolito ducked and made thrusts almost as swiftly as Alfred himself, but thankfully Brewer's training allowed him to parry every attack. He was also able to use a few tricks he learned to his advantage.

Brewer made a high thrust, only to slash low when the pirate went to block it. Diabolito brought his saber low to parry, which opened the door for Brewer to charge in and deliver a devastating blow to the pirate's chin with his free hand. Diabolito was staggered by the blow, which Brewer followed up by bringing the hilt of his sword up as hard as he could to the pirate's face. Blood spurted from his lip and nose, and the pirate went down. That's when Brewer made his first mistake of the day. Instead of running the pirate through as he lay on the deck, he backed off.

"Do you surrender?" he asked.

The pirate smiled. "You are a fool, Captain."

Brewer found out why the pirate said that when three of his minions charged him from behind their chief. Brewer was saved by Mac and two others, who shot down the attackers.

Diabolito was back on his feet quickly and on the attack. He pressed the British captain for all he was worth, but he could not find a way to get inside his defenses. The Englishman jumped to the attack with a speed that was not expected from one his size. The pirate winced and recoiled when his enemy's blade slashed his thigh. He dared not take time to inspect the wound, but he felt a warming moving down his leg which told him that he had to end this battle, and soon.

Brewer thanked God for his timely rescue by Mac and his men, and he set his jaw in his determination not to give the pirate another such chance. When Diabolito jumped back to his feet, Brewer dove in to the attack, trying every trick that Alfred had taught him until he finally succeeded in drawing blood from the pirate's thigh. Now he changed his game plan, to watch for a weakness due to the wound and to exploit it to the full. For a short time, his enemy did a good job in guarding his injury, but eventually the weakness in his leg showed in his fighting. The pirate made a thrust, which Brewer parried, landing on his bad leg, which gave way under him, causing him to fall to the deck. Diabolito promptly slashed with his saber to keep his enemy at bay and barely missed Brewer's hand with his blind attack. Brewer brought his blade down on the forearm of the pirate's sword arm. The pirate screamed and dropped his saber. Brewer quickly discovered that the force of the blow had not been sufficient to sever the forearm, and now his blade was lodged in the bones of the pirate's forearm. Diabolito instinctively reached up with his free hand and grabbed Brewer's jacket, hoping to hold him there until one of his men could come to his aid and finish the Englishman off. Unfortunately for him, Mac was quicker. He stepped in and buried his blade deep in the pirate's chest.

The pirate's dead hand released Brewer and fell to the deck. Brewer stood over his enemy, breathing heavily. Mac retrieved his saber for him from Diabolito's forearm and handed it to him. He nodded his thanks, too tired to speak. Brewer looked around and saw that his men were in control of the deck all the way to the forecastle, where a small group of pirates appeared to be fighting on. He touched Mac's arm to get his attention.

"Mac," he said. "The forecastle. Is that smoke I see rising?"

"Aye, sir," came the answer. "I'm afraid it is."

Alfred charged his adversary, determined not to allow him to escape again. Cofresi did his best to keep his distance, but he was only partly successful due to the blood and debris on deck. Alfred was silent and purposeful during his attack, paying no attention to the pirate's taunts, concentrating instead on pressing his own attacks. Cofresi tried the same trick that had saved him last time—breaking off, dodging and running below deck to see if he could find an ally. He was disappointed; the gun deck below held nobody alive to help him. His adversary was hard on his heels, so he was forced to turn and fight.

Eventually, Alfred's concentrated fury caused him to make a mistake. He got too close and allowed Cofresi to grab him by the front of the shirt, hurling him back across the deck to land among several bodies of what was once a gun's crew.

"You see, my little English dog!" Cofresi crowed. "I do not care for your rules of proper fighting!"

Alfred's hand felt a pistol in a dead pirate's belt. He pulled it without hesitation and shot Cofresi in the leg.

"Neither do I," he said as he rose.

Cofresi was down on one knee now, his hand pressing against the blood flowing from the wound in his thigh. "You swine!" he cried. "Stinking English swine! You knew you could not best me with the blade, so you resort to this! Curse you, you dog!"

Alfred searched among the bodies and found two more pistols. He used one to shoot the pirate in the shoulder of his sword arm. Cofresi screamed and dropped his sword, but he managed to stay upright. Alfred took a step forward and raised his remaining pistol.

"You have no ally to save you this time," he said. "And my philosophy of fighting is the same as yours: The only thing that matters is to win."

He shot the pirate between the eyes, and the body fell backward onto the deck.

Lieutenant Greene came up at that moment and found Alfred looking down on the dead pirate.

"Cofresi?" he asked.

Alfred nodded.

Greene grunted. "Too bad you didn't save him for the captain."

"I owed him," Alfred said simply.

Greene nodded. He turned to go and then stopped, sniffing the air.

"Alfred, do you smell smoke?"

Alfred raised his nose and sniffed the air. "Yes sir, I do."

"Let's get out of here! Alfred, I'm going on deck to find the captain." Greene turned and shouted, "Mr. Reed! Make sure our men and any prisoners get back to the ship immediately! Everyone off this ship and back to the *Revenge*!"

Simmons had managed to find himself a convenient hiding place between two guns. He had killed two pirates and then decided not to press his luck any further. He spotted his cozy little hideout and settled down there to wait the battle out. He heard Mr. Greene's call for the men to get off the ship, and he emerged from his hiding place. He didn't notice the hand come up beside him until it was too late.

"Mr. Simmons!" he called. "I've been looking all over for you! Glad to see you're safe, sir!"

"Hello, Tommy," Simmons said. "Let's get off this ship while we still can."

"That's going to be a little hard for you, mate," Tommy said. Before Simmons knew what was happening, the tar caught him by the arm and shoved the muzzle of a pistol into his ribs.

"What?" Simmons squeaked as the Tommy pulled the trigger.

Tommy knelt down beside the dying midshipman. "Scar said to look you up if anything ever happened to him," he said. "And, unlike you, he paid in advance."

Lieutenant Greene made it up on deck and found the captain leaning a little on Mac with his other hand to his head.

"Smoke below, Captain," he said. "I recommend withdrawal."

Brewer looked at him and nodded. Greene could see the man was almost played out between the fighting on the deck and his head injury. Greene saw the dead pirate at his captain's feet and noted that he was missing an ear. *Good,* he thought. *At least the Captain got his revenge.*

"Come on, Mac," he said. "Let's get the Captain back to the ship."

"Aye, sir." He steered his charge back toward the fantail.

"Let's go, you men!" Greene called loudly. "This ship is burning! Back to the ship! The pirate's afire! Back to *Revenge!*"

He stood by while the crew made their way past him. He noticed a few prisoners being herded aft as well; he knew implicitly he could trust Mr. Reed to deal with them. He also heard some splashes, and he turned to see a few pirates jump overboard, obviously preferring to try their luck with the sharks rather than the rope. Greene shrugged; that was fine with him. The way he figured it, either way, they would never bother English shipping again.

Greene made his way to the fantail at the end of the group of *Revenge's* survivors. He looked down to the sloop's deck and saw Mr. Reed standing there.

"Is the gun deck clear, Mr. Reed?" he called.

"Aye, sir!" Reed answered. "You're the only one left!"

Greene nodded and jumped over.

"Mr. Reed, I'm going aft. Get a party of men to push us away from *Pauline,* and make sure those prisoners are secured."

"Aye, sir."

On his way aft, Greene ran into the captain, still leaning on McCleary. Greene wondered what was stopping the man from collapsing completely.

"Captain?" Greene said. "We need to back away from the *Pauline* before the fire reaches her magazine, sir."

When Brewer looked at Greene, the dazed expression on his face told the first lieutenant that it was time for him to take over.

"Mac," he said, "take him below to his cabin and put him to bed. Send someone for the doctor; don't leave him alone. Ask the doctor to come see me after he's examined the captain."

"Aye, sir."

Greene continued aft. He found Mr. Sweeney on the quarterdeck.

"I have the deck," Greene called out. "Mr. Sweeney, get us out of here. Put the helm hard over."

Reed's men used pikes to push the ship off and past the *Pauline*, and *Revenge* pulled away from the pirate ship. And none too soon! They were only a few cable lengths away when the frigate exploded in a deafening roar that sent fire and debris hundreds of feet into the air.

"I wonder how much treasure they had in her holds?" Sweeney said, rubbing his jaw.

"Not enough to content them," Greene said, an edge to his voice.

Dr. Spinelli came up on deck and stretched before joining Greene and Sweeney.

"Pretty fireworks," he said, nodding towards the burning frigate.

"Yes," Greene said. "How's the captain?"

"His head had begun to bleed again. I changed the dressing and gave him another dose of laudanum to help him sleep. I'm more worried about the blurry vision he complained about. Hopefully, it won't persist when he wakes up."

"How long do you expect him to be down?"

"I would like him to rest for at least three days," Spinelli said. "Whether he listens or not, well, that is quite another matter."

"Thank you, Doctor," Greene said. Spinelli went below deck, and Greene turned to Sweeney. "Now, the question is, what do we do? We are hardly fit to fight another battle, either with pirates or a Spanish treasure galleon. We need time to make repairs before even thinking about either of those options."

"San Andres?" Sweeney suggested.

Greene nodded. "San Andres."

Sweeney smiled. "Aye, sir."

The ship's bell rang six bells. Greene looked around, assessing damage and resources. .

"Mr. Reed," he said. "Go below and get some rest. Relieve me at the turn of the first watch."

Reed nodded gratefully. "Aye aye, sir."

Work proceeded on what repairs could be made as the afternoon wore on. The watch bill was adjusted to compensate for the men lost in action, and Greene went ahead and buried those who had died on board. He felt bad for those who had fallen on the *Pauline* whose bodies were lost in the explosion; would it matter that they were not given a proper burial?

He was nearly at the end of his watch when Mr. Short approached him.

"Begging your pardon, sir," he said. "The captain sends his compliments and asks that you join him in his cabin at the end of your watch."

"My respects to the captain. Tell him I will be there as soon as I am relieved."

Lieutenant Greene arrived at the captain's cabin and found Mr. Sweeney and the doctor already waiting for him along with the captain. McCleary opened the door to admit him, closing it behind him and taking up his usual position just inside.

"Come in, Benjamin," Brewer said. The captain still had the bandage on the side of his head.

Greene took a seat on a sea chest, and Alfred presented him with a glass of port. This was the first time he had been in the captain's quarters since *Pauline* had put that broadside into them during the first part of the battle, and he was pleased to see that they had come through the ordeal relatively intact.

"So, Doctor," Brewer began, "what's the final tally?"

"In both battles combined," Spinelli replied, "we lost thirty-seven men dead. Another thirty-two are recovering from various injuries, and some of them have been released back to duty. Most of the dead were lost in the boarding action on the *Pauline*."

Brewer closed his eyes briefly when he heard the numbers. "Mr. Sweeney?"

The sailing master stirred. "We should make San Andres by tomorrow. A good part of the rigging will need to be reworked. We only did the patch jobs necessary to get us there."

Mr. Greene spoke up. "The carpenter would like to put a man over the side to check out the hull, sir. He thinks we're taking on water, but he can't find out from where while we are under way."

Brewer nodded and made a note on the paper before him.

"The sailmaker and his mate—he only has one left now— are getting a new set ready," Sweeney said.

"Very good," Brewer said. "Mr. Greene?"

Greene leaned forward, resting his forearms on his knees and holding his glass in both hands. "As you know, sir, we got hit hard. Lieutenant Tyler was killed by *Pauline's* broadside. I recommend that you promote Mr. Reed to acting-second lieutenant. I was very impressed with his conduct during the fighting. I will write you a report."

Brewer nodded and made another note.

"I have the updated watch bills ready for your review, sir. I had to shuffle some people around to make sure each watch was covered. We will need to take on replacements."

"So," Brewer said, "we give Mr. Reed a promotion to acting-lieutenant. Who does that leave as senior midshipman? Simmons?"

"Sir," Greene said, "Mr. Simmons is missing and presumed dead on the *Pauline*."

Brewer was surprised. "I didn't know that. Who do we have left? Mr. Short?"

Greene chuckled. "Doesn't being the *only* midshipman automatically make you the *senior* midshipman?"

"I suppose it does," Brewer said, unable to hide the amused look on his face. "Very well; Mr. Short shall be acting-senior midshipman for the duration of this voyage. Anything else for the present? No? Thank you, gentlemen."

Brewer rested his aching head in his hands as the men filed out. He did not notice that the doctor had kept his seat, so he was startled when he spoke.

"Is your headache worse?"

Brewer winced and looked over at his friend and tormentor. "Only when you surprise me like that. What do you need, Adam?"

"Oh, nothing, really. I just wanted to know when you were going back to bed and whether you needed more laudanum to help you sleep."

Brewer sighed. "I'm fine, Doctor, really. So, if you would be so kind..."

Spinelli sat back in his chair, the look on his face a mixture of concern and irritation.

"Very well," he said. "I did not want to resort to this again, but if I must... Mac!"

The big coxswain took two steps from the door and stood there with his hands behind his back. Brewer looked from the Mac to the doctor and back again.

"So, that's it, is it?" he said to McCleary. "I could charge both of you with mutiny, you know. I could put *you* in the brig!"

Mac shrugged. "Been there before, sir, and for worse causes, too."

Brewer looked at the doctor in exasperation. "You know, there was a time when he actually worked for *me*."

Spinelli leaned forward. "Look, William, there is nothing going on the rest of today and tonight. If you rest, you may feel much better come the morning. You may even feel well enough to oversee the start of repairs when we reach San Andres. Now, will you go willingly, or shall I have your nurse over there put you forcibly to bed?"

Brewer suddenly felt very tired. "You win. I'll go to bed."

"Good," Spinelli said as he rose. "May I tell Mr. Greene not to disturb you? Thank you. Keep your eye on him, Mac; you know what to watch for."

"Aye, sir," Mac said.

Spinelli smiled and waved, and then he was gone. Brewer sat there and looked at his coxswain, standing there like the Rock of Gibraltar, and two thoughts occurred to him. One was that he ought to clap him and his renegade surgeon in irons. The other was that he was lucky to have both of them. He sighed and went to bed.

CHAPTER 20

He slept like a baby, waking to find that the dawn had preceded him. Sleep's restorative powers proved even better than the doctor's prediction, as he discovered that his head hardly hurt at all and his vision had cleared. He sent for the doctor to come and examine the wound.

"So," Spinelli said as he removed the bandage, "you slept the whole night, did you? You recover from wounds quicker than most, Captain, I'll give you that. Now, let's see what we have here. Does this hurt?" He probed around the wound with his fingertips.

"No," Brewer said. "I feel the pressure, but there's no pain."

"Good. How's your eyesight? Do you have any trouble focusing on your books?" He pointed to the captain's library across the room.

"No, but they're out of order. I need to fix that."

"Very good. I feared that your blurry vision would persist, but such does not seem to be the case. I want you to report it to me immediately if you have another episode, sir."

Brewer nodded. "Understood. May I go on deck now?" he asked facetiously. He picked up his hat and left the cabin without waiting for an answer.

He stepped up on deck to find *Revenge* entering into the harbor at San Andres. The air was cool for the time of year, in spite of the sun shining down through a blue, cloudless sky. He walked over to Mr. Greene, who was speaking to the quartermaster.

"Good morning, Mr. Greene," he said.

"Good morning, Captain," Greene replied, as he and the quartermaster saluted. "How are you feeling this morning?"

"Much better, thank you. It seems the doctor knows what he's talking about when it comes to the benefits of sleep."

"Have you noticed we have company, sir?" Greene said.

Brewer turned around to see the *Semillante* berthed on the other side of the harbor with two of the missing luggars anchored beside her.

"Well," Brewer said, "I guess that explains why she never showed up to help with *Pauline*. She's taken a beating, that's for sure. My guess is that they'll try to make repairs and return to Martinique, although by the looks of her, Havana or Charleston might be more appropriate." Brewer began to pace the quarterdeck, chin down on his breast, hands clasped behind his back, eyes staring unfocussed at the deck before him. He ceased after only one circuit and looked at Greene with a smile. "Mr. Greene, what say we dispatch *Lieutenant* Reed to the Frenchman with another invitation to dine aboard *Revenge*? I know it's more properly their turn to play the host, but from here it looks like our house is a little neater than theirs. Pass the word for our new lieutenant, if you please."

Greene passed the word to a petty officer and turned back to his captain. "I see what you mean, sir. What size gun would you say that is run out from the starboard luggar? An 8-pounder? And five ports per side? Two of those could be a nasty handful, especially for a damaged ship."

Lieutenant Reed arrived and saluted. "You sent for me, Captain?"

"Yes, Lieutenant. I have two jobs for you. I want you to take a boat and row over to the *Semillante*. You'll find her berthed right over there behind two luggars. I want you to extend an invitation to their captain and first lieutenant to dine aboard *Revenge* this evening at the turn of the second dog watch. They may say something about it being their turn to play the host, but you tell them I insist. After that, I want you to row ashore and see if any orders or mail have been left for us."

"Aye aye, sir." Reed saluted and was gone.

Mr. Sweeney came back on deck. "Good to see you up and around, Captain."

"Thank you, Mr. Sweeney. Gentlemen, I want a detailed inspection of this ship and full list of damages that must be repaired. I'm returning to my cabin to write my report for the admiral, and I shall have to attach the list. Mr. Greene, let's get the man over the side for the carpenter to see if he can find a leak or shot hole we missed. Dismissed."

"Aye, sir," the two men said. They saluted and set off.

Brewer made his way back to his cabin and removed his hat and coat. As he laid them across his bed, he suddenly realized he was famished.

"Alfred!" he called.

Alfred appeared in the doorway. "Sir?"

"Have you anything for my breakfast?"

"Will ham, eggs, and potatoes be sufficient, sir?"

"Excellent! And coffee, if you please."

"Aye aye, sir." He retreated and went to work.

He was back within five minutes with the coffee and ten minutes after that with a plate piled high with the captain's breakfast. Brewer dug in, somewhat gingerly at first, but later on with the abandon of a man who had not eaten for nearly two days. When he was finished, Alfred cleared the table and refilled his coffee. Brewer got his writing materials out.

"This is one report I shall enjoy writing," he said. "El Diabolito is dead."

Alfred turned at the door. "And Roberto Cofresi, sir."

Brewer looked up. "What's that?"

"Roberto Cofresi is also dead, sir," the servant repeated.

Brewer opened his mouth but closed it again without speaking. He understood, and he looked at Alfred.

"I see. Thank you, Alfred."

Alfred bowed and left the room.

Brewer was about halfway through his report when Lieutenant Reed reported in.

"So, Lieutenant," Brewer said as he set down his quill, "how did it go on the *Semillante*?"

"Quite well, sir. Captain Roussin accepted your invitation, on the condition that your cook was still alive. I assured him that such was the case."

Brewer chuckled. "Anything for us ashore?"

Reed shook his head. "Nothing, sir."

"Ah. Report to Mr. Greene until the French are due to arrive."

"Aye aye, sir." Reed nodded to his captain and left.

"Alfred!" Brewer called, and that worthy appeared. "The French captain and first lieutenant will dine with us tonight. Can you be ready by the turn of the second dog watch?"

Alfred closed his eyes for several seconds. He opened them and said, "Yes, sir, but I shall need to make a trip ashore."

"Very well. Take Mac and a boat."

"Aye, sir."

He turned his attention back to his report.

BREWER'S REVENGE

It is my distinct pleasure to call attention to the gallantry of the Captain's servant, Alfred Thomas, who dispatched the infamous pirate Roberto Cofresi in single combat.

Brewer paused and looked down at the sentence, feeling that it was inadequate somehow and wishing he could do more. Alfred had saved his life in the first fight with Cofresi off Puerto Rico, and on the *Pauline* he had not hesitated to go after the man when he saw him again. Then Brewer remembered something, and he had to chuckle at the thought. The last time he bragged about his servant to the admiral, he lost the servant! So it may not be such a good idea to bring Alfred to Hornblower's notice.

One of the last things Brewer did was to attach a list of the dead or missing and presumed dead due to the explosion of the *Pauline*. One name pulled him up short.

Joshua Taylor, Leftenant

Brewer's heart went to his throat for a moment. The lad had had a bright future. Lad? Tyler was only five or six years younger than Brewer himself. Back during the wars, Tyler might have even had his own command before he was thirty. Brewer shook his head in disgust at the waste; well, nobody ever said life was fair.

The last name he wrote also gave him pause.

Noah Simmons, Midshipman

Brewer wondered about this one. Were their suspicions correct? Had he hired the assassin to kill Reed? Had Grant simply got in the way? Brewer sat back and sighed in frustration. They would never know the answers. The question now was, could he relax the security precautions around Mr. Reed? Sleeping arrangements were not a problem, as Reed could sling his hammock in the gunroom for the duration; in fact, Mr. Greene should have already moved him into Tyler's old quarters by now. Brewer chewed on his lip for a moment as he thought. His gut told him that it was safe now to release Kelly back to his normal duty—that was good enough for him.

As he sealed the report, Brewer wondered what the governor of Jamaica would think of his son's death. Officially, Simmons had died in a boarding action against notorious pirates—a hero's death. Thinking of Simmons and his father made Brewer think of his own father. What would he think if he got the news that his son had fallen before an enemy's sword? He was sure his mother and sister would weep and mourn for him, but what would his father do? Brewer honestly had no idea. His face burned with shame at the thought that his father had disowned him over joining the Navy. He prayed Heaven would give him the chance to make it right with the old man before something happened to either of them.

Captain Roussin and Lieutenant de Robespierre stepped on the deck of HMS *Revenge* at the appointed hour. Alfred outdid himself, serving platters of mutton, beef-and-kidney pie, a goose plump enough to be a blessing to Christmas dinner in any mansion in England, stewed potatoes, carrots, and cauliflower, accompanied by fresh baked bread and butter.

"Excellent, Captain, truly excellent!" Roussin declared enthusiastically.

When the feast was over, the stewards cleared the plates and bowls from the table, and Alfred came around and filled everyone's glass with wine. A steward followed him, offering cigars to those who would like them. Brewer looked with amusement on the two new members of the assembly. Lieutenant Reed had started out the evening looking a little uncomfortable as he sat next to Mr. Greene, but he'd soon warmed to his place. He sat quietly and listened, which impressed Brewer. Mr. Short was also there; Brewer had made an exception and invited him as the senior midshipman. The boy was a tad embarrassed when his voice cracked as he toasted the King's health, which raised several hints of laughter in the room, but Brewer made it up to him. After the boy sat down, his Captain rose and raised his glass in a toast to him and led the company in wishing Mr. Short a happy fourteenth birthday. Short grinned from ear to ear and raised his glass in return.

Brewer resumed his seat and lit his cigar. He puffed life into it and was soon sending clouds of smoke heavenward. He looked around to find his French guests doing the same.

"Captain, I do enjoy these cigars," Roussin said.

"Mr. Reed, arrange for our esteemed guest to take two dozen with him when he leaves," Brewer said.

"Aye aye, sir."

Roussin nodded and waved the cigar. "Thank you, Captain."

"Now, sir," Brewer said, "do you wish to go first, or shall I?"

"Oh, after *you*, my dear sir."

Brewer told the two French officers the story of the pursuit of the *Pauline*, how the repairs to her rigging came apart, and how she was boarded and taken. He also told of the smoke that warned them to abandon the ship and the explosion that followed.

Roussin listened without commentary. It was obvious they had hoped to retake their frigate and return to France with her as a prize.

"So," Roussin said, "El Diabolito is dead?"

Brewer nodded. "As is Roberto Cofresi."

De Robespierre spoke up. "You killed him as well, Captain?"

"Not I," Brewer said, as he motioned with his cigar toward the pantry door. "Alfred."

"The little cook?" the Frenchman said, astonished. "Remind me never to complain about the food."

"And you, Captain?" Brewer asked.

Roussin waited as the steward refilled everyone's glasses before he began his tale.

"It took us nearly two hours to make repairs and get under way after we parted company," he said. "We set off on a pursuit course but soon sighted a small group of sail to the west. You were already below the horizon, so I could not communicate with you. I decided to investigate the sighting. We found four of the missing luggars traveling two by two. This allowed me to attack them without being overwhelmed. We engaged the rearmost two; raking the first in the stern and one other volley broadside reduced her to a sinking wreck. The second raked us before we could turn, but our 18-pounders shattered her sides and she sank quickly. We were not aiming at the sails that time, but at the hull! We turned toward the second pair, but they hauled down their colors without a fight. I decided to return to San Andres to complete sufficient repairs to enable me to make Martinique with my prizes. Can you imagine the governor's face, Captain, when the *Semillante* sails into harbor with these two under her lee? It will be one for the ages, I promise you that!"

"I hope you get good prize money for them," Brewer said. "Any idea what happened to the other two?"

Roussin shook his head. "None. But with you sinking the *Pauline*, and our destruction of two of their six luggars and the capture of two more, they may be short of ships now to try to take the galleon."

"I'm not so sure," Brewer said. "Remember, Cochrane still has the *Valdivia,* and maybe those two luggars. We are talking about the man who took a Spanish frigate with little more than a schooner, don't forget, so he may be that bold again when it comes to the Dons." He thought for a moment. "When can you get under way?"

Roussin looked to his premier. "Two days, we hope," de Robespierre said. "We still have some holes to plug in the hull."

"Can you fight?" Brewer asked.

"Yes," the lieutenant said, "but not well and not for long."

"Mr. Greene?" Brewer asked.

"We need at least two days more than that, Captain," he said, "if you expect us to go up against a frigate again."

"You are expecting more fighting, Captain?" Roussin asked.

"Do you know Cochrane, Captain? No? Well, I have looked into his eyes. He is nothing to toy with, and he doesn't like it when his plans are interfered with."

"I see," Roussin said, with a dark look in his eyes.

"Well," Brewer said as he contemplated their options, "let's keep at it. Captain, can we speak again, the day after tomorrow? We can decide then if we have anything to worry about."

Roussin nodded. "Agreed, Captain." He rose, and his first lieutenant followed, as did Brewer and his company. "We shall bid you adieu, *mon ami,* and let us hope your fears prove unjustified."

Brewer's fears proved all too justified. Shortly after dawn the next morning, the *Valdivia* sailed into the harbor.

Brewer was immediately called to the deck. When he arrived, he used a glass to verify what he already knew to be true.

"Blast," he said. "Another day, and we might have been gone."

"Maybe the admiral's not on board, sir," Greene said.

"No such luck," Brewer said, pointing to the admiral's broad pennant unfurled high up on the mainmast.

"She's lowering a boat, sir!" Mr. Short called from the shrouds.

Brewer lowered his head and said, "*Mazel tav.*"

"Sir?" Greene said.

"Nothing." He put the glass to his eye. "A single officer. I think it's the same lieutenant who carried the message at Caracas."

"What will you do, sir?" Greene asked.

Brewer grinned. "Why, invite him to dinner, of course."

It was indeed the same Lieutenant Escobar who bounded aboard *Revenge.*

"Good day, *Capitan!*" he said. "A pleasure to see you again!"

"And to you, Lieutenant," Brewer said cordially. "What can I do for you?"

"Admiral Cochrane wishes to speak to you, *Capitan.*"

Brewer smiled and shook his head sadly. "Please convey my great respects to the admiral. Unfortunately, I am unable to leave my ship at present. By way of apology, please convey to your admiral my invitation to dine on board HMS *Revenge* today at the end of the forenoon watch."

Escobar was not pleased at all to convey the invitation, but of course he was trapped into the courtesy of accepting. He bowed dutifully, made his farewells, and quit the ship without delay. Greene stepped up to his captain and watched the Chilean's boat pull away.

"Well said, Captain," he said. "I don't imagine his admiral expected to hear that."

"We shall soon find out, Mr. Greene," Brewer said. "If you will excuse me, I need to tell Alfred that we'll have company for dinner."

Admiral Cochrane came aboard at the appointed hour, and Captain Brewer made sure he was received with all the pomp and ceremony accorded to his rank. Cochrane came aboard without an aide or flag lieutenant, so the two men adjourned to Brewer's cabin and the waiting feast. Cochrane complemented dish after dish, and Brewer brought Alfred out to be presented. The servant bowed with all dignity at the praise.

After the dished were cleared away, and the cigars and Madeira were served, the two men sat back in their chairs and smoked.

"So, my lord," Brewer asked, "what brings you to San Andres? I thought you had a galleon to catch."

Irritation flashed in the Admiral's eye, but he suppressed it with a smile. "Actually, Captain, I am in search of some of my ships."

Brewer nodded. "I imagine you found two of them sitting under the lee of that French frigate across the harbor."

"As a matter of fact, I did. Would you happen to know how they got there?"

"I would indeed, Admiral. Those two ships are part of a contingent of six allegedly stolen from Martinique by pirates. The frigate came upon four of them sailing in two pairs. She attacked the first two and blew them out of the water. 18-pound broadsides have that effect on luggars. These two are the second pair; they surrendered without the frigate firing a shot."

The Admiral's eyes were hooded and his visage was dark. "I see," he said. "I was also looking for a frigate. I believe you were looking for her captain the last time we spoke. You wouldn't happen to know what happened to her, would you?"

"I would, my lord. Before she encountered the luggars, we came across the French frigate in combat against another frigate. I identified the second ship as the one that ambushed my previous ship, the very one I was looking for when we last spoke. As we approached, the two frigates were engaged in a straight fight, exchanging 18-pounder broadsides. The frigate in the harbor here, the *Semillante*, was damaged and out of the fight temporarily. We managed to rake the *Pauline* twice and received a single broadside in return, which damaged us and allowed *Pauline* to stagger away from the battle. We made sufficient repairs to pursue. As we were in pursuit, we saw what appeared to be some patchwork repairs in *Pauline's* upper works come completely apart, which allowed us to catch up and rake her across the stern again. We boarded her and had just taken her when we were forced to abandon the ship due to smoke. A short time later, the ship exploded."

Cochrane was silent as Brewer finished his tale.

"El Diabolito is dead?" he asked quietly.

"Yes, my lord," Brewer answered just as quietly. "As is Roberto Cofresi."

"I see. Your doing?"

"Does it make a difference? My men."

Cochrane nodded. It was obvious to Brewer that the admiral was struggling to contain his temper.

"Captain," Cochrane said in a low, menacing voice, "I believe you owe me some ships."

"Not so, my lord. We lawfully attacked pirate ships in open waters in obedience to our orders."

"Blast your orders, sir! You knew I needed those ships!"

Brewer said nothing as Cochrane struggled to regain his control.

"Perhaps I shall be forced to just take what I need," the Admiral said. "I was once quite good when it came to cutting out ships, say, a sloop of war and two luggars?"

Now it was Brewer's turn to appear grave. He put down his cigar and rose.

"I promise you one thing, my lord," he said. "You will die trying. Thank you for your company, and good day."

Cochrane was surprised by the curt dismissal, but he smiled as he rose. He bowed, his eyes not leaving Brewer's.

He paused at the door. "A pleasure, Captain, as always. Hornblower has trained you well." He left the ship without another word.

Brewer sat at the table for a long time, trying to decide if the admiral was serious about his threat. He was still a peer of the British realm, after all, and the thought that he would deliberately attack a ship of the Royal Navy was difficult to comprehend. However, everything he knew about Lord Cochrane told him not to underestimate the danger he posed.

A knock at his door interrupted his thoughts.

"Enter," he said absent-mindedly.

Mr. Short came in. "Mr. Reed's respects, sir. *Valdivia* is leaving the harbor."

CHAPTER 21

"What?" Brewer was confounded. He rose and grabbed his hat. "Let's go, Mr. Short."

They arrived back on deck to see that it was true; *Valdivia* was indeed making sail. Brewer walked over and stood next to Sweeney and Mr. Greene.

"Now, what's he up to?" the Captain wondered aloud. "He can't just be abandoning his mission, not after the threats he's made."

"Threats, sir?" Greene asked.

"Lord Cochrane thinks we owe him some ships. When I disagreed, he threatened to cut out the two luggars and *Revenge*."

"He threatened to attack a ship of His Majesty's navy?" Greene sounded horrified. When Brewer nodded, Greene said, "Then the rumors are true; he is mad."

Brewer and Greene watched as *Valdivia* cleared the harbor and headed out to sea. The Captain turned and began to pace *Revenge's* quarterdeck. Greene's gaze went from the retreating frigate to his captain, back and forth, for several minutes. He tried to figure out what his captain was thinking and what it had to do with the Chilean frigate. Brewer told them of the mad Admiral Cochrane's threat to cut out *Revenge* and the two luggars. What more did anyone have to hear to know the man was insane?

Brewer stopped pacing and rejoined his first lieutenant at the railing. His eyes were hooded and his face serious, but he did not say anything at first. The two watched as the ship receded into the distance before Brewer finally stirred.

"Benjamin," he said, "pass the word for Mac and call away the gig. I need to speak to Captain Roussin on board the *Semillante* immediately."

"Aye, sir."

In short order, Brewer was standing on the deck of the French frigate being greeted by Captain Roussin.

"A pleasure to see you again, Captain," Roussin said. "I presume you are here to inform me about the frigate that just left the harbor, the one whose admiral visited your ship?"

"I am, Captain," Brewer said.

"Good. Please follow me to my cabin." Roussin led the way below decks to his cabin, where his steward provided them each with a glass of wine. "Now then, Captain Brewer," Roussin said as the two men sat on the cushioned settee beneath the cabin's stern windows, "I am at your disposal."

"Thank you, Captain," Brewer said. "This wine is excellent. I wish my tidings were as likely to be as well received. The officer you saw visit my ship was the Admiral Cochrane I spoke to you about earlier. He says he was looking for his ships, and he was none too pleased when he discovered what we had accomplished. He was very angry with me when I told him that both El Diabolito and Roberto Cofresi were dead. He saw the two luggars parked under your lee and demanded an explanation, so I told him what you told me about sinking the first two and capturing the other pair. He said I owed him for his lost ships. I pointed out that all we did was attack known pirate vessels. He then threatened to cut out the two luggars along with *Revenge*. I promised him he would die trying, and he left. The next thing I know, his ship sailed."

Roussin nodded slowly as he thought this over. "Do you think he has gone?"

Brewer frowned at the question. It was the basis of everything he had been thinking about since he watched the *Valdivia* sail out of the harbor. The more he thought it over, the less he liked the implications.

"No," he finally said. "I don't. My ship is damaged, so is yours; I think he is just mad enough to try to take at least the luggars back. I wouldn't think he would want to embroil Bolivar in a war with Great Britain by attacking *Revenge*, but I must not discount that possibility. He might assume that his rank will protect him, or that our ... disappearance could be accounted for I think he may be lurking just over the horizon, waiting for us to sail."

Roussin's brows were furled in anger and concern. He stared at the far wall for several minutes before sighing and turning back to his guest.

"Do you have a plan?" he asked.

"I do, Captain," Brewer said. "Can you sail tonight?"

Roussin thought it over for a moment. "Yes, but another day or two would be better."

"For us as well," Brewer said, "but I don't think it's a good idea to give Cochrane too many nights to carry out this threat. We sail as soon as it's dark. As we clear the harbor, we set course for Martinique. Sometime after midnight, we will part company, and *Revenge* will head for Port Royal. If *Valdivia* sees us leave, she can't chase both of us. One or the other will escape and report Cochrane's conduct."

Roussin thought it over for a moment. "And the luggars?"

"That is entirely your decision. Take them with you or leave them, as you wish."

Roussin nodded as he considered his options for a few moments.

"Very well," he said. "We shall try it your way. I shall take the luggars with me; they may be useful if *Valdivia* attacks." He stood. "So, Captain, we each have much to do before nightfall."

Brewer stood. "We leave with no lights, Captain, no signs at all if possible. I hope the town will be dark enough not to give us away."

Darkness was falling as Brewer stood on *Revenge's* quarterdeck. It would be full dark in less than thirty minutes.

"Are we ready, Mr. Greene?" he asked.

"Aye, sir," Greene said. "Lookouts report nothing in sight."

"Good. Let's hope it stays that way. "What about *Semillante*?"

"Ready to go, sir. Awaiting the signal."

Brewer nodded. He walked to the rail and stared into the darkness toward the open sea.

"He's out there, Benjamin, somewhere. I feel it."

"Cochrane?"

The Captain nodded again. "Our best hope is to find Admiral Hornblower and his two frigates. Even Cochrane isn't mad enough to take on those odds."

"I should hope not, sir."

Brewer began pacing the quarterdeck, his mind racing, trying to make sure that every last detail had been taken care of and every imaginable contingency anticipated. He frowned; there were so many that he could not provide for— his nightmare right now was for dawn to break and reveal *Valdivia* closing to pistol shot. He shook his head and shrugged his shoulders, trying his best to physically throw the image from his mind and concentrate on the task ahead. He plan was sound. They had to leave before Cochrane had a chance to try to cut out any of their ships.

Brewer noticed someone standing silently off to the side. It was Lieutenant Greene. Brewer paused and looked around to see it was full dark. How long had he been pacing?

"Are we ready, Mr. Greene?"

"Aye, sir. *Semillante* signals that she is ready. The anchor's hove short."

"Very well," Brewer said. "Mr. Greene, take us out. Mr. Short, signal *Semillante*. Gentlemen, I want silence on this ship once we get moving."

Brewer stood back and allowed his men to work. He heard the noise made by the capstan as it raised the anchor and wished it could be silenced. He cringed at the noises made by the unfurling of the sails and silently scolded himself for being so on edge. He could feel *Revenge* making headway now, she was coming around and heading for the open sea. He turned to see the two luggars following, *Semillante* in line behind them. So far, so good. Mr. Sweeney was standing beside the quartermaster at the wheel, rock-like and dependable. Once they had cleared the harbor entrance, Sweeney put the wheel hard over to starboard until their course settled down to due east.

Mr. Greene got the hands moving, making sail that would put distance between the ship and San Andres and Cochrane. He looked aft and could just make out the near luggar following suit and hoped that the other ships would do so as well.

Mr. Greene stepped out of the darkness. "So far, so good, sir."

"Have the extra lookouts been posted?" Brewer asked.

"Yes, sir."

"Very well. You have the deck, Benjamin, I shall be in my cabin working on my report for the admiral. Call me at midnight or if anything needs my attention."

"Aye aye, sir."

Brewer his way below. As the door closed behind him, he was suddenly exhausted, and his head began to pound. He sat down at his desk, and Alfred brought him a glass of port. Brewer thanked him and took an appreciative swallow. He put his forearm on the desk and laid his head on it. He closed his eyes, intending only to rest for a moment or two before starting his report on their departure from San Andres, but the next thing he knew, there was a knock at the door, and Mr. Short entered.

"Begging your pardon, sir, but Mr. Greene sends his respects and says to let you know it's time."

Brewer looked at him, dumbfounded. Had he slept the entire evening away?

"Very well, Mr. Short. I'll come."

Alfred entered. "I'm sorry, sir," he said, "but after seeing the way you came in and fell asleep so quickly, I just let you rest."

"It's all right, Alfred. You did nothing wrong." Brewer reached for his hat. "Can you bring a hot pot of tea up on deck in about an hour or so?"

"Tea, sir? Yes, sir."

Brewer stood. He still felt exhausted, although the pounding in his head had lessened. He made his way carefully up on deck. As he stepped from the stair, he noticed that there was very little moonlight, a fact that he hoped aided their escape.

Mr. Greene saluted. "Sir, do you wish to change course now, or do we wait?"

Brewer looked aft, but he could not see the luggar in the poor moonlight. He motioned for a glass and tried again. He saw the faintest hint of white and knew the ship was still there.

"Where are we, Mr. Sweeney?"

"Approximately thirty-five miles east of San Andres, Captain. Course to Jamaica would be northeast."

Brewer considered for just a moment. "Mr. Short, make the night signal to the luggar that we intend to alter course. Mr. Sweeney, as soon as the luggar acknowledges, lay us on a course NE for Port Royal, if you please."

The luggar acknowledged the signal, and Sweeney put the wheel over to larboard. He steadied the ship up on a course of NE. Brewer nodded approval but had a strange feeling in the pit of his stomach.

"Let's keep all the cloth on her that she'll stand, Mr. Sweeney. I don't want to waste any time."

"Aye, sir!"

The Captain looked around and saw that the new watch had come on deck to take over. Mr. Reed stood beside Mr. Greene. "Mr. Reed, you heard my instructions. Call me if I am needed. You have the deck."

"Aye aye, sir," Reed said. "Good night, Captain."

Brewer said his good nights and made his way back to his cabin. Mac was there to help him out of his coat, and Alfred had a quick meal of cold meat and wine ready for him. Brewer barely managed to change out of his clothes before he climbed into his bed and went straight to sleep.

"Frigate!"

Brewer's eyes snapped open at the sound of the word, shouted by the lookout to the deck below. He sat up and got dressed immediately and made his way to the deck. He found Mr. Greene standing at the fantail with a glass to his eye.

"What have we got, Benjamin?" Brewer asked. A hand offered him a glass.

"Good morning, sir. I was just about to send for you. Lookout spotted a sail on the horizon. All he could make out for sure were the topgallants, but he thinks it's a frigate. You can just see the sail two points to larboard, sir."

Brewer trained his glass along the given bearing, and, sure enough, he could just make out a bare patch of white on the horizon. He watched it long enough to make sure it was indeed heading for them.

"Coming right at us," he said.

"Lookout thinks so, too, sir."

"It's a cinch she's seen us then."

"Indeed, sir."

"Well," Brewer said as he handed his glass to a petty officer, "let me know if we can identify her. In the meantime, we keep going."

"Aye aye, sir."

Brewer returned to his cabin. Alfred had his breakfast ready, after which he worked on his reports and logs. He was almost finished when Mr. Short appeared at his door.

"Mr. Greene's respects, sir. Begging your pardon, sir, but the frigate is hull-up now. Mr. Greene asks that you come on deck."

He met Greene at the fantail. Short handed him a glass. He was not surprised by what he saw.

"The lookout has identified the frigate as the *Valdivia*, sir," Greene said.

So, Cochrane was going for vengeance. When Brewer lowered his glass, his face had a hard look on it. *So be it.*

"What do we do, sir?" Greene asked.

"We run for all we're worth," Brewer said. "Hopefully, we can hold him off until dark and slip away again."

Mr. Sweeney spoke up. "We're not sailing our best, Captain; I doubt we can hold him off that long."

Brewer looked at the mountain of sail above his ship, and then he looked at their pursuer.

"Well," he said, "let's do our best. Maintain your course; it's still our best chance to find help."

"Sail ho!"

"Where away?"

"Three points forward of the larboard beam!" the lookout cried. He pointed to the sighting.

Brewer, Greene, and Sweeney looked and picked out the dot of white barely visible on the horizon. They watched as it grew broader, as though the ship turned to run parallel with them, and then it disappeared below the horizon. The whole process took less than thirty minutes.

"What do you make of that, sir?" Greene asked.

Brewer shrugged and turned back to *Valdivia*. She was obviously gaining ground, however slowly. "Probably didn't want to get involved. We may never know. We have more important things to worry about." He studied the frigate for a moment. "What would you say, Benjamin? He should have us in range of his long nines in... what? Five hours? Perhaps six?"

Greene studied the approaching frigate for a moment before lowering his glass. "At the outside, sir. It won't be dark for nearly eight."

Brewer lowered his glass and began to pace again. Try as he might, there was nothing he could think of that would improve their odds. He could not run away, and his ship was not up for the fight. The only thing they could do was to run as fast as they could and pray for a miracle.

The tension grew on board as the day progressed. The men who were off-watch came on deck to watch their pursuer slowly close the gap on them. Brewer was on the deck throughout the day, and he could tell the mood of his crew was getting desperate.

It was about the turn of the first dog watch that they heard the first report of *Valdivia's* long nines. Her first shots were wide of the mark, and as they got better, Brewer had the sailing master make small changes in their course to try to throw the Chilean's aim off. In the end, it was for naught, because the gap continued to close.

Brewer looked at Sweeney. "Remember my old friend?"

"You mean the one who was so thankful?".

"Sail ho!"

"Where away?" Greene cried.

"On the larboard beam!" the lookout called.

They rushed to the railing and looked. Sure enough, it was a sail on the horizon, and it was heading their direction.

The next shot from *Valdivia's* long nine put a hole in the main course.

"It's two ships, sir!" the lookout cried.

They looked again and saw the small but growing field of white had indeed split in two. The next few minutes would tell who they were.

"They're British, sir!" the lookout called. "It's *Clorinda* and *Phoebe*!"

Brewer lowered his glass and smiled. "The admiral riding to the rescue like the cavalry at Waterloo."

The approaching frigates split in an attempt to bracket *Valdivia*, but the Chilean fired one last long nine and changed course to run southeast. The British frigates gave chase for a few miles before veering off to escort their wounded comrade home.

Captain Brewer stood at the fantail watching with pride and great relief as the two ships approached *Revenge*. When they caught up, they slowed their speed to match that of their wounded sister. Seeing *Phoebe* on his starboard side and *Clorinda* to port, Brewer never felt more secure. He was joined by Lieutenant Greene and Mr. Sweeney. Crewmen and officers from both frigates waved in greeting and congratulations, and his own men replied in kind. Brewer was interested to note an admiral's broad pennant flying from *Phoebe.*

"Signal from *Phoebe*, sir!" cried Mr. Short. "Our number! *Heave to! Captain come on board!* That's all, sir!"

"Kindly acknowledge the signal, Mr. Short," Brewer said. "Mr. Sweeney, heave to. Mr. Greene, kindly see to the gig, if you please."

"Aye, sir."

Brewer went below as the hands sprang to the rigging to take in sail. He entered his cabin to find Alfred laying out a clean shirt.

"I thought you might like to change before going to see the Admiral, sir."

"Quite. Thank you, Alfred."

The servant smiled. "A pleasure, sir, I assure you."

Brewer got dressed and picked up his reports to pass along to Hornblower. When he got back on deck, Mr. Greene reported that all was ready for him.

The ride to *Phoebe* was smooth, the sea being uncommonly calm for that time of year. Brewer sat in the stern sheets, suddenly conscious that he had forgotten his sword. *Just as well,* he thought. *Alfred probably hasn't had time to clean the blood off it anyway.*

He wondered if he would see Captain Roussin again. He hoped that the Frenchman had made it to Martinique without incident. Brewer thought it likely, since Cochrane had pursued *Revenge* so far north. Brewer shook his head in admiration; it took courage to take a 12-pounder frigate like *Semillante* into a broadside-to-broadside slugfest against an 18-pounder frigate like *Pauline.* Had Roussin not done that, Brewer doubted that *Revenge* would have shown up in time to engage the pirate and eventually sink her. He looked out over the calm sea and silently wished the Frenchman well.

When Brewer climbed on board *Phoebe*, he was met by Captain Lucius Clark. Brewer knew him by reputation. Clark had fought at the Nile and Trafalgar before making his name hunting French privateers in South American waters during the late war. The two officers saluted each other and shook hands.

"Captain Brewer," Clark said. "A pleasure to meet you at last."

"The pleasure is mine, sir."

"If you'll follow me? Admiral Hornblower is waiting."

Brewer followed his host below deck and into the presence of his mentor. Brewer came to attention.

"Captain," Hornblower said, "so good to see you again. It seems we arrived just in time."

"That you did, my lord."

"Was that Admiral Cochrane's Chilean frigate?"

"The *Valdivia*. Aye, my lord."

Hornblower grunted. "Firing on a British ship. That won't do anything to improve his standing at the Admiralty."

Brewer grinned. "No, my lord. Here are my reports. Except, of course, for Cochrane's recent attack."

"Thank you. Sit down, Captain. Smithers! Madeira for three!"

Brewer sat as the Admiral's steward brought their refreshment. As the man left, the Admiral raised his glass.

"A toast to HMS *Revenge*."

After the toast was drunk, Hornblower motioned to Brewer's reports. "I shall read these, of course, but summarize them for me, Captain."

Brewer set his glass down. "My lord, I am pleased to report to you the sinking of the pirate frigate *Pauline* and two pirate luggars, as well as the capture by the French frigate *Semillante* and two additional pirate luggars. I can also report the deaths of the pirates El Diabolito and Roberto Cofresi."

"Well done, sir!" Hornblower exclaimed.

"Sir," Brewer said, "I must also report the death of midshipman Noah Simmons. He was killed in the boarding action on the *Pauline*. Would you be so kind as to inform the Governor?"

"I'm sorry to hear that," Hornblower said. "I shall see the Governor when we return to Jamaica. I know he hoped for better for his son, but at least he can say his son died honorably—which is more than can be said of how he lived. Now, on to other matters. Your ship looks like she's been through it."

"Aye, my lord. An 18-pounder broadside or two will do that to a sloop of war."

The Admiral smiled. "Yes, well, we should have a dockyard clear within a week of our return. I will move *Revenge* to the top of the list for a refit. That will get you a spot of leave; what will you do with it?"

Brewer smiled. "If it can be worked out, my lord, I'm thinking of getting married. Would you be free for a trip to St. Kitts to perform the ceremony?"

"You've asked her?"

"Not yet, my lord."

Hornblower rose. "William, if the young lady says yes, you and I will go to St. Kitts."

Brewer rose as well. "As soon as *Revenge* is seen to, I'll tend to that, my lord."

THE END

About The Author

James Keffer

James Keffer was born September 9, 1963, in Youngstown, Ohio, the son of a city policeman and a nurse. He grew up loving basketball, baseball, tennis, and books. He graduated high school in 1981 and began attending Youngstown State University to study mechanical engineering.

He left college in 1984 to enter the U.S. Air Force. After basic training, he was posted to the 2143rd Communications Squadron at Zweibruecken Air Base, West Germany. While he was stationed there, he met and married his wife, Christine, whose father was also assigned to the base. When the base was closed in 1991, James and Christine were transferred up the road to Sembach Air Base, where he worked in communications for the 2134th Communications Squadron before becoming the LAN manager for HQ 17th Air Force.

James received an honorable discharge in 1995, and he and his wife moved to Jacksonville, Florida, to attend Trinity Baptist College. He graduated with honors in 1998, earning a Bachelor of Arts degree. James and Christine have three children.

Hornblower and the Island is the first novel James wrote, and it is the first to be published by Fireship Press. He has self-published three other novels. He currently lives and works in Jacksonville, Florida, with his wife and three children.

BREWER'S LUCK

BY

JAMES KEFFER

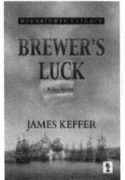

After gaining valuable experience as an aide to Governor Lord Horatio Hornblower, William Brewer is rewarded with a posting as first lieutenant on the frigate HMS *Defiant*, bound for American waters. Early in their travels, it seems as though Brewer's greatest challenge will be evading the wrath of a tyrannical captain who has taken an active dislike to him. But when a hurricane sweeps away the captain, the young lieutenant is forced to assume command of the damaged ship, and a crew suffering from low morale.

Brewer reports their condition to Admiral Hornblower, who orders them into the Caribbean to destroy a nest of pirates hidden among the numerous islands. Luring the pirates out of their coastal lairs will be difficult enough; fighting them at sea could bring disaster to the entire operation. For the *Defiant* to succeed, Brewer must rely on his wits, his training, and his ability to shape a once-ragged crew into a coherent fighting force.

PENMORE PRESS
www.penmorepress.com

Fortune's Whelp
by
Benerson Little

Privateer, Swordsman, and Rake:

Set in the 17th century during the heyday of privateering and the decline of buccaneering, *Fortune's Whelp* is a brash, swords-out sea-going adventure. Scotsman Edward MacNaughton, a former privateer captain, twice accused and acquitted of piracy and currently seeking a commission, is ensnared in the intrigue associated with the attempt to assassinate King William III in 1696. Who plots to kill the king, who will rise in rebellion—and which of three women in his life, the dangerous smuggler, the wealthy widow with a dark past, or the former lover seeking independence—might kill to further political ends? Variously wooing and defying Fortune, Captain MacNaughton approaches life in the same way he wields a sword or commands a fighting ship: with the heart of a lion and the craft of a fox.

PENMORE PRESS
www.penmorepress.com

Force 12 in German Bight

by
James Boschert

Considering that oil and gas have been flowing from under the North Sea for the best part of half a century, it is perhaps surprising that more writers have not taken the uncompromising conditions that are experienced in this area – which extends from the north of Scotland to the coasts of Norway and Germany – for the setting of a novel. James Boschert's latest redresses the balance.

The book takes its title from the name of an area regularly referred to in the legendary BBC Shipping Forecast, one which experiences some of the worst weather conditions around the British Isles. It is a fast-paced story which smacks of authenticity in every line. A world of hard men, hard liquor, hard drugs and cold-blooded murder. The reality of the setting and the characters, ex-military men from both sides of the Atlantic, crooked wheeler-dealers, and Danish detectives, male and female, are all in on the action.

This is not story telling akin to a latter day Bulldog Drummond, nor a James Bond, but simply a snortingly good yarn which will jangle the nerve ends, fill your nose with the smell of salt and diesel oil, your ears with the deafening sound of machinery aboard a monster pipe-dredging ship and, above all, make you remember never to underestimate the power of the sea.

–Roger Paine, former Commander, Royal Navy .

PENMORE PRESS
www.penmorepress.com

The Dragon's Breath

by

James Boschert

Talon stared wide-eyed at the devices, awed that they could make such an overwhelming, head-splitting noise. His ears rang and his eyes were burning from the drifting smoke that carried with it an evil stink. "That will show the bastards," Hsü told him with one of his rare smiles. "The General calls his weapons 'the Dragon's breath.' They certainly stink like it."

Talon, an assassin turned knight turned merchant, is restless. Enticed by tales of lucrative trade, he sets sail for the coasts of Africa and India. Traveling with him are his wife and son, eager to share in this new adventure, as well as Reza, his trusted comrade in arms. Treasures beckon at the ports, but Talon and Reza quickly learn that dangers attend every opportunity, and the chance rescue of a Chinese lord named Hsü changes their destination—and their fates.

Hsü introduces Talon to the intricacies of trading in China and the sophisticated wonders of Guangzhou, China's richest city. Here the companions discover wealth beyond their imagining. But Hsü is drawn into a political competition for the position of governor, and his opponents target everyone associated with him, including the foreign merchants he has welcomed into his home. When Hsü is sent on a dangerous mission to deliver the annual Tribute to the Mongols, no one is safe, not even the women and children of the household. As Talon and Reza are drawn into supporting Hsü's bid for power, their fighting skills are put to the test against new weapons and unfamiliar fighting styles. It will take their combined skills to navigate the treacherous waters of intrigue and violence if they hope to return to home.

PENMORE PRESS
www.penmorepress.com

Historical fiction and nonfiction
Paperback available for order on line
and as Ebook with all major distributers

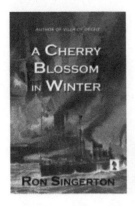

A CHERRY BLOSSOM IN WINTER
BY
RON SINGERTON

As the 20th century dawns, Japan is a rising power at odds with determinedly expanding Russia. In Moscow and St. Petersburg, aristocrats advance their political interests and have affairs as factory workers starve. Young Alexei Brusilov, son of an ambassador, accompanies his father to Japan and there falls in love with the daughter of a Japanese war hero. Despite threats and warnings, he pursues this forbidden romance, delighted to discover that Kimi-san returns his affection, until disaster overtakes them.

Amid the rising storm of revolution at home, Alexei returns to St. Petersburg to become a naval officer. A deadly rivalry with another cadet, a dangerous family secret, and friendships with revolutionaries imperil his career – and his life. Years later, Alexei finds himself aboard ship as the rusting and badly out of date Russian fleet is sent half way around the world to fight a modern and determined Japanese Navy. Will Alexei live to see his love again, or die under the blazing guns of the fast moving enemy cruisers?

"This is a sweeping work about the clash between Western and Eastern cultures, pretended morality, and grand passions struggling against heavily ritualized matrimony.... The author's observations about Russian society and his grasp of its good and bad points would likely have gained an approving nod from Tolstoy. This is first-rate storytelling!" —John Danielski, author of The King's Scarlet and Blue Water Scarlet Tide

PENMORE PRESS
www.penmorepress.com

Penmore Press

Challenging, Intriguing, Adventurous, Historical and Imaginative

www.penmorepress.com

Printed in June 2019
by Rotomail Italia S.p.A., Vignate (MI) - Italy